Quinlan looked down at the torn piece of a photo
he held in his hand.

Already two women had been unspeakably violated and killed because of it. Already the German
girl he loved was being stalked by a murder crew.
Already two men lay dead and Quinlan himself
had barely escaped an ambush.

How many more would die in the horror-haunted
landscape of post-war Germany before Quinlan
found the other pieces of the picture? And even
more terrifying, how many would die if he did
not . . . ?

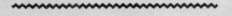

THE CANARIS FILE

"An exciting thriller, full of sharp twists and
surprises."

—*Milwaukee Journal*

Also by Walter Winward
from Jove

SEVEN MINUTES PAST MIDNIGHT
THE MIDAS TOUCH

THE CANARIS FILE

WALTER WINWARD

Published in hardcover as THE CANARIS FRAGMENTS

A JOVE BOOK

This Jove book contains the complete
text of the original hardcover edition.
It has been completely reset in a typeface
designed for easy reading, and was printed
from new film.

THE CANARIS FILE

A Jove Book / published by arrangement with
William Morrow and Company, Inc.

PRINTING HISTORY
Originally published in Great Britain in 1982
by Hamish Hamilton Ltd.
William Morrow and Company edition published 1983
Jove edition / November 1984

ISBN: 0-515-08065-9

Jove books are published by The Berkley Publishing Group,
200 Madison Avenue, New York, N.Y. 10016.
The words "A JOVE BOOK" and the "J" with sunburst
are trademarks belonging to Jove Publications, Inc.

PRINTED IN THE UNITED STATES OF AMERICA

For Rufus and Michael,
with love

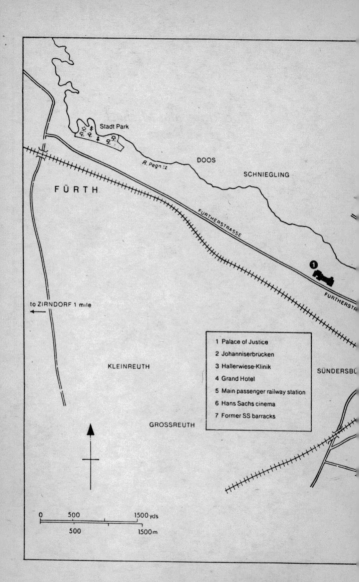

Stadt Park

DOOS

SCHNIEGLING

R. Pegnitz

FÜRTH

FURTHERSTRASSE

1

FURTHERSTR

to ZIRNDORF 1 mile

KLEINREUTH

SÜNDERSBÜ

1 Palace of Justice
2 Johanniserbrücken
3 Hallerwiese-Klinik
4 Grand Hotel
5 Main passenger railway station
6 Hans Sachs cinema
7 Former SS barracks

GROSSREUTH

0	500	1500 yds
	500	1500 m

WEIGELSHOF

NUREMBERG

R. Pegnitz

R. Pegnitz

HUMBOLDTSTRASSE

HUMBOLDTSTRASSE

HORST WESSELSTRASSE

ALLERSBERGERSTRASSE

Zeppelin Field

THE CANARIS FILE

PROLOGUE

∿∿∿∿∿∿∿∿∿∿∿∿∿∿∿∿∿∿∿∿∿∿∿∿∿

SOMEWHERE IN GERMANY
1943

BEAUTIFUL, BEAUTIFUL.

The two SS officers walked the length of the ware-house, stopping occasionally to discuss the objects of their admiration. They both agreed that, although the conception of the scheme was brilliant, its execution had surpassed their wildest expectations.

"What about the men who worked on the project?" asked the elder of the pair, who had arrived from Berlin only an hour earlier in response to a telephone call from his subordinate.

"Waiting to be dismissed, paid off."

"Then perhaps we'd better see that they are."

The senior SS officer counted fourteen men huddled against the far wall of the courtyard. Some of them were German, some French, a couple Belgian. *Strange*, he

1

thought, *that women had no skills in this field.*

To a man the fourteen were ill at ease. They knew the job was finished; they did not trust the SS. They had been promised their freedom in exchange for their talents, but they had all had experience of SS promises. With considerable anxiety they saw the massive gates swing open and a truck back in.

The two Belgians were quicker than their companions in recognizing betrayal. Even so, they were not quick enough.

At a shouted command from the junior SS officer, the truck's tailgate dropped, the canvas curtain was pulled aside from within, and the ugly snout of a belt-fed heavy machine gun appeared.

The machine-gun crew was commanded by an Oberscharführer. At a signal from him they opened fire, raking the far side of the courtyard. Even when all fourteen men opposite were either dead or dying, they didn't stop hosing the supine bodies until the belt was exhausted.

Afterward the Oberscharführer delivered the *coup de grace* to each, even if the man was obviously already dead. A single shot in the back of the head. He had to reload his Walther pistol twice. Then he marched smartly across to the two officers and snapped up his right arm in the Nazi salute.

"All finished, Herr Standartenführer," he barked.

"Burn the corpses," ordered the senior officer, "then report back to me. There is still much to be done."

ONE

GERMAN-DANISH BORDER
May 1945

LEAVING KÜPFERMÜHLE, A tiny hamlet near the Port
of Flensburg, he changed his mind about walking in the
woods and instead made for the hill overlooking Was-
sersleben, where he had a fine view of the harbor. The
earlier quarrel with his wife had left a nasty taste in
his mouth. She would calm down soon, however, and
before long she would come looking for him, expecting
to find him at their usual spot among the trees.

Although official documents gave his height as five
feet six or seven inches, he was in fact several inches
shorter. He had reached his fortieth birthday a month
before, but he looked much older, partly from under-
nourishment, partly because the shabby civilian clothes
he wore had been tailored for someone else. The ugly
scar that ran from the lower right-hand corner of his

3

mouth to below his right ear was an old wound; when he was anxious, as he was now, it turned pink and appeared fresh. Many of his companions of the last six years believed the scar honorably earned in a duel; it was, however, a legacy from a razor fight in 1924.

He smiled grimly. 1924 was also the year another man the world had yet to hear from was writing *Mein Kampf* in a Bavarian prison.

In an inside pocket he carried a passport made out to Wilhelm Hansen, occupation teacher, resident of Hamburg. To avoid its appearing suspiciously new, the issuing date was given as November 3, 1944. He also carried a *Wehrpass* in his real name, one that every German knew. The Hamburg Gestapo had insisted on this to prevent summary execution if he were picked up by the German military police, the Feldjägerkorps, as a deserter. Not that there was any danger of that now; neither the FJK nor the Gestapo existed anymore. The war had officially ended three weeks before on May 7. Hitler was dead, as was Goebbels. The Propaganda Minister had promised to protect the man with the scar, protect his wife also. Early in April he had seen the Teletype sent from the ministry: AT ALL COSTS THEY MUST BE KEPT OUT OF ALLIED HANDS.

He had to admit that the security services of the Third Reich had done their best, even after all was lost and the minister dead. He would stay free as long as possible, though it could only be a matter of time before he was arrested.

Still, he was no war criminal. Under international law as he understood it, neither he nor Margaret was a criminal of any sort. His greatest fear was that he would be executed out of hand when captured, that he would not be permitted the luxury of a trial in which to plead his cause.

A noise behind him made him start. He snapped his fingers at the emaciated dog, beckoning it toward him. It backed away snarling, hackles raised. *So, even the*

---

dogs, he thought, faintly amused.

He got to his feet and brushed himself off. He had been away long enough; by now Margaret would be anxious. After taking a final look at the harbor—something told him he would never see it again—he set off down the hill.

He was still half a mile from where he expected to meet his wife when, up ahead in a clearing, he saw two men in the uniforms of British Army officers. He was not alarmed. He had had several encounters with the occupation forces in the last few days, and so far no one had recognized him or even stopped him to ask for papers. He could, in any case, avoid the Tommies by a slight detour. They were gathering wood for a fire and seemed oblivious to anything besides the task at hand. For some reason he could never later fathom, he continued toward the two men.

Captain Lickorish and Lieutenant Perry, both of the Reconnaissance Regiment, Royal Armored Corps, looked up as he approached. They heard him say, in French, "Here are a few more pieces." A moment later he repeated the sentence in English. Then he walked on.

Perry was a German Jewish refugee, an interpreter. Like many European Jews serving in the British forces against Germany, he had changed his name to prevent brutality if captured. The sound of the scarred man's voice meant nothing to him. Captain Lickorish, however, had heard it too many times since the outbreak of war not to suspect the true identity of its owner. Even so, he could hardly believe that such a person would be casually walking through the woods.

When he relayed his suspicions to Perry, the interpreter was first to act. With Lickorish hard on his heels, he raced after the disappearing figure, who turned and smiled nervously back at them.

Perry glanced at Lickorish, who nodded.

"You wouldn't happen to be William Joyce, would you?" asked the interpreter.

At the Old Bailey trial which began on September 17, 1945, the attorney general, Sir Hartley Shawcross, asked Lickorish what happened when the prisoner was challenged. Lickorish answered, "He went to put his hand in his pocket, and Perry fired his revolver."

When his identity was questioned, any European accustomed to living under the Gestapo in 1945 would immediately respond by producing documentation. Joyce was reaching for his German passport in the name of Hansen when Perry, thinking that what might appear in his hand was a pistol, shot him. The single bullet passed through both Joyce's thighs, causing two entry and two exit wounds. As he fell to the ground he shouted, "My name is Fritz Hansen."

He was so confused or terror-stricken he had not even remembered that his adopted forename was Wilhelm. Not that it would have made any difference. A rapid body search revealed not only the Hansen passport but the *Wehrpass* in the name of William Joyce.

Outside of the remnants of the Nazi hierarchy and senior officers in the SS, the one man the Allies most wanted in custody was Joyce, otherwise known as Lord Haw-Haw, whose sneering voice had taunted the British with his nightly radio broadcasts for five years, who had warned every man, woman, and child in the United Kingdom that their days were numbered, their island doomed, their stubborn resistance futile. William Joyce, who knew, it was reputed, when clocks in English villages stopped and at what time, who preached the wisdom of surrender to the oncoming Wehrmacht, who attempted to spread defeatism, who set neighbor against neighbor, who broadcast lists of the dead after Luftwaffe raids before, it seemed, even relatives knew the fate of their loved ones; who would later claim he was not British at all but American and a naturalized German citizen *before* the United States entered the war. How dare anyone accuse *him* of treason!

No one who had lived in the United Kingdom during the dark days of 1940, when invasion seemed imminent, would ever forget Joyce's preamble to his nightly program, *Views on the News*, from Berlin: "Jairmany calling, Jairmany calling." Radio and stage comedians imitated his voice and intonation. "Jairmany calling" echoed across bomb sites and schoolyards, shouted by small scruffy children who knew not what they said. But Lord Haw-Haw was no joke, and twenty million adult Britons would willingly have knotted the noose and slipped the trapdoor that sent him to eternity.

This knowledge was uppermost in Joyce's mind when Perry and Lickorish handed him over to the nearest frontier post, after treating his wounds with field dressings. Although unable to walk and in a state of semi-shock, Joyce was fully conscious. He had no doubt he could survive a trial by jury; what worried him now was the possibility of a kangaroo court followed by immediate execution. The expressions of the dozen men in the guardroom, including two officers, were anything but friendly.

The senior of the officers, Major Otis Quinlan, who had been a free-lance journalist in peacetime, was quick to realize that he was sitting on top of a major news story. He would not be allowed to write it, of course, but in his wartime role as a member of the intelligence staff of General Sir Miles Dempsey's Second Army, he was certainly permitted to do a little preliminary interrogation. His future career in Fleet Street could not be harmed if he became known as the first man to get a statement from Lord Haw-Haw—preferably with no one else around. He was wondering how to get Joyce alone when the problem solved itself.

Far from thinking of a drumhead trial and a lynching party, the guard commander, a young lieutenant, was less interested in who Joyce was than where he had materialized from. In these first weeks after the war's end rumors abounded that Hitler was not dead but on the run, and the ports of North Germany (from which the erstwhile Führer could be spirited away via a small craft to a waiting U-boat and then to South America) were being closely watched. Less than a week before SS Reichsführer Himmler, wearing an eye patch and using the name Heinrich Hitzinger, had been picked up at Meinstedt. Two days later he was dead, having bitten on a cyanide capsule when confronted with his true identity.

Joyce was only too anxious to ingratiate himself with his captors. After complaining that he was in pain and receiving assurance that an army doctor was on the way, he revealed the location of the house where he and his wife had been staying for the last few days. His main concern was that Margaret Joyce be told his whereabouts, and his denial that anyone of importance was at the Kupfermühle address was ignored by the guard commander, who bundled almost his entire detachment into two Bren-carriers and a three-tonner and raced off for the hamlet. Afraid of missing anything, Perry and Lickorish went with the raiding party, leaving Quinlan, who volunteered with alacrity, and a Welsh lance corporal to look after Joyce.

Quinlan estimated he didn't have long. The nearest medical center was only minutes away, and doubtless the MO would arrive with half his staff in tow, all of them itching to get a look at the infamous Lord Haw-Haw. Meanwhile, Quinlan had a thousand questions he wanted to ask and no time to organize them. They came off the top of his head. Why had Joyce broadcast for the Germans throughout the war? When had he left Berlin? Had he seen Hitler recently? And Goebbels? Were they genuinely dead or in hiding?

Joyce was reluctant to say anything. Once the soldiers and the other three officers had disappeared, he felt more secure.

Quinlan pressed him. How had he got this far? Had he received help? Apart from the Kupfermühle house, were there any other hamlets in the vicinity sheltering fugitives?

"I have nothing to say at this time," replied Joyce haughtily, as though that settled the matter.

And well it might have done if the Welsh lance corporal had not dealt himself a hand.

"I don't know why you're bothering with the little bastard," he said in a singsong voice. "We should take him outside and shoot him. I lost a sister and my brother-in-law in the Coventry raids," he added fingering his Lee-Enfield.

Quinlan was about to tell him to shut up and mind his own business when he saw the flicker of panic in Joyce's eyes and recalled the collaborator speaking from Berlin during the evening of November 15, 1940, while Coventry was still burning, his voice jubilant at the destruction and death the Luftwaffe had meted out. The broadcast was one of his best remembered. He had detailed streets and buildings that were either damaged or destroyed, and even the names of some families who had died. The exactness of his information had given rise to the rumor that he had a battalion of fifth columnists all over England, men and women with shortwave radios in direct contact with Berlin.

"Maybe you're right," said Quinlan slowly, nodding at the Welshman. "We can always say he tried to make a run for it."

Joyce was lying prone on a stretcher. He raised himself up on his elbows, spluttering with indignation and fear.

"You would not be believed," he stammered. "A man with bullet wounds in both legs can hardly escape."

"Then we'll think of something else," said Quinlan lightly. "One thing's for certain: you're no use to us if you won't answer questions."

"I can't tell you what I don't know," protested Joyce.

Quinlan turned away from him.

"Do you have a round in the chamber, Corporal?" he asked.

The Welshman confirmed he did by bringing his rifle to his waist and flicking off the safety. Neither Quinlan nor Joyce had any doubt that, given the word, the lance corporal would gladly shoot.

"Wait!" shouted Joyce and broke into German, establishing first that Quinlan understood the language and guessing correctly that the Welshman did not.

Quinlan followed the avalanche of words with difficulty. He had a good working knowledge of German, but some of the more obscure and lengthy words defeated him. He understood Joyce to say that he had never met Hitler and had only talked with Goebbels on rare occasions, that he sincerely believed them to be dead. He was no more than a minor member of the Propaganda Ministry, he pleaded, and knew nothing about the former political and military leaders of the Third Reich with the exception of Admiral Wilhelm Canaris and Oberstleutnant (Lieutenant Colonel) Manfred Langenhain.

Quinlan pricked up his ears. The name Langenhain meant nothing to him. Canaris, however, was the onetime head of the Abwehr, military intelligence. No one was certain what had happened to him. Rumor had it that he had been hounded out of office in 1944, probably executed, and his entire organization taken over by the SS. On the other hand, if he were still alive and Joyce knew his whereabouts . . .

Quinlan had no opportunity to pursue the question. As Joyce finished speaking, the door to the guardroom was flung open and a Medical Corps colonel lumbered in, followed by half a dozen more junior officers.

The colonel pulled rank, quoted Hippocrates, and

took over. While Quinlan was not asked to leave—Joyce was still a prisoner and the medics were unarmed—it was made quite clear that no further questioning of the "patient" would be tolerated for the present. The Welsh lance corporal's expression was one of a child who has had his favorite toy confiscated.

Three days later, on May 31, Joyce dictated his first formal statement to Captain William Scarden of the Intelligence Corps at Lüneburg military hospital. After much string-pulling Quinlan contrived to be present. He was to be disappointed. Joyce, now confident he would not be executed out of hand, denied ever mentioning Canaris or an officer named Langenhain. Major Quinlan must have misunderstood.

Quinlan knew he had been conned and realized why Joyce, buying time until the medics arrived, had dropped into German. Because the Welsh lance corporal, the only other witness, did not speak the language, Joyce could repudiate, as he was now doing, the content of the entire conversation.

It was probably all bull anyway. Joyce would have said anything to keep the Welshman's finger off the trigger.

Quinlan decided to forget the whole episode. In a few months the traitor would be hanged and that would be the end to it.

What Quinlan did not know was that he was destined to meet Joyce again and, through him, become involved in an intrigue so bizarre that all written records of it would be destroyed by order of the highest authority and all surviving participants warned of the direst consequences should they ever tell what they had learned.

TWO

~~~~~~

NUREMBERG
November 29, 1945

LITTLE WAS LEFT to suggest that the city had once been the shrine of Nazism. After the Roehm purge—the Night of the Long Knives in 1934—it was Speer who stage-managed the party congress in September of that year, taking over the huge Zeppelin Field southeast of the Old Town to erect a massive stone structure thirteen hundred feet long and eighty feet high. Crowning the stadium was a gigantic eagle with a hundred-foot wing-spread and from every side hung thousands of swastika banners, twenty thousand in all. One hundred thirty searchlights were positioned at intervals around the auditorium, each with a range of five miles. When Goering complained about losing so much candlepower to propaganda purposes, Hitler backed Albert Speer. "If we can use such numbers for a gathering like this, the rest of the world will think we're swimming in searchlights."

Two hundred thousand party faithful crowded into the stadium that September evening. Leni Riefenstahl, the multi-talented actress and director, filmed the entire occasion using a dozen cameras. She called her documentary *The Triumph of the Will*, and everyone who saw it, supporters of the regime as well as implacable enemies, believed thereafter that Hitler's promise of a Thousand-Year Reich was no idle boast. Certainly no one would have suspected that in a dozen short years it would all be over and that Zeppelin Field, along with much of the rest of Nuremberg, would be a ruin.

Now, neither electric light nor heat existed in the majority of private houses and apartment buildings, which were, in any case, mostly bombed-out shells and low on the list of priorities for renovation. Whole families huddled together in any room that still had four walls. Tarpaulins, sheets of corrugated iron, and sometimes cardboard covered gaps in the roofs. Sanitation was at its most primitive and the danger of waterborne diseases ever present. The shops that still existed contained the barest rations, and most goods had to be queued for hours and eaten cold. Fresh water was obtained from standpipes at specific times or from bowsers when the conduits broke down. Luxuries such as cigarettes and chocolate were impossible to obtain outside the black market. Fraternization between the occupying troops and the Germans was strickly forbidden, but it went on nevertheless. For a pack of cigarettes, a bar of chocolate, or a pair of stockings, a man could buy whatever took his fancy in the way of women.

Nuremberg was in the American zone of Occupied Germany, and in spite of the fact that no GI had much sympathy for members of the defeated nation, US engineering battalions were working around the clock to get the basic utilities functioning, a task that was likely to take much longer than the few months they'd had. Since July the engineers had also been renovating the

Palace of Justice, where, on November 20, the International Military Tribunal (IMT) had begun hearings at which twenty-one leading Nazis were being tried for war crimes. Before October 25, the number was to have been twenty-two, but on that date Dr. Robert Ley hanged himself in his cell using a wet towel. Ley was the former head of the German Labor Front, a polite way of saying he ran the slave-labor program in which tens of thousands were worked to death.

Martin Bormann and Gustav Krupp were to be tried *in absentia*, the first because he could not be found, the second because he was reputed to be crazy.

Of the remainder, the most important were Reichsmarschall Hermann Goering, ex-Deputy Führer Rudolf Hess, Foreign Minister Joachim von Ribbentrop, and SS Obergruppenführer Ernst Kaltenbrunner, the chief, after Reinhard Heydrich's assassination, of the RSHA, the SS security services which included the Gestapo. Each of the twenty-one had pleaded not guilty to the charges contained in the indictment, but none had yet entered the witness box, nor would any for some time. Observers estimated the prosecutors would take six or eight weeks outlining the case against the defendants.

And what a case it was, thought Otis Quinlan, hurrying toward the comparative sanity of the Grand Hotel on Bahnhofstrasse. In the courtroom that afternoon, he had witnessed the horrors of Belsen, Dachau, Buchenwald, and other concentration camps as filmed by American and British troops when they overran Germany in the early months of 1945: the hideous piles of skeletal corpses unburied in open pits, the crematoria, the gas chambers. Perhaps worst of all was the footage of those who had remained alive either through luck or by some effort of will: their immense eyes, seemingly far too large for their shrunken, starving faces, their pathetic unbelieving smiles at being liberated from hell, the agonizingly slow pace at which they walked—or crawled. At more than one point the men and women in the darkened chamber were heard to gasp and sob openly.

Few of those in the dock could watch every reel of film. One defendant, Dr. Hjalmar Schacht, Hitler's financial wizard, sat with his back to the screen, refusing to look at all. Hess protested loudly that he did not understand what was going on. Only Julius Streicher, the one-time gauleiter of Franconia with his power base in Nuremberg, and Goering watched everything, though people who should have known better said in private that the Reichsmarschall kept his eyes on the screen because he genuinely could not believe what he was seeing.

There were many, far too many, middle-ranking Allied officers who felt that Goering should not have been in the same dock with men like Streicher and Kaltenbrunner. Remembering his record from World War I, when he commanded the famous Richthofen squadron and was awarded the Pour le Mérite, the German equivalent of the Victoria Cross or the Congressional Medal of Honor, these officers conveniently forgot that he was also the founder of the Gestapo, that he had looted Europe of many of its art treasures, and that he had joined the Nazis, giving their street-fighter image respectability, for no other reason than ambition.

The British were less sympathetic to the former head of the Luftwaffe than the Americans. The British remembered only too well those bleak days in 1940 when Goering's bombers pounded English cities day and night. They remembered also the brutal executions of fifty RAF officers recaptured after the mass escape from Stalagluft III at Sagan. Later Goering would profess not to have known anything of this slaughter until it was too late; but like much else the Reichsmarschall said, this too required all but the most gullible to reach for the salt.

Not yet having his own vehicle, Quinlan was hiking the mile and three quarters from the Palace of Justice to the Grand. He could have hung around the courtyard and easily bummed a ride, but at that moment he didn't want company, even though Allied officers in full uniform were not encouraged to walk the streets alone after dark. The dusk-to-dawn curfew imposed by the miltary government had proved impossible to enforce, and Quinlan personally knew of two totally unrelated incidents in which a captain and a major had disappeared, presumably killed by Germans unwilling to accept that the war was over.

Quinlan had arrived in Nuremberg from Schleswig-Holstein two weeks before, and four days later the IMT officially had begun to take evidence. He had used powers of rhetoric he had not known he possessed to get himself there. Seeing his name on the list of officers to be rotated home, he realized he wouldn't stand a snowball's chance in hell of witnessing the most momentous court case in history unless he did the fastest talking of his life. Going straight to the top, to General Dempsey himself, he finagled his way past battalion and divisional commanders in a manner that made him a few enemies and left more than one senior officer vowing to have young Quinlan's head for a paperweight.

The Second Army was being forgotten, he told Dempsey. It was stuck in a north German backwater while the real action was taking place down south. What was happening in Nuremberg was as much the concern of Second Army as of anyone else, but all they were going to receive were secondhand newspaper and radio reports. General Dempsey deserved to have a personal representative on the spot, reporting daily or weekly in the form of a bulletin that could be distributed to all ranks. That way, the troops who had fought their way from the Normandy beaches to the Danish border would not feel overlooked.

Did Major Quinlan have anyone in mind? queried

Dempsey. Perhaps an officer with journalistic experience? Quinlan had the grace to grin sheepishly.

Dempsey admired Quinlan's impudence. The proposition also had a certain appeal. Field Marshal Bernard Montgomery's Twenty-first Army Group, of which the Second Army was part, had been shunted out of the spotlight since the Supreme Allied Commander, Eisenhower, had made it clear in the early months of 1945 that Berlin was not the prime strategic objective, that the Anglo-French-American forces would stop at the river Elbe, leaving the Russians to take the capital of the Third Reich. Montgomery's counterargument that he could be in Berlin by mid-April had been rejected by Ike. Occupy Schleswig-Holstein, take Hamburg and the ports of Lübeck and Kiel, and hold tight: those were the orders. The decision had driven every Second Army senior commander mad with frustration. While George Patton and Alexander Patch were taking town after town down south and grabbing the headlines, the Twenty-first Army Group was left cooling its heels. Many thought Ike had political ambitions and it would do a future campaign no good at all to allow Monty to grab the lion's share of the glory.

Another factor in favor of Quinlan's suggestion was that since VE day the French and British occupation zones had taken a backseat to the American. While it was right and proper that Nuremberg (in the US zone), as the cradle of Nazism, should be the site of the trial, there remained the suspicion that some American senior officers looked upon the whole business as their own Tribunal. The British, French, and Russians were participating on sufferance.

Major Quinlan could therefore go to Nuremberg on full pay for as long as General Dempsey could swing it. Comprehensive bulletins would be expected weekly, though a seat in the press gallery from which to witness the proceedings might be difficult to obtain. Dempsey would, however, see what he could do. Twenty-four hours later he told Quinlan to be on his way and to seek out Colonel Eugene Masterson in Nuremberg.

Masterson, an old friend of Dempsey's, was currently a senior intelligence officer with Patton's Third Army, which, together with units of Patch's Seventh Army and members of the Counter Intelligence Corps (CIC), formed the occupying force in Nuremberg. The colonel told Quinlan to see his senior deputy, Major Ben Hadleigh, adding that if what he wanted was humanly possible to obtain, Hadleigh would make sure he got it.

Fortunately Hadleigh and Quinlan got along like ham and eggs, partly because, as it turned out, Quinlan had an American grandmother who had been raised not a dozen blocks from Hadleigh's home in Chicago. It was this same grandmother who had insisted that her only grandson's first name be Otis, not because of the elevator company but after the town in New Brunswick where she had honeymooned before the turn of the century. If their son were named anything else, her daughter and her daughter's English husband need not bother to attend the will reading.

Quinlan was a rangy twenty-nine-year-old with what an ex-lady friend had once called a studious if licentious face, like a medieval saint who had not quite made up his mind whether he wouldn't be better off running a bar. In college, he had been a cross-country runner and had boxed as a middleweight while getting a degree in English. Before becoming a free-lance journalist, he had spent a year in Germany, where he witnessed firsthand the rise of National Socialism.

He had some money of his own, and his ancestry was what he liked to describe as middle-class Anglo-American with around twenty percent Irish thrown in, which accounted for his near-black hair, for some reason going prematurely gray at the temples, and a temper with a low flash point. Since the invasion of Europe he had seen a dozen battles from a distance and a few more at much closer range. He considered himself neither especially brave nor crazy, but on more than one occasion he had picked up the nearest rifle and fought his way through hedgerows and villages. Being in intelligence meant he was usually away from the fighting. There was, however, a book to be written about this war, a good big novel, and he thought he had better find out what it was like at the front.

Hadleigh was Regular Army, commissioned from the ranks and already a major at thirty-one. He didn't talk much about his early years, and Quinlan got the impression his boyhood in Chicago had been tough. Taller than Quinlan, he was also twenty pounds heavier, none of them fat. He had a ready, broad smile, was always immaculately groomed, and was rarely seen without a Havana cigar, supplies of which were supposed to be as rare as gold dust. Rumor had it that he kept a couple of girls in the Sündersbühl district, south of the Ludwigs-Donau-Main Canal, for his own use and that of his special friends.

His primary job, in conjunction with CIC, was to seek out Nazis on the mandatory arrest list and turn them over for trial to the proper authorities. To this end he had let it be known that his door was open day and night to anyone who wanted to talk, perhaps to turn state's evidence in the hope of a lighter sentence. Apart from a handful of sprats, so far he had not been conspicuously successful. Which puzzled him. Germany must have had several million people who were members of the party. Of that number many would be dead; many more, however, had to be in hiding. Odd, therefore, that there were so few turncoats; odder still that only rarely did an innocent citizen come forward to report something suspicious, if for no other reason than to gain a pack of Luckies or a jar of coffee.

Many hated the conquerors, of course. Many more were just plain scared, which tended to support Gene Masterson's hypothesis that the hard-core Nazis were far from beaten yet. There were too few senior officers in captivity, too many junior officers and NCOs. Still, in Hadleigh's opinion, most of those on the wanted list would eventually be caught and hanged. In the meantime, he had it better than most, with his girls and his one or two deals on the side to keep him in loose change; fixing up the press seat for Otis Quinlan had hardly caused him to break sweat.

The oasis that was the Grand loomed up. The US engineering battalions had worked overtime here also; the hotel was a brightly lit miracle, for officers and their civilian equivalents, in the surrounding desert.

Quinlan mounted the steps and headed for the long bar adjoining the Marble Room. Inside, uniformed men and women were dancing to a small German band struggling with the latest American hit song.

Hadleigh was sitting on a stool halfway down the bar, staring at a glass of bourbon and a beer chaser, smoking the inevitable cigar. Quinlan joined him, as was his custom at the end of the day. Hadleigh had Max Judd, a first-class top sergeant, back at the base in case anything urgent happened.

The G-2 major signaled the barman with two fingers. *Set 'em up again, Joe.*

"Tough day at the office, honey?"

Quinlan grimaced as the sour mash hit the pit of his stomach. Good Scotch was hard to come by, even for the Americans, and he still wasn't used to bourbon.

"You can say that again. They had the films out. Dachau, Belsen, all points east."

"How did the animals take it?"

"Some easy, some hard. Schacht wouldn't look at any of them."

"Schacht's seen it from the inside, don't forget. He'll probably be acquitted."

"Inside information?"

"Just good guesswork. That's what I hope, anyway. I'm making a heavy book on the outcome. Schacht could cost me money if they deep-six the bastard.''

"Who're you making favorite to take the morning walk?''

"Eight'll get you five on Goering, Ribbentrop, Streicher, Frank, and Kaltenbrunner. Most of the rest I'm steering clear of until I see how they stand up in the box.''

"Even Hess?''

"Hess was in British custody for four years. That will probably be in his favor, though not if he spouts some of the crap he used to come up with in the old days. I'll wait and see what kind of an impression he makes.''

"Kaltenbrunner wasn't there again today," said Quinlan. "The word is he's suffering from spinal meningitis.''

"Which is the medical way of saying he's paralyzed with fear. He's in the One-sixteenth general hospital. Used to be an SD headquarters, so I guess he'll feel at home.''

"There'll be a few more in the hospital before this is all over, I'll wager.''

"Any idea who?''

"For the book?''

"For the book. You've got to have an edge if you want to come out ahead, and firsthand impressions won't hurt.''

Quinlan thought back to the first day of the trial, when the defendants were asked how they pleaded. Goering had tried to make a speech, but the president of the court, Lord Justice Sir Geoffrey Lawrence, had silenced him, having no intention of allowing the Tribunal to become a propaganda platform for the accused. Sulking, Goering had then stated that he declared himself not guilty in terms of the indictment. Hess had simply said no, and Von Ribbentrop had parroted Goering's words.

The erstwhile head of the OKW, the High Command of the German armed forces, Field Marshal Wilhelm

Keitel, was next to plead not guilty, and his declaration was followed by a statement from the president that Kaltenbrunner would have the opportunity to plead when he was fit. In the interim, the trial would proceed against him.

In quick succession Alfred Rosenberg, the violently anti-Semitic party philosopher; Hans Frank, governor general of Poland; Wilhelm Frick, minister of the interior; Julius Streicher; Walther Funk, the homosexual economist; and Hjalmar Schacht declared themselves not guilty.

The two senior naval officers came next, Karl Doenitz and Erich Raeder. Both announced themselves not guilty in clear voices. Baldur von Schirach, ex-Hitler Youth leader and later gauleiter of Vienna, echoed the words of Goering and Ribbentrop, while Fritz Sauckel, gauleiter of Thuringia being one of his many titles, wanted to dot the *i*'s and cross the *t*'s. "I declare myself in the sense of the indictment, before God and the world and particularly before my people, not guilty."

Generaloberst Alfred Jodl, Hitler's Chief of Staff, also felt a simple plea would not do. "For what I have done and had to do, I have a pure conscience before God, before history, and my people."

Franz von Papen, known to his captors as the Silver Fox and acting out the noun; Artur Seyss-Inquart, who had paved the way for Hitler's takeover of Austria and who later had served as Reichskommissar of Holland; and Albert Speer were content with simple pleas of not guilty.

The diplomat Konstantin von Neurath, Hitler's first foreign minister before the outbreak of war and later Reichsprotektor of Bohemia and Moravia, pedantically stated, "I answer the question in the negative."

Finally Hans Fritzsche, a member of Goebbels's Propaganda Ministry, had denied his guilt.

The four counts in the indictment against the defendants were: crimes against peace, war crimes, crimes against humanity, and being a member of a criminal group or organization.

No defense that a defendant was acting under superior orders was to be allowed on the first three counts.

Of those in the dock, Quinlan thought that Frank, Frick, Rosenberg, Sauckel, and Funk would probably require some form of medical treatment before the end. Kaltenbrunner was already hospitalized, and Hess was saying he recalled nothing. The military and the naval men would probably stick it out, while the remainder was anybody's guess.

He gave Hadleigh his opinion, adding, "Though I'd watch those wagers on Goering, Ribbentrop, and the others you mentioned if I were you. Talk is that the lawyers are going to question the validity of the whole thing, argue that it's impossible to have a fair trial when the judges are chosen from one side only, that of the victors. They're also going to submit that, according to international law in 1939, war was not an indictable offense. Neither were the SS, SD, and Gestapo criminal organizations. Their clients are being prosecuted under a law that was created only after the fact."

"How does that theory seem to you?" asked Hadleigh.

"Personally I'd have had this lot and quite a few more shot on sight, as Churchill apparently wanted to do. Stick 'em up against a wall and to hell with trials. But that evidently didn't suit your people or the Russians. Stalin particularly wanted a worldwide hearing to justify what he did in Poland and elsewhere. He's no fool, Uncle Joe. He knows damn well no one's forgotten that until the middle of 1941 he was Hitler's ally. The trouble is, if you start fooling around with the law and lawyers, it all becomes a matter of the fine print. Hitler himself said somewhere that he wouldn't rest until it became shameful for any German to be a lawyer."

"Sounds like a guy I used to know who was held back in sixth grade and tried to blow up the school for having lousy teachers," said Hadleigh.

"Nevertheless," grunted Quinlan, "you know and I know what the SS did in the camps, but if you let a lawyer tell the story, it'll come out that the Jews and the other poor bastards had to fight their way into the gas chambers while the poor helpless guards tried to keep them out."

"That sounds like cynicism, Major. By the way, how's the girl making out?"

The girl was Frau Gretl Meissner, a pretty mouse-haired widow in her middle thirties who had turned up out of the blue a month earlier and asked Hadleigh for a job, saying she had a fifteen-year-old son to support. She could, she said, type, take shorthand, answer the phone. She was also fluent in French and had a working knowledge of English. Hadleigh had checked her out, discovered that she had never had any Nazi sympathies, and hired her as a kind of general factotum. She worked twice as hard as his Third Army female clerks, and at present was "on loan" to Quinlan, sitting with him most days in the Palace of Justice press gallery, for which Hadleigh had got her a press card, and filling in for him when he had business elsewhere.

"I let her go early. I don't know whether it was the films, but she seemed upset."

Hadleigh looked at him inquiringly. "Nothing going on between you two is there?"

"Not a thing. I make it a rule never to fraternize with the help. Besides, she's too useful for me to get emo-tionally entangled. If I were really the stuff of which crooks are made, I could spend my days getting drunk and let Gretl do the work. She's that good."

Quinlan finished his drink. Before the refill arrived, Hadleigh was called to the phone by an orderly. When he returned, he finished his bourbon in one gulp and pushed away the beer.

"I have to head for the high sierras. That was the office. One of my informers came through and we've had a roundup of stooges."

"Anyone on the blacklist?"

"Not as it stands at the moment. You know the routine. They are not now, nor have they ever been, a member of the Nazi party or any affiliated organization. Christ, they've got Elks lodges in Nebraska with bigger memberships."

Hadleigh thought for a moment. "You doing anything special for the next couple of hours?" he asked. "If not, how would you like to help out? We've roped in half a dozen from what I can gather and it might be interesting. If we get through fast, we can go out on what's left of the town. I can't guarantee champagne or black silk sheets, but the girls are clean."

THREE

〰〰〰〰〰〰〰〰〰〰〰〰〰〰〰〰〰〰〰〰〰〰〰

NUREMBERG
November 29, 1945

THE FORMER SS BARRACKS on Allersbergerstrasse
where Hadleigh had set up his headquarters was also the
site of the biggest US Army base in Nuremberg. Quinlan had a room there and continued to be amazed,
even after two weeks, at how well the GIs lived. Once
through the gates and past the armed guards, he was in a
world completely different from the rest of the war-torn
city. Off-duty personnel walked around clutching cans
of beer and smoking whatever brand of cigarettes took
their fancy. In the PX, a fast-talker could buy whatever
he could afford, and black-market activity in Luckies
and Camels and canned Budweiser and Schlitz was a
cottage industry that would one day put the down pay-
ment on hundreds of homes and businesses. What was
truly astonishing, however, was the amount of electric

light shining throughout the compound. To the German men, women, and children who, defying curfew, congregated around the main gates in the hope of a handout, the illumination revealed just how impoverished their lives were.

Hadleigh skidded the Jeep to a halt beside a building that bore the official legend THIRD ARMY INTELLIGENCE. Underneath, some wag had chalked LUCKY BRAINS UNIT. During the war, Lucky was General Patton's personal choice of a code name for the Third Army.

Hadleigh's master sergeant, Max Judd, was waiting for them in the guardroom. Beyond this were rooms that served as offices, interrogation cells, and sleeping quarters.

Judd was a battle-hardened New Yorker whose German accent was atrocious but who could both understand and make himself understood and was, finally, with Hadleigh's patient help, getting the hang of tenses and genders. A thick-skinned thirty-year man who had joined the Army while still in his teens, he was a couple of years older than Hadleigh and looked as though he wrestled bulls for a pastime. Hadleigh had a handful of junior officers in his unit, but Judd was the man he relied upon as his second-in-command. Max had a street intelligence that was more valuable than anything the kids with college degrees could offer. He had fought with a combat regiment until shortly after D-Day, when Hadleigh, desperate for some real assistance with the thousands of prisoners being rounded up, had sent an urgent request to the brass for someone with more moxie than the Ivy Leaguers under his command, someone who could lean on the tough Waffen SS men being captured without worrying about the Geneva Convention or sleepless nights. Judd had been reluctant to come out of the firing line until Hadleigh had pointed out that he could do more to shorten the war from an interrogation hut than by leading bayonet charges.

Like Hadleigh, Judd favored big cigars. He waved the one he was smoking at the door as Hadleigh and Quinlan came in. Quinlan had had a few drinks with him and swapped a few stories. They got along well together—as well, that is, as anyone with Quinlan's background could with someone who had hustled his first buck on the streets before he had lost his baby teeth.

"Majors," he said.

It was generally "Ben" and it had got as far as "Otis" after a few beers, but for the present Judd was being formal.

"What's the score, Max?" asked Hadleigh.

"Got five of them in the Trough." The Trough was Judd's euphemism for the room where they kept all prisoners prior to in-depth interrogation.

"All together?"

"Shapiro and Kowalski are making sure they don't go into a huddle and exchange game plans."

"Who came through?"

"Schauff."

Hadleigh nodded. Walter Schauff was a fat fifty-year-old who'd once run his own bar and wanted to do so again, if he could get approval from the Americans. But a German wanting a license had to have a lily-white past and a recommendation from an officer. In Schauff's case, the price of that recommendation was cooperation.

Schauff had survived Hitler and the Nazis and had kept well away from anything that looked like a rifle or a front line by acting as a police stooge, informing the Gestapo about anyone with a loose tongue who did not subscribe to ultimate victory. He had changed little now that the war was over.

"Any possibles?" asked Hadleigh.

Judd shrugged his massive shoulders. Every intelligence outfit hoped to score big by capturing a senior SS or Gestapo officer with known crimes against his name. What mostly cropped up were petty criminals, former soldiers who had no intention of working in labor battalions, and men (occasionally women) who were living undercover, without registration or ration cards, for reasons that involved some minor peccadillo from years past in which the Allies were not in the least interested. However, Goebbels's propaganda in the closing weeks of the war—when he had broadcast that every male and female over the age of sixteen who had anything to do with the armed forces would be incarcerated for many years if not executed by the Allies—had been so influential that hundreds of Germans preferred starving in cellars and bombed-out buildings to registration.

The USAAF and the RAF had made the work of intelligence even more difficult by destroying tons of records in their bombings. Hadleigh was certain that many a man with a criminal past had slipped through the net solely because nothing on paper remained to prove he was other than what he claimed to be. The easiest thing in the world was to discard an SS uniform and don the clothes of a dead Wehrmacht soldier after relieving him of his paybook. Even the old test of examining everyone's upper inside arm for a tattooed blood group, once a sure sign of a fugitive SS man, no longer worked. Many of the senior ranks, with creditable foresight, had never been tattooed; others had found ways of removing the telltale marks.

"Let's take a look at what we have," said Hadleigh.

Judd hesitated.

"Come on, Max," prompted Hadleigh. "Major Quinlan and I have places to go if there's nothing here worth sitting up all night for. They didn't give me this bronze leaf to fill in forms."

Judd glanced from Hadleigh to Quinlan. He was plainly uncomfortable.

"Well, there's a slight problem," he said. "I told you we had five in the bag, but actually it's six."

"So what's the problem?"

"It'll be easier if I show you, Major."

Of the two doors in the guardroom, one led to the Trough, offices, and interrogation cells; the other to what were, in former days, punishment cells. Judd preceded them through this door.

Three cells stood on one side of a short corridor. Each was no bigger than a large pantry and each had a judas hole in its heavy soundproof door. Judd stood to one side and pointed to the first in line, indicating that Hadleigh should look inside.

The G-2 major squinted through the spy hole and stepped back instantly as though stung.

"Jesus Christ, Max. . . ."

Quinlan took his place. These days Hadleigh's outfit used the punishment cells as extra storage space for the massive overflow of files Third Army Intelligence was accumulating, but cell number 1 also held a young girl sitting on a pile of cardboard boxes. She was, Quinlan estimated, about seventeen, too thin by at least fifteen pounds, but pretty enough if you liked skinny teenagers who tied their hair back. The naked electric light bulb high on the wall and protected by wire mesh revealed a pale face and deep green eyes.

"What the hell's this, Max?" raged Hadleigh. "Haven't you read the goddamn rules about underage female prisoners? She screams rape and you put us all in the stockade until we're too old to care!"

"Sorry, Major, but blame Shapiro. He came back in the meat wagon with her. We'd arrested her father, and she said she wouldn't leave him because he's sick. When we tried tossing her out, she yelled blue murder. She calmed down when I said she could stay until we'd finished with her old man." He raised his shoulders apologetically. "It seemed the easiest way. She hasn't caused any fuss since we put her in there."

Hadleigh brought his temper under control. Wives, daughters, mistresses of arrestees frequently claimed their husbands, fathers, lovers were either sick or guilty of nothing. Tossing her back onto the street yelling her head off wouldn't have helped. The time was coming when the occupying powers would be looking for "good" Germans to take over the business of restoring some form of civil government, and the word from the top was not to rock the boat unnecessarily.

"Okay, Max, okay. You did right. Sorry I yelled. You say her father's in the Trough?"

"Yeah. Middle-aged guy Shapiro picked up in a house on Humboldtstrasse, between the Siemens factory and that burned-out cinema."

"What does Schauff say about him?"

Knowing that the girl and her father signaled trouble, Judd had the story at his fingertips. He referred to his clipboard.

"He claims the guy's name is Arndt and the girl's got the same name on her papers. He's not sure of his rank, but he remembers seeing him around Nuremberg during the war, in uniform. Arndt's got no identification and he's not registered."

"How did Schauff know where we could pick him up?"

"Said he saw the girl in the street, recognized her, and followed her. You know Schauff."

Hadleigh did. For a fat man Schauff could move like a wisp of smoke, and he worked to make an impression. He wanted that license badly.

"What about the daughter?" asked Hadleigh. "How does she check out for papers?"

"She's got a full house. Ration book, ID card, zone pass." Judd hesitated. "It looks like she was drawing rations for herself and splitting them with her old man."

"And that's all?"

Judd knew what Hadleigh meant. Prostitutes a good deal younger than Fräulein Arndt were on the streets, picking up a pack of cigarettes here, a slab of chocolate there.

"Not easy to tell without a thorough medical, but she doesn't look the type to hustle."

"They never do."

"Has Herr Arndt offered any explanation for his lack of cooperation?" Quinlan asked Judd. He knew from his own experience that men who had once been in uniform but were now hiding out, unregistered, usually had a damned good reason for doing so. Certainly a father who allowed his young daughter to share her already meager rations warranted investigation.

"Nobody's asked him for one yet, Major. I was waiting until Major Hadleigh got here."

"What about the others?" queried Hadleigh.

"Dreck," answered Judd. "The usual shit Schauff turns up to make his score sheet look good."

Hadleigh turned to Quinlan. "What d'you think? The girl'll keep, but Herr Arndt could be Martin Bormann."

Judd was not keen to allow Quinlan to participate in an interrogation. With a thirty-year hitch to complete, he wasn't about to buck standing orders.

"Major, with due respect, this is Third Army territory. I'm not sure the brass would go for letting outsiders in. No offense intended."

"None taken, Max," smiled Quinlan. To Hadleigh he added, "If you want me to take a walk, that's fine."

But Hadleigh hadn't made major because he smiled prettily.

"Crap. Max is just protecting me and worrying about that pension he'll be drawing around 1960. Besides, if Arndt has something he'd rather keep to himself, I'll be glad of the help. Okay, Max?"

"Whatever you say, Major. What about the kid?"

"She'll have to stay where she is for the time being. If it looks as though the interrogation will last all night, I'll think again, but if her father's got something to tell us, she might get in the way."

"And the other four?"

"You're sure they're just Schauff pulling shit?"

"As sure as I'll ever be."

"Then put them through the machine yourself. Are there any officers on duty tonight?"

"None I'd trust getting change for a nickel."

"I just wonder what you say about me when my back's turned."

On the way to the Trough he told Max that he and Quinlan would go into the good guy-bad guy routine. "I'll be the bad guy. When I'm through I'll come and give you a hand with the others."

They halted outside the door of the Trough and peered through the glass partition. With no prompting from Max, both Hadleigh and Quinlan identified Arndt without difficulty, a tall thin individual with iron-gray hair and an intelligent expression. In his late forties, he looked far from the best of health, but he was the only man in the room who could conceivably have worn a uniform with any sort of rank tabs. Max was right about how nondescript the rest were. Hadleigh made a mental note to have a quiet word with Schauff. He wouldn't get his liquor license this way.

Arndt did not seem surprised at being singled out and hurried into the nearest interrogation cell. Much bigger than the punishment cell, it contained a bunk, a wooden table, two upright chairs, and a chemical lavatory.

Hadleigh closed the door behind them and indicated that Arndt should sit on the bunk. The German did so, inquiring anxiously about his daughter.

Hadleigh ignored the question.

"Do you speak English?" he asked.

Arndt said he spoke a little. Hadleigh decided to converse in German. His accent was not much better than Judd's, but he had taken a six-month crash course in the language long before Pearl Harbor, and since June 1944 he had had plenty of practice.

"Now, Herr Arndt," he began, "or should I be addressing you as Sturmbannführer Arndt?" Sturm-

bannführer was an SS rank equivalent to major and
Arndt did not seem to like the association at all.

"I was not a member of the SS," he protested quietly.

"That's not the story we've heard." Hadleigh
dropped easily into his role of bad guy. For the moment
Quinlan said nothing. His turn would come later.
"We've got an eyewitness who will swear you were an
SS officer working out of police headquarters at num-
ber thirty-six Ludwigstrasse."

"Impossible. There can be no such eyewitness. I repeat, I was never in the SS."

"Nor the Nazi party either, I suppose," sneered Hadleigh.

"Nor that. He's a liar, your eyewitness."

"I never said it was a he," said Hadleigh, "but let's
assume it is, for the moment. He's proved pretty reliable
in the past. I have no reason to doubt his word this time.
There's one sure way of proving him right or wrong,
anyhow. If you're not Sturmbannführer Arndt and you
were never a party member, who are you really and
what have you been doing for the last six years? If
you've got nothing to hide, why haven't you registered?
Why have you been undercover, allowing the daughter
you seem so concerned about to sell herself on the
streets to keep you in food?"

"That's another lie . . ."

Arndt started to his feet angrily. He was no match for
Hadleigh, who planted a fist in his chest and pushed him
back on the bunk.

"Don't raise your voice to me, Herr Sturmbannführer," he growled. "You lost this fucking war and
that means you say please and thank you and watch
your goddamn manners. As to whether your daughter's
been on the streets or not, we'll soon have the answer to
that. I've sent for a doctor to give her a head-to-toe
physical, which includes a Wassermann. You know
what that is? It's the standard test for syphilis."

"You can't do that! She's only a child, just sixteen."

"I'm not in the least worried what the examination will do to one more Kraut hooker. What does concern me is how many GIs she infects."

"You bastard!"

Hadleigh hit him across the face. It wasn't a hard blow, more a dismissive insult. Even so Quinlan looked on uneasily. The G-2 major seemed to be playing his part with more conviction than was necessary.

"Mind you," said Hadleigh, "there's one sure-fire method of stopping all this before it starts, and that's to tell us what you did in the war. If you're not Sturmbannführer Arndt and you never worked out of Ludwigstrasse, just what have you been doing since 1939?"

"I have nothing to say," said Arndt quietly, wiping a speck of blood from his mouth. "I am guilty of no crime other than being a German. I also wish to point out, for the record, that I have a heart condition."

Hadleigh glanced at Quinlan. There was a damned sight more here than met the eye. Maybe Schauff had turned up trumps for once. Arndt couldn't know the bit about the medical was a bluff, and it didn't make any sense at all for him to allow his daughter to be humiliated unless he had a hell of a lot to hide.

"Screw your heart condition," jeered Hadleigh. "I don't believe one fucking word you're saying. As far as I'm concerned my information is correct and you're a former SS officer with probable crimes against his name. It'll take us awhile to run them down and make out a case against you, but we'll do it, make no mistake. Then we'll swing you from a fucking tree. In the meantime you're going to stay here until we've got a few more answers, and that daughter of yours is going to have her physical. If she's diseased, she's going to a women's prison and there she's going to stay. If she's clean—well, I've got a couple of boys on my staff who like making it with young girls."

Arndt sprang to his feet, screaming and cursing, spitting, throwing punches. He moved so fast for a man of his age who probably hadn't eaten a square meal in months that Hadleigh and Quinlan were caught unaware. After half a minute they subdued him by wrestling him to the bunk and holding him until they felt his muscles relax. Then they allowed him to sit up. His face was pasty gray, his breathing labored. *Maybe*, thought Quinlan, *the story about a heart condition was the truth*.

He beckoned Hadleigh to the far side of the cell.

"You'd better take it easy, Ben," he whispered in English.

Hadleigh nodded curtly. "Take over being the good guy."

"For Christ's sake take it easy," said Quinlan aloud, this time in German. "This isn't getting us anywhere. Let me talk to him. I don't care if he is SS. Since when did we start using their methods?"

"Since we saw Dachau and Belsen and Treblinka," answered Hadleigh. "And to hell with leaving him to you. You'll be feeding him coffee and doughnuts as soon as my back's turned. There's only one thing his sort understands and that's strength. Give him some of his own medicine; that's the way to deal with these bastards."

"Not while I'm around it isn't. If there's any more of this, there'll be a report going upstairs."

"Eat it," sneered Hadleigh. Nonetheless, he appeared to take the threat seriously. At least there was less venom in his tone when he added, "You Limeys are all the same."

"Half an hour," urged Quinlan. "Give me half an hour alone with him and hold off examining his daughter until I've finished. If he still refuses to talk, you can have 'em both."

Hadleigh pretended to think about it. Finally he agreed.

"Thirty minutes and not a minute more," he said from the cell door. "In thirty-one minutes I'll be back, bringing someone with more balls than you have, Major. Also in thirty-one minutes, the doc will be stripping Fräulein Arndt and prodding her with more instruments than you've ever seen. In sixty minutes, if he gives her a clean bill of health, I'm turning my men loose on her."

Hadleigh went out, slamming the cell door. He would give Max Judd a hand with the others while waiting.

Quinlan passed Arndt a cigarette and lit it for him. The German inhaled deeply and looked up at Quinlan with gratitude.

"Thank you," he said.

"Don't thank me," shrugged Quinlan. "He means what he says. Unless you start talking, he'll be back and I won't be able to help you. We're in the American zone and I'm a visitor. He might not be able to kick me out of Nuremberg, but he sure as hell can throw me out of this place. Then you and your daughter are on your own. What's her name, by the way?"

"Ilse."

"Okay, you and Ilse will have to face the music unless you can come up with a satisfactory explanation about why you were in hiding and why you didn't register according to the law."

"Allied law."

"But the law nevertheless. Come on, Herr Arndt." Quinlan adopted his most persuasive voice. "If you've got nothing to hide, you can at least tell me your rank and service arm."

"I never said I was in the services."

"You didn't have to. I've been in long enough myself to recognize a soldier when I see one."

"You may think what you wish, Herr Major."

Quinlan made a point of checking his wristwatch. He pulled up one of the wooden chairs and reversed it, sitting with his arms resting against the back.

"Look," he said, "I'm trying to help, but I need your cooperation. Consider it from Major Hadleigh's point

of view. Whatever you might think of Allied law, you're
in Nuremberg illegally because you didn't register. Add
to that the fact that you refuse to tell us your former
rank or service and you can see why Hadleigh is suspicious. About all we're sure of is that your name is
Arndt.''

"Not necessarily. Ilse's papers could be forged or
stolen.''

"We're not relying solely on Ilse's papers. Don't you
understand yet, Herr Arndt? You were informed on.
How do you think the Americans found you?''

"That is not possible. I have hardly been out of the
house in months.''

"Nevertheless, you were informed on. Believe me, we
do have a witness who remembers you from before the
war's end.''

Arndt's eyes widened in dismay when he realized
Quinlan was speaking the truth.

"That could not possibly be . . .''

"It could possibly be and is. It may take a while to
trace your background through him, but we can and
will.''

There was a tiny sigh of relief when Quinlan confirmed the informer to be male. It meant nothing to
Quinlan at the time, but he was to remember it later.

He tried a different tack. That Arndt knew something
he wanted to keep secret was no longer in doubt. Still,
he was tougher than he looked. He would probably hold
out forever unless the gloves came off. Though under-
nourished, far from the first flush of youth, and possibly sick, he possessed a determination that was almost
admirable. The weak link was Ilse.

"The war is over, Arndt,'' said Quinlan softly.
"None of us liked it, and things were done by the Germans that should never have been done. Any decent
man will see them as crimes and want the perpetrators
punished. Only those who committed the crimes or paid
lip service to the criminals will wish there to be no

retribution. I don't believe you fall into either of those categories.

"Let me tell you something about Major Hadleigh. He has seen Buchenwald and Dachau, and he is a man in a rage. He believes the whole German nation to be guilty because without the compliance of the people there could have been no Hitler, no SS. Those who now call themselves guiltless turned their heads when Jews were bundled off to concentration camps in the thirties. Many of you had Jewish neighbors and friends and didn't consider them lesser beings or stateless citizens until Hitler made killing them official policy. Then you went along. The corpses are real, the deaths unavenged. That is how Major Hadleigh sees it. The fate of one teenage German girl matters little to him if he can catch and hang some of the criminals who committed the atrocities."

Quinlan could see that his words were having no effect. He needed an extra gear.

"Let me tell you what will happen to your daughter if Major Hadleigh does not get some acceptable answers. She will indeed be examined by a doctor and pronounced clean. I know she'll be pronounced free from disease because I've seen her. I very much doubt she's been anywhere near a man. I would suspect her to be a virgin, which will make it worse.

"After what Major Hadleigh has seen in the camps, after what the guards did to the women there, the violation of Ilse will mean nothing to him, not if he suspects her father possesses information which he needs to do his job. Ilse will be taken to one of the larger cells—possibly the one next door to this, where you will be able to listen. Then any man who wants to will be permitted to do what he likes with her. I don't have to tell you that there are some appetites and tastes for the bizarre that not even a grown woman could survive, let alone a young child. Neither do I have to remind you that her unwillingness and fear will merely add spice to the occasion. Long before it's all over she'll be out of her mind —because her father was stubborn.''

"The Americans do not do such things," said Arndt dully.

His complexion had taken on a bluish tinge and his breathing was becoming labored. Quinlan hoped he wasn't overdoing it. He experienced only the mildest tremor of guilt when he saw the fight go out of the German, his shoulders droop, his features crumple. Nothing was going to happen to Ilse Arndt. If threats made her father talk, however, so be it. The memory of the afternoon's films was fresh in his mind, and Quinlan was more than willing to live with his conscience.

"I'm sick," mumbled Arndt, massaging his chest.

"You're also wasting time. You'll be given medical attention as soon as I have your full name, rank, and unit."

"And that's all?" Just getting the words out seemed to take an immense effort.

He wasn't stalling or faking, Quinlan was certain. But if he were allowed to see a doctor, any possibility of further information could be written off. He would be given treatment, pills, an injection. He would recover his strength and with it, possibly, his will to resist. Six months earlier on the German-Danish border, Quinlan had been unable to complete an interrogation because of doctors. It wouldn't happen again.

"To start with."

Quinlan made notes in the back of his diary. Twice he had to ask Arndt to speak up or repeat a sentence.

"My full name is Heinrich Adolf Arndt. My rank is— was—that of Hauptmann—captain. Since 1940 I have worked as a cryptanalyst for the Abwehr. Until this year, that is." In spite of his obvious pain, he managed a feeble joke. "Since May I have been unemployed."

"The Abwehr? You worked for Canaris?"

The reply was a long time coming.

"I knew Canaris, yes."

Arndt suspected he was dying. He could barely see his interrogator now through the thick curtain of red mist that clouded his vision. He thought his chest was about to burst, his heart explode. A terrible noise filled his head, a fierce buzzing that was growing louder and louder.

Quinlan tried a shot in the dark. For him the name Canaris was inextricably linked with the name William Joyce had denied giving him all those months before outside Flensburg.

"And your immediate superior was Oberstleutnant Manfred Langenhain, I believe."

My God, they knew of Langenhain! How was that possible?

"Yes, Langenhain." Arndt's voice was scarcely audible. "Please, I must have a doctor."

"In a moment, a moment."

"No . . ." Using all that remained of his strength, Arndt got to his feet. "Ilse . . ."

Quinlan caught him before he hit the stone floor, knocking over the chair and dropping his diary in the process. The official verdict would be a massive coronary brought on by extreme stress. The attack could have happened at any time. A healthier man might have recovered, but an autopsy would later show that Arndt was forty pounds underweight and that his body contained less than seventy percent of the minerals necessary to sustain life.

FOUR

~~~~~~

NUREMBERG
November 29–30, 1945

THE MEDICAL OFFICER had been and gone and the body taken to the morgue before Quinlan was able to tell Hadleigh and Max Judd what had transpired in the interrogation cell. He had no doubt that the threats against Ilse had caused Arndt's death; nor could he accept as mere coincidence that the name given to him by Joyce, now languishing in the death cell of Wandsworth Prison, London, was the same as Arndt's immediate superior.

"It's interesting," Hadleigh said finally, puffing away at his cigar, "but it's asking a lot to make a connection between Arndt and Joyce and Langenhain and Joyce. What you've got is as nice a case of happenstance as I've ever come across. No more than that, though."

Quinlan didn't agree. Hadleigh could call it happenstance or spinach; Quinlan was convinced there was more to this than chance.

"I mean, what *was* Arndt doing hiding out six months after the war's over?" the Englishman demanded. "Why did we have to go through that entire performance before he'd give me his full name? Christ, the Abwehr aren't war criminals. We want to interrogate them, sure, because as intelligence officers they can fill in a few blanks, but I haven't come across any of them playing coy before. They were serving soldiers, no more, no less."

Judd tried to say something. Quinlan waved him irritably to silence.

"Then there's Langenhain. I haven't seen the name in any file, yet this is the second time it's come to my attention in six months. So who is he? And what the hell was Arndt's big secret? He said he'd hardly been out of the house since May. Why? They were both living on the daughter's rations. Why? It doesn't make any kind of sense."

"It does to me." This time Judd insisted on being heard. "Even if we're not going to stick the majority of Abwehr officers in the dock, we are going to intern them until we're sure all they've been doing since 1939 is intelligence work. Who'd look after the girl if we'd put Arndt in jail? I haven't heard anyone mention a mother up to now. Maybe he stayed undercover to look after the kid."

"It seems to me it was the other way around," retorted Quinlan. "Ilse was looking after him."

"Speaking of which," said Hadleigh, "she'll have to be told about her father."

She would also have to be taken care of until they could decide what to do with her.

Hadleigh had no female personnel on his staff apart from Army clerks and Gretl Meissner. Counter Intelligence Corps did and there was little doubt that Ilse was going to need a woman's companionship after she heard of her father's death. The G-2 major wasn't at all happy at bringing in CIC and letting it become common knowledge that a death had taken place on Third Army property, but there were no other options.

While he placed the call, Quinlan volunteered to talk to the girl. Once alone with her in one of the offices, he could see that she seemed much younger than he had thought earlier, hardly a sixteen-year-old at all, closer to thirteen or fourteen. Yet she appeared to know what he was going to tell her long before he hesitantly found the words. She must have witnessed her father's gradual deterioration over the past six months and mentally prepared herself.

There were no hysterics. She cried a little while Quinlan looked on helplessly, wanting to reach out and comfort her but not knowing how. When the tears were over and she had wiped her eyes, he saw her make a conscious effort to regain her equilibrium. For an adult it would have taken a tremendous effort of will; for a young girl it was a magnificent feat.

He had not, of course, told her the entire truth. He mumbled something about a sudden heart attack, and she accepted his version without demur. The facts would come out later. Somewhere along the line an inquiry would have to take place, and then she would know. Tonight, however, was not the time. When she'd asked if she could see the body, Quinlan managed to persuade her to wait until the next day. He didn't add that Arndt was not a pretty sight and that it would be better to allow the morticians to add some cosmetic touches before she viewed the corpse.

He asked her where her mother was.

"She was killed in an air raid in 1944."

"Do you have any other relatives in Nuremberg?"

"I had an uncle and an aunt in Fürth."

"Who looked after you while your father was away?"

"Yes."

The professional in Quinlan wanted to pursue the question of Heinrich Arndt's absences. If the girl could remember dates or snatches of conversation, he might be a little closer to discovering the reason Arndt had been reluctant to tell him anything. The human being in the British major rejected the notion. Tomorrow or the next day would be time enough.

"If you'll give me your uncle's address, I'll see you're taken there tonight."

"You misunderstood me, Herr Major. I used the past tense. You see, they too are now dead. The terror fliers dropped their bombs with great accuracy. Of course, there's always my father's mistress. Her name is Hannah Wolz. When she's not with my father or whoring for the Americans, she sings in a place on Scheurlstrasse that used to be the Hans-Sachs cinema. But she wouldn't want me. She used to visit my father only when I was out. She didn't like me and I didn't like her. There's no one else."

Although they were terrifyingly stark words from a youngster who had just been orphaned, he detected no sarcasm or irony, nor any symptoms of delayed shock.

"Besides," she added in the same flat voice, "I should like to go home."

Quinlan searched his memory for the address where Judd had said Arndt and his daughter were picked up.

"To Humboldstrasse?"

"Yes."

The telephone on the desk rang. Hadleigh was on the other end.

"Did you tell her?"

"Yes. The quick brown fox jumps over the lazy dog."

"What?"

Quinlan glanced at the girl. There was nothing in her expression that told him she understood.

"Just checking if she speaks English."

"How did she take it?" asked Hadleigh.

"Too quietly. I think a doctor had better take a look at her."

"I'll arrange it. I've explained the situation to CIC and they're sending over one of their women operatives. She should be here any time. We'll rig up a couple of cots someplace and . . ."

"She says she wants to go home. To Humboldstrasse."

"Well, Christ—I don't know if that's such a great idea."

"It's what she wants, Ben. If the CIC woman will go along with it, I think it might be best."

There was a short silence.

"Well, okay," agreed Hadleigh. "I don't suppose it can do any harm. Will you stay with her until CIC arrives?"

"I'd rather not. Send someone down here, will you?"

When the GI came in, Quinlan told him to keep an eye on the girl and make sure she didn't do anything stupid. That done, he rejoined Hadleigh and Judd in the guardroom where the ever-alert master sergeant had a mug of coffee and a glass of bourbon ready for him.

"Thanks, Max."

"Rough, Major?"

"It's not something I'd like to do every day."

The mug of coffee was down to its dregs before the guardroom door opened and a very attractive, dark-haired woman in her late twenties came in. Like many CIC operatives, she was dressed in civilian clothes, a tailored two-piece suit which set off her trim figure to perfection. She gave her name as Angela Salvatini and produced her ID. Hadleigh examined it perfunctorily and handed it back.

"Where's the patient and what do you want me to do?" she asked.

Hadleigh introduced Quinlan and told him to give her the details. The G-2 major had already relayed the essential facts to CIC on the telephone. Quinlan explained that Ilse Arndt might need medical attention and wanted to spend the night in her own home.

"I don't know what sort of condition it's in," he added apologetically.

"Don't worry about it. Or about a doctor. I've had some training as a nurse and I've handled these cases before. A sleeping pill is probably all she needs."

"What about transportation?"

"I've got my own and a driver outside."

"They're starting to attract a better class of recruit to CIC," cracked Hadleigh. "Beautiful trained nurses with their own wheels."

Angela Salvatini refused to be baited. Instead she flashed him a dazzling smile. "I guess it was inevitable, considering how often we have to bale out Third Army Intelligence. Can I see the girl?"

"I'll take you along," offered Judd.

"I wonder where the bastards have been hiding Miss Salvatini," muttered Hadleigh after the door had closed. "She makes my clerks look like sumo wrestlers."

When Quinlan did not reply, Hadleigh clapped him on the shoulder. "Come on, Major, snap out of it. It's done now and there's not a damned thing you can do about it. What do you say we forget the whole fucking thing? It'll look better in the morning. Max can watch the store. I could use a diversion and I'm damn sure you could. If those girls of mine over in Sündersbühl haven't gone into business for themselves tonight—which Christ help them if they have—they should be very glad to see us."

Even though Quinlan wasn't keen on the idea, he allowed Hadleigh to persuade him that what he needed was another drink or two and the body of a compliant, experienced Fräulein.

The rest of the night was an unmitigated disaster. Quinlan's bedmate was one he'd had a couple of times

before—Ingrid, a sexy little dumpling who acted as
though she'd seen everything at least once and done
most of it twice. She tried all the tricks she knew to
please Major "Otters," but between Hadleigh grunting
away on the far side of the only habitable bedroom in
the house and his own private thoughts, Quinlan was
unable to respond. He was more than relieved when
dawn came.

Wrapped in a short silk robe from one of Hadleigh's
blackmarket sources, Ingrid took him into the kitchen
and made him a pot of coffee on a portable burner,
anxious to please in case he gave an adverse report
about her to "Major Ben."

After reassuring her that his lack of interest wasn't
her fault, Quinlan stepped out of the house into the cold
Nuremberg morning, thinking that the only thing worse
than a bombed city by night was a bombed city at first
light.

It was not quite 8 A.M., and a damp chill in the air
suggested snow was on the way.

Because leaving an unattended vehicle on the streets
overnight was not only an indictable offense but the
height of insanity if you wanted to find it with wheels
and tires the next morning, Hadleigh had had them
driven over the previous evening, his parting instructions being for a duty driver to pick them up around
nine. Quinlan could not wait. By nine he wanted to be
washed, shaved, and changed, and on his way to the
Palace of Justice.

The Sündersbühl district was a good two and a half
miles from Quinlan's quarters. While he could probably
have thumbed a lift, he didn't want strangers seeing a
British officer unshaved and unshowered. Besides, if he
walked, he would have to cross Humboldstrasse and he
could see how Angela Salvatini and Ilse Arndt were far-
ing. He recalled Max Judd saying that the Arndts lived
between the Siemens factory and a burned-out cinema.
He had no doubt he could find the address.

When he drew level with the factory, he saw two MP Jeeps and a military ambulance ahead of him. Some sixth sense told him they were parked outside the Arndt house. His stomach sank at the implications.

An American MP tried to bar his way and might have succeeded or suffered a broken jaw if Quinlan had not recognized Master Sergeant Judd among the knot of figures in the street. He shouted to get his attention, and Judd indicated that it was okay for the British major to come through. Judd was the senior NCO present. Two men in plain clothes were by his side. There were no prizes for guessing they were CIC.

"What's happened?" demanded Quinlan.

"Where's Major Hadleigh?" responded Judd. He pulled Quinlan to one side, out of earshot of the civilians. "Where the fuck's Ben?" he repeated. "I sent a Jeep for the pair of you."

Quinlan explained that he had left Sündersbühl about thirty-five minutes before.

Judd nodded. "That figures. I only got here myself ten minutes back. When I saw what had happened, I sent the Jeep straight over. The major should be here any time now."

"What's he going to find, Max?"

"You'd better see for yourself. And take a deep breath. It ain't pretty."

Judd led the way inside and up the creaking stairs, ignoring the questioning glances from the CIC representatives.

The Arndts' apartment was on the first floor above a bicycle shop. At one time there had been two more floors, but in trying to bomb the Siemens works the USAAF and the RAF had bracketed the target and many buildings on all sides of the factory complex were either completely in ruins or extensively damaged. The bicycle shop itself was boarded up, out of business for good by the look of things. Floors two and three, little more than gaping masonry, were no longer occupied.

Before someone had torn the place apart, Ilse Arndt
and her father had evidently done their best with what
remained—two rooms, plus a kitchen and a bathroom
from whose taps no water came. There was no glass in
any of the windows, which were covered with planks of
wood and tarpaulin. Illumination came from oil lamps.
Eight or ten were burning away, the majority probably
brought in by the two tough-looking MPs standing by
the bedroom door.

Quinlan looked around the living room in shocked
bewilderment. Practically every stick of furniture was
smashed, every item of clothing torn, every drawer up-
turned, every cupboard ransacked. Cushions had been
slashed, the stuffing scattered in all directions.

"We got an anonymous phone call just before eight,"
said Judd in a quiet voice. "Or rather the MPs did. A
woman said she'd heard screams coming from this address in the middle of the night, and hung up." He
shrugged. "It's not unusual. If you've lived in Nazi Germany for a few years, you learn to mind your own
business.

"The MPs came over, saw what had happened, and
hit the panic button for CIC. CIC called us, because it
was to us they'd loaned Angela Salvatini. Hang on to
your stomach."

Judd waved the two MPs to one side and preceded
Quinlan through the bedroom door. Quinlan would
remember the scene for the rest of his life. He had seen
some of the camps for himself and many more of the
atrocities committed there on film, but what greeted
him now was something straight out of hell.

Like the other room, the bedroom was a wreck, mat-
tresses ripped apart, bedding torn, drawers upended.
Ilse Arndt and Angela Salvatini were both naked and
very dead. It required little stretch of the imagination to
deduce that they had been raped, brutally and many
times. The position of each body gave that away. Nor
had whoever killed them settled for sexual assault

followed by swift dispatch. Both torsos were covered with cigarette burns, dozens of them, and the women had been severely beaten about the face. Both throats were cut, and both pairs of hands were nailed to the floor.

A doctor was trying to remove one of the six-inch nails when Quinlan ran out and was instantly and violently sick in the passage by the living room. Somewhere below he heard Ben Hadleigh's voice.

FIVE

∿∿∿∿∿∿∿∿∿∿∿∿∿∿∿∿∿∿∿∿∿∿∿∿∿∿∿∿∿∿∿

NUREMBERG
November 30, 1945

THE REMAINDER OF the morning developed into a
blistering argument between CIC and Ben Hadleigh,
with Quinlan an uneasy spectator. CIC had all the questions and Hadleigh few of the answers. *Sotto voce*, he
advised Quinlan to keep quiet too. This wasn't the moment to be voicing half-baked theories about Arndt, an
unknown Abwehr lieutenant colonel called Langenhain,
and the traitor Joyce.

Why, demanded the senior CIC officer, were they not
told that Angela Salvatini was wanted for more than a
routine overnight job? What were the full circumstances
surrounding the death of Heinrich Arndt? What had
Arndt said? What had taken place between the German
and this British major? Who the hell *was* this British

major and why was he allowed to interrogate a Third Army arrestee?

The questioning would doubtless have continued all day had not Hadliegh suddenly declared himself sick and tired of the whole lousy business and phoned his boss, Colonel Masterson.

The call was the first Masterson had heard of the murders. He knew, however, how to protect his own, and after a short, sharp argument on the telephone, the CIC men were on their way, their spokesman vowing that Third Army had not heard the last of them.

Hadleigh shook his head wearily when Quinlan wanted to continue the discussion of the previous night's horrifying events. There was much to talk about, but they'd think better after some sack time. They would all meet in Hadleigh's office that evening at seven-thirty.

Shaved and rested and wearing fresh clothing, Quinlan arrived early. Even so, Hadleigh and Judd were already there, the coffeepot on the boil, a small mountain of sandwiches on the desk.

Though spruced up, Hadleigh had evidently been put through the wringer by Colonel Masterson. Gesturing Quinlan to help himself to food and drink, he briefed him on how the meeting had gone.

"As expected, he chewed me out, telling me that CIC would have a field day over this. Maybe you don't know how it works in this man's army, Otis, but CIC and regular intelligence don't exactly hit it off. Half of them are bucking for jobs in this new organization Dulles is forming, the CIA, and they like to think they're the pros and we're the amateurs."

Quinlan, who had come across similar problems himself with the British Army's Special Investigation Branch, said he understood.

"Good," grunted Hadleigh, "because what I'm going to say next involves you specifically. Before we get down to cases, before we go over what happened last night—or what we think happened and why—there's something you and I have to get sorted out.''

Quinlan glanced across at Judd, puzzled, but the master sergeant was busy putting mustard on a sandwich.

''I don't know what the hell to make of the connection between Arndt, Langenhain, and William Joyce,'' Hadleigh went on, ''or even if there's anything to be made of it at all. Neither does Gene Masterson. If there *is* anything, you may be the only one who can put it together. Only you spoke to Joyce, and you were the last man to speak to Arndt. In other words, if this investigation—assuming there's something to investigate—is to remain in our hands and not CIC's, and if my career, and maybe Max's too, is not to go down the tubes, we're all going to need your help.''

Quinlan started to say something. Hadleigh held up his hand.

''Let me finish, Major. You can have your two cents' worth in a minute.

''While you were sleeping this afternoon, I got Gene Masterson to do the reverse of what happened when you first came down here. That is, ask General Dempsey a favor, ask if we could borrow you for a week or two or as long as it takes. By we, I mean Third Army Intelligence. More specifically, me. Your general said we could, providing you agreed. Apparently you were due to be rotated home before finagling your way to Nuremberg to cover the trials. Dempsey still wants the bulletins you promised him, though your head won't roll if they're not there every week. He said he'd leave the final decision up to you.''

There was really nothing to decide. True, Quinlan wanted to be sitting in the press gallery when Goering and the others were called to testify. The way things were going, however, the Allies would still be presenting the prosecution case up to and beyond the Christmas recess, and he wouldn't be there at all were it not for Gene Masterson and Ben Hadleigh. Gretl Meissner could take notes of the proceedings, and he could type up a report as and when he found time. Besides, he was indirectly responsible for Arndt's death and, because of that, young Ilse's. Third Army would have had to physically boot him out of Nuremberg before he gave up trying to find a few answers.

"You don't have to ask me, Ben," he said. "As long as I can have Frau Meissner on permanent loan, if you want me here, here's where I'm staying."

"Consider her yours. We can sort it out with her tomorrow."

They spent the rest of the session going over what they knew.

One: Hauptmann Arndt, for whatever reasons, had remained in hiding since the end of the war.

Two: Arndt had served in the Abwehr under Oberstleutnant Manfred Langenhain, about whom nothing more was known.

Three: William Joyce had also known, or known of, Langenhain.

Four: Ilse Arndt and Angela Salvatini had been raped, tortured, and killed and the Arndt apartment ransacked.

Conclusion to four: Some group—all the signs pointed to more than one or two—believed that something was hidden in the Arndt household and that Ilse and maybe Angela knew of its whereabouts.

"We all saw what was done to them," said Quinlan. "This wasn't any ordinary rape or burglary. They were tortured for information. The rape was incidental."

Hadleigh fumbled through his in-tray before coming up with the document he wanted. "I can give you an update on that. Prior to a full autopsy, first indications are that the burns and the rape took place several hours before the killings.'' He tossed the report on his desk. ''Which doesn't tell us who did it and what they were looking for.''

''And if they found it,'' added Quinlan.

''It also leaves another question,'' said Max Judd. ''Why did they choose last night? Arndt was in hiding for six months, presumably in the same place.''

''Maybe they didn't know where he was until last night,'' said Quinlan. ''Nobody else did.''

''So how did they suddenly find out?'' asked Hadleigh.

Judd had a possible answer. ''Schauff?''

Hadleigh shook his head. ''I don't think so. He's not the sort to work both sides of the street. I think they—whoever it is we're talking about—have been watching the main gates of the barracks. Remember, there's always a crew of people out there day and night, regardless of the curfew. Remember too that Ilse Arndt came in with her father and raised hell when Max tried to toss her out. That would have attracted someone's attention. Am I making any sense?''

''Keep talking,'' encouraged Quinlan.

''Let's figure it this way. Some group was looking for Anrdt. They knew he was in Nuremberg; they didn't know where. We've made the assumption up to now that Arndt was hiding from us. What if he was hiding from this unknown group? Although they can't find him, they assume sooner or later we will. What the hell have they got to lose by watching the gates anyway? Maybe they're not looking for just Arndt. Maybe they're looking for others too. They see Arndt and his daughter brought in, but only the daughter and Angela Salvatini leave. They follow them and see Miss Salvatini's driver leave. The way they tore the place apart, maybe they didn't want Arndt himself but something he had on him or hidden. That's a reasonable deduction because it would take around ten seconds for guys with their meth-

ods to find out from Ilse that her father was dead. Yet
they still ransacked the entire apartment. Any takers for
that theory?''

Quinlan nodded. Judd framed another question no
one had yet bothered to ask.

"We keep talking about 'they' in general. I think we
should be more specific. Don't we mean the SS or some
part of it? Everything about those killings bears the
mark of the SS.''

Hadleigh and Quinlan agreed.

"Okay," said the former, "let's say it's the SS.
Christ, there are still plenty of them around; we know
that much. If we had them all, I could go back to Chicago where the mobsters are civilized." He put a match
to the stub of his cigar. "Arndt had something this
group wants and they're willing to kill for it. SS or not,
we still don't know what or why.''

"Which means we're back to Canaris and Langenhain," said Quinlan. "And maybe Joyce too. Right,
let's forget Langenhain and Joyce for the moment. We
can't find one and the other's due to hang before long.
But there's a definite tie-in between Canaris and the
SS.''

Six months after the end of the war the facts concerning Canaris's fate were not fully known. All that the
Allies had established was that the ex-chief of the Abwehr had fallen from grace around the time of the July
Plot to assassinate Hitler, though whether Canaris was
part of the conspiracy remained a mystery. He was,
however, purged for being less than loyal to National
Socialism, and at the beginning of April 1945 he was
executed in the SS concentration camp at Flossenbürg
on the German-Czech border. The order for his execution could have come from only one of three people:
Hitler, Himmler, or the former head of the RSHA,
Ernst Kaltenbrunner. Himmler was definitely dead, Hitler almost certainly so, and Kaltenbrunner on trial for

his life in Nuremberg. Or rather he was suffering from spinal meningitis and presently in a military hospital in the city.

"Not that he'd tell us anything even if we were allowed to talk to him," said Hadleigh. "The friggin' judges are so anxious that everything be legal that, if anyone in the dock as much as *sneezes*, there are a dozen guys rushing toward them with the Kleenex. Apart from that, I hear Kaltenbrunner's denying everything. According to his deposition, he never even *heard* of the SS."

"Maybe they'd let me talk to Joyce," mused Quinlan. "He clammed up as soon as he knew he was safe back in May and claimed I'd misunderstood him. Now that his neck is on the line he might sing a different song."

"If there's anything to sing," said Judd.

Quinlan grimaced. "Maybe the answer is somewhere in Arndt's apartment, which is where we should be now instead of sitting around here."

"Not me." Hadleigh shook his head emphatically. His fatigue was beginning to show. Quinlan and Max had had some sleep; he had spent the afternoon with Gene Masterson. "Include me out. If there was anything there, it's been found or was never there in the first place."

"Maybe."

"Maybe, *sch*maybe. You play detective if you want to. Perhaps I'll join you when my mind's back in gear."

"Me, too," said Judd. "I've got a couple of yards of paperwork to catch up on."

Quinlan was in no way fazed. "Can I borrow a vehicle?" he asked.

"Sure," said Hadleigh. "Help yourself from the pool. I'll call through when you leave to tell 'em it's okay." He fished a buff-colored card from his jacket pocket and tossed it across the desk. "You'll need this also."

Quinlan picked it up and examined it. It was a laissez-passer authorized by Masterson himself, entitling Major Otis Nicholas Quinlan to go anywhere in the US zone without hindrance and to demand unqualified assistance from any member of the US armed forces, regardless of rank. There was a space for the bearer's signature at the bottom.

"I can just about start World War Three with this."

"I took a chance you'd want to stay on the team and had Masterson okay it this afternoon. You'll need it at the apartment. There are a couple of MPs on guard outside in case last night's visitors come back. They can watch the Jeep, so you won't need a driver. Unless you find Martin Bormann under the floorboards, don't bother to call. As of five minutes from now, I'm not available until morning."

Quinlan arrived at the bicycle shop on Humboldtstrasse just before 10 P.M. The MPs on guard were the pair he had seen earlier in the day outside the bedroom door. Although they recognized him, they insisted on seeing his pass.

"Sorry, Major," apologized one, handing it back and throwing a salute that was nearer a royal wave than anything from a drill manual, "but previous orders were that no one goes inside."

"No problem," smiled Quinlan. "Just watch the Jeep."

The oil lamps were extinguished and Quinlan spent five minutes lighting them. A fatigue party had made a reasonable job of cleaning the blood from the floor and walls, but what they could not eradicate was the smell of death.

Optimistically, Quinlan had brought his briefcase. After a quarter of an hour's search, he was willing to concede he'd find nothing to put in it. He prodded among the blood-stained cushions, chairs, and bedding and examined spare clothing and cupboards. He even prized off a couple of feet of wall paneling. To no avail.

Dousing each of the lamps, he returned to the street.

The snow that had threatened all day had now started to fall, small flakes that looked as though they would stick. It was no night to be driving around in an open Jeep. After thanking the MPs, who were shivering and cursing in the shop doorway, Quinlan flicked his headlights to full beam and headed for home.

He was still in third gear and had covered only a few hundred yards when he became aware that he was being followed. The driver of the other vehicle had tucked himself in on Quinlan's tail and there he was staying, headlights on. At first Quinlan thought it might be a patrol Jeep curious to know what kind of lunatic was driving around late at night in a snowfall. When he slowed opposite Kopernikusplatz, however, the car behind him slowed also.

Because the snow was restricting his vision, he was driving at less than twenty miles per hour, yet the pursuing vehicle made no attempt to overtake him. He soon discovered why.

At the Gudrunstrasse intersection, a second vehicle shot out from his left, causing him to wrench the steering wheel to the right to avoid a collision. Partly because of road conditions and partly because of his unfamiliarity with left-hand drives, he was slow to compensate, went into a rear-wheel skid, slid across the street, and stalled. Before he could restart the engine, the trailing car ground to a halt. Three men jumped out and ran toward him. From the second car two more figures emerged. Although it was hard to tell in the snow, they seemed to be carrying clubs. Or rifles. In German they called out to one another to hurry.

His heart beating rapidly, Quinlan was trying to decide whether to face his attackers or make a dash for it when they were on him. Something hard and heavy smashed against his temple. Before lapsing into unconsciousness he heard, with a jolt that hit him like an electric shock, the German voices joined by another that said, in English with a broad British accent, *"Nail the bastard!"*

In the distance he was vaguely aware of a blaring car horn and flashing lights. Then there was nothing but blackness.

When he came to, he was sitting in the passenger seat of the Jeep, his head thrown back, the snow wonderfully cool on his face. Ben Hadleigh was saying, "He'll have a mother of a headache in the morning, but he'll live."

Several minutes passed before he felt fit enough to talk. He shook his head to clear it. The Jeep was where he had stalled it; there was no sign of the other cars or their occupants and his briefcase was gone from the backseat.

He told Hadleigh and Judd what he remembered.

"It proves one thing, anyway," he concluded. "They haven't found whatever they're looking for. They must have thought I had—in the briefcase."

"But you hadn't?"

"There was nothing more in there than a couple of out-of-date maps." He concentrated on bringing his mind further into focus. "How come you two turned up when you did?" he asked. "Don't think I'm not grateful, but how come?"

"You can thank Max," said Hadleigh. "I was sound asleep when he woke me up with the notion that if I was bright enough to post a couple of guards on the off chance that last night's visitors would come back, they could be watching the Arndt place. If so, you were putting your head in a noose. We just hoped to God you'd take the obvious route home."

For the first time Quinlan noticed that Hadleigh was wearing only an Army-issue raincoat over his pyjamas and that his shoes were unlaced. "Did you get a look at them?" he asked.

"No." Hadleigh pulled his raincoat more tightly about him. "Even with the snow we could see what was happening a hundred yards away, so Max hit the horn and stepped on the gas. They took off in a hurry, and we had to decide whether to follow them or find out if you were okay.'' He grinned. ''Besides, there seemed to be a hell of a lot more of them than there were of us.''

Quinlan told them about the English voice he'd heard among the German ones.

Hadleigh whistled. ''Now what the hell do you make of that?''

Quinlan didn't know. What he did know was that he wanted to talk to Lord Haw-Haw. And fast.

SIX

‸‸‸

LONDON: WANDSWORTH PRISON
December 3, 1945

LONDON WAS COLD and wet, but even postwar auster-
ity and rationing could not dampen British spirits. The
islanders were nearing their first Christmas at peace for
six years and they were going to enjoy it. Although there
might not be much on the table, it could be eaten and
drunk without worrying where the next bomb or V-2
rocket would fall or whether that knock on the door was
a War Ministry telegram announcing the death in action
of a loved one.

William Joyce was in the condemned cell, where he
was prisoner number 3229. He referred to himself in letters to his wife, incarcerated in Holloway Prison for
Women, as Wandsworth William (as opposed to Wormwood Will after the prison Wormwood Scrubs, where
he was held while his Wandsworth cell was being pre-

pared). His trial at the Old Bailey had begun on September 17 and, despite a spirited defense by his leading counsel, Mr. G. D. Slade, KC, had ended on September 19 with a unanimous verdict of guilty. Prosecuting counsel was Sir Hartley Shawcross, presently head of the British contingent in Nuremberg.

Many argued that Joyce was convicted on a flimsy technicality, and at one time bookmakers were offering six-to-four on an acquittal. At the close of the first day of the hearing Shawcross had asked an eminent constitutional lawyer, Professor J. H. Morgan, whether the prosecution had any chance. Morgan had replied, "No, not unless the judge is prepared to make new laws."

The points of law that emerged during the trial were obscure to the layman, the verdict hinging on whether Joyce, as the holder of a British passport (no matter how obtained) at the time of his defection to the enemy, owed allegiance to the British crown. If so, in broadcasting for Germany, had he violated that allegiance? The jury decided he had. So did the Court of Appeal on November 7. He was guilty of high treason under the Treason Act of 1351, and the fact that he was the son of a naturalized American citizen or that he later adopted German nationality was not going to help him. He had joined Sir Oswald Moseley's British Union of Fascists, had claimed on the application form for his passport that he was a British subject by birth, having been born in Galway, Ireland, and had always thought of himself as British, even in his broadcasts, until thinking so became inconvenient. All he could hope for now was that the House of Lords, due to sit on December 10, would overturn the Appeal Court's confirmation of the original verdict. There was little chance of that. Joyce had turned on beleaguered Britain during its darkest hours, and it was not only the man in the street who wanted his head.

Realizing how hard it would be even to get permission to go to England, let alone see Joyce, Quinlan had enlisted Hadleigh's aid. As a Regular Army man of considerable experience, Hadleigh knew that the worst way to approach any problem was head-on. If the second stop was to get General Dempsey to make a few top-level phone calls to his political friends and the last step to obtain the British Home Secretary's permission to visit Joyce, the first step was to acquire some clout.

Hadleigh contacted both Colonel Masterson and CIC. The story he told each was the same: that a possible clue to the identity of the killers of Angela Salvatini might be found in Wandsworth Prison.

Masterson was more than willing to help, but initially CIC proved recalcitrant. They wanted in on the act and were only persuaded that as yet there was no act to get in on by a lot of fast talking from Hadleigh. When and if there was, they would be the first to know. In the meantime, would they be kind enough to make waves?

By midafternoon on December 1, Quinlan was making a direct appeal by telephone to General Dempsey, who was by now accustomed to peculiar requests involving his subordinate and who had, in any case, received several similar entreaties from American sources before he had finished his second cup of breakfast coffee. Dempsey was revered by those who served under him for his policy of either trust and delegate or fire, and he thought a lot of Otis Quinlan. He promised to do his utmost to help.

Even though the Home Secretary could forbid anyone outside immediate family to see a condemned man, in the peculiar tradition of British jurisprudence most individuals due to be executed were granted a far greater latitude facing death than, for the most part, they had ever had, or given others, in life. It was as if the law was saying, until we hang you we'll be nice to you.

The greatest obstacle might be Joyce himself, who could refuse a visit from anyone. Fortunately he remembered the British major from Flensburg and, with the sardonic humor for which he was noted (he had referred to Sir Hartley Shawcross as Hotcross and his trial at the Old Bailey as "a business trip to the city"), agreed to see the man who had threatened to have him shot six months earlier.

After that, wheels turned, strings were pulled, lines buzzed, cogs meshed, and Quinlan found himself on a plane for England, not at all sure what he intended to ask Joyce.

He was permitted to interview the former Lord Haw-Haw in an anteroom well away from the condemned cell. There was to be no smoking, nothing was to change hands, the conversation would be conducted exclusively in English, and two prison guards had to be present for security reasons. If any infraction of these conditions occurred, the guards had instructions from the prison governor to terminate the dialogue.

Quinlan was already seated on one side of a long wooden table when Joyce was brought in, dwarfed by the guards on either side of him. For some reason he was never later able to fathom, Quinlan stood up. Evidently amused and delighted by this involuntary gesture, Joyce said, "Sit down, my dear chap. Never stand in the presence of the dead."

He was plumper than Quinlan remembered and looked reasonably fit. His pale blue eyes were alert, eager even, and Quinlan reflected on Dr. Johnson's words: "Depend upon it, sir, when a man knows he is to be hanged in a fortnight, it concentrates his mind wonderfully."

Quinlan tried to recall how old he was: forty if memory served him, though he looked older. His hair was cut short in the prison fashion. The scar on his right cheek was hardly noticeable under the bare electric light.

Joyce took his seat on the opposite side of the table and clasped his hands while the guards retreated discreetly to the far side of the anteroom.

"And what can I do for Major Quinlan? I see you *are*

still a major. Promotion must be exceedingly slow now that there is no war to eliminate those at the head of the line.''

If Joyce was trying to bait him, Quinlan was unaware of it. The journalist in him was crying out to ask the thousand questions that would give him an exclusive story anywhere in the world if he could bypass the Official Secrets Act, and it was with difficulty that he brought his mind back to the matter at hand.

He reminded Joyce of their first meeting, how he had said he knew nothing of former leaders of the Third Reich with the exception of Oberstleutnant Manfred Langenhain and Admiral Canaris.

''Did I really say that? I can't imagine why unless it was because of the rifle that little Welsh corporal was pointing in my direction. He was Welsh, was he not? I seem to recall a malevolence in him reminiscent of all our cousins beyond Offa's Dyke. Of course, I had bullet wounds in both legs so I was perhaps slightly delirious. In any event, I did not mean it the way you apparently took it. I did of course meet many of Germany's leaders, notably Dr. Goebbels. I really cannot say why I singled out those two gentlemen for mention apart from the fact, as I said a moment ago, I judged your leek-eating underling's intentions to be less than friendly.''

He had always had that curiously stilted way of talking, and prison had evidently done nothing to diminish it.

Quinlan was conscious that the interview could get wildly out of hand if he allowed Joyce to dictate the pace. The little man was obviously quite proud of his facility with the English language and would be anxious to compensate for the small opportunity he had to exercise it in prison.

Quinlan had conducted interrogations before and knew the theory and practice of selective memory. Equally, he understood that, no matter how calm and superior Joyce might appear on the surface, deep inside him was the knowledge that he was shortly going to die. He would have to be handled with kid gloves if anything was to be gained.

Keeping his voice as neutral as possible, he told Joyce what, to the best of his recollection, his precise words were in the border guardroom. "You didn't exactly say you had never met anyone else. What you did say was that you *knew nothing about* former military and political leaders of Germany with the exception of Langenhain and Canaris."

"The implication being I had intelligence on their recent whereabouts and activities?"

"Yes."

"Hmmm."

Always keep your subject off balance was the golden rule of every interrogator. In this instance Quinlan disobeyed it. Joyce was not someone dragged in off the streets who could be browbeaten. He was a man with nothing to lose. At the flick of a finger, on a whim, he could close the interview. Quinlan's one hope was to keep him interested, allow him his vanity, encourage what was evidently a prodigious memory, make him *like* the man on the opposite side of the table.

But the traitor's next statement floored him.

"As I recall," said Joyce, "you asked the Welsh corporal if he had a round in the chamber. You also implied that if I was shot you could always say I had tried to make a run for it, and who would question the word of a British officer, especially when the cadaver was the infamous Lord Haw-Haw."

Quinlan's heart sank. He had feared all along that, if Joyce could remember mentioning Langenhain and Canaris, he would also remember the circumstances. He considered briefly trying to bluff it out by maintaining those words had been said in the heat of the moment, but something told him to play it straight. At the back of his mind he recalled a piece he had read in the *Manchester Guardian* at the time of the Old Bailey trial.

The commentator had written that the impression he got was of Joyce wanting to be thought of as British through and through. Never mind what the excellent Mr. Slade was pleading for the defense, Joyce was as British as village greens, pints of dark ale, red London buses, smog, and hot chestnuts from a brazier. Had he been allowed on the witness stand, there was little doubt (in that commentator's opinion) that Joyce would ever have denied broadcasting for Germany. He would have said yes, certainly he had, to reaffirm to the British people his belief that their true friends were in the Reich, their real enemies among them and in government. He was a man who would hope to see in his obituary the sentiment that he had always played the game honorably.

Quinlan took a chance.

"You're right," he said. "Your memory does you credit. I can't say at this distance whether I would have allowed the Welshman to shoot you, but yes, it was in my mind."

There was a short silence before a flicker of a smile crossed Joyce's face.

"Good," he murmured. "That's the only answer I would have accepted." He paused. "May I ask you the purpose of your visit and the reasons for your interest in Canaris and Langenhain?"

"I'm afraid not."

"I'm not likely to shout it from the rooftops, you know," teased Joyce.

"Nevertheless . . ." said Quinlan.

Joyce glanced across at the guards, who were listening with total fascination. This was heady stuff. What a story they'd have for the pubs and the family, a British Army officer wearing the green insignia of Intelligence asking the most notorious prisoner in the land about Hitler's chief spymaster.

"Canaris is dead, I believe."

"So we understand."

"And Langenhain?"

"That's for you to tell me."

"I'm not at all sure, Major Quinlan, that I have much to tell. I never met either of them, you know, although I heard them being discussed around the beginning of April this year. In Berlin."

BERLIN
April 1945

Word came from on high that the Reichsrundfunk English Language Service, the propaganda department for which Joyce worked, was to move out. Berlin was too dangerous for men and women who still had a useful function to perform. The city was on the verge of becoming a smoking ruin. The Soviet ground forces were almost within artillery range, the Allied bombers over night and day. The firemen were barely able to control one lot of fires before another conflagration started elsewhere, and the TENO platoons (*Technische Nothilfe* or Technical Emergency Help) were stretched to breaking. Everywhere Berliners looked, buildings that had been standing unscathed the day or week before were now tableaux of yawning masonry. The Führer kept on encouraging the people of Germany not to desert him, to remain and fight the Mongolian hordes from the east. There was little fight left in them, and none at all in the majority of the English language broadcasters.

Herr Winkelnkemper, the Foreign Service director, first suggested Dresden as the new base of operations, and Gauleiter Mutschmann conducted one of Winkelnkemper's representatives over every availabe building in the city. But the February raids by the combined forces of the USAAF and the RAF had virtually destroyed the capital of Saxony and the idea had to be abandoned.

Finally the Propaganda Ministry decided that the

English Language Service would be moved to Apen, a town midway between Bremen and the Dutch frontier. Most of the staff preferred to risk the consequences of falling into Anglo-American hands rather than be taken by the Russians. The lone voice pleading to be allowed to stay, to fight to the death if it came to it, was that of William Joyce.

Now a Volkssturmmann, a member of the Home Guard comprising the very old and the very young and those not fit enough to fight with a front-line regiment, Joyce had a violent argument with his wife, Margaret, in their apartment the morning before they were due to leave.

He was drinking brandy straight from the bottle, and as always when the real world did not accord with his fantasies (he had once thought he would return to England with the victorious Wehrmacht as gauleiter of London), he became irrational.

"The troops can't run away and neither can the aged and infirm," he shouted, "so why should I? You go if you want to. I'm staying."

His wife tried to reason with him. Although as dedicated a supporter of National Socialism as her husband, the former Margaret Cairns White, daughter of a Lancashire businessman of Irish lineage, was frightened of her husband's rages, the more so when he was drinking.

They *must* go, she argued gently. He was employed by Reichsrundfunk, and if he did not do what Toni Winkelnkemper said, he would soon be unemployed and penniless.

Joyce refused to see reason. Taking the bottle of brandy with him, he retired to the bedroom and fell asleep in his clothes.

When he awoke it was midafternoon and his wife had gone. A handwritten note on the dressing table told him that she was visiting friends and would be back later.

In spite of the picture depicted of him in the British press, Joyce was no physical coward. But Margaret was

right. If he disobeyed Winkelnkemper's orders to go to
Apen with the others, not only would his contract with
Reichsrundfunk be terminated but he might soon receive a visit from the Gestapo. The Third Reich, battling
for its life, would give short shrift to individuals who
would not do what they were told. The only man who
could possibly grant him authorization to stay was Dr.
Goebbels.

After washing and shaving and putting on a clean
shirt, he made his way across town to the Propaganda
Ministry on Wilhelmstrasse, taking streetcars where they
were running and walking where they were not.

The huge building which faced the eastern windows
of the Reich Chancellery had received several direct hits
during the previous night's air raid, and dust and debris
were everywhere in the massive lobby. The official behind the desk where all visitors were obliged to report
was less than helpful. He knew Joyce by sight of course,
as did every member of the Propaganda Ministry and
most Berliners of any rank.

"Impossible, Herr Joyce," snapped the official.
"The Reichminister does not see anyone without an ap-
pointment. If you care to send in a written request, I will
see it's forwarded via proper channels. Other than that I
cannot help."

"It's a personal matter which cannot be delayed,"
tried Joyce.

The official sighed wearily.

"There are three million Berliners who all have personal business which cannot be delayed. You are merely
three million and one." Smiling slyly, for Joyce's fond-
ness for the bottle was well known, he added, "I suggest
you decamp to the nearest bar and write your request
there."

Outside, Joyce considered the virtues of the idea. His
mouth was dry and he needed a drink. A short walk
away was the Adlon Hotel, famous before the war as an
international watering hole for the rich and influential

and even now a meeting place of the powerful. He would kill two birds with one stone: quench his thirst and hope to bump into someone who could help him remain in Berlin.

Miraculously, the Adlon was untouched by bombs. Its windows were filigreed with tar paper and the entrance was sandbagged to the second floor, but it was still there.

Inside the great hallway, with its priceless tapestries and crystal chandeliers, he paused for a moment, faced with a sea of uniforms representing all the services and an equal number of civilians. Many of the latter were with women who only could be their wives, though scattered among the uniforms were pretty little blond creatures, laughing, giggling, as anxious as the men they accompanied to make hay while the sun still shone. Liveried waiters hurried from group to group bearing trays. The drinks were almost exclusively champagne.

Feeling considerably underdressed in his shabby suit, Joyce searched the lobby for someone he recognized, his gaze at last alighting on a trio of men huddled deep in earnest conversation. Two of them, senior SS officers in full uniform, were unfamiliar to him, but the third, in plain clothes, he knew well. All three had their backs to him as he sidled up in time to hear the older of the officers say, "Canaris is finished. It's that bastard Manfred Langenhain who bothers me. He skipped before we could pick him up, and he's dropped right out of sight. If we don't find him, we're in trouble."

"You can leave Oberstleutnant Langenhain to my people," said the second officer confidently. "He can't remain in hiding forever."

"It's not forever I'm worried about. It's the next few months. He could pass on this information to dozens of others. We could finish up not knowing who the hell to look for."

At this point the third man, conscious of someone behind them, turned and saw Joyce. His eyes widened in dismay and he greeted Joyce's ingratiating smile with a scowl.

The two officers turned also. The older of the pair recognized Joyce.

"Well, well," he grinned, "the celebrated Lord Haw-Haw. I thought you people had moved out."

"Not yet," said Joyce. "In fact I'm rather hoping not to go at all."

"Determined to die for the Reich, eh? Admirable, admirable."

The third man whispered anxiously to the older SS officer who seemed unconcerned.

"I don't think Herr Joyce heard anything of major importance, did you, Herr Joyce?"

"Nothing," lied Joyce.

"I thought not. Even if he had, he has his own neck to worry about now."

"I'm not in the least worried about my own neck," blustered Joyce.

"Again admirable—if unique." The older officer glanced pointedly at his wristwatch, a beautiful creation in twenty-two-carat gold. "I'm afraid we have much to discuss, Herr Joyce, otherwise I would invite you to join us. If you will therefore excuse us. . . ."

LONDON: WANDSWORTH PRISON
December 3, 1945

". . . As you know," concluded Joyce, "I didn't stay in Berlin. I went with the others to Apen."

"And that's all?" Quinlan was unable to disguise his disappointment. "That's all you heard?"

"I'm afraid so."

"Did you learn the names of the two SS officers?"

"No."

"But the third man, the one in civilian clothes. You said you knew him."

"So I did."

"Who was it?"

Joyce shrugged. "It can be of no importance now."

"It might be to me."

"I think not."

Quinlan knew that Joyce had said all he was going to, and little enough it was. He was no further ahead than yesterday. Two SS officers and a third man had been planning the capture (and presumably the execution) of Oberstleutnant Langenhain, who apparently possessed information they preferred kept secret. What the information was would probably remain a mystery, as would Langenhain's fate. With Arndt dead and Joyce unable or unwilling to fill in the gaps, he might never learn who had killed the Abwehr captain's daughter and Angela Salvatini or who was responsible for the attack on himself three days before. The chain had run out of links unless there was something in the Arndt apartment everyone had overlooked and unless . . .

In his excitement he almost snapped the pencil with which he was taking notes. Of course! What a damned fool he was! With all the drama of the previous seventy-two hours he had completely forgotten . . .

He packed his notebook and pencils into a brand-new briefcase, courtesy of the Third Army. *There must be words for situations like this,* he thought grimly.

But apart from that, Mrs. Lincoln, how did you enjoy the play?

"I'd like to thank you for your cooperation," he offered lamely.

"Think nothing of it, Major Quinlan. I've enjoyed our talk. It would be pleasant to think we might meet again, though I doubt it."

Quinlan stood up awkwardly. He was wondering, in spite of everything, whether he should offer to shake hands when Joyce solved the problem for him by abruptly getting to his feet and indicating to the guards that he wished to return to his cell. Not until much later

did Quinlan realize Joyce had perceived his dilemma
and purposely left the table quickly to save him embarrassment.

NUREMBERG
December 7, 1945

Quinlan was left cooling his heels in London for three
days before his number came up for a return flight, and
even that was delayed by a dozen hours because of a real
pea-souper of a fog. With money in his pocket, seventy-
two hours in the capital was an unexpected bonus. He
managed to contact an old girl friend who, happily, was
between affairs. They had a decent dinner at the Ritz
and spent the night together. Part of his mind, however,
was in Germany.

He arranged with an RAF acquaintance for a signal
to be sent to Third Army when he was airborne, and
Hadleigh was at the military airfield to greet him on the
afternoon of December 7 with the news that Schauff,
his informer, had been found dead two days before, his
throat cut. Hadleigh had also sent in a specialist team to
tear the Arndt apartment to shreds. They had come up
with nothing. When he was able to get a word in,
Quinlan told him about Arndt's mistress, the woman
whom Ilse had not liked: Hannah Wolz.

SEVEN

wwwwwwwwwwwwwwwwwwwwwwwwwwwwwwwwww

NUREMBERG
December 8-28, 1945

BUT OF FRÄULEIN WOLZ there was nary a whisker nor
a feather to be found. The manager of the Hans-Sachs
cinema on Scheurlstrasse confirmed that she had sung
there, adding grumpily that she had not turned up for
work "since a week ago last Friday." These girls, his
tone implied, who could trust them? "Not like us men,
eh, German, American, or British?"

On hearing the date Quinlan experienced a sense of
dread. Last Friday week was November 30. During the
small hours of the twenty-ninth and thirtieth Ilse Arndt
and Angela Salvatini had been killed.

The Hans-Sachs cinema no longer showed films. The
projection equipment had been damaged in an air raid
and replacements were impossible to come by. Besides,
there was more money to be earned by converting the

building into a club. Ignoring the fraternization prohibition and the need for a license, the enterprising owner had ripped out the tip-up seats, installed a bar and a small stage, and let it be known he had the finest singers and strippers in the entire zone. He obviously had hefty clout somewhere, because when Quinlan and Hadleigh visited the place beer and hard liquor were flowing like there was no tomorrow, while onstage a young redhead a few pounds underweight was peeling off her clothes to music from a hand-cranked phonograph and raucous shouts and whistles from the audience.

As a demonstration of the erotic, it compared with watching paint dry. For the spectators, however—most of whom had not been anywhere near a woman for as long as they could remember—it was Marlene Dietrich in *The Blue Angel* in spades.

The majority of the clientele were enlisted men. Hadleigh recognized many of them. Located near the Allersbergerstrasse barracks and just across the main railway line from the Grand Hotel, the Hans-Sachs was ideally situated for individuals tired of their quarters and getting drunk with each other.

The manager had introduced himself as Herr Lorenz. He was a small, worried-looking Pickwickian character, the sort to be kept well away from a party rally or uniform for fear of tarnishing the *Übermensch* image of National Socialism. He had, he claimed, run the cinema for a quarter of a century and had tried to keep its standards of the highest "even during the unpleasantness of the last few years." Lamentably, projection equipment could not be obtained; otherwise, he seemed to be implying, the cinema would revert to showing movies at once. Circumstances being what they were, however, one had to make a living as best as one could. If the two officers would be his guests, he would be pleased to seat them at the best table and serve them the finest brandy. He would also arrange for two of the prettier performers to join them after their acts.

By some trick of inflection, he achieved making this last statement both salacious and prudish, like a clergyman telling blue jokes apologetically to keep his congregation in church. Hadleigh guessed afterward that he was the proprietor as well as the manager and keeping his ownership quiet in case of trouble with the authorities. In that eventuality he could plead he was only an employee.

They declined refreshment and entertainment. What they wanted was Fräulein Wolz's home address. Presumably Herr Lorenz could provide it.

Herr Lorenz was reluctant until Hadleigh threatened to have the MPs there in thirty minutes and the whole place closed down for good within the hour. Besides, the Allied majors appeared to want nothing more than to conduct a little private business with his star attraction. They did not want to arrest her or persuade her to join a rival establishment.

Hannah Wolz had a room on the second floor of a boardinghouse in the northern suburb of Weigelshof, close to a well-known orphanage. For humanitarian reasons the USAAF and the RAF had steered clear of it. Thus most of the buildings in the vicinity were undamaged. The sub-power station had also escaped the bombs and continued to provide electricity, a rare luxury for private houses.

The landlady had not seen her tenant for a week or so, a not-unusual occurrence. Fräulein Wolz kept strange hours, although she was clean and quiet, did not receive men in her room, and the rent was paid until the end of December. She had no objection to the two officers looking over the room. The Allies had won the war, hadn't they? They could do what they wished.

She was on the point of leading the way when Quinlan held out his hand for the passkey, making it clear they did not require company, just directions.

Hannah Wolz's lodgings were small, no more than a studio, with the bed neatly made, the tiny table covered

with a bright yellow cloth. In a free-standing wardrobe
under whose front legs were wedged pieces of newspaper to balance it, several skirts and dresses hung.
Underwear, handkerchiefs, and the like were folded in a
chest of drawers, which seemed to indicate Fräulein
Wolz had not packed and left for good. A quick search
of all her belongings told them nothing.

"She's probably dead," surmised Hadleigh. "A
woman in present-day Germany doesn't leave her
clothes behind through choice."

Quinlan disagreed.

"How would they know who she was or where to find
her? They didn't know where Arndt lived until the night
he died. The landlady says she never entertained men,
and Ilse said something about her father's mistress only
visiting him when she was out. Ilse might have told her
killers about the Hans-Sachs cinema. I doubt if she
knew the existence of this address."

Hadleigh shrugged. "Have it your own way. My feeling is that these guys are one jump ahead of us all along
the route. Anyway, she's not here, so what's the next
move?"

"Hope she turns up, I guess. We can ask the landlady
and Herr Lorenz to contact us if she comes back. Apart
from that I haven't a clue."

"So in the meantime we forget it?"

"I don't see what else we can do. I'd better see what
Gretl Meissner's up to and reacquaint myself with the
Palace of Justice anyway."

"I'll second that. I'm still on Third Army payroll. If I
don't start earning my per diem by clearing my desk,
someone upstairs might conclude I'd make a good
civilian."

As it happened, before twenty-four hours had
elapsed, Third Army had more to think about than one
G-2 major. On December 9, while driving between
Frankfurt and Mannheim with his Chief of Staff,
General George S. Patton was seriously injured when

the Cadillac in which he was riding collided with a military truck.

Although he had formally handed over command of the Third Army to General Lucian K. Truscott on October 7, to the officers and men who had served under him since Normandy Patton *was* the Third Army. The news of his injuries—head wounds and what appeared to be partial paralysis—shocked everyone.

In a Heidelberg hospital the medical team that operated on him found that his neck was broken. Bulletins concerning his progress were posted daily on notice boards down to company level, and within a few days he seemed to be making a full recovery. Nothing could kill Old Blood and Guts.

During the middle weeks of December, Hadleigh was too busy to give Hannah Wolz's disappearance more than a passing thought. Quinlan was also heavily occupied, attending the daily sessions of the Tribunal and making sure his bulletins to General Dempsey went out on time.

In the Palace of Justice the prosecution's case had become such a catalog of dreadfulness that the world press was no longer making the revelations headline news. Indeed, many of the journalists rarely bothered to attend more than once or twice a week, relying upon borrowing colleagues' notes for their columns. The defendants were not due to take the stand until the new year, and hearing Sir Hartley Shawcross and Sir David Maxwell-Fyfe, together with Chief Justice Jackson, lading counsel for the United States, recite long lists of atrocities had become tedious. Blood and gore need counterpoint; lows to balance the highs. In their anxiety to give a fair trial to the defendants and insure that the entire chronicle of Nazi crimes was officially documented for history, the Allied prosecutors had succeeded, for the moment, in making the Tribunal a non-event.

On December 18 William Joyce was told that his ap-

peal to the House of Lords had failed, though their
lordships' reasons, the final irony, were not to be given
until a later date. Joyce's execution was set for January
3, and he knew he would never learn the grounds for the
dismissal of his appeal.

After the governor had left his cell, Joyce thought
briefly of Major Quinlan and the identity of the third
man in the Adlon Hotel. Keeping it a secret no longer
mattered—or would not matter in a couple of days.
Maybe he'd make an official statement and ask that it
be forwarded to Quinlan.

The IMT adjourned for the Christmas recess on
December 20. One of the last pieces of evidence to be
presented by counsel for the United States was, from
Buchenwald, a large piece of tattooed human skin that
one of the overseers had fashioned into a lampshade.

After such a horror, the gathered journalists, radio
commentators, film cameramen, judges, counsel, inter-
preters, and military personnel were relieved to quit the
courtroom. Those who drank anesthetized their senses;
those who did not drink wished they did.

Since December 19 General Patton had been experi-
encing difficulty with his breathing, though his doctors
were not unduly alarmed. At a few minutes before 6
P.M. on the twenty-first, however, he died of acute heart
failure. Supposedly his last words were, "This is a hell
of a way for a soldier to go."

An endless procession of GIs came to pay their
respects at the Villa Reiner, where he lay in state. After
a funeral service on the twenty-third, he was buried in
the US Military Cemetery at Hamm, Luxembourg,
where he joined six thousand other men of the Third
Army.

Those members of code-name Lucky who survived
him went on a gigantic binge. Old Blood and Guts
would not have wanted a small thing like his death to
spoil their Christmas. Beginning on the evening of the
twenty-third, booze flowed like water.

Otis Quinlan saw none of it. His main reason for being in Nuremberg was at an end until the Tribunal reconvened, so he applied for some home leave. General Dempsey granted him five days from the twenty-second, reminding him that he was still on temporary loan to Colonel Masterson and should report back to Third Army Intelligence on the twenty-seventh.

Apart from two days in July, Quinlan had not seen his parents since before D-Day. He spent a quiet Christmas with them, the rest of his furlough occupied with traveling to and from Germany. He was amused to observe that, even after such a short time with the US Army, he no longer noticed his mother's American accent, which she had stubbornly retained after over thirty years in England.

For Hadleigh and Max Judd the duty roster did not work out too well. Over the holiday both found themselves at their desks every day, including Christmas. Their first break came on the twenty-seventh, when they were invited to a party by a Soviet intelligence colonel they had had dealings with in the past and had got to like, Yuri Petrov, whose apparent function in Nuremberg was to insure that nothing happened to the Soviet members of the Tribunal. Hadleigh suspected he was also involved in a little espionage on the side. He was pleasant enough, however, and, with Gene Masterson's permission, Hadleigh had allowed him occasional access to the Sündersbühl girls, who had orders to report any conversation that might indicate the Russian was there for reasons other than pleasure.

The party comprised a dozen Soviet officers and the same number of Americans, and was held in the Grand, where Quinlan found them when he flew in. On being introduced, Petrov invited him to join them, handing him a glass of vodka and immediately proposing a toast to lasting friendship between the Soviet Union and the United Kingdom.

Six vodkas later they were toasting eternal comradeship between all peace-loving peoples, and December 27 passed into history with most of the gathering unsteady on their feet.

On December 28 Hannah Wolz turned up for work.

EIGHT

‿‿‿‿‿‿‿‿‿‿‿‿‿‿‿‿‿‿‿‿‿‿‿‿‿‿‿‿‿‿‿‿

NUREMBERG
December 28, 1945

HERR LORENZ'S INFLUENCE (the source of which Ben Hadleigh was determined to discover before another week was out) extended to having a telephone when few private lines were available. He called shortly after 8 P.M. and announced that Fräulein Wolz had walked in ten minutes before and started changing for work.

"Of course, in the old days she would not have been given her job back," he intoned pompously, "but these are difficult times and my customers have missed her."

"Did she say where she's been for the last four weeks?"

"No, Herr Major. I asked for an explanation, naturally. She said it was none of my business."

"And you didn't tell her we were inquiring about her?"

"Not a word. I called you instantly, as instructed."

Hadleigh couldn't resist it.

"Who supplies your booze and protection, Lorenz?"

A fit of coughing took place at the other end of the line.

"Herr Major?" Lorenz managed eventually.

"Skip it. Act as if nothing has happened. What time does she go on?"

"Almost immediately."

"Don't let her leave if she finishes before we arrive."

"There will be no danger of that. She does several more spots later in the evening."

"We'll be there in fifteen minutes."

He was about to ring through for Max when he remembered the master sergeant was away overnight in Tübingen, just across the demarcation line in the French zone, delivering a truckload of Lucky Strikes which Hadleigh had bought surreptitiously for a tidy sum. In exchange, Max would pick up several crates of perfume from their contact there, perhaps some lipsticks too. Cigarettes, booze, and cosmetics were worth their weight in gold in the zones of occupation, and while quantities of the first two were readily available, at a price, in and around Nuremberg, the French had cornered the market in scents, lipsticks, and face powder.

Wheel and deal, sell and buy, give some, take some. That was what made the world go around. The only items Hadleigh refused to deal in were narcotics and medical supplies.

When Hadleigh arrived in the Jeep, Quinlan was in his quarters typing up a report of the trial to date before transmitting it to Second Army HQ. He was mildly hungover from the drinks in the Grand and he needed no arm-twisting to abandon the Olivetti, not when he learned that Hannah Wolz was no longer on the missing list.

Lorenz was waiting for them at the entrance, slightly

concerned that the Allied majors were just a little too eager to get in touch with Fräulein Wolz, that maybe she had broken some law and was about to be taken away for interrogation or worse. Business had dropped off alarmingly during her absence. A few illicit clubs like his could provide liquor and strippers, but there was only one Hannah.

Quinlan reassured him that, as far as they knew, the Fräulein had committed no offense.

"I have reserved a table for you near the front, gentlemen."

"Forget it," said Hadleigh. "We'll find our own way around."

"I think you might change your mind," murmured Lorenz slyly.

Apart from a pianist and a bass player in the wings, the beautifully svelte Hannah Wolz was alone on stage, sitting on a barstool and bathed in a soft pink spot emanating from what had once been the cinema's projection booth. Her ash-blond hair was straight, parted in the middle and cut to the shoulder. She was dressed in a figure-hugging, full-length black evening gown, décolleté and slit on one side, revealing long self-supporting dark stockings and a breathtaking glimpse of pale thigh. One leg was on the lower crossbar of the stool, the other on a second, higher rung. Her hands were clasped around the upper leg. On her feet she wore three-inch heels with ankle straps.

They guessed her age at twenty-three or so, her height around five feet four inches. Her face was a near-perfect heart, her lips full. They would find out later that her eyes were blue-gray, the color of cigarette smoke.

Without the aid of a microphone and in German, which doubtless few of her audience understood with any degree of fluency, she was singing a universal song about a soldier and his lost love. If her voice would never set Broadway or the West End of London ablaze, something about her delivery managed to convince every listener that her words were for him alone.

Several hundred men were jammed into the auditorium—at the bar, at the tables, and standing—and they gave her their silent, undivided attention with none of the catcalls or ribaldry that greeted the strippers. Except for the muted clinking of glasses, no one made a sound until she was finished. Then the audience erupted, whistling, shouting, stomping, appealing for more.

She accepted the adulation with a dip of her head and a slight, sad smile.

"Christ," muttered the American, with a sidelong glance at Quinlan, "no wonder Lorenz's customers were missing her."

She sang three more songs before, in a broken English accent that was a delight, she thanked the men for their kindness and promised to return later. When she left the stage through the wings and a big-breasted stripper came on with her bump-and-grind act, the GIs expressed their disapproval in the usual manner.

The two majors sought out Lorenz and asked to be directed to Hannah Wolz's dressing room, which turned out to be a converted office and hers exclusively. The strippers shared an adjacent one.

Not really knowing where to begin, Hadleigh kept things simple, telling her of Arndt's death and the murders of Ilse and an American security agent, speaking in German when Hannah admitted that her command of English was less than adequate. Her name, he added, was given to Major Quinlan by Ilse.

Close up, they saw her eyes had a quality of vulnerability that she somehow injected into her songs. If her male audience lusted after her, they also wanted to protect her.

She knew, she told them quietly, of Herr Arndt's death and that his daughter and another woman had been murdered. She was about to call on Herr Arndt on the afternoon of November 30 when she saw the military police outside the bicycle shop. She asked one of the civilian bystanders what had happened, and in the manner of such things the crowd knew almost as much as the authorities. After she learned of Arndt's death and the murders, the thought uppermost in her mind was to get as far away as possible. She had been staying with friends in nearby Fürth since the thirtieth and had returned only that day because money was short and she needed to earn her living.

Quinlan found her actions most odd. He said as much in a tone that surprised Hadleigh by its severity. Her lover dies and his daughter (with whom admittedly she did not get along) is killed, and she calmly goes to stay with friends. Instead of doing what most women would have done—breaking down or at least waiting around for the funerals—she disappears.

"My . . . Herr Arndt made me promise on many occasions to go away instantly if"—she hesitated—"if anything happened to him."

Quinlan seized on this.

"Does that mean he was expecting something to happen?"

"I . . . I don't know. I think he always considered the possibility, though he never spoke of his fears. He was such a proud man. I have a good job and a legitimate ration book, but he would never let me take him as much as a loaf of bread. He and Ilse lived on her rations."

"That doesn't sound like pride to me," said Quinlan sharply, "taking the food out of a sixteen-year-old girl's mouth because he's too frightened to register with the authorities."

"That's because you didn't know him, Herr Major."

Her voice was unsteady. Quinlan felt like a bastard for asking his questions and making his statements without a spark of compassion. When he examined his motives later, he came to the conclusion he had over-reacted because of her loveliness. She produced a gut feeling within him he didn't understand and didn't like.

On the way across in the Jeep he and Hadleigh had

debated how much to tell her and decided it would have to be most, if not all, of the little they themselves knew. The killers of Ilse Arndt and Angela Salvatini would not hesitate to torture and murder Hauptmann Arndt's mistress if they knew where she was and if they thought she had the information they were looking for.

Not really sure—it seemed a most peculiar relationship—how close she and Arndt had been, Quinlan brusquely expressed his regrets at the former Abwehr captain's demise, even while reminding himself that Hannah Wolz could be the key to the whole business.

"Have you been back to your lodgings yet?"

"No. I came directly here from Fürth." She indicated a small suitcase in the corner of the dressing room. "Am I to be told why you're asking all these questions?"

Hadleigh took over. Quinlan was being too heavy-handed, and that wasn't the way to handle this woman. "We believe Herr Arndt possessed information or documents of great value," he said. "His daughter and the United States security agent were murdered because the killers thought that Ilse, at least, knew what the information was or where the documents were. It seems they were mistaken."

"But you think I might have this information, these documents?"

"According to Ilse you were . . . er . . . close to Herr Arndt," said Hadleigh delicately.

Her big eyes looked at him inquiringly.

"Ilse told you I was her father's mistress."

It was a statement and Hadleigh elected not to beat about the bush.

"Exactly that."

"You knew Herr Arndt held the rank of Hauptmann in the Abwehr during the war, did you not?" asked Quinlan.

"Of course, though he spoke little of his work."

"But you do know the Abwehr was the intelligence arm of the Wehrmacht?"

"So I understand, though it's not something a German girl pays much attention to. Any more, I suppose," she added with a surprising toughness in her tone, "than an English or an American girl would care about the spy services of her own country."

Hadleigh suppressed a grin.

"What we're trying to establish, Fräulein Wolz," Quinlan went on, "is whether Arndt said anything to you or gave you anything for safekeeping that could possibly explain why his daughter was killed. I should add that if you do know anything, it would be advisable to tell us. Sooner or later, Ilse's murderers will undoubtedly find out about you, and your one chance is to help us get to them before they get to you."

"You're saying my life is in danger?"

"It could be. It very well could be."

She paused, studying each of them in turn before abruptly coming to a decision. Walking over to her suitcase, she kneeled and opened it. Rummaging through the contents, she took out a plain manila envelope, eight inches by five inches, and held it to her breast.

"He gave me this," she said, "with instructions to keep it with me at all times. If anything happened to him, I was to hold on to it until Oberstleutnant Langenhain—"

"Wait a minute, wait a minute," interrupted Quinlan. "Oberstleutnant *Manfred* Langenhain? You know him, you've met him?"

"Of course. Several times right here in Nuremberg. Before the end of the war, that is. I haven't seen him since."

She appeared to have lost her train of thought.

"Please continue," encouraged Quinlan.

"I don't suppose it matters now," she went on. "The envelope was sealed, but I opened it when I learned Herr Arndt was dead. It may be what you're looking for. I don't know. It certainly seems to have no value."

She hesitated for a moment before handing the envelope to Quinlan, who could barely disguise his disappointment when he saw that it contained no more than a torn fragment of color photograph measuring two inches by two inches and depicting an irregular section of island or islands with sea on three sides. The fourth side was hard against one edge of the photograph and would have shown the rest, or another part of, the island or island group had the picture been intact.

It had evidently been taken with a powerful camera—at least the definition was perfect—from an ordinary atlas, but there was no way of telling what or where the island was. The photographer had erased all distinguishing marks such as towns and lines of longitude and latitude.

Whoever had mutilated the picture had also made certain that the remaining outline would furnish no clues to the island's whereabouts by reference to a world map. For that matter, what was shown did not even have to be an island. It could equally have been the coastline of a country or a continent. As was presumably intended, without the missing pieces it meant absolutely nothing.

Flipping over the photograph Quinlan saw the word KIKA handwritten in ink on the back. That too meant nothing.

He handed the fragment to Hadleigh.

"And this is all Arndt gave you?" he asked Hannah.

Again there was a moment's hesitation before she answered.

"Not quite all," she said finally. "There was also an address, which he asked me to keep separate from the photograph. If something happened to Herr Arndt and Oberstleutnant Langenhain did not appear after a reasonable period, I was to contact a Herr Helmut Bachmann in Munich and give the envelope to him."

"*Herr* Bachmann?" queried Quinlan. "No rank?"

"I was never told a rank."

"Where in Munich?" asked Hadleigh.

"I don't remember the exact address. It was written

down for me. It's on a piece of paper I use to prop up one leg of the wardrobe in my apartment, inside an old newspaper.''

They remembered the wedges of newspaper and cursed themselves for making such a perfunctory search of the room. Not that the name and address would have meant anything to them at the time.

"There's one other thing," said Hannah. "No, perhaps two. Herr Arndt told me not to worry if Oberstleutnant Langenhain never turned up or if I could not trace Herr Bachmann. After January tenth, he said, it wouldn't matter. He never explained what he meant by that.''

"January tenth next year, 1946?" said Hadleigh.

"Yes.''

"And the second thing?" asked Quinlan.

"I was never Herr Arndt's mistress," she said after a long pause. "Like Ilse, I was his daughter.''

NINE

~~~~~~

NUREMBERG
December 28–29, 1945

THE STILLNESS IN the dressing room was broken by
Hannah reaching for a cigarette from a packet on the
table, an American brand, a Camel. Hadleigh leaned
forward to light it for her.

"You might as well tell us the rest," he said. "As
Arndt's mistress you might have been in danger. As his
daughter you certainly are."

"I was what you would call a love child," she began.
"My father was already married to Ilse's mother when I
was conceived and, though Ilse was not of course born
at the time, there was no question of a divorce.

"I didn't know of my father's existence until late in
1944 when my own mother died. I had always been led
to believe he was killed in a road accident when I was
very small. She explained why there were no formal

photographs of them together by saying they were destroyed in a fire. She had a couple of snapshots of herself and Herr . . . I mean my father, but they could have been of any young man. Everything I'm telling you I learned from him, of course. I suppose my mother felt ashamed I was illegitimate.

"She never told him she was pregnant. They had a brief affair in the autumn of 1922, and then it was over. It wouldn't have stood the test of time anyway, even though he was a handsome man in his youth and she was a beautiful woman."

There could be little doubt of that, thought Quinlan. *Like mother, like daughter.*

"When she died," Hannah went on, "I had to go through her papers, where I found my birth certificate. Mother Gerda Wolz, father Heinrich Arndt. I wasn't shocked; more disappointed that I'd had a father all those years without knowing it. Neither did I know whether he was still alive. He was, of course, and living, when on leave, right here in Nuremberg, not four miles from my mother's house in Fürth. It's no longer standing, that house. It was destroyed by an Allied bomb, which is why I live where I do."

All this was said without a trace of bitterness.

"It took me a little while to track him down," she continued, "until earlier this year, to be exact. I judged he would be in the military and contacted the authorities. They were reluctant to cooperate at first, but finally they gave me his address. After that it was just a question of waiting until he came home on leave."

"They gave you his Humboldtstrasse address?" asked Quinlan.

"No. At the time he was living in the Gibitzenhof district. He and Ilse didn't move into the apartment above the bicycle shop until March this year, though he kept the Gibitzenhof house."

Quinlan nodded. That figured. A man in hiding would have one address for the official records and another, unknown to the authorities. What Hannah Wolz could find out so could anyone else.

"Did he ever mention where he was stationed, where his base was?" asked Hadleigh.

"He never spoke of his work at all, not even when the war was over. Neither did he tell me why he rarely went out. He said it was better I didn't know." She sighed deeply. "I suppose I thought he was wanted for war crimes. Once that idea was in my head, I decided it was better not to press him. I'd only just found him. I didn't want to lose him again to an Allied court." She looked at them anxiously. "He wasn't a war criminal, was he? He had nothing to do with those dreadful camps we read about?"

"Not as far as we know," answered Hadleigh. "In fact, I'd say it was almost a certainty."

"I didn't think so," said Hannah in a relieved tone that made it clear the thought had crossed her mind.

Quinlan had a question, the obvious one. It might be irrelevant, and it was more out of curiosity than anything else that he posed it.

"I don't understand the reason for the subterfuge. Why didn't Arndt acknowledge you as his daughter and tell Ilse she had a half-sister? Why allow her to believe you were his mistress?"

Hannah stubbed out her cigarette in an ashtray.

"You didn't know Ilse," she explained. "She was going through a difficult time. Her own mother was killed in an air raid shortly before mine died. She was insanely possessive about our father. At least, that's what he believed. He never told her I was his mistress, of course. That was a deduction she made for herself. She could accept him, we agreed, receiving visits from another woman while she was out. She would not have accepted a half-sister appearing from nowhere and claiming a share of his affections."

Thinking it over, Quinlan concluded there was more to it than that. Hannah had been entrusted with the photographic fragment and Bachmann's address, which were of vital importance to Arndt no matter how trivial they might seem to anyone else. If anything happened to him, Ilse could become a potential target. There was no getting around that; his enemies would know he had a daughter. But what she didn't know she couldn't reveal. He must have been worried sick wondering if he should have tried to get her away, far from easy under the occupation laws. Freedom of movement was restricted. While adults could, and did, flout the rules almost at will, it would be asking a lot of a sixteen-year-old girl to go to a different town or district and fend for herself. Arndt was doubtless hoping that, if he kept his head down, no one would find him or Ilse until it didn't matter.

Except: until what didn't matter?

Only the killers knew what had taken place in the Humboldtstrasse apartment before Angela Salvatini and Ilse had mercifully died. The CIC agent could have told her attackers nothing because she knew nothing. Arndt may have reasoned, however, that Ilse, under torture, would reveal the existence of a half-sister. She might not say anything about a mistress.

On the other hand, there was no evidence to suggest that she hadn't. Hannah had disappeared very quickly the following day. Possibly the killers knew of her but were unable to trace her. If that were so, she was in grave danger.

Quinlan examined the fragment of photograph again. Could it really be part of something so important that it had already cost at least three lives? With his own a fourth if Hadleigh and Max had not intervened?

There was a timid knock on the dressing-room door. Herr Lorenz inquired from the corridor when Fräulein Wolz would be ready to go on again. The men had missed her and were demanding more.

Hadleigh told him to go away and come back in five minutes. He added to Hannah, "You mentioned you'd met Langenhain several times. When was the last?''

She had to think about it.

"Before the end of hostilities, I believe, and before the move to Humboldtstrasse. Around the end of March.''

"Did you hear what he and your father discussed?''

"No. On each occasion I was asked to leave so that they could talk in private.''

"Did Langenhain know of the true relationship between you and Herr Arndt?'' asked Quinlan.

"I very much doubt it.''

"Or your Weigelshof address or where you worked during the war? I presume it wasn't here.''

"I wasn't. No, to the best of my knowledge Oberstleutnant Langenhain knew nothing more about me than my given name.''

"Your instructions nevertheless were to hand over the envelope to Langenhain if anything happened to your father?''

"Either that or contact Herr Bachmann, yes.''

"But how could you,'' demanded Quinlan, "if Langenhain knew nothing more than your first name? How would he find you or you him?''

"I've really no idea. Perhaps I've misled you. My father didn't say that the *moment* something happened to him I must both leave my job and seek out Herr Langenhain. He implied I should hold on to the envelope *in case* I was contacted or I could get to Munich to see Herr Bachmann. Although he was a sick man, I don't really think he expected to die before he saw Herr Langenhain again.''

Which perhaps he wouldn't have done, thought Quinlan, *if I hadn't overdone the threats*.

Hadleigh sensed his discomfort and came to the rescue.

"But he never did see Langenhain after March?''

"No.''

"How can you be so sure?''

"I knew my father well even on such short acquaintance. He was always agitated for several days after a meeting with the Oberstleutnant. I noticed no such agitation after March."

Quinlan held out the fragment of photograph.

"When did he give you this, before or after March?"

"Oh, a long time after. Not until this past autumn."

"So it could have come from Langenhain in the first place?"

"I expect it could. The idea never occurred to me."

Lorenz was still outside in the corridor. He tapped again on the dressing-room door.

"*Please*, Fräulein," he begged.

"May I continue my act?" she asked.

Hadleigh nodded. "But come back here when you're through."

"Am I under arrest?"

"No. We may have more questions for you."

She swished out of the room. In her heels she was almost as tall as Quinlan.

A moment or two later they heard the distant roar of approval from the auditorium.

Hadleigh bit the end of a fresh cigar and put a match to it. When it was well lit he said, "Curiouser and curiouser, even if I can't see the bottom line."

"For the moment, the bottom line is keeping her out of the morgue. You'll have to take her in or she could wind up like her half-sister."

"Forget it." Hadleigh shook his head. "Where the hell would I put her in Allersbergerstrasse? Half the guys out front are billeted there. If they got to hear she was in the barracks, I'd have a riot on my hands."

"You can't let her go back to Weigelshof."

"Not even if I detail you as a twenty-four-hour guard?" Hadleigh grinned.

"Not even then, much as the idea appeals. I wouldn't find her presence hard to get used to."

"Me neither. Okay, I'll give it some thought. In the

meantime, let's get down to cases. There's something about this whole business that's puzzling the hell out of me."

"Just one something?"

"One more than all the rest. Her father was a serving officer in the Abwehr, right? So was Langenhain. Now furloughs are hard enough to come by in peacetime, for Christ's sake, but at that stage of the war leave would be canceled all around. Yet here are Arndt and Langenhain meeting regularly in Nuremberg just a few days before the Third and Seventh armies overran the city. Arndt lived here, fair enough. We've heard nothing that indicates he was based here, though, so how come he was more or less a permanent fixture in Gibitzenhof or Humboldtstrasse after February? He seems to have had an awful lot of freedom for a lousy captain. Langenhain was a light colonel, which might give him certain movement privileges. But Arndt I can't figure."

Quinlan thought he could.

"Remember what Joyce told me about the meeting in the Adlon, that the SS officers were worried because Langenhain had dropped out of sight? It's my guess Arndt did the same, took French leave. They were up to something, the pair of them, something that was bothering the hell out of the SS."

"More than just the pair of them would be my guess," Hadleigh conjectured. "That piece of photograph has to have brothers and sisters someplace. It looks like a quarter of the original you're holding, perhaps a sixth. There are three or five other fragments somewhere."

"And together they'd add up to what? A picture of an island or islands or a section of mainland? A place where the SS has stashed some loot or documents? And what about this word KIKA on the reverse? What's that, part of a code, the name of a person, the name of the island or a town?"

Hadleigh frowned. "You're asking me questions I can't answer, but there's one I can. Until you spoke to Joyce we were only guessing that the SS was in on this. Now we can be ninety-nine percent certain that they're involved. They're also probably not a dozen or so miles from where we're standing."

"Which makes it imperative we put Hannah Wolz out of their reach. We'd better check with Lorenz to see if anyone else made inquiries about her during her absence."

Lorenz confirmed that there had been many, many inquiries.

"Dozens of them, daily."

Hadleigh explained that that was not what they meant. They were not interested in horny GIs who wanted to know when their favorite fantasy would be back.

"Any Germans or anyone you didn't recognize as a regular customer?"

"No Germans, although there was one man who spoke the language fluently in an accent I couldn't place. I thought at first he was English, but his pronunciation was like nothing I'd heard before."

Quinlan recalled the broad northern voice saying "nail the bastard" on the road back from Humboldt-strasse, and gave a passable impression of a Yorkshire-man asking the time of day in German.

"Yes," said Lorenz, "something like that. He was wearing a uniform with a civilian raincoat over it. I couldn't see any marks of rank, just his khaki trousers. He didn't have a cap."

"What precisely did he say?" asked Quinlan.

"And when was it?" added Hadleigh.

Lorenz's brow furrowed as he tried to remember. He wished this American and this Britisher would go away and leave him in peace, let him get on with the business of making a living. How could he possibly have known when he voted for Hitler back in the thirties that he would end up running little more than a brothel for foreigners?

"Herr Lorenz," prompted Quinlan.

"Yes, yes, I'm thinking. It was, I believe, the first evening Fräulein Wolz did not appear for work. I didn't pay him much attention at the time, apart from his strange accent. Many others were also inquiring why she wasn't singing. When I told him I had no idea where she was, he asked me if I knew where she lived. I said I did not. My customers frequently tried to find out Fräulein Wolz's address. I never gave it."

"You gave it to us," accused Quinlan.

"Only because the Herr Major threatened to close me down. Besides, you were obviously on official business."

And equally obvious, thought Hadleigh and Quinlan simultaneously, was that Ilse Arndt, before she died, had told her killers of Hannah Wolz's existence and where she worked. She could not have given them her address. Heinrich Arndt would have made sure she never knew it. If he could not protect one daughter because she was too young to send away, he could protect the other.

"And you never saw him again?"

"Never."

"Which doesn't mean to say he and his bunch haven't got this place under surveillance," Hadleigh speculated when they left Lorenz and went into the auditorium. To the customary hush Hannah was singing about a rose which died a little each day her lover was away. It should have been corny. It wasn't.

He jerked his head in the direction of the stage. "You're right about putting her out of reach. What they'd do to her doesn't bear thinking about. One of us had better spend the night with her up in Weigelshof—and I mean that in the purest possible way—until we can come up with something better." He sighed a long sigh.

"It'll have to be you. *No todos los días son días de fiesta.*"

Quinlan's command of Spanish was limited. "Which means?"

"Not every day can be a party. I've got to watch the store. Don't forget to pick up Bachmann's Munich address."

In spite of Lorenz wanting his leading lady to do the midnight spot, as she always did, they insisted she quit after her second session, close to eleven o'clock.

They repeated to Hannah that they believed her life to be in danger and urged her to agree to Quinlan's staying with her until morning. Tomorrow they would try to find her somewhere safer to live, though where that would be neither of them had any notion. Short of keeping her in protective custody until the entire business was sorted out, they could do little to prevent someone determined enough from getting to her. Hadleigh hadn't the manpower to give her around-the-clock protection. Nor could he justify it to Gene Masterson even if he had.

Hannah accepted the arrangement with only the mildest protest. They stood in the corridor while she changed into her street clothes: low-heeled black pumps, a skirt and sweater which had seen better days, and a hooded gray cloak. The latter reminded Quinlan of the outer garment some nurses wore back in England, and she confirmed that she had spent much of the war in the DRK, the German Red Cross, her base being the Hallerwiese-Klinik.

"I didn't train to be a nurse. At school I always wanted to be an entertainer, a singer. Then the war came along and spoiled it all. I'll never get further than Herr Lorenz's now."

Outside it was snowing lightly. The Jeep's driver had had the good sense to put the top up and was stamping his feet to keep warm.

"Second item on the agenda is to get myself a decent

vehicle," muttered Hadleigh, shivering at the sudden drop in temperature.

The first item was for Quinlan to draw from the Allersbergerstrasse armory something that packed more of a punch than his Webley.

"Just in case," said Hadleigh.

Unnoticed by them, their departure was observed by two men sitting in a parked unmarked Opel sedan on the far side of Scheurlstrasse. they made no attempt to follow the Jeep, however. They had other things on their mind.

The armory was locked. Hadleigh spent forty minutes tracking down someone with a key.

Quinlan chose a box-fed Thompson .45 submachine gun and three 30-round clips of ACP ammunition.

Hadleigh remained behind while the driver took Quinlan and Hannah to her boarding house. The PFC at the wheel did not know the route, and because the snow had thickened even Hannah had difficulty recognizing familiar landmarks.

North of the river Pegnitz they got lost several times before the Jeep dropped them outside the house at almost 1 A.M. The PFC roared off while the return route was fresh in his head. He had had more than enough for one evening, though from what he had seen of the Fräulein, he judged the British major to be one lucky son of a bitch.

Hannah had a key to the front door. Frau Schrieber, the landlady, was accustomed to her peculiar hours. She was also something of an insomniac as well as being excessively anxious. She invariably opened the door to her own rooms, ground floor back, when she heard someone enter.

"To make sure I'm not bringing a man in," said Hannah with a hint of mischief.

But on this occasion it remained closed, although a light was shining through the crack under it. Quinlan felt the hairs on the back of his neck stiffen. He'd had the same feeling a dozen times since June 1944, in the hedgerows of Normandy and the narrow streets of German towns. Frau Schrieber could be in the john or boiling a kettle and not have heard the key in the lock. He didn't think so. Something was wrong.

The hallway was almost pitch black and it took several moments for his eyes to become accustomed to the darkness. He did, however, remember the layout of the house from his previous visit.

Directly opposite the front door the stairs led to the upper floors. To the right of the stairs, where he and Hannah were now standing, a narrow corridor ran the length of the house to Frau Schrieber's rooms. Hers was the only apartment on the ground floor.

He passed Hannah her suitcase and cocked the Thompson.

"Keep your head down and don't move a muscle until I tell you," he whispered.

To her credit she did as he commanded without question.

From the stairs to Frau Schrieber's door was a distance of some thirty feet. Keeping flat against the right-hand wall, Quinlan moved slowly along the corridor. He was thinking how foolish he was going to look if the old woman suddenly appeared in her nightgown, when the door was flung open and a man's voice shouted in German, "For Christ's sake don't shoot the girl!"

He realized later that their reluctance to risk harming Hannah before she could tell them what she knew saved his life.

Blinded by the light from Frau Schrieber's rooms, Quinlan let his instincts take over. He dropped into a crouch and squeezed the Thompson's trigger.

Within the narrow confines of the corridor the noise was deafening. Above it, he heard answering shots coming from the doorway, a man's shriek of agony, and Hannah screaming behind him.

Half a clip had gone before he released the trigger. He now had a choice of moving either backward to the safety of the stairs or forward. He elected to go on, covering what remained of the thirty feet in a couple of strides and jumping over the prone and bloody figure of a man blocking the doorway as he did so.

Frau Schrieber was bound to a chair, and gagged. She was fully conscious, her eyes wide with terror. Edging swiftly toward her, intending to use her as cover, a thickset fair-haired man was waving an automatic pistol in Quinlan's direction. He loosed a couple of shots that missed their target by several feet before Quinlan pumped a short burst into his upper torso.

Then the lights went out, literally and figuratively. One moment the room was flooded with electricity, the next it wasn't. Even as Quinlan turned upon hearing footsteps behind him, something very hard hit him across the back of the head.

He recovered consciousness to find Ben Hadleigh standing over him and the room full of heavily armed GIs, a sergeant in command.

"This," he managed, "is becoming a habit. What the hell hit me?"

Frau Schrieber was sobbing in a corner, drinking greedily from a GI flask which obviously contained anything but water. Close by, eyes averted, Hannah was standing amid the ruins of her suitcase. One of its metal corners was dented.

"She did and that did," said Hadleigh.

"I'm sorry, Herr Major," the girl apologized. "When the shooting stopped, I switched off the lights from the main switch by the front door and hit out at the first thing I saw."

Quinlan nodded his acceptance of her apology. It was a gutsy performance from someone who had been screaming a few seconds earlier and who could just as easily have run into the street.

"What brought you here?" he asked Hadleigh.

"Herr Lorenz. He called twenty minutes after you left and said he'd been beaten unconscious by a couple of Germans—these two, I presume, but we'll get a formal identification later—who forced him to give them Fräulein Wolz's address. They would have killed him from what I can gather if a couple of the strippers hadn't heard the ruckus and started screaming. My guess is they watched us leave and, what with the time we took at the armory, got here before you. They're both dead, by the way. I didn't tell you to start World War Three."

Quinlan struggled to his feet, holding his head.

"Who are they?"

The sergeant answered that. He and a couple of GIs had dragged the corpses into the corridor for examination.

"SS, Major. Blood-group tattoos below their armpits. No other ID on them."

"Which settles for once and for all who the bad guys are," said Hadleigh. "Come on; we'll leave the sergeant to clean up here, pick up Bachmann's address from Fräulein Wolz's room, and make tracks."

"Changed your mind about putting her up in the barracks?"

"No, we'll take her to Sündersbühl. If she doesn't mind sharing a house with a couple of hookers, that's probably the safest bet. I'll put a guard on the door for tonight."

They were speaking in English, but Hannah realized they were discussing her immediate future.

"What about tomorrow and the next day?" asked Quinlan.

"Tomorrow—later today rather—we'll pay a visit to Herr Helmut Bachmann in Munich. The Fräulein goes with us. For all we know Bachmann is Langenhain in another hat and only Fräulein Wolz is in a position to recognize him. Besides, I'd like to get the pair of you out of Nuremberg. Together you're more lethal than

Bonnie Parker and Clyde Barrow. Sleep as long as you like. I want to take Max along in case we run into trouble, and he won't be back before noon.''

As it turned out, Quinlan was destined to be awakened at 10 A.M. Hadleigh had an army signal form in his hand.

"Sorry to rouse you from your beauty sleep, but I thought you'd want to see this. It's come the long way around and because of Christmas it's been held up right down the line. Should I read it? It's addressed to you via Third Army.''

Quinlan struggled to full consciousness.

"Go ahead.''

"It's by-lined your Home Office and states that in a private conversation with the governor of Wandsworth Prison William Joyce revealed the identity of the third man in the Adlon Hotel to be John Amery.''

Quinlan was now wide awake. Son of Leo Amery, Churchill's wartime Secretary of State for India, John Amery was the founder of the Legion of St. George, later known as the British Free Corps, whose volunteers, recruited from POW camps in Germany and Occupied Europe, had been controlled by and fought with the Waffen SS.

Then he remembered something else.

"Oh, Christ.''

"Right,'' said Hadleigh. "I recognized the name and checked the newspaper files for the date before I came over. They hanged Amery at Wandsworth on December nineteenth.''

TEN

~~~~~~

NUREMBERG
December 29, 1945

MAX DROVE THE Mercedes staff car Hadleigh had commandeered from the pound of captured vehicles. It had once belonged to panzer Generaloberst Heinz Guderian, though Captain Jim Pepper, the officer i/c the compound, had pronounced it fit only for a museum. Hadleigh knew different. Jim Pepper had his own beady eyes on it and was keeping all comers at arm's length until he figured out a way to ship it back to the States, where it would cause a sensation in Poughkeepsie.

Hadleigh made a deal with him: a dozen bottles of the perfume Max had brought back from Tübingen in exchange for a loan of the Merc. Pepper thought of what he could do with twelve bottles of scent and quite suddenly the car was in perfect running order.

"But make sure I get the damned thing back in one piece."

Sure, Jim.

"And take it easy on the gas pedal between fifty and sixty m.p.h."

Right, Jim.

"She's a bit sticky on her steering above eighty."

Okay, Jim.

"For Chrissake, let's get out of here before he tells us how to burp it," moaned Hadleigh.

Max had not returned from the French zone until two-thirty, after which it had taken time to bargain for the Merc and stash the remainder of the scent where no one would find it. They were therefore late leaving Nuremberg and, in a light snowfall, did not reach the Berlin-Munich Autobahn until dusk.

Quinlan had spent most of the morning and early afternoon on the telephone and looking through old Third Army newspaper files, refreshing his memory on the subject of the British Free Corps and its founder. He related his findings in German so that Hannah, sitting next to him in the back, would also understand. In the front passenger seat, Hadleigh translated the more obscure nouns for Max and filled the massive interior of the Mercedes with cigar smoke.

At the Bow Street committal proceedings, John Amery had pleaded not guilty to the charge of high treason, contending that he was a Spanish citizen, naturalized during the Spanish Civil War. His subsequent trial at the Old Bailey, which had taken place a month before, on November 28, had lasted a mere eight minutes. Moments before it was due to begin, he had called his defense counsel, the same Mr. Slade who had defended Joyce, down to the cells and said he was changing his plea to guilty, which gave him no recourse of appeal to a higher court. Before passing sentence of death, Mr. Justice Humphreys asked Mr. Slade if his client fully understood the implications of his plea. Slade said he did. The reason for the change of heart was never publicly established, though rumor had it that Amery had made an honorable decision to save his distinguished family from the agony of a prolonged hearing and the attendant publicity. If that was so, the volteface was remarkable, for Amery had caused his parents nothing but trouble for most of his life, his misdemeanors ranging from petty fraud to bankruptcy in 1936. After that, he had left England for Spain, where he ran guns for Franco.

At the outbreak of World War II he went to France, where he joined up with the Gagoulards, the French Fascists. Throughout 1941 and much of 1942 he offered his services to the Nazis, who, after first ignoring his entreaties, relented in October of that year and invited him to Berlin. In the capital he volunteered, over dinner at the Hotel Kaiserhof with a high-ranking official of the German Foreign Office and Dr. Friedrich Hansen, a member of Hitler's personal staff, to raise what he called the Legion of St. George, a force of British POWs, to fight the Russians. He was also permitted to do some propaganda broadcasts.

Introduced as the son of a British cabinet minister, he made a long speech imploring the British to form an alliance with Germany to fight the "twin enemies" of Judaism and communism. In a later broadcast, answering the accusation of treachery made in London, he said that treason could never be defined, in wartime or at any other time, as an ardent love of one's own country—which nullified his claim to Spanish citizenship.

Eventually he quarreled with his paymasters and left them. Any purpose his broadcasts served, he argued, was undone by William Joyce, who sneered at and threatened the islanders instead of courting them. The official version for the split was somewhat different. Amery could not break old habits and ran up huge debts in Berlin, the stores, hotels, and restaurants always being told to send the bills to Dr. Hansen.

Amery returned to Paris, where, encouraged by the French collaborator Jacques Doriot, he rehashed his ideas for the Legion of St. George.

At the beginning of April 1943, after defeats at El 'Alamein and Stalingrad, Berlin was willing to listen and approved a brigade of fifteen hundred. Around this time Amery's mistress, a hopeless alcoholic, died after a heavy drinking spree, choking on her own vomit. Although apparently distraught, while taking her cremated ashes back to her birthplace in France, he met another young Frenchwoman. Before the train journey was over, he had proposed they live together.

On April 21, the day after Hitler's fifty-fourth birthday, Amery began his recruiting drive at the St. Denis internment camp outside Paris. It was far from successful. Most of the inmates shouted him down; some threw rocks. At the end of the session he had three converts.

He was bitterly disappointed. The prophet was without honor even outside his own country. Quickly losing interest in his brainchild, he dropped out of sight with his new mistress. Little more was heard of him until he was captured by partisans on the road between Milan and Como at the end of April 1945.

But the Legion of St. George was established. It continued to attract recruits, though other men were doing the recruiting. It was part of the Wehrmacht until late in the war, when control passed to the SS, whose field-gray combat uniforms it wore with the addition of collar patches depicting three leopards and a Union Jack on the upper-left sleeve. A cuff band bore the words British Free Corps in Gothic letters.

"There were never very many of them—nothing like the fifteen hundred Berlin envisaged," Quinlan concluded as the huge Mercedes ate up the hundred-odd miles between Nuremberg and Munich. "A total of several hundred would be my guess, mainly on the eastern front." He glowered at Hadleigh. "And you can take that superior grin off your face. The unit wasn't exclusively British in spite of its title. There was at least one American among them, probably more.''

"Probably more is right," nodded Hadleigh. "I remember the one we captured, a guy named Hale from Michigan. Got ten years a while back. But there are other names we haven't accounted for, guys who are still missing, who were taken out of their POW cages for reasons other than the usual treatment from the Gestapo and never heard of again. Anyway, we've now solved the problem of who it was visited Lorenz and the English accent you heard the night they bushwhacked you on the way back from Humboldtstrasse.''

What wasn't explained was how remnants of the BFC and the SS were now tied together, nor what the two SS officers and John Amery were talking about in the Adlon Hotel back in the spring.

Damn Joyce for being so secretive! cursed Quinlan silently. He had concealed Amery's identity for no other reason than vanity. He would have hated to think that a British Army officer was visiting Wandsworth Prison to see someone besides himself.

By all accounts Amery had mixed with the top people in Berlin and was permitted unlimited freedom of movement in Occupied Europe, living high off the hog, while Joyce was stuck with Büro Concordia. Joyce would have resented that while at the same time envying Amery's aristocratic background. The former Lord Haw-Haw had grown up with a huge chip on his shoulder. Even in the old, prewar days, when the British upper classes considered it fashionable to flirt with fascism, he was never accepted by the more blue-blooded of the Mosleyites. They referred to him as that funny little man with the scarred face, but in Wandsworth Prison he was king. The other inmates spoke of William Joyce, not John Amery.

Hannah was bewildered by it all. Englishmen fighting with the SS and somehow, now, a threat to her? She had never heard of such a thing, she said, though she knew about the Dutch and Flemish SS divisions, the Estonian and the Norwegian.

"Munich in fifteen minutes," grunted Max from the wheel, purring with pleasure at the response he was getting from the Mercedes.

Quinlan told Hannah that most other people had never heard of the British SS unit either.

"It's not something we brag about. In any case," he added to Hadleigh, "although I'm obviously wrong, I thought they were all dead or in captivity."

One who was emphatically not in captivity was the Yorkshireman who had advised "nailing" Quinlan. Now aged twenty-seven, he was born William Riordan, though the ID he carried and the uniform he wore belonged to Captain Eric Spencer, who to Riordan's certain knowledge was dead. The papers were for emergencies only. Spencer would be on someone's AWOL sheet and an alert MP might recognize the name.

Riordan had watched the Mercedes leave the Allersbergerstrasse barracks before beginning the mile and a half walk to the Grand, his head deep inside the turned-up collar of his overcoat to keep out the bitter wind and the snow. His transportation was elsewhere in the city for the moment.

Twenty minutes later he arrived at the hotel, where he had to wait for another fifteen to use one of the phones. He asked the operator for a number and, when connected, gave the name of the person he wanted to talk to.

Thirty seconds elapsed before a voice at the other end said, "Yes?"

Riordan did not identify himself.

"The Grand in half an hour," he said curtly.

"I'm not sure I can make it."

"Be there," said Riordan, and hung up.

He left his overcoat, cap, and swagger stick in the

cloakroom, brushed a speck of lint from his lapel, and walked into the bar.

"What can I get you, Captain?" asked the barman.

"A small beer, please."

When served, he left the counter and sat at a table near the door, where he had difficulty, a few minutes later, convincing an RAF squadron leader looking for a friendly face that he was waiting for someone and did not want company. In a room filled mostly with Americans he felt conspicuous in his khaki battle dress, which was an open invitation to any other Britisher to strike up a conversation. His accent, however, precluded wearing a US uniform. Neither should he have worn the rank tabs of an officer, for before his capture by Rommel's forces in North Africa in 1942, he was a sergeant with the 51st Highland Division. Afterward, he was one of the first to succumb to the temptations of an easier life by enlisting in the British Free Corps. Others who had done the same had lived to regret it. Now incarcerated in British prisons or waiting to come to trial, they doubtless wondered why they hadn't stuck it out. Riordan didn't. Although no believer in National Socialism, the BFC and the SS had offered him a route out of the dreary discipline of a POW camp and promised him more. They still did.

His contact was five minutes late and looked around anxiously before spotting Riordan. This was no place to be seen with a fake British officer.

They got straight down to business, keeping their voices low.

"Where have they gone?" demanded Riordan. "I saw Quinlan, the Americans, and what I take to be the Wolz woman leave in a Mercedes."

"Munich."

"We should have been informed."

"It wasn't possible. I didn't know myself until a short while ago. I'm not told everything."

"Where in Munich?"

"I don't know."

"That isn't an answer I accept."

"It's nevertheless the only one I can give. I know who they hope to see but not where."

"Who then? Who?" he repeated when a response was not immediately forthcoming. "You know the consequences if you hold anything back."

"A man called Bachmann. I think his given name is Helmut."

"But no address."

"None that I heard. You don't understand how difficult it is."

"If you're lying . . ."

"I'm not, I swear it. There's something else I can tell you to prove it. Quinlan was in a gun battle last night, over in Weigelshof. I didn't hear it all, but two men were killed, two Germans."

"Their names?" asked Riordan, though he was fairly certain he could supply the answer to that himself.

"No names. From what I overheard they carried no identification papers."

"And what is the significance of Weigelshof?"

"I believe it's where Hannah Wolz lived."

"Lived?"

"You saw yourself, she went with them."

"But she has to live somewhere when they return."

"Of course, but I don't know where."

Riordan elected not to pursue the matter, unimportant now, in any case. Hannah Wolz had obviously had Arndt's fragment all along. She would by this time have handed it over to Quinlan and the Americans. Why else would they be going to Munich? Bachmann had to be the second link in the chain.

"You will have to do better than this," he said coldly. "We won't be strung along with things you believe or think or assume—or things you don't know. We have to have hard intelligence before the event, not afterward. Bear that in mind."

"I can't leave as and when I choose. I don't have that much freedom."

"Then make it. Remember the alternative."

"I'll try to let you know when they return."

"I need to know more than that. I need reports on their conversations, their attitudes, if they're elated or depressed."

"If only I knew what you were really looking for, it would be easier. I could ask Quinlan. He's the most trusting of the three."

"You'll do nothing of the kind," said Riordan. "There will be no direct questioning. You know the conditions. If you're suspected or arrested, it's the same as if you betray us."

Riordan glanced furtively around the bar, aware that his voice had risen an octave. Besides, they had been sitting together too long.

"Go now," he said quietly, "but remember what I said. It's the boy's life."

Frau Gretl Meissner got to her feet and smoothed her skirt.

"Please," she asked, "may I see him?"

"You know that's not possible. He's in good hands and healthy. He'll remain healthy as long as you do as you're told. It won't be for much longer, either way. Now leave."

She answered Riordan's smile with a forced one of her own. Anyone watching would have assumed that a British officer and his lady friend were making arrangements for later.

She went down the steps and into the street, hating herself for betraying Quinlan and Major Hadleigh but knowing there was no other option. Unless she did as she was told, Riordan and his SS friends would murder Willi.

Riordan gave her a five-minute start before collecting his overcoat, cap, and swagger stick. Outside he walked south along Frauentorgraben, looking over his shoulder every so often until a Jeep carrying Third Army markings pulled up and a cheerful American voice called, loud enough for anyone in the vicinity to hear, "Give you a ride someplace, Captain?"

"Thanks," said Riordan. "I'd appreciate that."

Once aboard the vehicle he added, "Kramer and Wildehopf are dead. They must have picked up the Wolz woman's trail last night and followed her home. Unfortunately Quinlan was with her and they were killed in some sort of shoot-out. Quinlan, the Americans, and Hannah Wolz are now on their way to Munich to see a man named Bachmann. Have you heard him mentioned before?"

"No," answered the driver.

"Maybe one of the Krauts knows him."

The driver grinned. "Don't let the Krauts hear you call them Krauts."

"Fuck 'em. They don't bother me."

At the wheel, twenty-five-year-old Frank Hallam wondered if that was the truth. Riordan was tough enough—he'd seen that with his own eyes—but the Germans were also hard men.

A native of Milwaukee and later a corporal with the 2nd Canadian Division before being taken prisoner of war after the raid on Dieppe in August 1942, Hallam took a left turn at the wooden markers and headed southwest for Grossreuth, a fifteen-minute trip.

"If they've gone to Munich, does that mean we go to Munich?"

"Someone, maybe," answered Riordan, "but not us."

"What if this guy Bachmann has another fragment and they get it?"

"So they get it. By the looks of things they've got Arndt's already."

"We don't have much time. What is it, ten, twelve days tops?"

"Less. We have to move well before January tenth.

But if we don't have much time, neither do they. Even if they get Bachmann's fragment and the others, they still have to decipher their meaning. They don't stand a chance.''

Hallam acknowledged a wave from an MP in a slicker at a junction.

"Bet I make it stateside before you do!" he yelled.

"Don't push your luck," cautioned Riordan.

Hallam shrugged over the wheel. "What the hell. I'm as American as he is."

"I'm more concerned about the Jeep."

"Same thing. When I was in England in '42 we used to lose around a dozen vehicles a week from Second Division. You know, guys going out on the town and forgetting where they parked the thing. My guess is it's the same around here. Worse. Remember how we picked this one up? Nobody gives a fuck. Uncle Sam's paying and you can bet your ass two-star generals and above have sold off a whole fleet of Caddies."

"Nevertheless," said Riordan, "no point in taking chances."

Hallam tossed a sideways glance at him to see if he was kidding. He wasn't. Dumb Limey son of a bitch. He was right, though. Too close to blow it.

"Do you ever think of the old days?" he asked out of the blue.

"Never."

"Never? Sometimes I have a hankering for them."

"For the States?"

"No, for the corps, with the rest of the guys before the war was over. Christ, we had some times."

ELEVEN

~~~~~~

BERLIN/HILDESHEIM/
DRESDEN/SALZBURG
1943–1945

ONCE THEY UNDERSTOOD they would get few recruits
for the Legion of St. George by propaganda, the German brass came up with a different idea: the special
camp. Commandants of regular POW camps were invited to select non-troublemakers for a two weeks' stay
in a camp where all discipline would be relaxed, extra
rations provided, and brothels established. There were
two camps: one for officers, the other for enlisted men.
The former was known as Special Detachment 999 and
based in a villa in Zehlendorf, a southwest suburb of
Berlin. There the incoming officers were greeted by the
commandant, Herr Dr. Falkner, and told that the facilities available were simply Germany's way of giving
POWs a rest from the rigors of normal camp life. The

inmates were provided with recent copies of British newspapers and taken on sightseeing tours of Berlin. Compulsory lectures warned them of the threat the Soviet Union posed to all "civilized" nations. No attempt was made to indoctrinate them with the virtues of Nazism.

The senior British officer cautioned his subordinates against being taken in by this display of German generosity, and when the question of joining the Legion eventually cropped up there were few takers.

In the aftermath of increased Allied air force activity over Berlin, Special Detachment 999 was moved from Zehlendorf in the autumn of 1943 to a wired-off section of Stalag 111A at Luckenwalde, where it would be safe from bombers, because the RAF and the USAAF knew of the POW camp there. At the end of September the Germans shut it down altogether because of its lack of success.

The special camp for NCOs and enlisted men was first attached to Stalag 111D at Steglitz, another suburb of Berlin. Later it was transferred to Genshagen, southwest of the capital. Here almost three hundred POWs were accommodated in three large huts, with a fourth used as kitchens and a dining hall. Set in a pleasant country estate, by mid-July 1943 it had a full complement.

Recruiting for the Legion did not seriously begin for another month. When it did, the volunteers fell into three categories: those who were unwilling to give up this newfound luxury; a lesser number who believed the Allies would lose the war; and a few who were terrorized by stronger personalities. They were a mixed bag, mostly British but with a sprinkling of Commonwealth troops and Americans.

Once committed, they had to sign a declaration that they had no Jewish blood. In turn they received assurances that they would never be called upon to face their own countrymen. The Legion was being formed solely to fight bolshevism.

Later in the year they moved to a permanent base in Pankow, where they were allowed their own canteen which served beer and spirits. A portrait of the Duke of Windsor when he was King Edward VIII dominated one wall. Discipline was minimal; as long as the recruits kept themselves clean and tidy and did not cause trouble when drunk, the Germans were content.

Toward the end of 1943 the OKW (the German High Command), the SS, and the German Foreign Office met to decide what to do with the fledgling Legion. Present also were some of the original volunteers, among them Bill Riordan and Frank Hallam, who had met at Genshagen, together with two other Britishers who could be regarded as founding members: ex-Corporal Tom Granger, a hard, twenty-six-year-old tankman captured at El 'Alamein, and ex-Corporal Harry Laidlaw, a thirty-year-old dour Scot taken prisoner in the early North African fighting. This quartet formed the hard core of the Legion, a fact an SS Sturmbannführer took note of during the discussions.

The first gripe Riordan and the others had was John Amery, still the Legion's nominal leader. They wanted him out, and their request was agreed to in principle.

Next came the question of a unit title. The tankman Granger had noted that the Germans frequently referred to the volunteers as the British Legion, which was unacceptable because of the ex-serviceman's organization in the UK of the same name. Nor did the Legion of St. George find approval among the turncoats. Apart from that being Amery's idea, Saint George was the patron saint of England, which could well deter potential recruits from Wales, Ireland, and Scotland.

Granger proposed they be allowed to petition Hitler to call themselves the British Free Corps, which was agreed to by the senior German officer present.

The formal document read:

We, the true soldiers of Britain, wish to swear allegiance to the Führer and to the German Reich. We volunteer to fight side by side with the Germans against the enemies of Europe. For this purpose, the undersigned make application for the corps to be called the British Free Corps.

The only non-Briton at the meeting, Frank Hallam, had no objections. It didn't matter to him what the hell they were called.

When the subject of uniform was raised, Riordan was quick to point out that, if they wore their original khakis, it might be tempting for a German commander to use the corps in an intelligence capacity in the West, if and when the Allies invaded Europe. If the Germans genuinely intended them to face no one except the Red Army, surely field gray was the answer.

After consultation the German brass agreed, detailing the Waffen SS representative present to supply regulation breeches and tunics, the latter minus SS runes. In place of these, three leopards would be used as the collar patch insignia. The brassard would be a Union Jack shield on the upper-left sleeve.

A proposal that the corps members, who would be fighting alongside Waffen SS troops, should have their blood groups tattooed under their armpits in the customary manner was rejected by Riordan and the others. If they were ever captured, a tattoo would earn them summary execution.

The last item on the agenda was that of the corps commander. Since no officers from Special Detachment 999 had been tempted into doing more than broadcasting propaganda, Riordan was hoping for the honor. The SS vetoed his request, insisting that the CO be German. They chose Hauptsturmführer Johannes Roggenfeld of the SS Panzer Division Viking, giving him St. Michael's monastery at Hildesheim as corps headquarters. Once a lunatic asylum, it had been commandeered by Himmler as a center for maintaining cultural bonds between Nordic nations and rechristened Haus Germanien. The BFC moved there in February 1944.

While Roggenfeld busied himself with the massive administration problems of the new unit, the Big Four (as Riordan, Hallam, Granger, and Laidlaw were now known) concentrated on discipline, banishing the easy days of Genshagen and Pankow. Parades were held daily at 8 A.M., followed by physical training and lectures. Many recruits had had enough within a couple of weeks and applied to be returned to their POW camps. Others replaced them, but the corps's combat strength never rose beyond sixty or seventy during this period.

In April their uniforms arrived and pay was regularized to one Reichsmark per day regardless of rank, with a further thirty RMs a month from a separate SS account. The corps had yet to hear a shot fired in anger, however, and there was not even a whisper of it being sent to the Russian front. The Waffen SS (the field commanders as opposed to the deskbound political officers) could find no use for it. In spite of everything the corps was still too small.

By August Roggenfeld was thoroughly disenchanted with the BFC. After all the trumpeting and ballyhoo and a predicted brigade of fifteen hundred, his command remained around company strength. He had several titanic arguments with his superiors and was eventually dismissed, his replacement being Hauptsturmführer Eric Jupp, who had lost a leg in Russia. A few days after he took over orders came through for the corps to move its base to Dresden, where it arrived at the beginning of September.

The SS was very proud of the Dresden barracks. Begun in 1936, its every building was centrally heated and the enlisted men's quarters were close to luxurious. All ranks received grade one-alpha rations, the highest food scale in the German armed forces, which caused Himmler, toward the end of the year, seriously to consider disbanding the corps. Its members were eating but not fighting.

After a series of long and bitter arguments with the Foreign Office, which convinced the Reichsführer that dissolution would be a major propaganda defeat, Himmler relented, which enabled Riordan and his immediate circle to breathe again when the news came through. Disbandment would have meant either a return to a POW camp or absorption into a Waffen SS line regiment with no guarantee their outfit would not be sent west against Anglo-American forces at some point.

Toward the end of January 1945 Riordan held a secret meeting with his three principal henchmen. The Allied advance across Europe was proving unstoppable. Germany's promised "wonder weapons" were propaganda fantasies. The writing was on the wall for the Third Reich and, with it, for the BFC, which was already falling apart. Half a dozen corpsmen had deserted a week earlier and later had been picked up in Czechoslovakia by the Gestapo. Another dozen had volunteered for the Waffen SS, some as combat troops, some as medics. And the US Eighth Air Force raid on Dresden on January 16 was a forerunner of worse to come. For more than one reason, Dresden was no longer a desirable place to be, nor was continued membership in the corps an attractive proposition.

The trouble was, Riordan argued, their options were virtually nil. To desert would put them in the hands of the Gestapo. Even if it didn't, sooner or later they would be captured by the Russians or the Anglo-Americans, who would either execute them or put them in prison for the rest of their natural lives.

The Big Four considered themselves to be hard and practical men and flight without purpose or objective did not appeal to them. Neither did staying put, waiting to be overrun or conscripted into the Waffen SS. They were at a complete loss regarding their next move until

February 6, when there appeared in Dresden, bright and shiny in an immaculate uniform with SD (SS Security Service) sleeve patches, the same Sturmbannführer who had sat in on the December 1943 meeting and who had taken note of the BFC ringleaders' names. He introduced himself as Heinrich Scharper, and he was not in the city by chance. He had full authority to take Riordan to Berlin, if the ex-sergeant wanted to go. He would not be coerced. Neither would he receive any explanation until he got there.

Riordan consulted with Hallam, Granger, and Laidlaw. The consensus was that they had nothing to lose by agreeing, even though Laidlaw maintained that Berlin probably wanted Riordan to organize the remnants of the BFC for some sort of death-or-glory mission on behalf of the Reich. When this was put to Scharper, he denied it. He also took great pains to reassure them all that Riordan would soon be back, possibly with something encouraging to report. They were not to mention the conversation to any of the others, however. This—whatever "this" was—was for the Big Four only.

Riordan and Scharper traveled by road, arriving in Berlin on the evening of the sixth. Scharper's driver dropped them at the Adlon, where the Sturmbannführer ushered Riordan to a suite on the third floor, a Wehrmacht overcoat covering his BFC uniform. Inside he was introduced to Standartenführer (SS Colonel) Hugo Sternberg and reacquainted with John Amery.

Riordan had always considered Amery to be a milksop dilettante and was fully prepared to dissociate himself from any scheme which had the cabinet minister's son as a leading participant until it became apparent that Amery was there on other business and just about to leave. After he had gone and the champagne was poured, Sternberg explained that Amery was not involved.

"It was he who jogged Scharper's memory when we realized we would require English-speaking personnel who could be trusted absolutely. Other than that he knows nothing of why you were brought here.''

"I wouldn't have thought Amery would recommend me for whatever you've got in mind,'' grunted Riordan. "He hates my guts.''

"He didn't recommend you. Quite the reverse. Which is why we concluded you might be the man we want.'' Sternberg smiled as though he were the sole possessor of a mildly funny story. "Sooner or later Amery plans to return to Italy. I think he believes it will go better for him if he is captured there.''

He put an American cigarette in a long ebony holder and patted his pockets. Scharper supplied the light.

"What I am about to tell you involves my taking a great risk,'' Sternberg said to Riordan, "and you should fully understand that once told you are committed. In other words, I am asking you to pledge yourself before hearing what I have to say. You will be responsible for the others in your group also.'' He referred to a typewritten document. "Hallam, Granger, and Laidlaw.''

They conversed in German, which, after twenty months with the BFC, Riordan spoke fluently if with an accent.

"You can't ask me to vouch for them,'' said Riordan roughly, deliberately omitting Sternberg's rank.

"Let me put it another way,'' murmured Sternberg, ignoring the discourtesy. "If what I have to tell you appeals, I leave it to you whether or not you pass it on to Hallam, Granger, and Laidlaw, or any other three you can trust. But we have calculated we are going to need four of you. Fewer will give us no backup should anything go wrong; more will make us top-heavy. Bear in mind that you are all, you British Free Corps people, now in great danger. You will either be killed in the fighting to come or taken prisoner by the Allies. Either option seems somewhat limited.''

Sternberg was right, of course, which was why he, Riordan, was in Berlin.

"Let's hear what you have to say."

"You understand you will not leave this building alive if, having heard, you decline to participate?"

"I understand."

For over an hour Sternberg and occasionally Scharper talked while Riordan listened, outlining a scheme of such daring and imagination it took Riordan's breath away. By 10 P.M. when the meeting ended he was so full of enthusiasm for the project that he wanted to return to Dresden immediately. Scharper persuaded him to remain in Berlin overnight, and for his pleasure provided a sumptuous dinner, two bottles of malt whiskey, and the services of a Swedish countess whose sexual appetite left Riordan exhausted.

With the same driver at the wheel, he and Scharper drove back to Dresden the following afternoon. During the small hours of February 8 the Big Four left Dresden forever—not too soon, as it turned out, for on the thirteenth and fourteenth of that month the RAF and the USAAF leveled much of the city. Without leadership, surviving corpsmen were drafted into the Waffen SS with no argument. The great majority were killed in the final days of fighting in Berlin.

In civilian clothes, the BFC quartet was driven to Austria where they were installed in a country villa owned by a titled Austrian who had managed to convince everyone who knew him that he was and always had been an anti-Nazi. To support the strategem the SS had, on several occasions throughout the war, taken him into custody. If the villa was ever subjected to more than casual scrutiny when the Allies overran Salzburg, there was a well-concealed underground bunker on the estate. There were also other "safe" houses in Bavaria and Austria, many apparently owned by implacable enemies of the regime.

From time to time Sternberg and Scharper put in an appearance, and around the second week in April two names started to dominate their whispered conversations: Canaris and Langenhain. A few days later Riordan heard Amery referred to and challenged Sternberg, fearing that the cabinet minister's son was about to become part of the group. The Standartenführer assured him otherwise. He and Scharper had simply arranged a further meeting with Amery in the lobby of the Adlon because Amery knew by sight a man the SS wanted to interview, Oberstleutnant Langenhain.

During the third week in April Sternberg and Scharper took up residence in the villa, bringing with them four SS NCOs. Canaris and Langenhain were no longer mentioned.

The last few days of the month and the beginning of May were anxious ones for the villa's occupants. The news that Hitler was dead did not seem to affect the Germans; the fact that Patton's Third Army was now in Salzburg did. But as had been predicted, the anti-Nazi reputation of the villa's titled owner was well known to Allied intelligence. While the illicit houseguests were in the underground bunker, the premises and grounds were subjected to no more than a perfunctory search by US troops, whose commander had, in any case, other things on his mind.

A few miles east of Salzburg were the salt mines at Alt Aussee, where a vast storehouse of looted art treasures was kept. Once German resistance in the city was overcome, the MFA&A (Monuments, Fine Arts and Archives) detachment with the Third Army, spearheaded by tanks, drove at speed for the mines, worried that the SS had orders to destroy everything as an act of vengeance. They made it just ahead of the advancing Soviet forces.

The official end to the war in Europe came with the signing of the unconditional surrender document by Generaloberst Jodl. On hearing of this over the radio and from the loudspeaker vans that toured the center and outskirts of Salzburg, the villa's occupants felt a sense of relief. They were all on the mandatory arrest list, of course, and doubtless, when things calmed down, there would be a massive manhunt for the thousands of individuals not yet in captivity. In the meantime, at least the shooting had stopped and the strategy outlined in the Adlon a step closer to beginning.

Riordan wanted to know when. Sternberg told him there was no hurry. They were not yet a full complement. Perhaps it would be months before the time was right. In the interim they had everything they wanted here, did they not? Their host had blackmarket contacts; there was as much food as they could eat and alcohol as they could drink. Lack of women was a problem, naturally, but it would be unwise to ferry in whores. Women were talkative bitches.

To move prematurely would not only be risky but could prove counterproductive. The existence of their plans, which had been laid with great care several years before, was known only to a few, all evidence eradicated. Patience was the order of the day.

And might well have remained so had word not filtered through to the villa early in June that one of the men for whom they were waiting was in custody.

TWELVE

~~~~~~

NUREMBERG
December 29, 1945

NOT AS LARGE or as sumptuous as the Salzburg villa,
the house nevertheless stood in its own grounds midway
between the southwest suburbs of Grossreuth and Kleinreuth, shielded from the main road and surrounded on
three sides by a high hedge. The fourth side backed onto
open fields and the nearest neighbors were half a mile
away. The entire area had escaped much of the heaviest
bombing.

The SS had owned it (and backup houses in Fürth and
Zirndorf) since 1937, though the name on the title deeds
was Frau Elke Niemeyer, a woman in her fifties whose
husband was under arrest in the Russian zone, accused
of war crimes in Mauthausen concentration camp.
While privately believing that ex-Hauptsturmführer
Niemeyer would be executed before long, Sternberg had

promised on arrival to look into ways of either freeing
or defending the man. In the meantime, Frau Niemeyer
would kindly keep to the small gardener's cottage, ignore the comings and goings at the main house, and not
enter unless invited. She was not to leave the grounds
without permission and casual callers were to be discouraged.

Visitors would not be a problem, Frau Niemeyer had
informed Sternberg when the SS colonel first appeared
toward the end of September. Since the war's end, her
so-called friends had shunned her, wanting nothing to
do with a woman whose husband was connected with
"those terrible camps."

"Though they were willing to sit at his table and beg
favors in the earlier years."

Sternberg had clucked sympathetically, told her not
to worry about rations (which he could obtain easily on
the black market with the funds at his disposal), and
had hardly set eyes on her since. For her part, as long as
she was fed and occasionally supplied with alcohol, she
was more than happy. She would be sorry to see them
go.

The house was a three-story structure containing six
bedrooms spread equally between the upper two stories.
In one of these fifteen-year-old Willi Meissner was
handcuffed to a heavy iron bed. A majority had wanted
to kill him, to save them the trouble of having to super-
vise and feed him. Sternberg had vetoed that notion. If
Gretl Meissner ever became difficult or uncooperative,
she might need a gentle reminder, such as a high-pitched
scream over a telephone as one of her son's fingers was
removed, to bring her back into line. For the moment,
Willi Meissner was more useful alive than dead.

On the ground floor were three living rooms, the
largest serving as a common room for the occupants.
After Hallam parked the Jeep alongside two others
carrying Third Army markings, he and Riordan made
their way toward the house. From the shrubbery Tom

Granger whistled a soft greeting. Sternberg had ruled that someone should always patrol outside during the hours of darkness. He had learned a long time ago that caution paid dividends.

The common room was illuminated by oil lamps, and Riordan saw at once that everyone was present. Apart from Harry Laidlaw, the remainder of the group were Germans. Having lived in their company for eight months, Riordan knew them as well as he knew himself. He didn't trust any of them farther than he could spit. They needed the Big Four for the foreseeable future; after that, each member of the quartet would be well advised to watch his back.

At the head of a long oak table sat Sternberg, impressive looking even out of uniform. He was tall and lithe, and his hair had turned silvery gray at the temples, making him look older than his forty-four years. On his right Heinrich Scharper cradled a goblet of brandy, judging by his eyes and past experience not his first of the night, though he could hold his liquor. Somewhere in his late twenties, he was a heavyset man who would one day have a weight problem—if he lived that long.

Over by the curtained window Oberscharführer Oskar Flisk was buffing his nails with a handkerchief. In his early thirties, Flisk was one of the four SS NCOs Sternberg and Scharper had brought to the villa in April. His constant attention to personal hygiene and a deceptively mild manner made him an unlikely candidate for the rank of a senior sergeant in the SS. Nevertheless, Riordan knew him to be hard and ruthless beneath the affable exterior; knew also he had been part of the team that had executed Canaris. As had Unterscharführer Kurt Zander, standing next to him. Zander smiled a lot when there was little to smile about. Without a shadow of a doubt, in Riordan's private opinion, he was a psychopath looking for a victim. He was another of the Salzburg four, the other two being Kramer and Wildehopf, now dead.

Rarely was the pair who completed the German contingent found far away from one other, though there was nothing sinister or homosexual in their relationship. Formerly tank drivers with the SS Panzer Division Totenkopf, Hans-Dieter Kleemann and Anton Isken were not only the youngest of the Germans but the last to join the group. Sternberg had found them in Salzburg, in a "safe" house, in midsummer, on their way down the SS escape line to Italy. The Standartenführer had close connections with the men who ran the Odessa route and had received their permission to approach and proposition Kleemann and Isken when he realized that two others who were supposed to make the Salzburg villa rendezvous were either dead or in captivity.

The tankmen were both in their early twenties and alike enough in Aryan good looks to be brothers. They were generally sent elsewhere when something important was being discussed, which seemed not to bother them at all. Their blue eyes shone with fanaticism and their voices dropped to a whisper whenever the late Führer's name was mentioned. They would have died, willingly, if Riordan was any judge of character, protecting the reputation of the Third Reich's founder.

Seated down the table from Scharper, Harry Laidlaw grinned through broken teeth at Riordan and Hallam, relieved to see them back. The Scotsman was a willing and rugged fighter, weaned on violence in the Glasgow slums. No one would have put his intelligence much above average, however. His command of German was the least adequate of the Big Four and he felt uncomfortable being able to catch the meaning of only two words out of three.

Riordan helped himself to a brandy from the bottle at Scharper's elbow.

"Kramer and Wildehopf are dead," he announced without preamble. "According to Gretl Meissner, they were killed last night. Quinlan and the others are on their way to Munich with Hannah Wolz. They're looking for a man called Bachmann, given name probably Helmut.''

Scharper's eyes betrayed his alarm.

"Were Wildehopf or Kramer carrying anything to connect them with us or this house?''

"According to Frau Meissner, no. They had no papers or IDs on them at all.''

"That's something, I suppose,'' grunted Scharper.

Sternberg cursed under his breath, less concerned about the deaths of Wildehopf and Kramer than the loss of two able-bodied men. Theirs was a small-enough group anyway. Losing a sixth of it would make everything that much harder.

"Damn it,'' he repeated. "Where did all this happen?''

"Over in Weigelshof, where Hannah Wolz lived.''

"Lived?'' questioned Scharper.

"I asked Gretl Meissner the same thing,'' said Riordan. "They've taken her to Munich, as I just told you. They'll move her to a new address when they get back. If Kramer and Wildehopf could find her, and that's what we have to assume happened, so could anyone else. She was lucky last night because Quinlan was with her. He can't be with her all the time. They'll move her when they return.''

"What about the Opel Kramer was driving?'' asked Flisk.

"The Americans must have it.'' Riordan tossed back his brandy. "If they haven't, it will be stripped into a thousand pieces by now. In either event, it's lost to us.''

"Stupid bastards,'' swore Scharper. "What the hell did they think they were playing at?''

"They must have picked up Hannah Wolz's trail somehow or found out where she lived. Unfortunately for them she had an escort.''

"Bachmann,'' murmured Sternberg. "Bachmann. He holds the second fragment, presumably. Does the name mean anything to anyone?''

It did not.

"But we can take it for granted he's another damned Abwehr man," said Scharper. "Christ, I hope Canaris is rotting in hell. He's been dead for eight months and he still haunts us."

"I think we can also take for granted the fact that Langenhain did not know the second name," added Sternberg. "Either that or he was a braver man and a better liar than we thought."

Kurt Zander remembered the day they had finally caught up with Langenhain in mid-April, how long it had taken him to die.

"No, he did not have the second name," he said slowly, smiling cynically. "Believe me, if he'd known of Bachmann, he would have told me. He'd have willingly killed his own parents if I'd commanded him in the end, the way he begged me to kill him after I broke his wrists."

"Enough," said Sternberg brusquely, glaring at Zander. The sooner he no longer had to deal with sadistic gutter rats like the Unterscharführer, the better. But he concurred that Langenhain had known only of Arndt.

"Do we go to Munich, some of us?" asked Flisk.

"We do not go to Munich, none of us," answered Sternberg. "It would be far too dangerous and asking for trouble. We don't know where this Bachmann is or even whether he's alive. Nor have we anything to gain. Without the first fragment, the others are useless, and the Americans must have obtained the first from Hannah Wolz or they would not know the whereabouts of the second."

"What if they find Bachmann and he gives them the second?" Scharper wanted to know.

"That still leaves two others. Even if they find them they have to work out what it all means. We have twice as much information as they do, and I'd wager we would not solve the riddle overnight. Canaris was very clever. Or Unterscharführer Zander not so persuasive with the old man as he was with Langenhain.''

"That's not true," muttered Zander, his eyes narrowing at the implied rebuke. "The circumstances with Canaris were very different. If I'd been allowed a free hand, we would not be sitting here now."

"Perhaps not," said Sternberg. "In any case, it's of no consequence, water under the bridge. We must, however, be told when Major Hadleigh and his party return from Munich and also where Fräulein Wolz is to be kept. We can presumably rely upon Frau Meissner to provide us with that information?"

"I'll make sure of it," growled Riordan. "She knows what will happen otherwise."

"Then in the meantime, gentlemen," concluded Sternberg, "I suggest we concentrate on our own business. There is still much to be done. I need not repeat that I should like to bring the date forward. That, however, does not depend upon us. We can only hope it is fully understood in other quarters that we have to move well before January tenth. I'm rather hoping for the third or fourth, but at the very outside it must be Monday the seventh."

THIRTEEN

~~~~~~

MUNICH
December 29–31, 1945

THEY DROVE INTO Munich from the north, down through the Schwabing district via Schleissheimerstrasse where, at number 34, Adolf Hitler had first lived above a tailor's shop on arriving in the Bavarian capital as a student in May 1913. In number 106 an earlier revolutionary, registered as Meyer, had spent a year at the turn of the century studying Marx. His given name was Vladimir Ilyich Ulyanov; the world would later know him better as Lenin. Anyone given to irony could scarcely find a better example.

They had to ask their way opposite the technical school on Elizabethplatz. Although Max had packed an Army-issue street map, it was way out of date and some of the roads and buildings listed were no longer recognizable.

The MP who gave them directions after referring to a typewritten sheet said that Sedanstrasse, where they hoped to find Helmut Bachmann, was on the other side of the river Isar and that all the bridges were open to light traffic. To get there, he added chattily in his best guidebook manner, they should follow the signs for Haidhausen. Once across the river they should turn left at the massive Bürgerbräukeller on Rosenheimerstrasse, from where Hitler had launched his Beer Hall Putsch in 1923. First on the left was Steinstrasse, which was open, and at the end of that Sedanstrasse. They couldn't miss it.

"Though don't expect to find much," said the MP.

They discovered what he meant when they reached the street, cruising down it with the Merc's headlights blazing. Every block was a ruin. Nothing was left of Sedanstrasse, certainly nowhere for anyone to live.

Quinlan was sick with disappointment. They'd wasted a trip. If they'd picked up a telephone or used the wireless, they'd have known in a moment that Sedanstrasse was no longer anything but vast mounds of snow-covered rubble.

"I don't know what I was expecting," he said disconsolately. "Well, that's that."

But Hadleigh had different ideas. If Bachmann had been sitting in his house when the bombs landed, they were out of luck. On the other hand he could be a prisoner, having surrendered or been captured when Patch's Seventh Army stormed the city—in which case he would be on file somewhere.

"No reason why he should be," muttered Quinlan, speaking in English. "Arndt kept his head down for six months. Maybe Bachmann did too and is still doing it."

"Well Jesus H. Christ," exploded Hadleigh. "If that's the postwar bulldog spirit, no wonder you're going to lose the empire. Arndt had the SS on his tail and Ilse and Hannah to worry about. Anyway, what the hell can we lose by checking? We've got to report in and find somewhere to bunk down for the night.''

They recrossed the Isar and stopped a mobile Jeep patrol. Hadleigh flashed his credentials and asked to be directed to his opposite number in Seventh Army G-2. The corporal wasn't sure where intelligence had its HQ but his driver got on the radio and had the answer within minutes.

''It's Major McLusky you want, Major. He's based over at the infantry barracks south of Oberwiesenfeld airfield.'' They knew where the airfield was; they had passed it on the way in. ''But he isn't there right now. His office says your best bet is the Bavaria Hotel at this time of night.''

The corporal told them to follow the road they were on, Bayerstrasse, until they reached the Hauptbahnhof, the main railway station. The Bavaria Hotel was a couple of hundred yards off to the left. There were Seventh Army signposts at the station.

''The Third, Forty-second, and Forty-fifth divisions have got some of their brass living there. Just follow the markers.''

Munich gave the impression of being much brighter and more full of life than Nuremberg. In spite of the bitter cold, hundreds of people were on the streets, German civilians as well as armed troops. Max suggested that it had something to do with Christmas just being over and New Year's around the corner. Hadleigh begged to differ.

''No, things are changing fast. In a couple of days we'll be talking about the war that ended *last* year.'' He was still speaking in English and Hannah wasn't following him. ''Whatever any of us might think about the Germans, we've got to help them rebuild the country we knocked down before some clever bastard in the Kremlin decides these are ideal conditions for a revolution.''

Judging by the stenciled signs on the wall by the entrance, the Bavaria now functioned as part hotel, part command post. The forecourt was packed with vehicles, civilians as well as military, and Max spent several minutes finding a vacant slot for the Mercedes. He and Hannah stayed with the car. Hadleigh didn't want to tread on anyone's corns by inviting a German girl inside, no matter how beautiful she was.

He asked a Seventh Army staff sergeant who stood behind a desk beneath a notice reading ALL PERSONNEL ON OFFICIAL BUSINESS REPORT HERE for Major McLusky, and a dogface was sent to fetch him. While waiting, Hadleigh confessed that a little of his earlier optimism about tracing Bachmann was fading. By the looks of things Sedanstrasse was a ruin long before Arndt had told Hannah that that was where she would find Bachmann. Which must mean, at the very least, that Arndt hadn't seen Bachmann or Munich for some months prior to the end of the war.

McLusky appeared with a glass in his hand. Above his left breast pocket were two rows of campaign ribbons. He was a beefy man in his late thirties. Over a much-needed drink in the bar, Hadleigh explained their business in Munich.

"Has this guy Bachmann got a rank or a record?" asked McLusky. "Any strikes against him?"

"Not as far as we know. I'm only guessing, but he could have been Abwehr, maybe a middle-ranking officer."

"Well, that narrows the field—if we've got him or had him and if he confessed to being Abwehr."

"There's no reason why he shouldn't," said Quinlan. "They were clean enough."

McLusky had taken in Quinlan's uniform and noticed his English accent during the introductions. Clearly he was puzzled.

"What's the British interest in this?" he asked. "For that matter, what's the tie-in between the British and Third Army?"

They decided to lay it on the line, tell McLusky about Arndt, the murder of Arndt's younger daughter and Angela Salvatini, the fragment of photograph, Quinlan's shoot-out with a couple of unidentified SS men, the probability that remnants of the SS and the British Free Corps were working together.

If it all sounded incredible, fortunately McLusky was an old hand and accustomed to the bizarre.

The Seventh Army major scratched his head.

"Well, there's no easy way of doing this. All I can suggest is that you go over the records I have back at the office. It'll be a helluva long job. They're stored in a room the size of a small conference hall. We must have processed twenty or thirty thousand individuals in and around Munich alone, most of them in the few weeks right after the war when we were all a bit keener, when we expected to find Himmler and Bormann and maybe Hitler himself right under our noses. We've slackened off a bit in recent months." He shrugged apologetically. "Inevitable, I guess. Anyway, that's the first problem, the sheer volume of files.

"The second problem," he went on, "is that not everyone we hauled in gave us his real name to start with. You wouldn't believe the number of guys we came across who claimed to have lost their IDs."

"I believe it," said Hadleigh.

McLusky grinned amiably. "Yeah, I guess you would at that. Anyway, some of them gave us phony names because they had something to hide and some because they wanted to make it as hard as they could for us to introduce a form of military government. The trouble is, if a joker gave us the name of Schmidt to begin with and later we discovered his name was Braun, we only need one dogface with a hangover to say, 'Fuck it, I'm not hunting through that stack of files to find the original Schmidt and change it,' and we're left with a Braun *and* a Schmidt, two guys who are really one."

"What happened to all the people you processed?" asked Hadleigh. "The individuals, I mean, not their files."

He knew how Third Army operated, but each outfit had its own way of doing things.

"Those with three strikes against them we put in the stockade to await trial," McLusky explained. "To listen to the radio and read the newspapers, you'd think the only court case that matters is going on in Nuremberg. But the smaller fry—if you can call any of those bastards small—are being tried up and down the country right now, or about to be. That's the first category.

"The second category are those we're still not sure about—guys who've changed their stories a dozen times or claim they spent the whole of the war in the fire service or issuing ration cards. There are more of those than you might think. Even if we know almost one hundred percent that one of them was a camp guard or a senior Nazi official, we still have to hunt down witnesses to verify it. That's not easy. Anyway, those we've got locked up in the Oberwiesenfeld pound. It's surrounded by dogs and armed guards, but I sweat when I think what might happen if they decided, regardless of the consequences, to break out one dark night. If we shoot them "trying to escape," the Germans are going to turn around and ask what the hell's so different between us and the Nazis. Since Bachmann was Abwehr, he's unlikely to be in the first two categories. Sadly, the last two are the biggest."

The third category, McLusky told them, consisted of military personnel who had fought only as soldiers and could prove it.

"Those we put in labor battalions to clean up the mess the air forces and artillery made, though we've more or less finished with that now. We need skilled people today, not muscle. Guys who can drive bulldozers and cranes, man telephone exchanges, repair fuel and water conduits, staff power stations, fight fires, run schools and colleges, maintain generators. Patton got roasted by the newspapers back home and by some of the brass here for allowing proven Nazis to occupy key posts, but what else was he supposed to do? The fact is that many of the better-educated and skilled Germans joined the party. If we don't let them get on with the business of running the country, we'll be here till 1990, and the US taxpayer's going to have something to say about that. So is Mrs. Jones from Omaha, Nebraska, who's wondering when her little boy's coming home to apple pie and ice cream. We hear a lot of talk about making Germany pay reparations. How can they pay and what with if they haven't got any industry?

"The last category is military and civilian personnel who were too sick or worn out to be of any use in a labor battalion. We sent them packing, back to their civilian jobs if they still existed or on to the streets if they didn't."

Hadleigh remembered a fifth category from his own experience. "And there were those who, for one reason or another, were never picked up and processed at all. Not war criminals as such but guys who can get along by hustling, who don't need ration cards or who're in the rackets."

McLusky looked at him shrewdly.

"Yeah, there are those," he agreed. "I guess most of us have done a little black marketeering from time to time. Small stuff—stockings, French perfume, booze, cigarettes. The German heavies deal in currency, medical supplies, forged papers, vehicles, and gasoline. Anyhow, let's not be too pessimistic. If Bachmann passed through our hands under his own name, we'll have a record of him somewhere."

Quinlan shook his head in dismay at the thought of having to plough his way through twenty or thirty thousand names. McLusky told him it was not as bad as that.

"We've got them classified under various headings, those we were able to pin down, that is. General SS, Waffen SS, Wehrmacht, police, SA, Todt Organization, party members. And so on. While we're far from able to say for certain that everyone we cleared was not part of a criminal organization, I think we can assume that anyone not in the SS, the SA, and so forth would hardly claim that distinction. Which takes care of thirty or forty percent of the dossiers. We've got a section on Abwehr personnel also. You could try that first. You might get lucky."

"How is everything filed?" asked Quinlan.

"By job and organization as far as possible. Within the subsections it's pretty random. We tried alphabetical order, but with guys coming along and taking files and adding to them, I wouldn't lay money that Bachmann's not with the Z's. Neither would I trust the card index. You should start there, however."

"And the sooner, the better," said Quinlan.

"Now?" asked McLusky incredulously.

"Why not? Neither Major Hadleigh nor I can stay in Munich more than a couple of days. The quicker we begin, the quicker we'll find out."

"How big's your team?"

Hadleigh explained that apart from the two of them, he had only a senior G-2 noncom and a German girl.

"It shouldn't matter that she speaks almost no English since all we're looking for is a name on a dossier. We'll need accommodations and food for the four of us. We'll sleep where we work and the favor's returnable any time you're in Nuremberg."

"Which God Almighty forbid," intoned McLusky. "I can maybe lend you a couple of my boys," he offered, "but a couple is tops." He put on a long face. "Christ, I don't think you know what you're letting yourselves in for."

"We'll take our chances."

McLusky nodded slowly, coming to a decision.

"Okay, if you're determined to do it, we'd better get going. I'd probably have got taken to the cleaners in the poker game anyhow."

"There's no reason to drag you into this," protested Hadleigh.

"You're going to need someone to show you where everything is, point you in the right direction. Three guys and a Fräulein who doesn't speak much English won't get very far without help. I'll bet the woman's a middle-aged spinster too, huh?"

Hadleigh and Quinlan grinned at one another.

McLusky canceled his own transport and traveled with them in the Mercedes, his jaw dropping a foot when he saw Hannah.

The Oberwiesenfeld military training ground and barracks was ten times the size of Allersbergerstrasse in Nuremberg and had at one time housed infantry, reconnaissance, observer, anti-tank, and signals regiments of the SS as well as of the Wehrmacht. The building where Seventh Army interrogation records were kept was as big as a warehouse. Olive-green filing cabinets stood in row after row, separated by narrow corridors. Quinlan groaned out loud at the magnitude of the task facing them.

To start with, McLusky set them up with bunks in two anterooms adjacent to a washroom and shower. Rather than expose Hannah to what would undoubtedly be a stream of ribald comments in the general mess area, he arranged to have meals sent across three times a day. He detailed PFCs Martin and Toogood to help, and also provided half a dozen bottles of bourbon, a case of beer, and a coffee machine.

At ten-thirty they started on the card index, which produced seven Bachmanns but no Helmut. Four were designated as SS, two were women, and the last a major general in the Luftwaffe.

McLusky took the airman's dossier to check it out,

returning around midnight with the news that Wilhelm Bachmann could hardly be the man they were looking for. His wartime job was senior Luftwaffe liaison officer with the *Hauptamt fur Kriegsopfer*—the Main Office for War Victims. He was sixty-eight years old and currently in a military hospital, slightly out of his mind. Nothing in his dossier indicated that he had ever lived anywhere near Sedanstrasse; nor did he seem the type to have been trusted with anything that required a cool head and steady nerves. He was a desk man, a World War I flier who had kept his nose clean and been rewarded with regular promotions and nonsensitive posts. He might be worth interrogating if no Helmut Bachmann materialized, though everyone agreed that this could hardly be the man Arndt had told Hannah to contact.

The Abwehr dossiers produced no Bachmanns, not even a name which, in transcription, could have been misspelled. The gods of fortune were not going to assist. It was going to be a long job.

As McLusky had suggested, they ignored the sections that dealt with the SS, SA, police, and so forth, making the assumption that Bachmann would not be a member of a hard-core Nazi organization, nor claim to be. Standing at the filing cabinets, they concentrated on the remainder, working their way from drawer to drawer, from front to back, putting a white chalk mark on each cabinet that had been examined so that effort would not be duplicated and no one have to be awakened and asked if a specific cabinet was completed; for it had been agreed, as fatigue was their worst enemy, that anyone who felt weary could retire, no questions asked.

Time passed, food arrived, coffee and bourbon were consumed, bunks occupied. December 30 came and went and so did most of December 31 without any sign of Helmut Bachmann's name appearing on the cover of a dossier.

By 10:30 P.M. on the evening of the thirty-first, there were only half a dozen cabinets, a few hundred files, remaining.

Quinlan slammed the bottom drawer of a cabinet shut, stood up, and flexed his aching muscles. A few feet away, Hannah smiled sympathetically. Hadleigh, Max Judd, and PFC Martin were resting.

"Time for a break, I think," said Quinlan.

Hannah joined him at the center table, on which a pot of coffee was regularly filled. From where he was standing, PFC Toogood glanced enviously across at the British major, watching Quinlan fill a cup and light a cigarette for the German girl. She was a beauty. She was also, by the looks of things, spoken for.

Quinlan didn't quite see it that way; nor was he sure he wanted to. He was very attracted to Hannah Wolz, much more than he wanted to admit to himself. He also acknowledged that some sort of tenuous relationship had grown up between them over the previous forty-eight hours. They now addressed each other by their given names and they were aware of each other physically. During their breaks they had talked extensively, told each other something of their prewar lives. He was the first Englishman she had ever known. She questioned him endlessly about London's theaters and famous places of entertainment she had only read about. She expressed a keen interest in his parents, their home and life-style, which brought him back to reality. No doubt they could have got to know each other a lot, lot better were it not for Arndt's death, the father she had lost after such a short acquaintance.

She did not know the full story. She believed that he'd suffered a heart attack in the Allersbergerstrasse barracks; she was unaware that Quinlan's fierce interrogation, his threats against Ilse, had caused it. Part of him wanted to tell her the truth before she found it out elsewhere; the other part accused him of being a romantic fool. Let sleeping dogs lie. He was not sure he could.

"We've almost finished," she said, cutting into his thoughts.

"Yes. We seem to have wasted our time."

"There are still a few hundred files to be examined."

"I doubt we'll find Bachmann's name among them."

"But wouldn't it be the height of irony if his was the last dossier?"

"Also the height of coincidence, which I'm afraid I don't believe in." Quinlan sipped his coffee. "Herr Bachmann's either buried in an unmarked grave or alive and elsewhere in Germany."

"Then we return to Nuremberg tomorrow?"

"I expect so. Early. We have to find somewhere other than the rooming house in Weigelshof for you to stay. Nor would I advise you to return to Herr Lorenz."

"I have to earn my living. As for somewhere to live, the girls in Sündersbühl were very nice to me."

Her eyes twinkled mischievously. She obviously knew how "the girls" supported themselves and had probably guessed, if Ingrid hadn't told her straight out, that he occasionally shared one of their beds. To change the subject, he asked her if she was quite sure her father had given her nothing more than Bachmann's name and address.

"No rank or branch of service that might help us?"

"I wish he had," she said sincerely. "I wish I could tell you more. I've been racking my brains for several days now, trying to recall if he said anything about Herr Bachmann when he gave me the slip of paper bearing his address. If he did, I've forgotten it. Perhaps he meant to at a later date. He couldn't have known he would die before then."

Quinlan took a deep breath. There would never come a better time than right now to get it off his chest. He stumbled over a word or two and occasionally repeated himself as he told her, quite quietly, the full circumstances of Heinrich Arndt's death, sparing himself nothing. When he had finished there was a long, long silence.

"I see," said Hannah eventually.

Whether she would have said any more, become bitter or sullen or accusatory, he was never to find out, for at that moment the door leading from their sleeping quarters was flung open and, from the far end of the records warehouse, Hadleigh and Judd appeared.

"For Christ's sake," shouted the G-2 major, "it's almost New Year's. Were you two going to let us sleep through it? How far have we got to go?"

Not knowing whether to bless or curse the interruption, Quinlan pointed to the half dozen remaining filing cabinets.

"Then let's run through the damned things as quick as we can," said Hadleigh. "It's unlucky to take unfinished business into a new year."

At the end of it, Helmut Bachmann's dossier had still not materialized. McLusky rolled up with a canvas holdall full of champagne just as they were finishing. PFC Toogood was anxious to join the enlisted men's celebrations, and McLusky dismissed him. It was then eleven-forty.

"No luck?" inquired McLusky.

Quinlan told him no, no luck. "We've seen everything, have we?"

"Everything bar the criminal organizations' dossiers. And the morgue file," he added as an afterthought.

Hadleigh and Quinlan turned on him.

"The morgue file?" they chorused.

"Yeah, the stiffs. Guys who've died in captivity from accidents, illness, malnutrition, fights, guys repaying old debts. There are only a couple of hundred."

"But they're not here, not in the warehouse?" accused Quinlan.

"Well, no," admitted McLusky hesitantly. "You see, if someone dies or is killed, we pull his file and keep it separately over in the morgue building. Oh, Christ," he groaned, "you don't think Bachmann's one of those?"

"It's possible," said Quinlan grimly. "Let's hope so anyway," he added in a lighter tone, seeing McLusky's downcast expression.

The morgue was on the far side of the main compound. They drove there in the Mercedes, McLusky at the wheel, headlights probing the newly falling snow.

McLusky spoke to the noncom i/c the morgue, who directed them to a tiny anteroom containing just two filing cabinets, the dossiers in alphabetical order. The fifth name they came to was Helmut Bachmann, rank Hauptmann, branch of service Abwehr, condition deceased.

McLusky read aloud as he flicked through the dossier. Bachmann was picked up in Munich on May 10, seriously ill with pneumonia aggravated by malnutrition. He was taken to a military hospital where, on May 16, he died and was cremated. No formal interrogation had taken place because he was too ill to answer questions. The dossier details were taken from papers found on him.

"What happened to those papers, his personal effects?" demanded Quinlan.

"They're kept here, Major," answered the noncom.

"SOP," said McLusky. "Nonsensitive material such as photographs, letters, personal diaries, and stuff we retain, after examination, in case a relative turns up to claim them. It's part of some bright PR guy's hearts-and-minds campaign to show the Germans the US Army and government are not like the Nazis."

Hadleigh said Third Army did the same, mentally kicking himself for not having remembered it earlier.

Bachmann's effects were in an adjacent room, in a US Army-issue tin box the size of a bank deposit box, numbered and tagged alongside several hundred identical boxes. The contents consisted of letters, Bachmann's paybook and Abwehr pass, a gun-metal cigarette case and lighter, a few hundred now-useless Reichs-

marks, a leather wallet containing a picture of a smiling
Bachmann next to a young woman holding a small,
grinning infant. At the bottom was a torn fragment of
color photograph, attached by a pin to a piece of paper.
The fragment measured approximately two inches by
two inches and depicted an irregular section of island or
mainland with sea on three sides. Quinlan had Hannah's fragment in his pocket; he had no need to com-
pare the two pieces. They were obviously from the same
original, and again all distinguishing marks such as
towns or bays, lines of longitude or latitude, and clues
to where the island or island group or section of mainland actually was had been erased.

On the reverse side of the fragment, handwritten as
before, was the word KIKA.

The sheet of notepaper gave a name and address:
Klaus Butterweck, Tirpitzufer 72/76, Berlin. No prizes
were being offered for guessing that Herr Butterweck
had, or used to have, the third fragment.

Not that that knowledge was going to be much use to
them. Tirpitzufer 72/76 was as well-known an address
to Allied intelligence as the Gestapo HQ on Prinz Al-
brechtstrasse or the Foreign Office on Wilhelmstrasse,
being the one-time headquarters of Admiral Canaris's
Abwehr. It stood a couple of hundred yards on the British side of the border that separated the British sector
from the Soviet. Rather, it *had* stood there. Like the
Gestapo building, it had been flattened by bombs and
artillery before the end of the war.

In any case, Hadleigh pointed out, Butterweck
wouldn't be there now even if Tirpitzufer still existed.
As the original occupiers of Berlin, the Russians treated
the city as their own, paying scant respect to demarcation lines. Furthermore, long before the official bound-
aries were drawn up, the Red Army had captured or
killed key personnel unfortunate enough to be in the
capital when it fell. If Butterweck was still alive, which
must be considered doubtful, he was in Soviet hands.

"Berlin," moaned Quinlan. "Of all the damned luck!"

"What about Yuri Petrov?" suggested Max.

"I suppose he might help," said Hadleigh doubtfully. "We can try him, anyway."

They were brought out of their gloom by the sudden blowing of klaxons outside. The year 1946 had arrived.

McLusky had had the foresight to bring the canvas holdall with him and the morgue noncom provided paper cups. When they each had champagne, McLusky raised his drink in a toast.

"Happy New Year."

Quinlan looked at Hannah, whose eyes were elsewhere.

"Happy New Year," he said to no one in particular.

FOURTEEN

~~~~~~

NUREMBERG
January 1, 1946

WHEN THEY GOT back early in the afternoon to the
Allersbergerstrasse barracks, Hadleigh was greeted with
a sheaf of Most Immediate signals from Gene Masterson.

One: Where the hell had he been for three days? Permission to go to Munich did not include permission to
take the scenic route, nor take his own goddamn time
about returning to duty. The US Army wasn't paying
him to go schlepping around Germany like a tourist.
Major Hadleigh was either Army or civilian. If Army,
he should remember the adage about not trying to buck
the system. If he wanted to be a civilian, that could be
arranged.

Two: The whole outfit had gone to hell in his absence.
Five of his enlisted men—their names were appended—

had seen the New Year in in style by gate-crashing a bash at the Grand Hotel reserved for officers and their guests only. Four of them had started a fight with a bunch of journalists, laying into them with bottles, ashtrays, and stools. The fifth had insulted the ladies present by exposing himself and yelling, "I'm the easiest lay in town. Come and get it."

Three: Two other enlisted men were AWOL, neither tail nor whisker seen of them since 6 P.M. on December 31.

Four: A Sherman tank and its crew were missing, vanished off the face of the earth. While not strictly a G-2 problem, all units were being asked to assist and would Hadleigh look into it. The Third Army had had this trouble before, with guys joyriding in tanks down the Autobahns until the gas ran out of the machine and the liquor out of the crew. This time the guilty parties were in for it—thirty years in the stockade for openers.

Five: If discipline was a problem and Major Hadleigh could no longer handle his outfit, perhaps the said major might like another posting, say in the Aleutians.

There was a *six, seven,* and *eight* also. Quinlan left Hadleigh muttering something about what they all needed was a brand-new war. These problems never existed during hostilities.

Quinlan drove Hannah across to the Sündersbühl house in the Mercedes, making sure he was not followed. For the time being, they had decided she should be safe enough there.

Amid some opposition from Hannah, they had also advised her not to return to Herr Lorenz's for a week or so. When she asked whether "a week or so" meant a week or two or a month, Quinlan had to confess he couldn't say. According to Arndt, January 10 had some significance. She should stay away from the club until then. After that, they would think again.

Short of rescinding her work permit, they had no legal grounds to keep her from singing had she elected to ignore their advice. Fortunately the events in Weigel-shof the night before they left for Munich had con-vinced her to take seriously the threat against her life. Nevertheless, she told them, she had to support herself. With her meager savings she could just about survive for ten days. After that, she would be penniless.

Quinlan wanted to say he would lend her money. The words stuck in his throat. Throughout the journey from Munich she had remained silent, and she was still silent as they drove across Nuremberg. He didn't need oracu-lar powers to divine what was occupying her thoughts.

He chose not to bring the subject out into the open for the present. She would either get over his part in her father's death or she would not. Time would be the healer, not words. He could do nothing apart from try-ing to solve the whole mystery, remove the threat. To begin with that meant tracking down Klaus Butterweck, for which he was going to need Colonel Petrov's help.

A red-faced bear of a man in his forties, Lieutenant Colonel Yuri Alekseyevich Petrov could be found in the Grand Hotel most evenings. While his colleagues con-gregated around the bar, drinking themselves into insen-sibility, Petrov was generally in the Marble Room, on the dance floor. As second-in-command of the security team that protected the Soviet members of the Interna-tional Military Tribunal, he had discovered Western-style dancing on his arrival in Nuremberg and had become quite an expert, capable of wearing out with his enthusiasm several partners during the course of an evening. The democracies were self-evidently decadent, he had decided early on, but nowhere in the USSR could an officer of his rank hope to get so close to so many at-tractive women. Normally it would have taken an inter-national crisis or a personal directive from Stalin to get him off the floor. For Major Quinlan, however, he was willing to make an exception. Quinlan was Hadleigh's friend, and Hadleigh allowed him access to the Sündersbühl girls when his needs became more basic and urgent than cheek-to-cheek waltzing. The American major had made it clear during a telephone conversation earlier that he would appreciate a little cooperation.

Since Quinlan spoke no Russian and Petrov no English, they conversed in German, retiring to the bar and ordering drinks. They had no difficulty in finding an empty table. Most of the serious drinkers were still getting over their New Year's Eve excesses and would not surface for a hair of the dog until later.

Keeping it brief, Quinlan recounted everything he knew. The Soviet colonel might enjoy the high life in the Grand and give the impression of being a hedonist, but he was a professional to his fingertips, as tough as old boots. He would soon detect if he were being told anything less than the whole truth. Besides, Quinlan wanted to intrigue him, capture his interest. Petrov would be unlikely to assist unless he could see something in it for himself.

"So all we can guess," Quinlan concluded, "is that Klaus Butterweck's last base was Tirpitzufer. Whether he's dead or alive we have no way of telling. If he's dead, that's probably the end of it. If he's alive, he may have the third fragment and know where the fourth is. The way the picture, literally, is building up, it appears there are only four."

"But Tirpitzufer or what remains of it is in the British sector of Berlin," said Petrov.

"The British sector, like the Americans and French sectors, only came into being after your forces had overrun the city. You were there first. If Butterweck was still in Berlin when you occupied it, you'll have him, not us."

"It's possible, of course," mused Petrov, stroking his jowls, "but more than likely he's dead, either killed during the heroic Soviet advance or by the SS. When the SS absorbed the Abwehr, they settled a lot of old scores.

From what you've told me, anyone connected with these fragments was no friend of the SS. Butterweck is in his grave. Leave it.''

But Quinlan would not.

"You can't be certain of that," he insisted. "He could be alive in one of your camps."

Petrov raised his beetle eyebrows.

"Camps? You're confusing us with the Nazis. I know of no such camps."

Quinlan bit his tongue at the lapse.

"All right, in protective custody then. Or being debriefed by your intelligence people."

He did not add "being debriefed prior to being turned." The Soviets had taken tens of thousands of prisoners back to the mother country, mostly as slave labor. At some future date, to a fanfare of trumpets, they would release a good percentage as a "gesture of humanity." In the meantime, of course, hundreds would have gone over to the Soviet cause, either out of genuine conviction or because of threats. The Anglo-Americans would then discover they had a legion of agents in their midst and no real way of ascertaining who was an authentic repatriate and who a spy. The hot war was over, the cold one about to begin. Highly trained ex-Abwehr operatives skilled in the intelligence game would be invaluable. Quinlan had no doubt that, if Butterweck had survived the war, the Soviets would not have put him up against a wall and shot him. But that very argument, of course, was the one good reason why Petrov could refuse to help. Unless he, Quinlan, could up the stakes a bit.

"Major Hadleigh and I believe it's important for all of us to find out what these fragments mean," he went on while Petrov remained silent. "Why elements of the SS and the British Free Corps are willing to kill to get hold of them. We don't know how big the SS contingent is. There could be dozens, even hundreds of them. You must agree we have a duty to put them out of business permanently by seeing them hang."

Petrov frowned at the implied rebuke. If Major Quinlan was suggesting that the Soviet Union did not know where its duty lay, his expression conveyed, Major Quinlan was mistaken.

"Hundreds of them?" he queried aloud.

Quinlan shrugged. "We have no idea."

That worried Petrov. A unit of SS gangsters roaming around loose in Nuremberg spelled trouble. If Butterweck was alive and in the process of being turned, perhaps broken to make him more malleable, what difference would it make if Quinlan saw him? None. In fact, it might be advantageous. When the Abwehr man was returned to non-Soviet Germany one day to face a routine grilling by Anglo-American intelligence, what better than to have on file a report by a British major stating that he had interviewed Butterweck in 1946 and found the Abwehr officer showing signs of ill-treatment? (Petrov had no doubt what his condition would indicate.) Few would suspect Butterweck to be working for the Soviet Union if he had suffered while a POW. And if there was something to be gained from these mysterious fragments, so much the better.

Priorities, that was the name of the game. Petrov recalled an American joke he thought humorous. One GI says to another, "What's the first thing you're going to do when you get home?" The second answers, "First I'm going to the nearest cathouse, take off my boots, drink a crate of beer, and get laid. Then I'll take off my pack."

Priorities. He would make a few inquiries about Butterweck. If the man was alive, perhaps a meeting could be arranged—carefully monitored, of course.

"These fragments, the ones you already have. Would we be given access to them assuming a third can be traced?"

Quinlan had them in his shirt pocket, and there they were staying. He was not about to hand them over or even let the Russian see them until he had some sort of commitment.

"I see no reason why not."

Petrov grinned, showing teeth yellowed by tobacco.

"British double-talk. Does that mean yes or no?"

"It means yes—if you come up with Butterweck and in the next day or two. None of us has any idea what Arndt meant by January tenth, but the date was important enough for him to mention."

"A day or two is out of the question," spluttered Petrov. "If we have Butterweck, he could be anywhere in our zone of Occupied Germany or the Soviet Union. Which is not," he added sarcastically, "a tiny island like Great Britain. I'll need two weeks simply to trace his name."

"Two weeks is too long. Let's not beat around the bush, Colonel Petrov. Butterweck was Abwehr. Your people will have Abwehr personnel segregated from the run-of-the-mill German. You should be able to find out whether you have Butterweck merely by picking up a telephone."

"You give us too much credit."

"I think not. Anyway, I know you'll try. You could prevent a tragedy. If the SS, for example, plans to murder the Tribunal judges, including the Soviet representatives—*especially* the Soviet representatives—on the way to the Palace of Justice sometime before January tenth, I wouldn't like to be in your snow boots."

Petrov shuddered at the thought while considering such an eventuality unlikely.

"The judges are heavily guarded traveling to and from the Palace. Besides, the fragments have been in existence since before the end of the war. No one knew then what form the Tribunal would take, nor where it would be held. I am more than willing to concede that many Germans, and not only surviving members of the SS, would drink a toast if the judges were killed. Nevertheless, their deaths would have something to do with the fragments."

"But you'll do what you can as soon as you can?"

"Of course."

"Beginning now?"

Petrov glanced at his wristwatch, a handsome gold Omega which said a lot about his subscription to the doctrine of "from each according to his ability, to each according to his needs."

"Perhaps not quite now. In the Marble Room there is a Belgian countess working for a French news agency. She is a superb dancer of the old-fashioned waltz, as light as a feather. Unfortunately she has an American lover and leaves early each evening. However, I'm working on her."

Quinlan couldn't resist teasing the Russian.

"I don't know what Uncle Joe would have to say—a Soviet colonel prancing around a dance floor with European aristocracy."

"Marshal Stalin knows little of the finer things of life, and if you repeat that I shall deny it. To him, power is an end in itself."

"Colonel Petrov, you're a snob."

"But a Communist snob."

From the far end of the long bar Riordan, in his British captain's uniform, watched them leave before joining the line for the telephone.

In the forecourt Quinlan offered Petrov a lift. The Russian declined. He had his own transportation. Quinlan watched the taillights disappear in the January gloom before climbing in the Mercedes. On impulse he decided to make a final check of the Sündersbühl house before returning to the barracks.

All was quiet outside, and he resisted the urge to knock on the door. Instead, he drove once around the block to satisfy himself there were no suspicious-looking vehicles in the vicinity, then made for home.

In the distance, across the canal, he could see the searchlights illuminating the Palace of Justice and the jail. The Christmas recess was not quite over; the Tribunal not due to reconvene until the coming Thursday. Even so, security was as tight as ever. In passing, he wondered what the defendants were doing, whether any of them were thinking that 1946 could be the year in which their lives ended.

Some were, some were not.

From his cell Goering eyed with distaste the GI peering through the grille and attempted, by a system of mnemonics, to commit to memory everything he wished to say to his defense counsel, Dr. Otto Stahmer, when they next met. He would have made written notes had the Americans not had a peculiar attitude toward pencils, fearing that a sharpened point could be used as a suicide tool. As if the only holder of a Reichsmarschall's baton in the Third Reich would contemplate such an unworthy exit from the world!

In the adjacent cell Hess was muttering quietly to himself. The GI at the grille was never sure whether he was genuinely crazy or faking. He doubted if Hess himself knew most of the time.

Farther along the brightly lit corridor, no one had any doubt, to judge by the number of medical men in attendance, that Kaltenbrunner was unwell again. Whether he was scared stiff, as many suggested, or really suffering from spinal meningitis was open to question. The doctors resolved to take no chances and arranged to transfer the Obergruppenführer as soon as possible, not to the 116th general hospital on this occasion, where facilities were inadequate, but to a civilian clinic. The trial could and would proceed in his absence.

Julius Streicher was convinced, and repeatedly said so in a loud voice, that all the guards—everyone in the prison, for that matter—were Jewish. As far as the Beast of Nuremberg was concerned, most people on the planet were Jews or working for Jews.

Of the remaining defendants only one was looking forward eagerly to the resumption of the trial: ex-Governor General of Poland Hans Frank, who was anxious to continue purging himself in public, having told anyone who cared to listen that he regarded the Tribunal as a God-bestowed world court, destined to examine and punish and bring to an end the terrible age of suffering under Adolf Hitler. The same Hans Frank had once gone on record as saying, "We must not be squeamish when we hear a figure of seventeen thousand Poles executed."

Riordan arrived back at Grossreuth just after 9 P.M. with the news that Quinlan and the others had returned from Munich. "I gather they've found Bachmann's fragment," he said.

Sternberg was unimpressed. "They will not find and decipher the others in time."

"They might. We've heard nothing that tells us we can go for the third or fourth. It will have to be the seventh. That gives them almost a week."

"You're certain they have Bachmann's piece of photograph?"

"Not certain. The Meissner woman cannot ask direct questions for obvious reasons. She picks up what she can."

"It would be useful to know," mused Sternberg.

"There is a way, perhaps," said Riordan, and told Sternberg where Hannah Wolz was staying.

FIFTEEN

~~~~~~

BERLIN
January 3–6, 1946

QUINLAN AND PETROV flew to Berlin in a Douglas
C-47 troop transport carrying Soviet markings, one of
the hundreds sent to Marshal Stalin by the Americans
during the war under the Lend-Lease Act, whose termi-
nation in August 1945 supposedly meant the return of
unpaid-for hardware to the United States. So far Uncle
Sam had not figured out how to persuade Uncle Joe to
comply.

They were not the only passengers. The aircraft was
packed with Soviet brass and noncoms sitting side by
side against the fuselage and looking decidedly uncomfortable in each other's company. There were also
one or two civilians who seemed to be under arrest;
at least they were isolated at the forward end of the
airplane, their every movement watched by armed

guards. When asked by Quinlan who they were, Petrov shrugged evasively and muttered something about enemies of the state.

The windows were blacked out. Whether this was customary or because much of the flight was at low level over Soviet-occupied Germany, Quinlan never discovered. In any event, he saw nothing of the ground until they landed at Tempelhof airfield, strictly speaking in the British sector but used by the Soviets.

Petrov had moved with remarkable speed in tracing Butterweck. After spending most of January 2 in his quarters making a halfhearted stab at completing his report, Quinlan had come around to thinking that his conversation with the Russian in the Grand was likely to be the last he heard on the subject. Even if Petrov managed to work up some enthusiasm for the task, it could take days to track down the former Abwehr operative, assuming he was still alive. Quinlan was therefore startled to receive a telephone call at 10 A.M. on the third, shortly after hearing on the radio that William Joyce had been executed that morning in Wandsworth Prison. Petrov stated that Butterweck was indeed alive and "somewhere in the Soviet Union." Arrangements were being made to fly him to Berlin as soon as possible, where Quinlan would be allowed to interrogate him. The personal effects on him when he was captured would also be made available, though at this moment it was not possible to say whether they included a fragment of a photograph.

Petrov made it clear he could not give a precise hour, or even day, when Butterweck would arrive, but a special flight was leaving Nuremberg for Berlin that afternoon. They could both be aboard it if Quinlan wished. Quinlan had jumped at the opportunity.

They were met at Tempelhof by a uniformed Starshiy Leytenant, senior lieutenant, who ushered them to a

waiting Opel staff car which, in spite of a recent paint
job, still bore signs of its previous German owners.
Quinlan began to suspect that Petrov was more influential than he cared to admit, for two-star generals were
left waiting for transport while the Opel sped off toward
the distant, ruined city.

The lieutenant drove, with Petrov next to him in the
passenger seat. Quinlan sat in splendid isolation in the
back. After a brief conversation with his subordinate,
Petrov turned and announced a slight delay in getting
Butterweck to Berlin.

"How much of a delay?"

"Twenty-four hours, perhaps a couple of days. I
apologize but these things happen."

Speaking no Russian, Quinlan had not followed the
dialogue between Petrov and the lieutenant. Had he
been able to do so he would have learned that Butterweck was not yet in a fit state to be seen by outsiders.
In the special camp for former Abwehr officers near
Kharkov, he was proving a troublesome convert to
Soviet-style communism, unlike, in a different camp,
ex-members of the SD and the Gestapo, who switched
sides with astonishing alacrity (and were accepted with
open arms by the Soviets) once they were captured.

The procedure to break Butterweck's will to resist was
standard: periods of solitary confinement and interrupted sleep to disorient him, and short rations. In the
opinion of Kharkov's chief psychologist, the prisoner
should not be seen by outsiders at the present time.
Changing the routine could set back the treatment by
several months.

The psychologist was overruled. As far as Petrov's
superiors were concerned, Quinlan's request could not
have come at a more opportune moment. With a full
belly and fresh linen Butterweck would realize what he
had to gain by cooperating, how reasonable his would-
be paymasters could be. Not for a few more years would

the technique become known as brainwashing. The camp commandant was allowed forty-eight hours to prepare Butterweck for a meeting with a British officer. He was to be given fresh clothes, shaving equipment, and three high-protein meals a day.

Tempelhof was several miles south of the city center and, during the drive in, Quinlan was staggered at the destruction the air raids and the Soviet ground assault had inflicted. Munich and Nuremberg looked like landscaped gardens by comparison.

Much of the southern suburbs was wasteland, though the devastation there was minor compared to the area around the Brandenburg Gate. Here there was scarcely a habitable building in sight, and gangs of German men, women, and adolescents were still clearing, eight months after the war, mountains of rubble with their bare hands.

Petrov seemed totally unmoved and chatted away cheerfully, translating the signs in Cyrillic script for Quinlan's benefit. On the left was what remained of the former Gestapo headquarters on Prinz Albechtstrasse. Farther up Wilhelmstrasse on the right was the Propaganda Ministry, opposite what remained of the Reich Chancellery and Hitler's infamous bunker. Separated from the chancellery by a square was the one-time Nazi Foreign Office, whose chief incumbent, Von Ribbentrop, was now on trial for his life in Nuremberg. On the corner of Pariserplatz stood the battered remains of the Adlon Hotel. Over there, just in the British sector, was the Reichstag. Farther west was the once-beautiful Tiergarten, most of the animals in its world-renowned zoo now dead.

The Opel headed northeast and entered the suburb of Wiessensee, where it stopped before a relatively unscarred building that had evidently once housed a school. Now, however, instead of children on the grounds there were tanks, pickup trucks, and half-tracks. At the gates were two uniformed sentries who, seeing Petrov's rank insignia, saluted smartly and waved the Opel through.

Bringing the car to a halt, the lieutenant-driver hopped out and opened the door for Petrov, who beckoned Quinlan to follow.

"What is this place?" asked Quinlan.

"Part barracks, part interrogation center, part administration block for Marshal Zhukov's First Belorussian Army Group. It used to be a residential school and we were fortunate to find the dormitories more or less intact. We have also converted several other buildings into private sleeping quarters for high-ranking officers and their guests, which includes you and me. The enlisted men eat in the dining hall and two of what I believe were called senior common rooms are now mess areas for officers. There are also a bar and a brothel."

Quinlan was surprised at the bland manner in which this admission was delivered. He had somehow never connected the great worker state with overtly indulging in anything so base as copulation.

"A brothel?"

"Of course. Two of them, to be exact. One for the enlisted men, another for the officers." He grinned cynically. "We don't want the diseases picked up by the rabble to be passed on to their superiors now, do we? Although I must confess there hasn't been a venereal infection on the premises in my time. They're all good, clean German girls willing to give their bodies to the occupiers in exchange for food and shelter."

"They must be kept busy," said Quinlan shortly.

He had meant the comments to be ironic, but Petrov took him literally.

"Not at all. Someone should write a paper on it one day. You would be surprised how little interest the girls generate, now they are so readily accessible. The Russian soldier is, perhaps, accustomed to the spice of a little rape. So far we've been unable to come up with a solution that satisfies his fantasies without damaging the goods. Well, not officially. Unofficially there are one or two girls who seem to enjoy being manhandled. However, that too has its drawbacks. After a beating it takes several weeks before the girl is, shall we say, open for business once more.''

"Are you sure you should be telling me all this?" asked Quinlan, amazed at how frank the Soviet colonel was being.

"Why not? It's only what the democracies think of us anyway. There is little I can tell you that actually happens which is not exaggerated one hundredfold in the lurid imaginations of the Americans and Englishmen.''

Quinlan preceded Petrov through a door and found himself in a long corridor that immediately brought back memories of his own childhood. Cyrillic script denoting military function on classroom and study doors or not, there was no disguising that this had been a school.

"What happens when the students come back?" he asked.

"Why should they do that?" Petrov was genuinely puzzled.

"To complete their education."

The Russian laughed openly.

"My dear comrade, the kind of education the average German child will need in the foreseeable future will not be found in a classroom. It's all around them, among the debris. There they will learn the only lessons worth knowing, about what it's like to be conquered. The sins of the fathers will be visited upon the children unto the third and fourth generation.''

Quinlan was not at all surprised that Petrov could quote from the Second Commandment.

"For now, maybe," he said, "but sooner or later that will all change."

"You think so? If I had my way, it would never change. I would leave Berlin exactly as it is today, its citizens scrabbling among the ruins with their bare hands, a permanent reminder to future generations that there is a price to be paid for everything."

Quinlan shivered involuntarily. The man who spoke these words was a totally different Petrov from the one he had known in Nuremberg. Gone was the lover of good living, the man who spent hours on the dance floor wooing Belgian countesses. In his place stood a dedicated servant of Moscow.

Petrov recognized the silence for what it was.

"You disapprove? Where is good old Yuri Petrov of Nuremberg, you ask yourself. Well, he's still there, Major Quinlan, alongside the Yuri Petrov who took part in the retreat to Moscow, who returned when our armies advanced to find the village where he had grown up no longer existed, who identified the bodies of his mother and his sisters among a mountain of rotten corpses, who heard from the few survivors how an SS Einsatzgruppen had swept through the village with their flamethrowers, burning the men and houses, raping and mutilating the females, even the very old and the very young. Can you imagine the terror a twelve-year-old girl must feel when a fully grown man approaches her with only rape on his mind? To be killed outright is better. You in the West sometimes forget just how many lives we lost in the Great Patriotic War. The figure was twenty million dead. Can you conceive of that? *Twenty million*. In battle, by starvation, through summary execution, in extermination camps. Half the population of Great Britain. Fifteen percent of the United States. Almost twice as many men, women, and children as there are in the whole of Norway, Sweden, and Denmark combined. You are here in Berlin, comrade, because of those twenty million. While a single SS butcher survives, the dead will remain unavenged. If former

Abwehr agent Butterweck, however unwittingly, has information that will lead to the apprehension and execution of *just one* SS private, none of us will have wasted our time.''

As if embarrassed by his outburst, Petrov walked Quinlan to his quarters in silence. On leaving he said he would return later in the evening to take Quinlan to the mess hall. In the meantime, he would appreciate it if Quinlan did not wander around the complex.

Quinlan had no intention of doing any such thing. Although his quarters were small and contained nothing more than a large bed, a washbasin, and a handmade wardrobe, he was tired and fell asleep in his uniform.

He was awakened by Petrov at seven forty-five. While he shaved, the Russian chirped away like a blackbird, his earlier saturnine mood forgotten.

Dinner was a sumptuous affair served by liveried flunkies at long linen-covered tables, each seating twenty. Petrov sat at the head of one of these and, despite Quinlan's obvious unease at being the only non-Russian in the mess, insisted the British major occupy the honored position on his right.

They dined on beluga caviar served with iced Russian brandy (a combination Quinlan found bizarre but pleasing), a wonderful fish soup, and fresh trout followed by a choice of venison or wild suckling pig. A cornucopia of exotic fruits topped off the meal, Petrov confiding that the fruits were flown in twice weekly from the Middle East. There was little wine but enough vodka with each course to float a fleet. Too much for Quinlan who, pleading fatigue, begged to be excused and retired early.

The following morning there was still no word of Butterweck, but Petrov expressed the hope they would hear something before the day was out.

To pass the time, Quinlan was given an escorted tour of the barracks and, more from boredom than any other reason, joined Petrov in a marathon drinking session, where his stock rose several points in the Russian's estimation for his ability to keep pace, vodka for vodka. Later Petrov suggested they visit the whores. Quinlan declined.

Still, it seemed that Petrov was not going to let him get away without sampling some of the delights offered, for in the small hours of January 5, while Quinlan was still asleep, a girl no older than seventeen joined him in bed. In spite of the warning lights flashing in his head that his antics could well end up on film, he thought to hell with it and took full advantage of the lush, young body even though for much of the time, in the semi-darkness, the image in his mind's eye was that of Hannah Wolz.

The girl was gone when Petrov awoke him at 8 A.M. Grinning lasciviously and expressing the hope that Quinlan had enjoyed his entertainment, the Russian announced that Butterweck was on his way and would arrive before noon.

The Abwehr officer was brought into the room set aside for his interrogation under armed guard. The senior lieutenant in command handed Petrov a dossier, saluted, and left with his men.

Petrov read aloud from the dossier as though Butterweck were not within earshot.

"Klaus Emil Butterweck, born Berlin April 20—I see he shares his late Führer's birthday—1915. Which makes him what, thirty. Looks older. Profession before enlistment lawyer. Abwehr rank Oberleutnant. Served with the Brandenberg Division before being seconded to Tirpitzufer—where he almost certainly had regular contact with Canaris himself. There's much more," he said to Quinlan, "but I don't know how relevant his past is. Do you want to see the dossier?"

"Is it in Russian?"

"Yes."

"Then I don't."

Butterweck certainly did look older than thirty, thought Quinlan. Hardly surprising after eight months in Soviet hands. There would be no caviar and fresh trout where he had come from.

He was a smallish man, five feet seven or eight, and considerably underweight. His fair hair was thinning and his eyes, though intelligent, looked dull and defeated. His appearance reminded Quinlan of the sort of photograph of a dead man one sometimes sees in newspapers, one touched up by the police artist in an effort to get the public to identify him. He was wearing a civilian suit a size too big.

Quinlan was wondering how to begin when Petrov anticipated him by laying the ground rules.

"This interrogation," he said formally, in a manner that suggested the entire interview was being recorded by hidden microphones, "must relate solely to relevant matters and is not to touch upon questions regarding Butterweck's health or his treatment since he became a legitimate prisoner of war. You are not to ask where he is currently being held or the nature of his life there. Neither will the prisoner—who has been instructed to cooperate fully otherwise—offer any information that is not directly requested unless it is germane to the matter under consideration. Any contravention of these conditions will oblige me to bring the interview to an immediate end. There will be no others. The floor is yours, Major."

Quinlan summarized some of the events that had brought him to Berlin, leaving out the fate of both Arndt and his daughter. Neither did he mention Hannah. Butterweck was unlikely to know of her existence. He simply gave the Abwehr Oberleutnant three names: Langenhain, Arndt, and Helmut Bachmann, adding that his, Butterweck's, name had come to light because of a scribbled note attached to the fragment of photograph found among Bachmann's belongings.

"Bachmann is dead?" Butterweck's voice was curiously soft, as though he had spent hours talking to no one but himself, which indeed was the case.

"Yes," answered Quinlan. "In Munich directly after the war."

"A pity," muttered Butterweck. "He was a good man."

"Irrelevant," snapped Petrov. "Kindly do not make unsolicited comments."

"Did you know Arndt?" asked Quinlan.

"No, not personally. I had seen him around Tirpitzufer and elsewhere, of course, but I wouldn't say I knew him. Oberstleutnant Langenhain I knew well, though not in connection with this business."

"What business?" demanded Quinlan.

"The photograph fragments. I take it that's why I have been brought here. You wouldn't have mentioned Bachmann's otherwise."

"You will have to speak up," barked Petrov, removing all doubt that the session was being recorded. "I can hardly hear you."

"The photograph fragments," repeated Butterweck. "Those Admiral Canaris distributed."

Quinlan felt his pulse race with excitement.

"Just begin at the beginning and tell me what you know."

"There's very little to tell. I didn't know Helmut Bachmann was involved, nor Arndt nor Oberstleutnant Langenhain. But that's the way the admiral would have wanted it."

"To the point, please," insisted Quinlan.

Butterweck frowned as he tried to remember.

"I can't recall the exact date, but it would have been during the spring of 1944. Admiral Canaris called me into his office and told me that the Abwehr was breaking up, that the SS were plotting to take it over and probably imprison, perhaps execute, him. He gave me the fragment of photograph and told me to take good care of it. If anything happened to him, if he were murdered by the SS, someone would approach me and ask for it. That someone would have further instructions, information that might perhaps be of value to me personally.''

"How would you know this person was genuine?" asked Quinlan.

"Because he would have other fragments. I was to hand over mine and direct him to the holder of the fourth fragment.''

Quinlan took a deep breath.

"You have that information, the holder of the fourth fragment?"

But Petrov interrupted before Butterweck could answer.

"Why did Canaris choose you?"

"Who can tell? I was close to the admiral; he knew me to be loyal when loyalty was at a premium.''

"Presumably so too were Hauptmann Arndt and Langenhain?'' queried Petrov. "And Bachmann.''

"Arndt I can't answer for, but I believe so. Certainly Bachmann was loyal to the admiral personally and Oberstleutnant Langenhain was a close friend.''

Quinlan tried his original question again.

"And the fourth man, the one who has the fourth fragment—he can be put in the same category?''

"Your tenses are wrong, Herr Major, but yes, Oberleutnant Straub was in that category.''

"What do you mean, my tenses are wrong?" asked Quinlan, knowing the answer before it was given.

"Straub was killed in Berlin during the last days.''

"And his fragment?''

"Destroyed with him, I imagine.''

No matter, thought Quinlan. *Three were better than two and, like a nearly finished jigsaw, they should be able to build up the whole picture from the three quarters.*

"But you still have your own fragment?" he asked hopefully.

"I'm afraid not." A spark of defiance entered the Abwehr officer's voice. "We lost many things when Berlin was overrun—homes, friends, personal effects. My fragment was in a wallet that was taken from me when I was first captured. It was doubtless consigned to some Russian fire as being of no value."

"That's enough," rapped Petrov.

"As you say." Butterweck meekly lowered his head.

Trying hard to conceal his disappointment, Quinlan continued his questioning.

"The word KIKA is handwritten across the back of the fragments in my possession," he said. "Does it mean anything to you?"

"Certainly. Admiral Canaris wrote it across the back of my fragment too. Also Straub's. To guarantee authenticity. Few outside the Abwehr would know that KIKA was the *nom de guerre* adopted by the admiral when acting as an agent in Spain during World War One and between the wars. It was what he termed his 'yesterday name.' Admiral Canaris was a man who loved an ironic joke. I suppose it pleased him to use his yesterday name for some future project."

"But you don't know what that project was?" asked Petrov.

"No. I was simply a cog in the wheel."

"Nevertheless, you did see Straub's fragment, didn't you?" probed Quinlan, thinking back to Butterweck's words a moment or two before. "You said Canaris had written across the back of it, as he had across yours. Which means you saw it or discussed it."

"Both," said Butterweck. "Although my orders from the admiral were to speak to no one about the matter until I was contacted, I knew, because he told me, that Straub held the next fragment. The final one."

"Why final?"

"It's an assumption. Straub did not have a fifth name. I therefore assumed he was the last link in the chain."

"That's the second time you've implied there were only four fragments. How could you possibly know that?" asked Quinlan.

"By comparing my section and Straub's it was obvious the original photograph had been divided into quarters."

"So you compared them. In spite of your orders from Canaris you discussed the matter with Straub before you yourself were approached."

"There seemed no reason not to. The war was almost over." Butterweck shot a glance at Petrov. "The Soviets were at the gates of Berlin. We had nothing to gain by waiting any longer. For all I knew the fragments Straub and I had might save our lives."

"And you examined each other's?"

"Of course."

"Then you could draw a rough outline of both of them?"

"I can draw you a *precise* outline of both of them, Herr Major. Straub and I looked at them so often, trying to divine what they meant, that I could draw them in twenty years' time."

"For God's sake," cried Quinlan, half rising from his seat, "why didn't you say so in the first place!"

"I was instructed at the start of this interview not to offer unsolicited comments," murmured Butterweck slyly.

Petrov went to the door and called along the corridor. "Bring pen and paper."

Either Butterweck's memory was not quite so good as he claimed or it had been affected by his periods of isolation. He made over twenty attempts before he pronounced himself satisfied, that, to the best of his recollection, what Quinlan and Petrov saw before them were facsimiles of the fragments he and Straub had once possessed. They were drawn larger than the pair Quinlan had in his pocket, and they were not in color. But Quinlan could see that when scaled down they would dovetail with his own.

"Is there anything else you have omitted to tell us because the question has not been posed?" asked Petrov. "You may answer freely on this occasion."

"Nothing except . . ."

"Carry on."

"It's hardly material."

"We'll be the judges of that."

"Well, apart from telling me I would not be contacted unless he was dead, the admiral also said that I was not to worry if no one *ever* contacted me. After January tenth, 1946, he said, it would no longer matter. I regret I do not know whether today's date is before or after January tenth or even whether it is January at all."

"Enough," said Petrov, and called for the guard to take Butterweck away. "He is to remain in the barracks until I order otherwise," he added.

Quinlan could see the pattern now. Langenhain, the linkman and Canaris's trusted friend, had been briefed to contact Arndt if and when the admiral was executed or otherwise died. Arndt would lead to Bachmann who would lead to Butterweck, and so on. But Langenhain had panicked and decided to jump the gun while Canaris was still alive. Either that or he assumed that once in Flossenbürg Canaris was as good as dead anyway.

The outstanding question was, what did it all mean?

"I think the moment has come to live up to your end of the bargain," said Petrov, when they were alone.

Quinlan had forgotten the agreement made in the Grand.

"Bargain?"

"You have the drawings of Butterweck's and Straub's fragments. We should now see if they all fit together."

Half an hour later Quinlan had scaled down Butterweck's drawings. He took the two pieces of photograph from his pocket and assembled the whole. The result was imperfect. Either Butterweck's originals were inexact or his own cartographic skills inadequate. Nevertheless, what emerged was a rough outline of an island; to be precise, one large island surrounded by a number of smaller ones. What did not emerge were lines of longitude or latitude or any other clue to the whereabouts of the group. Neither, even if they could have pinpointed the spot, did they know what it meant. What had Canaris intended to convey? And what was the significance of January 10?

"I'm completely baffled," said Quinlan eventually. "I don't know what it means."

"Perhaps a large-scale world atlas would help," suggested Petrov.

Quinlan had his doubts. "We could start there, I suppose, but there must be tens of thousands of islands throughout the world, some as big as Cuba, some as small as cays. We'd be looking for a needle in a haystack. Besides, the original photograph seems to have been blown up, magnified, twenty or thirty times. A world atlas showing features on this scale would occupy a building."

"We might perhaps narrow it down," proposed Petrov. "Remember what Butterweck said about Canaris's yesterday name, how he used it in Spain and how he was fond of an ironic joke. I don't speak English as you know, but I have a little knowledge of Spanish from Civil War days. *Islas Canarias*—"

"The Canary Islands," Quinlan interrupted him. "It's a thought. He could have been making a pun on his own name."

Petrov's men could not find a large-scale world

map, but one of them unearthed a stack of students' atlases from a cupboard. None of the Canary Islands looked remotely like the montage in front of them.

They flicked from page to page in the hope of stumbling, by chance, on something that struck a chord, but as Quinlan had predicted, the needle remained firmly in the haystack.

After a while they concluded they were tackling the problem back to front. They required the help of a specialist military cartographer, which Quinlan suggested Ben Hadleigh could provide.

"But you will keep me informed of progress," said Petrov. "I would be within my rights to confiscate Butterweck's drawings since they were made by a Soviet prisoner of war on Soviet-occupied territory. However, that would leave each of us with only half a possible answer and a lot of memorizing to do."

Quinlan agreed that anything Ben Hadleigh's people came up with would be passed on to Petrov.

"Though even if we identify the island," he added wearily, "we're still only halfway there. Is it a jumping-off point for SS men on the run? Is something or someone hidden there? Why is the SS involved with the British Free Corps? The permutations are endless. The only people who could give us the answer are Canaris, who's dead, and Langenhain, who's missing, either dead or in a camp somewhere."

"He's not in our hands," said Petrov. "I checked when inquiring whether or not we held Butterweck."

"What will happen to Butterweck now?" asked Quinlan.

"Have you finished with him?"

"I can't see he can help us further."

"Then he'll be taken back."

"Back where?"

"You know better than to ask that."

"But we, the West, will see him again one day, won't

we?'' said Quinlan mischievously.

"That I couldn't say." Petrov's expression scolded Quinlan for breaking the rules.

Because they could not obtain space on any aircraft flying out of Berlin that day, it was late afternoon on the sixth before Quinlan and Petrov arrived back in Nuremberg. The Russian had a car waiting for them and dropped Quinlan off at the Allersbergerstrasse barracks before continuing to his own destination.

Thirty seconds after walking into Hadleigh's office, Quinlan had forgotten about Canaris, Butterweck, fragments of photograph, and much else. A grim-faced Hadleigh informed him that earlier in the day Hannah Wolz had been abducted from the Sündersbühl house by three German-speaking men.

SIXTEEN

~~~~~~

NUREMBERG
January 6, 1946

WITH A SUPREME EFFORT Quinlan managed to erase
from his mind the image of Hannah in the hands of
those who had killed Ilse Arndt. "Tell me about it."

There wasn't a lot to tell, Hadleigh informed him. He
and Max were catching up on some paperwork in the office when a wireless message came through. A mobile
patrol in the Sündersbühl district claimed they had a
hysterical young German woman in the Jeep. She'd
flagged them down in a state of great distress. About all
they could get out of her was that she had to talk to
Major Hadleigh. At once.

"It was Ingrid," said Hadleigh. "I couldn't make
much sense out of what she was saying over the radio,

but when she mentioned Hannah I knew we were in big trouble.''

Telling the patrol commander to take his directions from the woman and meet them at the Sündersbühl house, he and Max had driven over there as fast as they could.

''They were outside,'' continued Hadleigh. ''Ingrid wouldn't go in.''

He and Max soon discovered why.

The other regular occupant of the house, Helga, was lying across the bed, her throat cut. Of Hannah Wolz there was no sign.

''We were a while piecing it all together,'' went on Hadleigh, ''because Ingrid was in no state to answer questions until the medical officer here gave her a shot to calm her down. When she could talk, she told us that around three-thirty or four—she's a bit vague on time— there was a knock on the door. Though I'd given them all strict instructions to open up to no one without confirmation of identity, Ingrid looked out of the window and saw a US Jeep—yes, a fucking Jeep—parked outside and three guys in what seemed to be US or British uniforms. She unlocked the door and in they came.''

Hadleigh shook his head in despair.

''Now it starts to get confusing. From what we can gather, they identified Hannah without difficulty and shut off Helga's screams by killing her. Somewhere around this time Ingrid made a run for it. She's not sure how she got out, but she did and kept on running. The rest we saw for ourselves. Helga dead, Hannah vanished. In spite of the uniforms and the Jeep, they all spoke German. We might not have found out about it for several days if Ingrid hadn't got away.''

''You mean neither you nor Max nor anyone else has been making regular checks while I was in Berlin?'' said Quinlan incredulously.

''I've been over there twice, Max not at all.'' Hadleigh shrugged in futile apology. "What the hell difference would it have made if we'd been out there ten hours out of twelve? If they knew where Hannah was, they'd only have to wait until we left to make their play."

"But twice in four days! Christ!"

Hadleigh swallowed his annoyance. Anyone could be wise after the event. "In the first place," he explained patiently, "we've been busy, and in the second place we thought it safer. They got to Ilse Arndt and Angela Salvatini easily enough, found out where Hannah worked and where she lived. Frequent visits to the same house would have aroused their suspicions if they've got the barracks under observation, and six times a day wouldn't have been enough if they knew where she was from another source."

"Meaning what?"

"Meaning if they've got inside information."

"You're kidding me!"

Hadleigh looked at Max uneasily.

"I hope so."

Quinlan fought down a sudden surge of panic. Hannah had been missing for an hour, perhaps an hour and a half. She might already be dead or undergoing the most terrible suffering at the hands of her captors.

"Where's Ingrid now?" he asked.

"Here. Under sedation in a private room in the women's infirmary. She's got a couple of bruises, but mostly she's just terrified out of her wits. The MO's prognosis is that she'll be okay, although he wants to keep her sedated for twenty-four hours. We've spoken to her, Otis. She couldn't tell you any more than she's already told us."

Quinlan's fingers beat a nervous tattoo on the arms of his chair.

"What action have you taken so far?"

"Not a lot," confessed Hadleigh, explaining that he

and Max had only got back to the barracks with Ingrid twenty minutes ago. "I've put out a general alert for all mobile patrols to stop and hold any Jeep carrying three men in Allied uniforms and a girl. I don't hold out much hope of success. It's Sunday. It's dark outside. They won't still be driving around. Wherever they were heading, they'll have got there."

Hadleigh decided this wasn't the moment to add that he was almost as much concerned about the uniforms and the Jeep as he was about Hannah. However, it made him uneasy, knowing that members of the SS were riding around Nuremberg as though they owned it.

Quinlan hammered Hadleigh's desk top in frustrated rage.

"How," he asked of no one in particular, "how the hell did they know where she was? I'll swear to Christ no one followed me when I first took her to Sündersbühl. I was as careful as hell."

"Me too," said Hadleigh. "I made sure nothing was behind me on both occasions."

There was a long silence.

"So," said Quinlan finally, "they've got someone on the inside."

"Max and I was talking it over before you arrived. Apart from the three of us, no one knew you were taking her to Sündersbühl. We discussed it here in the office—you, me, Max, and Hannah. No one came in, no one went out."

"What about Ingrid and Helga?"

"For Christ's sake," groaned Hadleigh, "that's clutching at straw! You're trying to say that a couple of little hookers are somehow wired into the SS? It won't wash."

Quinlan agreed reluctantly, knowing that every moment they spent talking could be another moment of agony for Hannah.

Unaware that he was clenching his fists until the

knuckles whitened, he cast his mind back to the day they returned from Munich. Hadleigh was right; the four of them had debated Hannah's temporary accommodations behind closed doors. To the best of his recollection they had never even mentioned the exact address, merely saying that she should be safe enough for the time being with Ingrid and Helga.

On the way out he and Hannah had passed Gretl Meissner in the corridor. Remembering that he was about to meet Yuri Petrov and that a trip to Berlin could result, he had sent Hannah on ahead while he briefed Gretl to look after things in the Palace of Justice if he wasn't back before the IMT reconvened on the third. Gretl had asked if he wanted the whole proceedings taken down verbatim or whether, since none of the defendants would as yet have taken the stand, thumbnail sketches of their reactions to the prosecution witnesses would suffice. He had replied, "Let me think about it. I'll jot down a few notes *when I get back from Sündersbühl.*"

Christ.

"Gretl Meissner knew I was taking Hannah to Sündersbühl," he said, slowly and painfully relating the circumstances of the encounter. If anything happened to Hannah because of his own stupidity, he would never forgive himself. "Does she know where the house is?"

Hadleigh wasn't sure, but thought so.

"I never made it a big secret where Ingrid and Helga lived. She's probably heard me mention the address one time or another. But that's crazy," he added plaintively. "She couldn't possibly be in touch with the SS. Jesus, she's got a confirmed record of anti-Nazism. You think I didn't check her out before hiring her? Why would she do it?"

"Maybe she didn't," said Quinlan. "There's only one way to find out for sure. Is she around?"

"It's Sunday. She doesn't work Sundays."

"I'll go get her," offered Max.

"We'll all go," said Quinlan.

Hadleigh did not think that was a good idea. Quinlan would undoubtedly agree if he were thinking straight that interrogating suspects in their own environment, where they felt secure, was poor tactics.

"It's a twenty-minute trip there and back. If she's got anything to hide, this is the place to sort it out. You'd better bring her son in also," he added as Max reached the door. "If we've gotten around to suspecting Gretl, we may as well include Willi."

While Max was away, Hadleigh asked if the Berlin jaunt had proven fruitful. Although Quinlan had never felt less like talking in his life, he knew Hadleigh was only trying to help take his mind off Hannah. In any case, the fragments in his shirt pocket were somehow tied into her disappearance.

He spread them across the desk and explained what had transpired during his cross-examination of Butterweck.

"There's a cartographic unit somewhere in Nuremberg," Hadleigh said eventually, "working with US Army and German architects to see if this city can be rebuilt to look the way it did. Give me a minute."

He spent six on the telephone while Quinlan paced the office. Finally Hadleigh hung up.

"They're based over in Fürth. I've told them what we want and they've agreed to go through their files as a matter of urgency."

"The islands may not be in Germany, may not even be in Europe," Quinlan cautioned.

"That doesn't matter. These guys travel with everything on microfilm, the entire box of tricks. Their aerial photographs of Nuremberg and Fürth are the size of a postage stamp. They can put the world into a couple of suitcases. If this island group exists and is not part of Canaris's imagination, they'll find it. They've even got

gizmos called computers—electronic gadgets. I don't
understand how they work except that you punch a
bunch of information in one end and out comes the
answer at the other."

Hadleigh put the two photo fragments, Butterweck's
original drawings, and Quinlan's scaled-down versions
into a manila envelope and scribbled a name and address across the flap. He summoned an orderly and told
him to take the package over to the dispatch rider's
pool. It was urgent. If the DR stopped for a beer on the
way, he'd find himself on KP for a month.

As the orderly went out, Max and Gretl came in. One
glance at her face was enough to tell them how the SS
had known where to find Hannah.

Slowly and tearfully she informed them that, one day
in the middle of November, her fifteen-year-old son,
Willi, had not appeared for his evening meal. She was
approached later that night by a German-speaking for-
eigner who disclosed that Willi was being held hostage as a guarantee of her future cooperation. This man
knew she worked in the Allersbergerstrasse barracks,
even for whom she worked. He had obviously studied
her movements and her companions carefully.

At first all she was asked to do was listen for the name
Arndt. When Arndt died she was told to report anything
she overheard concerning a Fräulein Hannah Wolz.
While she behaved, Willi would live. If she disobeyed
orders, he would be killed.

"He is my only son, Herr Major," she said to Hadleigh between sobs. "I couldn't let anything happen to
him."

Sitting there weeping, she presented such a pathetic
picture that Quinlan had to remind himself that her
treachery might well have killed Hannah. Keeping his
voice hard, he asked her how she passed on her information.

"If I had anything to tell them, I called the Grand Hotel and left a message for Captain Eric Spencer. Although I don't believe it to be his real name, it's the one used by the man I usually meet, an Englishman. He telephones the Grand each evening at six-thirty and asks if there are any messages for Captain Spencer. If there are, he knows to meet me there one hour later."

"You say Spencer is the man you *usually* meet," said Quinlan. "Does that mean you sometimes meet others?"

"Yes and no." She lowered her eyes, unwilling to face Quinlan. "Obviously I could meet Captain Spencer in the hotel only if neither you nor Major Hadleigh was in Nuremberg. Otherwise you would become curious at seeing me with a man in British uniform."

"He wears the uniform of a British Army captain, then?"

"Yes."

"Go on," said Quinlan.

"If you or Major Hadleigh was in Nuremberg, I would say in my message that I could not meet Captain Spencer in the hotel that night. He would understand this to mean that the meeting was to take place at the alternative rendezvous, the Hauptbahnhof."

"You still haven't told us whether you met others apart from Spencer," Hadleigh reminded her.

"I do—did. Captain Spencer always made the rendezvous if the meeting was inside the hotel. If outside, it could be either he or any one of two or three other men, sometimes a German, sometimes not."

"Do you have names for these others?"

"No."

"What does Spencer's cap badge look like?" asked Quinlan with a flash of inspiration.

She did not understand. "His cap badge?"

"Yes. You must have seen him with his cap on at some time. What was the badge in the center?"

Twisting her sodden handkerchief into knots, Gretl tried to remember.

"A sort of gun, I think," she managed eventually. "A cannon on large wheels."

"Royal Artillery," said Quinlan, snapping his fingers. "He's wearing the uniform of a gunner captain. We should check whether an RA captain by the name of Spencer has been reported AWOL in Nuremberg in recent months. The name could be genuine, the phony Spencer keeping the original owner's papers in case he was ever asked for ID."

Hadleigh questioned the validity of that theory. Every MP in Third Army territory had a list of Allied officers and men posted AWOL. The fake Spencer would be taking a hell of a risk, walking around with the papers of a man who would be arrested on sight.

Quinlan broke into English, which Gretl would find difficult to follow at speed.

"Christ, Ben, we're not talking about minor criminals, pick-pockets or car thieves. Taking risks is a way of life for these people. If they've got the balls to commit a couple of murders, maybe more, have a crack at me, kidnap Willi Meissner and Hannah, they're not going to worry about a few lousy papers."

Hadleigh accepted that, adding that he could not see where it would get them, knowing whether or not a Captain Spencer was listed as AWOL.

Quinlan disagreed vehemently.

"Ingrid said the three men who snatched Hannah were wearing British or US uniforms. They must have got them from somewhere. If we can check not only on Spencer but on how many other officers and men have gone AWOL in the last few months, talk to each one's CO to see if he was the type to do a vanishing act, we should get an idea what size team we're up against. Fathom that and we might be able to fathom what they're up to and where they, and Hannah, are." Quinlan paused for breath. "I tell you this," he continued, "the thought of the SS and the BFC wandering around Nuremberg in Allied uniforms gives me a funny feeling in the pit of my stomach."

Hadleigh confessed his own disquiet. Every one of the Tribunal judges had received crank death-threat letters since the trial had opened. Maybe the guys who had abducted Hannah weren't cranks. Kill the judges and their alternates and there went the trial for another year, after which the climate of public opinion might have changed, the world occupied with more pressing matters such as Stalin's territorial ambitions. Defendants who would draw the death penalty in six months' time or whenever the present hearing ended, in eighteen months could get just a hefty jail sentence.

Nevertheless, how the hell *could* anyone get at the judges? Their residences were heavily guarded, they were escorted to and from the Palace of Justice by enough hardware to fight off a division, and the Palace was ringed with armed troops whenever the court was in session.

"I've no idea," admitted Quinlan. "But they've proved they're ruthless, and they've got uniforms and at least one Jeep."

"They might also have a tank," said Max, reminding them of one of the Most Immediate signals from Gene Masterson. The Sherman was still missing.

That clinched it for Hadleigh.

"Get on the phone to the MPs, Max. Use my name and talk to Colonel Cahn in person. Don't go into details. Just ask him if he has a Captain Eric Spencer, Royal Artillery, on his wanted sheet. If he has, ask him to send over a complete breakdown of all absentees from, say, October last year. Forget about French, Russian, and so on. Concentrate on British and American. Use the phone in your own office."

"Right," said Judd, and went out.

Hadleigh rubbed his eyes wearily. None of it made any sense, he said. How did a missing gunner captain connect with Canaris and the fragments? What had Canaris meant about January tenth? What was the BFC involvement? "I don't see those boys going in for death-or-glory stuff."

Neither did Quinlan. He had had a similar conversation with Yuri Petrov before they flew to Berlin. Everything *was* connected somehow, but he was damned if he could see where.

He reminded Gretl that she had been telling them how she passed on information. Had she ever met Spencer or any of the others away from the Grand or the Haupt-bahnhof? In other words, did she have any idea where their base was, where they might be holding Hannah? She did not.

She looked at Quinlan fearfully, sensing his anger.

"Sometimes," she said, her voice little more than a whisper, "I had nothing for them but they wanted something of me. In that case they would call me here if it was urgent or come to my home if it was after my normal hours."

Hadleigh shook his head in amazement. He had grown stale since the end of the war. Gretl Meissner and her contacts had been conducting their business under his nose.

"When did they ask you about Fräulein Wolz?" said Quinlan. "Today? This morning?"

"No. Last Tuesday, the day you returned from Munich. Captain Spencer telephoned me—here. I was late leaving because I had a lot to do." She held back a sob with difficulty. "I had nowhere to go anyway."

"How did they know we were back?" asked Quinlan. "From you?"

"No. When he called he immediately suggested the station rendezvous. I got the impression he had just left the Grand."

Where doubtless he witnessed my conversation with Petrov, thought Quinlan, trying to recall seeing a gunner captain in the bar. He could not.

"So you met him at the Hauptbahnhof?"

"Yes."

"And told him where Hannah was?"

The only confirmation was a tearful nod.

"You've probably killed her," said Quinlan bitterly. "You've probably killed her the way you killed Ilse Arndt and Angela Salvatini."

"No!" protested Gretl, shaking her head with horror. "That wasn't me. I couldn't have told them where Herr Arndt lived because I didn't know. I didn't even know he was dead until I came in the following day."

"She's telling the truth, at least on that score," said Hadleigh. "I can check the log if you like, but I'm pretty certain she was with you in the Palace of Justice when Arndt was brought in."

"You must believe me," cried Gretl. "They sometimes have a man watching the gates, in the crowd."

Quinlan beckoned Hadleigh to one side, where they held a rapid, whispered conversation in English. Gretl Meissner had committed no crime for which she could be punished in a court of law. Although she had taken the soft option, she was more victim than culprit. If they could persuade her to help them, there was a possibility that Hannah and Willi Meissner would come out of this alive.

Quinlan let Hadleigh explain what was required of her.

"The time is now ten minutes to six," said the American major. "You'll use this phone to call the Grand, where you'll leave a message telling captain Spencer you can't meet him at the hotel tonight. If we understood you correctly, that's the code for arranging to meet him at the station at seven-thirty."

They would have preferred to use the signal advising

the fake Captain Spencer that the rendezvous with his contact was at the Grand. As he presumably knew, however, the Hadleigh at least was in Nuremberg, he might smell a rat and not put in an appearance at all, now that they had Hannah. For that matter, the phony gunner captain did not have to turn up in person since the meeting was outside, but that was a risk they would have to take.

"I don't think he calls on a Sunday," said Gretl. "He knows I don't work that day."

"Never calls?"

"I don't know. Since I've never left a message for him on a Sunday, I'm not sure whether he telephones or not."

"Let's hope he does today," muttered Hadleigh grimly.

But Gretl had still not agreed to cooperate. "They'll kill my son," she wept quietly.

Quinlan was not in the mood to indulge her. "There's a good possibility he's already dead," he informed her bluntly. "In any event, do you really expect them to set him free when you're no longer any use to them? Your only chance of seeing him alive is to help us find their base."

And a devil of a slim chance that is, thought Quinlan. The odds were heavily against tailing whoever made the rendezvous back to where he came from. Still, that would have to be played by ear. They had an hour and a half to make their preparations and stake out the station. Nothing would happen before seven-thirty. Nothing *at all* would happen unless Gretl agreed to work with them.

He and Hadleigh spent a further five minutes convincing her where her best interests lay. Finally she nodded her head.

After making the call, she was taken to an empty office where she would be guarded by a GI until the time came to move. She was not, they told her, under arrest.

Max Judd returned from his conversation with the MPs at six-fifteen. Since the beginning of October forty-six soldiers had gone AWOL. All but nineteen had been accounted for and taken into custody. Of those nineteen four were British, the remainder American. Two of the British were officers; so were two of the Americans. One of the British officers was a Captain Eric Spencer.

"Though it's going to take me a hell of a long time to check with each CO and find out how many were genuine absentee material," Max wound up.

Quinlan told him not to bother now.

"My faith in the modern-day soldier is restored. I was expecting many more than nineteen, a couple of hundred. I doubt if every one of those nineteen is linked with the opposition, which means, if I'm looking at this thing properly, they're not in Nuremberg in battalion strength. We can rule out anything that requires more than a handful of men."

A few minutes after six-thirty Quinlan was all for telephoning the Grand to see if Spencer had called in. Hadleigh advised him not to.

"They might have a man in the hotel. Christ knows, they've been running rings around us up to now. If we do anything out of the ordinary, we could blow the whole ball game."

Although the waiting and inactivity were driving him mad, Quinlan gritted his teeth and agreed.

A little later, as they were preparing to leave, the cartography unit rang through from Fürth. Its spokesman said they'd had a stroke of luck in identifying the island group. One of the team had spent some weeks surveying it for use as a possible base during the time of lend-lease, and had no doubt that the fragments depicted a volcanic archipelago in the South Atlantic, a British possession. Only the chief island, Tristan da Cunha,

was inhabited; the rest were too tiny. In case they were
interested and wanted to look it up on a map, Tristan da
Cunha's location was 12 degrees 30 minutes west, 37
degrees south.

None the wiser for the information, Quinlan now saw
what Butterweck had meant about Canaris's ironic
sense of humor. Tristan, lover of Isolde, was a legen-
dary Wagnerian hero.

SEVENTEEN

~~~~~~

NUREMBERG
January 6, 1946

THE GRANDFATHER CLOCK in the hall showed ten
minutes to seven when Riordan returned to the Grossreuth house after telephoning the Grand. The phone he
called from was in a garage about half a mile away and
was one of only a couple of dozen in the area. The garage proprietor had applied to the military authorities to
have it reconnected in July 1945 and, to his astonish-
ment, the work was done the following day. The British
captain used it regularly with the proprietor's full approval. The officer paid well.

On entering the common room Riordan inclined his
head at Sternberg and thumbed over his shoulder. The
former Standartenführer followed Riordan into the
passage, closing the door behind him.

"There was a message," said Riordan, keeping his

voice down. "The station rendezvous."

Had Quinlan or Hadleigh known the identity of their chief adversary, they would have been amazed to witness his reaction. Sternberg's face cracked into a broad smile.

"So," he said, "we have guessed well. I was beginning to worry. Not picking up the Wolz girl until today was masterly."

"We can thank Scharper for that."

Sensing Riordan to be the bearer of important tidings, the others looked up expectantly when he and Sternberg reentered the common room. Sternberg kept them waiting, studying each of them in turn. The next few minutes were vital to the overall plan.

Oberscharführer Oskar Flisk, a chain-smoker who scorned the use of a cigarette holder as an affectation, was characteristically attending to his hands, cleaning the nicotine from his fingers with a small piece of pumice stone. Nearby, Unterscharführer Kurt Zander was on his knees, lovingly field-stripping an automatic pistol, the parts spread out on a sheet of newspaper. Sitting at one end of the long oak table, Heinrich Scharper held a goblet of brandy up to an oil lamp, examining the liquor for impurities. Judging by the color of his cheeks, he had refilled the glass during Sternberg's short absence. The SS colonel made up his mind to have a word with his second-in-command at an opportune moment. Although Scharper could outdrink any of them without impairing his faculties, he was perhaps overindulging.

At a low table by the window the German tankmen, Hans-Dieter Kleemann and Anton Isken, were playing a two-handed card game. They were absurdly young to have fought a hard war with the Totenkopf Division, thought Sternberg. Youth had been valued out of all proportion in the Third Reich. Their lack of years was no handicap in the current venture, of course, though Sternberg was reassured to have Granger, the British tankman, at his disposal. Granger was something of a braggart. If a man were to believe all his stories, he was single-handedly responsible, before being captured, for the destruction of Rommel in North Africa. Nevertheless, he had proved himself tough and fearless in the past few months, as had the Scotsman Laidlaw, now standing over the cardplayers and offering gratuitous advice in an appalling German accent.

Sternberg scanned the room for the American Hallam before remembering he was on picket duty on the grounds. Riordan had doubtless already spoken to him on the way in; if not, he could be brought up to date later.

"There appears to be an unforeseen last-minute complication," Sternberg announced finally. "Comrade Riordan has just learned that the Meissner woman wishes an urgent meeting at the Hauptbahnhof. He cannot make the rendezvous personally since we still have much to discuss. Zander, you know her by sight. You and Flisk will have to go."

As though on cue, Riordan objected. "You're forgetting, Zander and Flisk still have to check the weapons. They've been their responsibility all along and we can ill afford malfunctions now."

Sternberg clicked his tongue in annoyance. "Of course. My mind is on other matters."

His eyes wandered around the room until they alighted on Kleemann and Isken.

"You've spoken to her, Kleemann. It will have to be you. Get changed and take Isken with you. Use the Jeep with the Sixth Armored Division markings."

A rendezvous was always made in pairs, one man to drive and look after the Jeep, the other to make the contact. But usually one of the Big Four went along, to take care of a chance roadblock or inquisitive MP.

Kleemann protested that neither he nor Isken spoke more than a few words of English, and those with heavy accents.

Sternberg cut him short.

"This is an emergency. I need Laidlaw, Granger, and Hallam here. They will be in the vanguard tomorrow and they must rehearse and rehearse again until their roles are second nature. Go now."

Kleemann and Isken glanced at one another before getting to their feet. They had served for long enough in the Totenkopf Division to learn that a man didn't question twice an order from an SS colonel. Besides, these were risks they had agreed to accept, and small they were compared with what was to come.

They left the room to change their clothes. When they returned ten minutes later Kleemann was wearing the uniform of a Third Army corporal, Isken that of a PFC.

"The meeting is for seven-thirty," Sternberg told them. "Listen carefully to whatever Frau Meissner has to say and return here directly. I shall expect you no later than eight-thirty. Take no chances."

"You may be assured of that, Herr Standartenführer," muttered Kleemann with unaccustomed humor.

The men in the common room waited until they heard the Jeep drive off. Apart from Frank Hallam, patrolling outside, and Riordan, Zander, and Flisk, who had kidnapped Hannah Wolz earlier in the day, the others were in civilian clothes. As the note of the Jeep's engine died in the distance, Sternberg indicated that the time had come for the rest of them to change.

When those concerned returned to the common room, Sternberg was attired as a US infantry major and former Sturmbannführer Heinrich Scharper as a US lieutenant. Tom Granger had on a Royal Artillery bombardier's uniform that didn't quite fit, while Harry Laidlaw wore the second-best khaki of a one-time private in the Royal Army Medical Corps. Zander and Flisk were already dressed as Third Army sergeants. Every one of the original owners of the uniforms were dead, murdered and disposed of by those now impersonating them.

Sternberg considered it unfortunate that they presented such a motley collection, but that couldn't be helped. They'd had to take what they could where they could find it.

Zander glanced toward the ceiling, licking his lips at the prospect of what was to come.

"The girl and the Meissner brat, Herr Standartenführer."

"I leave them to you and Flisk. Bring the girl, kill the boy. We'll meet you outside."

Gagged and handcuffed to the opposite end of the iron bed from Willi Meissner, Hannah listened to the heavy tread of footsteps on the stairs. Since her abduction that afternoon, she had lost all track of time. They had not harmed her. They had knocked her unconscious in the Sündersbühl house, and when she came to she was here. Wherever here was.

In a different bedroom from the one she was now in, two of them had questioned her while a third had mauled her sexually in an effort to get her to talk.

More frightened than she had ever been, even during the worst air raids, she had told them what they wanted to know. Everything. About Quinlan. Hadleigh. About Max Judd and their trip to Munich. About the photo fragments, Bachmann, and Klaus Butterweck. About her father.

They had asked her about her past and she had told them that too. About her mother, where she had lived during the war, what she had done.

She had confidently expected to be killed. Raped first, then killed. She knew these men, their sort. She had seen too many of them in the past not to know them.

The silver-haired one—the leader, it seemed—had reacted to something she said and held a hasty conference with the man in the British captain's uniform. They had started to laugh delightedly, chuckle, whisper unheard. And then they had brought her to this room, chained her to the bed opposite the boy, and left her alone.

Until now. Now, perhaps, they were going to kill her.

Flisk came in first. For a moment she didn't recognize him in his uniform. For a moment she thought the Americans were there and she was safe. Then, seeing his cruel eyes, she remembered him as the one who had run his hands all over her body, squeezing, probing, all the while saying it would be better if she told them what they wanted to know.

"Time to leave, Fräulein," he grinned, unlocking the handcuffs but not removing the gag. Again she felt him touch her, fondle her breasts, stroke her buttocks as he pushed her ahead of him.

Behind her, he stood very close as they reached the door. She could feel his erection through the material of his trousers.

"Don't take all night about it, Kurt," she heard him say over his shoulder.

Zander gazed into Willi Meissner's terrified eyes. He would have enjoyed nothing more than taking all night about it.

It was odd, he thought, increasing the pressure with his thumbs on Willi's larynx, how those who were about to die knew it long before they felt the physical presence of approaching death. Something in the executioner's demeanor told the victim all hope was lost.

There, there, he murmured softly to himself as Willi's eyes started to bulge and strangled animal yelps were heard through the gag. *There, there.*

EIGHTEEN

∿∿∿∿∿∿∿∿∿∿∿∿∿∿∿∿∿∿∿∿∿∿∿∿∿∿

NUREMBERG
January 6–7, 1946

A TINY FIGURE in gray, Gretl Meissner stood just inside the east entrance of the Hauptbahnhof, opposite the old post office building. Since the reopening of road and rail communications is a major priority on the agenda of any conqueror in an occupied country, train services had long been back to normal. Although the station still carried the scars of bomb and artillery damage, it was not only functioning again but crowded with both civilians and military personnel, all wearing that semidazed expression rail travelers everywhere have, cocking their heads for announcements, gazing anxiously at arrival and departure bulletin boards, asking questions of uncaring porters and US Army transport officers.

Quinlan had agreed with Hadleigh that they should
not stake out the Hauptbahnhof with half the Third
Army as backup. The objective was not to apprehend
whoever made contact with Gretl but to follow him. A
convoy of trucks would only arouse suspicion. If they
were successful in finding the base, they could call up
reinforcements before making any further moves. Thus
only the two of them and Max were watching Gretl
Meissner, who was, they agreed, the weak link in the
chain.

They had briefed her with a phony story. Whether she
would prove convincing was another matter. She was to
tell her contact that American intelligence had recovered
four fragments of photograph that were somehow connected with the late Hauptmann Arndt. These were now
in Hadleigh's office safe. She could not remove them
for any length of time without the alarm being raised;
she could, however, photograph them if she had a suit-
able camera. Could her contact provide one? If so and
she gave them what they wanted, would they set her son
free?

They were standing some thirty or forty yards from
one another and the same distance from Gretl to keep
her under constant surveillance from different angles.
At twenty-five minutes to eight, with each of them
wondering whether Spencer had called the Grand, they
observed a youngish US captain approach the German
woman. It became apparent after a moment that he had
mistaken her immobility for importuning, that what he
was trying to do was see if she was free for a couple of
hours. When she shook her head vigorously and turned
her back, he moved on.

Five more minutes passed before Judd, who was nearest the station entrance pretending to read a newspaper,
quite suddenly folded it into a roll and tapped it against
his palm. Quinlan and Hadleigh scanned the crowds and
simultaneously picked out the man Max had spotted.

He wore a US uniform with corporal's chevrons, but he had never spent any time in the American military. Straight-backed, he carried himself like a recent graduate from boot camp. A Marine Corps drill sergeant would have wept with joy at his carriage, except this man's alma mater was the Wehrmacht or the Waffen SS.

Kleemann took his time approaching Gretl, who had not yet seen him. He didn't like these station meetings, even though Sternberg assured him time and time again that the safest place to hide a fake Reichsmark was among genuine paper currency. On a platform swarming with uniforms, no one was going to take any interest in one more GI corporal.

Satisfied that all was well, Kleemann went up to Gretl. He saw she had been crying recently, probably over that brat of hers.

"Frau Meissner," he said politely.

Her mind elsewhere, Gretl started at the interruption to her thoughts.

She recognized Kleemann, whose name she did not know, from previous meetings. Her first reaction was one of disappointment.

"I was expecting Captain Spencer," she managed.

"The captain is otherwise occupied. Please inform me why you made the call. And smile, Frau Meissner. You look like the chief mourner at a funeral."

Hesitantly, stumbling over her words, Gretl told him about the fragments, how they were in the office safe, how she needed a camera to photograph them.

Kleemann frowned. He had heard about these fragments, heard Sternberg, Scharper, the Englishman Riordan talking about them. But no one had ever explained to him their importance.

"Let me understand this," he said patiently, keeping his voice soft because they were conversing in German. "The Americans have all four fragments in the Allersbergerstrasse barracks. You can't steal them. You need a camera to photograph them."

"Yes. It's most urgent."

Gretl started to crack. She clutched Kleemann's sleeve.

"You must get me one at once. Then I can have my son back. He's well, isn't he? Please tell me he's alive and well."

Kleemann tried to loosen her grip.

"Frau Meissner," he hissed. "You are attracting attention."

Everything happened very quickly after that.

Gretl refused to let go of his sleeve. This man, this German, was her one link with Willi, without whom she was going out of her mind.

Panicking, Kleemann attempted to prize her fingers loose and back off. From their various vantage points, Hadleigh, Quinlan, and Judd could see and hear some sort of argument taking place and instinctively began to move in.

Already nervous and made more so by Gretl's hysterical persistence, Kleemann sensed the jaws of a trap closing around him. Wrenching himself free from her grip and throwing her to the ground, he ran for the exit. In the east forecourt Isken was waiting in the Jeep.

Not knowing what had happened but seeing their quarry trying to escape, Quinlan and the others raced after him. Suddenly they were shouting. In the space of a few seconds it had all gone wrong.

Kleemann gained the forecourt a dozen strides ahead of Judd, screaming at Isken to get moving. Isken tried to. At the third attempt the plugs sparked and the motor caught, by which time Kleemann was alongside, swinging himself aboard.

"Go! Go! For Christ's sake, go!" he bellowed.

Isken engaged first gear and let out the clutch. The Jeep careened forward, sideswiping a stationary Mercedes. It was gaining speed when Judd appeared on the driver's side. Always the man to take the direct route wherever he was going, Judd wasted no time trying to wrestle for possession of the steering wheel. Grabbing the windshield stanchion with his left hand, he slammed his right fist into Isken's face.

The master sergeant was off balance and thrown clear as the Jeep yawed out of control. Semiconscious, blood pouring from his mouth, Isken was no longer able to steer. The vehicle crashed into a line of parked cars, hurling Isken against the windshield and pitching Kleemann on to the sidewalk. Before he could get to his feet, Hadleigh planted a foot on Kleemann's back, pinning him to the ground, and cracked him over the skull with his pistol when he continued to struggle.

Seconds later Quinlan arrived, shouldering his way through a gathering throng of mystified spectators. One of the Germans was unconscious and Max was dragging the bloody driver from his seat. But the plan had gone terribly wrong. Gretl's spooking her contact could well be the signature on Hannah's death warrant.

Back at Allersbergerstrasse, Quinlan argued in favor of third-degreeing the Germans, breaking their fingers one by one if necessary in order to get them to talk. Hadleigh disagreed. There were more ways of skinning a cat than with a blunt knife. Extreme measures were generally countered, at least to begin with, by extreme resistance. Besides, he wasn't sure Quinlan could carry out his threat. Nor did they have much time. Whoever had dispatched the Germans would be expecting them back. If they didn't reappear within a reasonable period, that could be the last of Hannah. And of Willi Meissner, whose mother was under sedation in the infirmary.

"Have you a better idea?" Quinlan wanted to know.

Hadleigh thought he had, one that had worked in the

past and might do so again. Especially with young
Germans who wore their aggressive masculinity like a
badge, and more especially with men who would be facing a charge of murder.

Max Judd had supervised the strip-and-search, finding SS blood-group tattoos under each German's armpit
and relieving them of papers in the names of Corporal
Jerry Thompson and PFC Edward J. Strickland.
Thompson and Strickland were on the AWOL list. No
one doubted that they were dead.

In the classic manner of interrogations they had separated the two Germans, putting one, Kleemann (though
they had no idea of either's real name yet), in the
Trough, the larger cells, the other, Isken, in the punishment cell that had housed Ilse Arndt the night her father
died. Judd considered Kleemann to be the shakier of the
pair, the one more likely to break, not least because of
the blow on the head he had received from Hadleigh's
pistol.

There was to be no good guy-bad guy routine. They
hadn't the time. After telling Max to seek out Privates
Bennett, Guthrie, and Johnson and keep them in the
guardroom until they were needed, Hadleigh picked up
a near-full bottle of bourbon from his desk.

"Maybe he could use a drink," he said.

At this point Quinlan had only the faintest glimmer of
the American major's proposed tactics.

Kleemann looked up anxiously as the cell door
opened. Apart from a blanket around his shoulders, he
was naked and felt vulnerable. His head throbbed, but
he was more than ready for his interrogators. A man did
not swear the SS blood oath unless he had proved
himself.

Quinlan took a backseat. Literally. He pulled the
wooden chair to the far side of the cell and sat on it,
arms folded. After a while Max reappeared and stood in
the doorway.

"What division?" asked Hadleigh casually. "Das Reich, Leibstandarte, Totenkopf?" He named the three premier Waffen SS divisions, flattering Kleemann.

"I have nothing to say," muttered Kleemann sullenly.

"Please yourself," said Hadleigh, "but the only definite charge against you as of now is illegal possession of US Army property. We're too busy here in Nuremberg to bother about such matters. If that's all you're guilty of, you'll be put in the pen with the others pending a formal indictment. Probably you'll draw no more than a couple of weeks on a labor gang and in six months' time there'll be a general amnesty. All those not guilty of war crimes will be released. On the other hand, if you were not Waffen SS, maybe you were on the staff of one of the camps."

"I was a front-line soldier," said Kleemann. "I had nothing to do with the camps."

"Regrettably everyone is saying that," murmured Hadleigh. "The only stories we're inclined to accept are those that can be proved. I tend to believe you were a front-line soldier. You don't look the type to have served in Dachau or Mauthausen. But I need proof for my superiors. Name, rank, number, and unit is all we want for the moment."

"To hell with you," sneered Kleemann. "You know I'm no ordinary SS man. You were waiting for us at the station. The Meissner woman talked and you set a trap. It's unfortunate I walked into it, but there it is."

Quinlan tossed a glance at Judd. If this was the weaker of the two, God help them if they had to tackle the other one.

Hadleigh was unperturbed.

"You're right about the trap, of course. We did set up Gretl Meissner. We were expecting the fake Captain Spencer, however. No doubt he preferred someone else to take the risks."

"I don't know any Captain Spencer."

"And I don't exactly believe that."

Hadleigh moved up a gear.

"Neither, now we're down to it, do I believe you were Waffen SS. You have, shall we say, a certain femininity about the features. Not combat material at all."

Kleemann felt his cheeks redden at the implication he was homosexual. That was a fucking lie, he wanted to shout. He'd had more than his fair share of women.

But he kept his rage to himself. The American was trying to goad him into doing something stupid.

"You were probably in the camps," went on Hadleigh, not raising his voice at all. "You're a killer anyway, and what's a few more deaths? Someone murdered a woman and a young girl on Humboldtstrasse in November, though I doubt you had anything to do with raping them first. The uniform you were wearing wasn't handed over to you voluntarily. Neither were Corporal Thompson's papers. You were at Dachau or Buchenwald or Mauthausen or one of the others, and we have ways of dealing with people like you that do not involve lengthy trials. You'd better take a drink or two while I tell you about it."

Kleemann ignored the proferred bottle. He had been willing to die before and he was willing to die now. Giving this *Ami* major his name, rank, number, and unit wasn't going to help him.

"So go ahead and shoot me."

Although he knew it to be an act, Quinlan shivered at Hadleigh's smile.

"We're not going to shoot you. That would be too easy. Later we may hang you, but first you're going to undergo a somewhat unpleasant experience. I don't care whether you're homosexual or not. Neither will several men I have in my command. Between you and me they're animals. They belong in the stockade, which is where they'll be if they ever fail to carry out an order

I give them. I can tell them, for example, to sexually assault you. They've done it before with recalcitrant suspects. They don't like it, but they do it. They prefer that to ten years behind bars. I hope you understand what I'm talking about.''

Kleemann did. In spite of himself he shuddered with revulsion.

"I don't believe you."

"A pity," murmured Hadleigh. "Max, get them, will you?"

Hadleigh remained silent, allowing the terror to build up in the German until Bennett, Guthrie, and Johnson appeared. They were the biggest and maybe the ugliest GIs on the base. Quinlan had seen them around, heard them talk. He knew that Hadleigh was lying in calling them animals.

"Get him ready, Max," said Hadleigh.

Kleemann tried to hold on to his covering. Max backhanded him across the mouth and removed the blanket, tossing it onto the cell floor. Fear of the most primitive kind overtook Kleemann. He clutched his genitals with both hands and retreated on his bunk to the corner where it met the wall.

"This is not just," he protested.

Had he not been serious, they would have laughed in his face.

"Take a drink," said Hadleigh soothingly. "It'll make it easier."

Hadleigh watched the SS man's eyes. There would come a fraction of a second when the German would be torn between wanting the alcohol and wanting to protect himself. When he judged the moment to be right, Hadleigh instructed Max to hand back the blanket. Kleemann grabbed it and wrapped it around him, encasing himself in its security.

Hadleigh held out the bottle of bourbon. Kleemann reached for it and drank deeply, despising himself for his weaknesses but needing the liquor.

"Maybe now you believe I'm telling the truth," said Hadleigh, leaving the bottle with the German. "Let's begin with your name, rank, number, and unit."

What harm could it do? thought Kleemann. He and Isken were finished as far as the job was concerned.

Hadleigh jotted the information down in longhand on a pad and made the German repeat his rank and unit.

"Scharführer. SS Panzer Division Totenkopf."

Hadleigh was not slow to make the connection between the identity of the division and the missing Sherman.

"You were a tank driver?"

"Yes."

"And your friend, your comrade?"

"He should be telling you himself."

"I'd rather you told me."

Kleemann hesitated only momentarily.

"Anton Isken. Same rank, same division. I regret I don't know his number."

"But he too drove tanks?"

"Yes."

Hadleigh beamed, a schoolmaster giving a mental pat on the head to a bright pupil.

"Good. We progress. Now all I need to know is your business in Nuremberg and the whereabouts of Fräulein Wolz and Frau Meissner's son."

Kleemann shook his head.

"That wasn't part of our bargain."

"Herr Major," prompted Hadleigh.

Hadleigh was taking his time, and Quinlan's anxiety about Hannah was as strong as ever. Nevertheless, he had to admire the manner in which the American was handling the whole business. Kleemann was on the run now. By a combination of alcohol and threats Hadleigh was attempting to substitute one figure of authority, himself, for another, Kleemann's commanding officer. And not once had he raised his voice.

"Herr Major," repeated Hadleigh.

"That wasn't part of our bargain . . . Herr Major."

"Not part of our original bargain, agreed," said Hadleigh cheerfully, "though I have to point out you failed to give me your name and unit until I explained the alternative." He inclined his head toward the silent Bennett, Guthrie, and Johnson, who must, thought Quinlan, have played these roles before. "Therefore we no longer have a bargain. So, the information I require, if you please."

Kleemann was drinking mechanically while Hadleigh spoke. He had consumed four or five good double measures in the space of a few minutes.

"That I can't do," he stammered, slurring his words. "Herr Major."

"That I can't do, Herr Major. You don't understand what you're asking. . . ."

Hadleigh leaned forward and removed the bottle from Kleemann's fingers. The German let it go without protest.

"I'm afraid it's you who does not understand, Scharführer Kleemann," he said softly. "All right, Max. He wants to play it the hard way."

Taking his cue, Max grabbed the blanket and pulled it from Kleemann's shoulders. When the German tried to resist, Max cuffed him about the head lightly, the sort of blow a parent would give to a truculent child or over-playful dog. And all the more effective for that.

"Bennett, Johnson," said Judd, snapping his fingers.

Like well-rehearsed actors, the two huge GIs came into the cell and seized Kleemann without ceremony. The German kicked out and shouted, but he was no match for their strength.

They whipped him over onto his stomach as easily as most men would a ten-year-old. While Bennett pinioned his arms and placed a knee in the middle of Kleemann's back, Johnson forced his legs apart in an inverted V.

Kleemann's eyes were wide open, staring horrified at

the cell door where Guthrie was very slowly unbuckling his belt, leering as he did so.

The German began to whimper and plead. Ashen, Quinlan hoped he would never hear such a sound again.

Guthrie moved out of Kleemann's line of sight, glancing anxiously at Hadleigh, who mimed him to silence. After a two-second beat, he placed the bourbon bottle against the German's buttocks.

"All right, all right, all right! I'll tell you, I'll tell you."

There were tears in his eyes when Max helped him to sit up and handed him back his blanket. He looked at the master sergeant with the gratitude of an infant.

Hadleigh waved Bennett, Guthrie, and Johnson away. They knew the routine. There were beers for them in the guardroom, where they would wait in case they were needed again. Which was unlikely.

Quinlan heard Guthrie say, as they disappeared along the passage, "One day that fuckin' Major Hadleigh's gonna go too far and one of them Krauts ain't gonna say uncle."

His hands shaking, Kleemann accepted the bottle once more and drank deeply. But not too deeply; Hadleigh saw to that. He wanted Kleemann compliant, not incapable.

"Let's begin at the beginning," he said, his voice the same melodious baritone it had been throughout. "First, I want to know if Fräulein Wolz and Willi Meissner are still alive and where they're being held."

There was no fight left in Kleemann. He had looked into the innermost reaches of his soul and found he was mortal. To answer the American major's questions was a catharsis, and once he started talking nothing was going to stop him.

Fräulein Wolz and Willi Meissner were alive when he left the Grossreuth house, he informed Hadleigh, giving him the address.

Max did not have to be told what his next job was. He was out of the door like a greyhound, to check the address on a map and round up men for the raid. Stealth was no longer on the agenda. They would hit and hit fast.

Hadleigh next asked about the number of individuals in the house. Kleemann recited their names as though in a trance.

There was Frau Elke Niemeyer, who ostensibly owned the property and whose husband was under arrest in the Soviet zone. She was the willing accomplice of Standartenführer Sternberg, Sturmbannführer Scharper, SS NCOs Flisk and Zander. The names of the British Free Corps contingent were Riordan, Granger, Hallam, and Laidlaw. He was not sure of their former ranks. Two other SS men, Kramer and Wildehopf, had been killed at the end of December. But the major knew that, of course.

"And that's the lot?" asked Hadleigh. "An original dozen and no more?"

"Yes." Kleemann's eyes had begun to glaze over, part booze, part relief that his manhood was not to be violated. "We were the last to join the battle group, Isken and myself."

"Battle group!" chorused Hadleigh and Quinlan in unison.

"Yes."

Even when they heard it they didn't believe it. The SS and the British Free Corps men, down to a total of eight now, were in Nuremberg to make an attempt on the lives of the Tribunal judges and simultaneously try to free the defendants from the dock of the Palace of Justice. Final details were to have been worked out that evening and the operation was to take place at 10:30 A.M. on Monday, January 7, a little over thirteen hours away.

"You're lying," snapped Hadleigh.

"I'm not. I swear it," said Kleemann, and it became obvious after a moment that he wasn't.

Spearheaded by the Sherman tank and backed up by two Jeeps and automatic weapons, the group was to hit the Palace of Justice as the judges were taking their seats. The action was to be sudden, swift, and bloody, with surprise the key. Who would suspect a small convoy of vehicles with US markings and personnel in Allied uniforms until it was too late? He and Isken would have been driving the tank. It made no difference that they were now in custody. One of the Englishmen, Granger, had driven tanks in the Western Desert.

"Where's the Sherman now?" asked Hadleigh. "Grossreuth?"

"I don't know. In all truthfulness I don't," Kleemann added plaintively when Hadleigh made a gesture of disbelief. "Isken and I were not part of the team the night of the ambush. We were told privately by Standartenführer Sternberg that we were too valuable to risk on a venture that could go wrong. He could always try for another tank, but he couldn't find two more SS drivers if we were killed or captured. Let the Englishmen take the risks, the Standartenführer said. Granger drove the tank to a secret location."

"But why keep it secret from you now?"

"You don't understand the Standartenführer. Everyone was told only as much as he needed to know, in case anything went wrong."

As indeed had happened this evening, thought Quinlan. Sternberg was obviously a cunning opponent. If Kleemann and Isken had known the location of the tank, the SS colonel would not have it as a potential weapon come tomorrow.

But the whereabouts of the Sherman was not the only item the Standartenführer had kept from Kleemann. Quinlan tossed the names Arndt, Langenhain, Bachmann, Butterweck, and Straub into the dialogue. They meant nothing to Kleemann. He had heard the first three discussed from time to time; he did not know who they were. Neither did he understand the significance of the photo fragments. As for Tristan da Cunha, he didn't even know it was an island in the South Atlantic.

"As I have explained, we were told only what the Standartenführer wanted each of us to know."

When they had time they would grill the other captive, Isken. Hadleigh doubted he knew any more than Kleemann.

Accompanied by two GIs to stand guard over the prisoner, Max appeared in the doorway and announced that they were ready to roll.

Hadleigh had one more question. He had a lot of telephoning to do and he wanted to be sure of his facts.

"Let me get this straight. Tomorrow morning this SS colonel is going to attack the Palace of Justice. I find it hard to believe that even fanatics would contemplate such a suicidal scheme, but answer me this. If you were not in custody, would you have driven the Sherman, regardless of the consequences?"

"Of course."

"Jesus Christ," said Hadleigh with feeling.

In the passage Max said he had a Jeep, two armored personnel carriers, and a company of GIs in two trucks standing outside. He'd located the house, which stood on its own grounds, on a street map. They should have no difficulty finding it.

"I've got a funny feeling you're not going to find anything," said Hadleigh gloomily. He consulted his wristwatch. "It's now nine-twenty. From the Hauptbahnhof to Grossreuth is a fifteen-minute drive. The meeting with Gretl was set for seven-thirty. If all had gone according to plan, Kleemann and Isken should have been back by eight o'clock. Allow for a margin of error of a quarter of an hour and they're sixty-five minutes overdue. If I were this Standartenführer Sternberg, I'd have headed for the hills long ago. Sorry, Otis, but that's how I read it.''

"Then what the hell are we hanging around for?"

Hadleigh held up his hand as Quinlan headed for the exit.

"We're hanging around because I'm not coming with you. You and Max can lead the operation. If I'm right and they're gone, I've got to call Gene Masterson. If Kleemann's telling the truth—and that's the way it looks—these lunatics are serious.''

They hit the house from all sides, finding the dead body of Willi Meissner in one of the upstairs rooms and a bewildered Frau Niemeyer in a cottage on the grounds. She could not give them the exact hour the main house was vacated. She had heard several vehicles start up some time before, perhaps a couple of hours. She had paid no attention. They were always coming and going. She was also most indignant when Quinlan informed her she would be taken into custody on a charge of harboring war criminals.

Quinlan was simultaneously dismayed and relieved that Hannah was still missing. If they'd wanted her dead, he reassured himself, she'd have been there alongside poor Willi Meissner. On the other hand, they might have taken her to amuse themselves during the small hours before the assault. He refused to dwell on that possibility.

Leaving a senior NCO to tidy up the details, he and Max raced back to Allersbergerstrasse in the Jeep. Giving Hadleigh, who was on the telephone, the thumbs-down, they made for the Trough and Hans-Dieter Kleemann. The German protested that he had no knowledge of a backup house, and they believed him. Perhaps Isken could tell them more. For the moment, however, they had to accept that Battle Group Sternberg had disappeared.

*   *   *

Isken refused to talk even when confronted with Kleemann. He raged and spat at his fellow tankman and finally had to be dragged out, yelling that he would find a
way of settling accounts with Kleemann.

They were in no way fazed by Isken's lack of cooperation. They had no reason to believe he knew any more
than Kleemann. Besides, they had other matters to think
about.

Counter Intelligence Corps had been called in now, as
had Colonel Masterson and Third Army brass up to
three-star-general level. In accordance with their agreement, Quinlan had also left a message for Yuri Petrov
to phone him.

Shortly after midnight Gene Masterson appeared in
person. The word from the brass was to play it by ear.
The judges would be warned of a possible attack and
security arrangements tightened. The trial, however,
could not be postponed for even a single day just because a handful—he emphasized *handful*—of fanatics
was on the loose. If the German public learned that the
Allies were running scared, the Tribunal would become
a laughingstock and lose all credibility.

In any case, he added, this SS colonel surely must
have concluded that Kleemann and Isken had been captured and made to talk and would therefore call off the
assault.

Hadleigh wasn't so sure. Anyone crazy enough to
conceive such an idea was also crazy enough to carry it
through. Besides, there were many aspects of the whole
business that left him uneasy. Why were members of the
British Free Corps involved? They were not renowned
for heroics. What was the significance of the fragments?
What did they mean and why was the opposition so anxious to get hold of them? Canaris had been dead since
April 1945. Before that he was incarcerated in Flossenbürg and other camps for ten months. He could not

have known in 1944 of a potential plot to assassinate the Tribunal judges. In 1944 neither the judges nor the Tribunal existed.

And what the hell did the reference to Tristan da Cunha mean? Or the date January 10?

Masterson agreed that the information in their possession was far from complete. Nevertheless, they had to go on what they had. Hadleigh concurred.

"I'll cordon off the Palace of Justice so tight a flea won't get through. If they're going to come in, they're going to go out dead."

NINETEEN

~~~~~~

NUREMBERG
January 7, 1946

HADLEIGH WAS AS good as his word. By nine o'clock
a ring of steel surrounded the Palace of Justice, the
forecourt jammed with tanks, half-tracks, armored personnel carriers, and troops on foot. Snipers were positioned on the upper floors of the old Wehrmacht stores
HQ opposite the palace and on the roofs of several
buildings on Maximilianstrasse.

The entrance to the prison where the defendants were
held when not in court, and which backed onto the
Palace, was blocked by a three-ton truck. Astride the
tailgate, two GIs manned a belt-fed heavy machine gun.
On either side of the three-tonner, shielded by the entrance pillars, were bazooka teams. A hundred yards

farther north the river Pegnitz was patrolled by gun-
boats.

The judges, their alternates, prosecution and defense
counsel, and other court officials had been contacted
during the night. All had agreed to cooperate by being
in the palace by eight-thirty. Everyone else who had
business in court—stenographers, translators, radio and
newspaper journalists—had their credentials closely
scrutinized before being allowed in. A forgotten pass
meant nonadmission, with no exceptions, no matter
how familiar the face.

Hadleigh had first suggested blocking off the main
road on which the palace stood, Fürtherstrasse, for a
hundred yards in either direction, and all side roads
emptying into it. Masterson had counseled otherwise.
The brass had decided that the members of Battle
Group Sternberg were to be dealt with, if possible, once
and for all. The object was to let them get close, but not
close enough to do any damage. If they were foolish
enough to make the attempt in spite of the loss of
Kleemann and Isken, Third Army did not want to scare
them off before they were in the net. Otherwise they
might try again tomorrow or the next day, and such
elaborate security arrangements could not be repeated
without causing major logistical headaches.

All tank movements within the area were forbidden
from eight forty-five, armored unit commanders being
informed that any mobile Sherman approaching the
Palace after that time would be fired on without warning. Hadleigh had wanted to prohibit the movement of
Jeeps and trucks also, but that was vetoed on the
grounds of impracticability. None were to be allowed
into the Palace forecourt after nine o'clock, however.

Since learning of the plot in the small hours, Yuri
Petrov had become, in Hadleigh's words, "a royal pain
in the excretory opening of the alimentary canal." The
Russian colonel had wanted to draft several battalions

of Soviet troops and was furious when turned down by Gene Masterson, who knew only too well that allowing the Soviets in was a hell of a sight easier than getting them out. Petrov had finally agreed with bad grace that security matters should be left to Third Army and CIC, though he made it clear that, if a disaster occurred, Moscow would know at whose door to lay the blame. Masterson had the distinct impression that the *Pravda* print workers had already set up their linotype.

AMERICANS STAND IDLY BY WHILE SOVIET JUDGES ARE MURDERED

By nine-thirty everyone with business inside the Palace had been admitted, according to the MP lieutenant detailed to check off names against a master list. Latecomers were to be turned away, except there were no latecomers. Although only a handful of men knew the reason for the extreme security measures, the peculiar sixth sense that journalists develop over the years had told them that something was up. For the first time since before Christmas every seat in the press gallery was occupied.

As 10 A.M. approached so did the Third Army's first problem: snow. Within minutes Nuremberg and environs were in the grip of a blizzard which reduced visibility to twenty or thirty yards.

Huddled deep inside their overcoats and taking shelter against the elements in the lee of a truck, Hadleigh, Quinlan, and Judd were discussing this new worry when Colonel Masterson sought them out.

"Any ideas, Major?" asked Masterson, returning Hadleigh's salute.

"We still have thirty minutes, sir. Maybe it won't last."

"Major Quinlan?"

"I can't see them bringing the time forward, sir,"

said Quinlan. "The judges don't sit and the defendants aren't brought up from their cells until ten-thirty. Even if Sternberg wanted to take advantage of the cover the snow will give him, his group would be blasting a courtroom empty of all VIPs if they attacked earlier." He grunted with disgust. "I'm starting to believe they're really going to try it."

"Safer that way," said Masterson. "If nothing happens, the men have had a useful exercise. Still, I'll double the roadside guard. The men on the rooftops won't be able to see a damned thing and a tank could be among us before we knew it."

"I'll give the order," offered Hadleigh.

"No, it had better come from me." Masterson winked broadly. "The infantry is already a touch pissed off that G-Two is running the operation." He tapped the silver eagle of rank on his shoulder. "I'll need this to persuade them to do as they're told."

No sooner had Masterson vanished beyond a curtain of snow than Yuri Petrov appeared, flanked by two junior lieutenants. Judging by his opening remarks, he was playing to the gallery, for the benefit of his subalterns. He was guarding his back in case anything went wrong, talking for the record.

"What do you intend doing about the snow, Major Hadleigh?" he asked in German.

Hadleigh saw that the two subalterns understood the language.

"What do you expect me to do, Colonel? Give an order for it to go away?"

"That is insolence, Major, and will be reported as such to your commanding officer."

Hadleigh gritted his teeth. He could do without Yuri Petrov in this mood. Nevertheless, Petrov outranked him.

"All right, I apologize. But whatever the representative of the Soviet Union might think, the United States has no control over the weather. We're doubling the guards at the roadside, which is about as much as we can do with the forces available."

"If Colonel Masterson had accepted my offer of Soviet troops, you would have had more than enough men to patrol the entire length of Fürtherstrasse."

"That's something you should take up with Colonel Masterson."

"I intend to at the appropriate time. For the moment I have made a written report that my offer of cooperation was rejected by American security. If any harm befalls Major General Nikitchenko or any other member of the Soviet delegation, there will be the gravest consequences."

"Stick it in your ear."

The phrase did not translate well and Petrov asked Hadleigh to repeat himself. The G-2 major did so, ignoring Quinlan's cautionary shake of the head.

"Nothing will happen to them," he said, trying and failing not to lose his temper. He had been up for much of the night and his nerves were frayed. "A gnat couldn't get through that cordon, so for Christ's sake don't bother me with trivialities. Unlike the Red Army, ours is competent."

Petrov turned purple. His eyes bulged with incredulity and the veins in his temple throbbed. When he tried to say something, the words stuck in his throat. His two aides shuffled their feet uncomfortably, waiting for the explosion.

Quinlan leaped to Hadleigh's defense. Petrov was behaving like a boor, but the American had overstepped the bounds of propriety.

"If I may have a word with you in private, Colonel Petrov."

Petrov allowed himself to be led to one side, where he and Quinlan put their heads together and held a whispered conversation. Finally the Russian nodded and beckoned curtly to his lieutenants. The three of them disappeared through the snow.

"Thanks," said Hadleigh. "What did you say to him?"

"I told him you were thinking of importing a couple of girls from the French zone and that one of them had a title. You know what a snob he is. If he wanted to continue receiving invitations to Sündersbühl, it would be well if he forgot all about the last couple of minutes. I also told him he could safely leave security in your hands."

"I wish I was that confident," said Hadleigh moodily. "Thanks again, but this snow is a real pain."

"It's the same for them as it is for us."

"You may be right, except I have a little worm gnawing away at my guts that's warning me they're one jump ahead of us again."

Quinlan kept silent about his own fears. However, he too felt that Battle Group Sternberg had an ace up its sleeve that would not be revealed until it was played.

The same blizzard that was whiting out central Nuremberg also blanketed the satellite town of Fürth as Sternberg, Riordan, and the others left the backup house at ten-fourteen, slightly ahead of schedule because the snow, though useful in other respects, would slow them down.

Sternberg, Riordan, Zander, and Hannah were packed into the first Jeep, with Hallam at the wheel. Scharper was in command of the second vehicle, with Granger driving.

Although the most direct route to Nuremberg was Fürtherstrasse, this was not the road they took. Instead they crossed the river Pegnitz west of Stadt Park. From there they would drive through the suburbs of Doos and Schniegling, skirt the cemetery using Schnieglinger-strasse, and enter Nuremberg from the north.

During the previous forty-eight hours Riordan and Hallam had made the run several times, allowing for various kinds of delays. Despite the snow, they should be at their destination within a few minutes either side of ten-thirty.

Sitting in the back between Sternberg and Zander and wearing a hooded gray cloak which one of her captors had produced, Hannah listened in silence while the silver-haired SS officer repeated her part in the coming proceedings, reiterating his warning that she would be killed out of hand if she attempted to raise the alarm. She believed him. She also now understood why they hadn't harmed her in any way. She did not expect to come out of the morning alive, however, regardless of an earlier promise that they would free her once her usefulness was at an end. She was therefore determined to make a run for it if the opportunity presented itself.

Riordan asked over his shoulder if Scharper and the others in the second Jeep had had it impressed upon them that on no account were submachine guns to be used at their destination. There had been trouble over this before they left Fürth, Scharper and Flisk arguing that having automatic weapons was pointless if they were to be left in the Jeeps. But finally Riordan had got his way. Those in officer's uniforms would carry service revolvers; those dressed as enlisted men, rifles. The submachine guns were to remain in the care of the drivers, Hallam and Granger, to be used only in the event of an emergency.

Sternberg confirmed that Scharper and Flisk would obey orders.

"How are we for time?" he asked.

Riordan checked his watch and peered through the windshield in an attempt to identify a landmark. He also glanced at the speedometer.

"We're running a bit behind."

"Snow's worse than I thought," said Hallam, con-

centrating fiercely on what he could see of the road
ahead.

"We can afford to be a little late," said Sternberg.
"What we can't afford is going into a ditch."

"We can't really afford either," said Riordan. "Let's
not underestimate the Americans. Whatever else they
are, they're not fools."

That sentiment was not shared by Ben Hadleigh as
ten-thirty arrived without a sign of anything happening.
Mostly on his say-so, several hundred extra troops and a
couple of million dollars' worth of hardware had been
drafted to surround the Palace of Justice. Sure the brass
and Gene Masterson had made the final decision, but on
his recommendation. Well, his and Quinlan's, who had
no official status here.

Hadleigh could visualize the entry on his service
sheet. "This officer is prone to acting hastily and on in-
sufficient data."

At ten thirty-two with the snow still falling in thick
flakes, he sent Max to find Gene Masterson.

"Sternberg won't be running on schedule," said
Quinlan, reading his mind.

"Neither he nor they will be running at all," lamented
Hadleigh bitterly. "They've called the whole thing off,
as I should have concluded last night. With Kleemann
and Isken missing and presumed captured, they decided
not to risk it. The odds were stacked against them in the
first place. They became totally unacceptable once we
had two of their men. They've postponed it until another day, when they think our guard's down. More
likely they've abandoned the whole idea. Gene Masterson's going to have my head."

Quinlan said it was a bit early to conclude nothing
would happen. He added that the sort of men they were
up against were not the kind to give up without a fight.

Hadleigh disagreed.

"It's precisely because they *are* who they are that they'll back off now they suspect we're waiting for them. Murdering a few defenseless people and kidnapping Hannah doesn't mean they're the stuff of which posthumous heroes are made."

"You could be wrong. You heard what Kleemann said last night, that he was prepared to attack regardless of the consequences. They might have got close enough to loose off a couple of rounds from the Sherman's big gun before anyone grasped what was going on, maybe even kill a few people in the courtroom. After that, however, they'd have been cut down pretty fast. We may call it fanaticism, even lunacy, but we've got to grant there's an element of bravery involved. Some of them would have been killed."

"Not if they used the tank in the vanguard and then escaped in the Jeeps during the confusion," argued Hadleigh. "They'd have been wearing Allied uniforms, don't forget. Most of the GIs around here would think twice before shooting at a friendly uniform and a tank with US markings. If we hadn't grabbed Kleemann and Isken, there's a sporting chance they wouldn't have suffered a single casualty. A few quick rounds from the Sherman, then away in the Jeeps. If Kleemann and Isken didn't make it, that's tough titty. My guess is that they were expendable. The whole affair would have been over in a minute."

"You're forgetting that they were also planning to release some of the defendants."

Hadleigh shook his head, mystified.

"That's the part that doesn't make sense. In and out I can understand—a swift offensive and a swifter retreat. But attempting a rescue is illogical. What the hell would they do with the defendants? Why the hell would they want them? Goering was sacked by Hitler and discredited toward the end of the war. He was lucky not to be shot by the SS. He's only a pretty big man in the dock because Hitler, Himmler, and Goebbels are dead. Goering wouldn't rate the first team if we had the others.

"Then there's Hess. He's been a traitor in every true Nazi's eyes since he flew to England in '41. He's also a little crazy. Why would the SS want him except to put a noose around his neck? Keitel and Jodl are Army, Raeder and Doenitz Navy. Frank claims he's found Jesus and the first thing Rosenberg would want is a stiff drink. The only man the SS could conceivably be interested in as one of their own is Kaltenbrunner. . . ."

Hadleigh's jaw dropped a foot when he realized the full implication of what he was saying. Wordlessly, he gaped in horror at Quinlan, whose expression altered from one of bewilderment to one of alarm as he too finally understood.

Obergruppenführer Ernst Kaltenbrunner, head of the SS Reich Main Security Office and Himmler's second-in-command, was not in the dock. *He wasn't even in the prison.* He was in the hospital, the Hallerwiese-Klinik. Battle Group Sternberg was playing its hidden ace on the other side of the Pegnitz, a mile and a half away in Hallerwiese.

Suddenly Hadleigh was yelling at the top of his voice for Max and Gene Masterson. Even as they appeared through the snowstorm Quinlan was racing for the nearest Jeep, cursing his stupidity.

Sternberg had been a step ahead once again. Kleemann and Isken were not privy to the real plan. Hadleigh was right about their expendability. Sternberg had deliberately sacrificed them, knowing they would break under interrogation. How Sternberg had outguessed Third Army Intelligence, how he had known he was sending Kleemann and Isken into a trap, would have to wait until later. But there was never a plot to hit the Palace of Justice and kill the judges. No wonder the whole scheme had seemed like lunacy. It *was* lunacy! All along Sternberg had intended going for Kaltenbrunner, who was conveniently suffering from some sort of illness, who had been in the hospital once or twice before and who was now there again, whose whereabouts were common knowledge. Anyone who cared to listen to the news bulletins knew he was in the Hallerwiese-Klinik, the hospital where Hannah Wolz had worked during the war. There had to be a connection between that fact and not finding her dead beside Willi Meissner. There had to be.

Battle Group Sternberg arrived at the Hallerwiese-Klinik at ten forty-two, twelve minutes behind their deadline because of weather conditions. Even so they did not hurry. They parked the two Jeeps side by side in the forecourt, as though they were just ordinary visitors.

Under the pretext of paying a call on a sick friend, in his British officer's uniform Riordan had checked out the clinic as soon as he learned Kaltenbrunner was hospitalized there. Although he hadn't managed to get anywhere near the former Obergruppenführer, he had ascertained that Kaltenbrunner occupied a private room on the second floor of the wing that overlooked Hallerwiese. A couple of friendly questions to a chatty houseman had elicited the information that the guard surrounding him was pitifully small: two GIs outside the door and another in the room. The Americans were less concerned about someone trying to liberate him than about a suicide attempt.

Hannah Wolz had proved to be an unexpected bonus when the cross-examination of her the previous afternoon had revealed that she had worked for the German Red Cross in the hospital during the war. Her presence would enable them to climb the stairs to the second floor and get close to the guards outside Kaltenbrunner's door without arousing suspicion. She would give the raiding party an air of authenticity, dressed as she was in the nurse's cloak. If all went well, no one would know Kaltenbrunner was gone until the time came for his next medication or guard change.

Including Hannah, five of them were to go in. Riordan to lead because he was familiar with the layout of the hospital; Scharper and Zander because they both knew Kaltenbrunner from the old days and would be able to convince him, should he have any doubts about accompanying them, what was in his best interests; Laidlaw because they needed an extra man whose native tongue was English and because he had drawn the uniform of a private in the Royal Army Medical Corps.

The others were to remain outside, ready to give covering fire to the raiding party if things did not go according to plan.

At ten forty-three Riordan led the way through the entrance door, one hand gripping Hannah's elbow. With an irritable gesture that was not entirely feigned, he waved aside a uniformed porter who seemed about to ask if he could help them.

Also at ten forty-three a small convoy of vehicles, klaxons blaring, crossed the river Pegnitz via Johannis-erbrücke and swung right into Grossweidenmühl-strasse, half a mile from the hospital. In the leading Jeep, with Max Judd at the wheel, were Quinlan, Had-leigh, and Gene Masterson, the latter furious that they had been duped, that in all the preparations and confer-ences during the small hours no one had considered that the target could be Kaltenbrunner. That sort of over-sight had lost many a battle in the past and might do so again. He hoped the orders he had given for someone to call the hospital immediately and warn the guards that under no circumstances was *anyone* to be allowed near Kaltenbrunner were being obeyed. He would not find out until later that the blizzard had brought down nu-merous telephone cables and that the hospital's number was registering as unobtainable.

In spite of Hadleigh's cursing and urging Max to go faster, the road conditions made speed impossible. Already a truckful of troops three vehicles behind had ploughed into the south side of Johanniserbrücke, blocking the bridge. Farther back, in his own stationary staff car, not knowing what was going on because no one had found time to tell him, Yuri Petrov pounded the seat with impotent rage.

TWENTY

∿∿

NUREMBERG
January 7, 1946

ARRIVING AT THE second floor unchallenged, Riordan called for a halt. The next couple of minutes were the most dangerous. Hannah Wolz could ruin the entire plan if she chose that moment to scream, if she failed to fully understand the consequences of any foolhardy action on her part.

"You look like a nurse," he whispered fiercely, "behave like one. If there's any shooting, you'll be the first to die."

Hannah nodded her acceptance of the conditions. She remembered this part of the hospital well. Nothing had changed. Unfortunately the corridors in the west wing all led away from the central staircase and lifts. The only exits at the furthermost ends were fire escapes. To get at one of them it was necessary to cpen a heavy iron door, which would take time. But she'd try that or something else if they took their eyes off her.

Riordan peered through the glass partition in the swing doors. Except for two GIs lounging outside a room at the far end of the corridor, some fifty yards away, there was no sign of life.

"Let's go," he said over his shoulder.

The GIs, both PFCs, glanced up as they heard the swing doors swish open. They saw a motley crew coming toward them: a British captain, a US lieutenant, a US sergeant, and a British medic. And a very lovely woman whose cloak was still wet from the snow.

"Looks like the pig's got visitors," muttered one.

"Not according to the schedule," said the other suspiciously. Nevertheless, he was reassured by Hannah's cloak.

Riordan overheard the last sentence and knew he had to get the guards off balance and keep them that way. When he was still fifteen feet from them he called, "It's about time you challenged me, isn't it?"

Both sentries sprang to attention at his imperious tone. Neither wanted to go on report for failing to observe standard operating procedure.

"We were just about to do that, Captain," said the first PFC.

By then the quintet was level with them, and no one had to tell Scharper and Kurt Zander what to do next. They had rehearsed this a score of times in the Grossreuth common room, with Hallam and Granger taking the part of the sentinels. They had to get themselves and the Americans out of the corridor without too much noise before anyone appeared from an adjacent room.

While the two young GIs' attention was on Riordan, who was fumbling in his jacket pocket for a nonexistent laissez-passer, Scharper and Zander slipped behind them, the former drawing his pistol, the latter reversing his rifle so that the butt was forward. They were all swift, clean movements occupying only fractions of seconds; so were the savage blows to the base of each skull which felled the guards. There was a muted "Hey" from one of them, but that was all.

Scharper and Zander caught them as they dropped, while Laidlaw was on hand to retrieve their rifles before they hit the floor. *So far, so good,* thought Riordan, rapping on Kaltenbrunner's door with his knuckles and pushing Hannah ahead of him as he barged in.

Kaltenbrunner and his bedside guard were not alone. A doctor was examining the Obergruppenführer, who was lying on the bed, naked to the waist. The three men looked up in alarm at the sudden intrusion, in time to see Scharper and Zander drag the unconscious bodies of the guards into the room, and shut the door.

The bedside guard was sitting on a chair several feet from Kaltenbrunner, chewing gum and nursing his M1 carbine across his knees. For a moment he remained motionless, unable to comprehend what was happening. When it registered, he tried to get to his feet and swing the carbine into a firing position. He was several seconds too late on both counts.

As an RAMC private and therefore a noncombatant, Laidlaw was not permitted under international law to bear arms. The rifle he carried slung over his shoulder when he entered the hospital should have told an intelligent observer that all was not well. Arming him, however, was a risk they had all decided to take for two reasons. The first was that extra firepower might be needed at some juncture; the second, that the Scot had categorically refused to be the only man in the battle group without a weapon.

The bedside guard was not even halfway out of his seat when Laidlaw slammed him across the temple with the rifle muzzle, knocking him to the floor and causing a fearful open wound. For good measure he followed up with several vicious kicks to the side of the injured man's head.

Concurrently, Riordan dealt with the doctor, pistol-whipping him into insensibility. A French civilian, part of the team that was endeavoring to ascertain what, precisely, was wrong with Kaltenbrunner, the physician was no match for Riodan's brute strength.

So far the whole action had taken less than a minute, and inside the room not a word had been uttered. Now Scharper decided to make his voice heard. From the look of horror on Kaltenbrunner's face, he thought the newcomers were an Allied assassination squad there to settle once and for all the matter of his nonappearance in the dock.

"It's Scharper, Herr Obergruppenführer," he said. "Do you remember me? We've met many times."

If the lantern-jawed Kaltenbrunner, a giant of a man over six and a half feet tall, was genuinely ill, for the moment it did not show. He sounded as mentally alert as anyone on trial for his life could be when he told Scharper that of course he remembered him.

"Zander too," he added in his Austrian accent. "I don't know these other two or the woman."

Scharper explained quickly that Riordan and Laidlaw were friends, formerly British Free Corps; they'd discussed the necessity of using such individuals last year, before the war ended. The woman was not to be trusted; she was a hostage.

Kaltenbrunner had a thousand questions to ask. Scharper cut them off as politely as he could.

"Later, Herr Obergruppenführer. For the present we must hurry and get you out of here. Do you have street clothes?"

"No. The bastards took them away from me."

"No matter. A dressing gown?"

"In the closet."

"Excellent. You'll be a little cold for a while, but cold is better than the alternative."

"You have a plan?"

"We originally intended bandaging your head and taking you through the front entrance in a wheelchair.

The blizzard, however, is an unforeseen bonus. We won't risk the front. We'll use the fire escape. The snow will cover our movements.''

Kaltenbrunner was on his feet now, towering above the others, attempting to compose himself. Although something about his manner chilled the blood, his voice nevertheless held a note of incredulity when he asked if they really had come to free him.

"Of course," answered Scharper. "Did you ever doubt it?"

"At times. I expected someone to try when I was in the hospital before."

"We were not ready and the other place was too well guarded."

Kaltenbrunner permitted himself a glimmer of a smile.

"And doubtless you were hoping to find all the fragments before the tenth, which would have made my rescue superfluous and your risk unnecessary. It's as I thought, Scharper, precisely as I thought."

And too close to the truth as far as Scharper was concerned.

"Quickly now," he urged, handing Kaltenbrunner his robe. "There's no time to waste."

Nor was there, for even as Scharper was speaking they all heard the wail of klaxons two stories below, leaving no one in doubt that the Americans had at last figured out the Palace of Justice strategem.

"You seem to have waited too long, Scharper," said Kaltenbrunner calmly.

"Ask him for the number," prompted Riordan, talking as though Kaltenbrunner were not present. "Ask him for the number contained in the fragments."

Not bothering to don his robe and seemingly in no hurry, Kaltenbrunner shot Riordan a look that would have withered lesser men.

"You'll hear no number from my lips, whoever you are. Do you think I'm a fool? The information I possess is my sole remaining bargaining counter with the Allies. I would have preferred to be free so that we could all enjoy the fruits of earlier labors, but don't underestimate my intelligence or think captivity has softened my brain. You wouldn't be here now if you had solved the riddle of the Canaris fragments.''

Gesturing Zander to check the corridor, Scharper noted with dismay the use of the perfect tense—"I would have preferred to be free."

"With respect, Herr Obergruppenführer," he said, "your release is of paramount importance to those of us who served under you in the SS. As you point out, the information in your possession could be used to bargain with the Allies. Even if we had successfully recovered the fragments, there would have been nothing to prevent you from telling your story to the *Amis* before the tenth."

Kaltenbrunner shook his head.

"You're a plausible individual, Scharper. You always were. I do not, however, need a crystal ball to read your mind. If you had obtained the number, the documents would have disappeared. The Americans would then have thought they were listening to the ravings of a madman looking for ways to save his neck. They'd have had to take my word that what I was telling them was the truth." He smiled grimly. "I do not think they're inclined to take my word on that or any other matter."

"Corridor's clear," called Zander from the door.

"We've no time for all this shit," growled Riordan, addressing Scharper. "If he won't tell us, he won't. Let's get him the hell out of here."

Kaltenbrunner refused to move. Instead of putting on the robe, he allowed it to fall to the floor and sat on the edge of the bed.

"You're too late. You don't stand a chance of getting me out of the building alive. Do you really believe they won't have thought of the fire escapes? You've missed your opportunity by ten minutes."

Scharper was sweating now.

"Herr Obergruppenführer, you *must* come with us. The blizzard will give us cover. We have transport in the forecourt, where Standartenführer Sternberg is waiting. But we must hurry."

"So, Sternberg is still alive."

"He is—and anxious for your safety."

Kaltenbrunner snorted with laughter.

"The only thing Sternberg was ever anxious about was his own skin. And you mistake your man if you think he won't make a run for it as soon as he senses danger."

Kaltenbrunner wiped a fleck of spittle from his chin and repeated that the opportunity to flee had gone.

"The Americans would like nothing better than to shoot me while trying to escape, leaving them one less German in the dock, the one they fear most. Because when I give my testimony, Scharper, heads will roll. Allied heads. I have irrefutable proof that some of the most respected businessmen in the United States covertly cooperated with industrial leaders of the Third Reich throughout the war."

"You will not be permitted to give that in evidence, Herr Obergruppenführer," said Scharper.

"You think not? Wait and see. In any event, I have something else the Allies would be pleased to hear about, do I not? Had you arrived half an hour earlier none of it would have mattered. I spent months feigning my illness and weeks contriving to be treated in a civilian hospital from where I could be rescued. But you're too late, Scharper. I must look out for myself now."

Scharper stared at Riordan, horrified. Kaltenbrunner was planning to stay behind and sell out to the Allies in the hope of beating the gallows. Whether he could prove collaboration between German and US industrialists was of no concern to Battle Group Sternberg. The key to the Canaris fragments was.

In the distance Riordan thought he could hear shouting. They had to move. If Himmler's deputy would neither accompany them nor talk to them, neither would he be talking to anyone else.

He cocked his revolver.

"We'll have to kill him."

When it sank in, Scharper's reaction was not at all what Riordan expected.

"You can't."

Riordan turned the Webley on Scharper.

"What do you mean, can't? With him dead we've still got three days. Leaving him alive to talk to the Americans means we're finished now."

Scharper was reaching for his own sidearm, a Colt .45 automatic. Kaltenbrunner was the senior SS general alive, the natural successor to the Führer and Himmler. There were thousands, perhaps tens of thousands, of former SS men still at liberty, some in South America, others in Germany and elsewhere in Europe. One day, when their so-called crimes were forgotten, they would all meet again. Heinrich Scharper did not want to be known as the man who participated in the killing of the keeper of the flame, in spite of what was at stake. They had a few more minutes. They'd get Kaltenbrunner out somehow.

Riordan's eyes were on the Colt, which Scharper was beginning to point in his direction. Whether the German intended using it, he didn't wait to find out. *Christ,* he thought, *they're all mad,* and shot the SS major in the chest. The bullet's impact hurled Scharper backward as though he were a discarded rag doll.

The noise of the explosion was so deafening and totally unexpected that momentarily everyone was shocked into immobility—except for Kaltenbrunner. While Scharper clutched his chest and gazed with utter disbelief at the blood oozing through his fingers, Kaltenbrunner sprang from the bed and made for the bathroom, moving with astonishing speed for a man of his size. He kicked the door shut and engaged the lock. Too late, Riordan spun around and fired a couple of shots after him.

With Laidlaw temporarily rooted to the spot and a thunderstruck Zander bending over Scharper, the path to the corridor was now clear. Hannah seized her opportunity, realizing she would never get a better one. While Riordan strode over to the bathroom, intending to shoot off the lock and dispatch Kaltenbrunner once and for all, she raced for the passage, slamming the door behind her, and ran toward the central staircase. Before she was halfway there, the swing doors were thrown open and a posse of uniformed men charged through, headed by Quinlan, Hadleigh, and Gene Masterson. Behind her she heard the sound of gunfire.

"Get down!" screamed Quinlan.

From their position in the forecourt, Sternberg and the others in the two Jeeps had also heard the klaxons in the distance and observed the arrival of the convoy's vanguard.

"Christ," swore Hallam, "how the hell did they get here so fast? What do we do now?"

Sternberg counseled patience, though inwardly he was far from calm.

"The Americans must know we have Jeeps. Any vehicle traveling against the general flow of traffic will be stopped and its occupants questioned. In a few more minutes the forecourt will be chaos. We'll move then. Fortunately visibility is still poor."

"What about Kaltenbrunner, Riordan, and the rest?"

"If they're not here in five minutes, they won't be coming."

Neither Quinlan nor Hadleigh was familiar with the geography of the hospital. Masterson, however, had conducted an interrogation of a dying German civilian on the premises several months before. He recalled that there were fire escapes on each floor and at least four exits including the main doors. Although most of the convoy was still held up at the bridge, they had sufficient numbers to cordon off the building.

Leaving Max to organize and deploy the ground troops, Hadleigh led the way through the main entrance, followed by Quinlan, Masterson, and half a dozen GIs. Without breaking stride he demanded the location of Kaltenbrunner's room from the startled porter, pulling the man along by the lapel when he had difficulty finding his voice. Valuable seconds were wasted while the elderly German stammered out the required information. In answer to Masterson, the porter added that four men in a mixture of British-American uniforms and a woman dressed like a nurse had entered the hospital a few minutes earlier.

They reached the second floor and pushed through the swing doors in time to see Hannah racing toward them. As Quinlan bellowed at her to get down, three figures emerged one after the other from a room at the far end of the corridor. Two of them, one armed with a rifle, dropped into a crouch and began shooting, while the third fumbled with the bar that opened the fire-escape exit.

Flat against the wall, Quinlan shouted not to return the fire for fear of hitting Hannah. He saw her fall and, unable to contain his anxiety any longer, ran toward her, oblivious to the bullets ricocheting off the walls around him. He was crouched over her within seconds, shielding her body with his own. He winced involuntarily as behind him the GIs discharged a fusillade over his head. When the shooting stopped and he looked up, the last of the fugitives was going through the heavy iron door, closing it behind him.

To his relief Hannah seemed unhurt. She had simply fainted, her mind unable to compete with the bedlam around her.

While Masterson went into Kaltenbrunner's room,

Hadleigh ordered one of the GIs to return to the ground floor, find Max Judd, and inform him that three men were making a run for it by way of the western fire escape. He instructed the remaining GIs to stay where they were.

"No point in charging through after them in case they're waiting for us on the other side. They're not going any place."

Which was not strictly speaking true. Although outside on the catwalk none of them could see for more than a few yards in any direction, Riordan suspected, as Kaltenbrunner had done, that the Americans would have the fire escapes covered. The time had come to look after number one.

"We still stand a chance if we move fast," he said, his head bent against the snow. "You first, Harry," he added to Laidlaw. "Once you're on the ground, make for the road and come into the forecourt as though you've just arrived. If Sternberg didn't get out when he heard the klaxons, it's my guess he's where we left him. If not, it's every man for himself. I'll see you at the Jeeps. Move it, for Chrissake," he snapped.

Still shaken by the experience of being shot at, though the fusillade had been aimed high to avoid the woman, Laidlaw hesitated. He was a follower, not a leader; fine in a pack but inadequate alone. After a moment's indecision, however, he nodded and started down. Soon he was lost in the snow.

"Now you," Riordan told Zander. "I'll bring up the rear in case they try to break through the door."

For Riordan to have knocked Zander unconscious and pushed him from the catwalk would have been a simple matter, except it did not suit the Englishman's plans. He needed confusion on the ground, and Laidlaw by himself would not create enough.

"Do you go next or do I?" he demanded, when the German seemed reluctant to move. "If you don't want the second spot, I'll take it. You can be tail-end Charlie."

That did not appeal to Zander. Besides, he wanted to report to Sternberg that Riordan had shot and perhaps killed Scharper. If Riordan told the story first, it would come out differently.

Without a word he slung his rifle over his shoulder and followed Laidlaw.

Riordan waited until he disappeared before starting upward, using the fire escape to climb to the fourth floor. At the third he heard rifle shots followed immediately by the unmistakable chatter of automatic weapons. So much for Zander and Laidlaw.

At fourth-floor level he levered up the iron bar of the fire-escape door and stepped into the hospital. He could hear the sound of raised voices and running feet coming from below. The corridor here, however, was quite empty.

Pausing only to holster his pistol and brush as much snow as possible from his jacket, he made his way toward the central staircase. He reached the first floor without incident, but was then confronted by three GIs running up the stairs toward him.

"Check the third-floor east wing," he improvised. "Major Hadleigh thinks some of them might have slipped through that way."

"Right, Captain." They did not give him a second glance. They had all heard of the Limey officer on the team.

The entrance lobby was a madhouse, with more GIs —the bridge now unblocked—arriving by the minute. White-coated doctors together with nurses and administrative staff were trying to make some sense out of the tumult. No one had time to answer their questions. One of the doctors, a German instructing a member of his staff to find the officer in charge, was older and seemed more senior than the others. Riordan button-holed him.

"I need your help," he said quietly, feigning a poor

German accent. He coolly walked the man away from the group. "Do you speak English?"

The German said he did. "What is happening?" he added. "Why are all these soldiers here?"

"There's been an attempt on the life of your most notorious guest."

"Kaltenbrunner?"

"Kaltenbrunner. Whoever tried to kill him may still be in the building. We have to make certain all the exits are covered. Is there a back way out?"

"Of course. Through the kitchens."

Riordan was about to ask the doctor to show him the route when he realized he was making a grave mistake. Hadleigh would have posted men on the kitchen exit by now. Anyone trying to use it would arouse suspicion. He had to be bold or nothing. No one was taking the slightest notice of him in the lobby.

"Perhaps you could show me all the exits from the outside," he said. "I want to be sure we've men on each and that the ground-floor windows are covered. I'm sorry you're likely to get damp, but this is an emergency."

Riordan did not allow the doctor's mild objections to deter him. Keeping his head down and talking complete nonsense about security, he propelled the man across the lobby, where the main entrance was guarded by two PFCs carrying carbines. Riordan made for the younger of the pair, who was plainly unwilling to prevent a British captain from leaving the building. Clearly this was not the enemy he had been briefed to detain.

Without breaking off his monologue to the doctor, Riordan grabbed the PFC by the arm before he could ask for identification and ordered him to accompany them.

Outside pandemonium reigned, with vehicles arriving every few seconds. Riordan was reassured by the sheer numbers. If Sternberg had not panicked and left when the first of the trucks appeared, he would not be trying to get out now.

The storm was breaking and visibility was up to sixty or seventy yards when Riordan saw the Jeeps where he had left them. Telling the PFC to go with the doctor and make sure all exits and low-level windows were covered before reporting back to the lobby, Riordan strolled across to Sternberg's Jeep and climbed inside. He indicated with a slight movement of his hand that Granger and Flisk were to remain in their own vehicle for the present.

"What happened?" asked Sternberg grimly. "We heard the shots from here."

Riordan told him in as few words as possible about Kaltenbrunner's reaction to the rescue party, how he had refused to accompany them or reveal the number contained in the Canaris fragments. Zander, Laidlaw, and Scharper were either dead or in custody. Riordan did not bother to add that he had shot Scharper, nor that, if Laidlaw and Zander were dead, he was the one who had sent them to their graves.

"I was lucky to get this far myself," he ended, all the while peering through the windshield for signs of anyone taking too close an interest in them.

"What about the woman?" asked Sternberg.

"She escaped in the confusion. I fired at her and saw her fall. I don't know whether I hit her."

"If she's alive, she'll tell the *Amis* about the Fürth house."

"Of course."

"There's always the one in Zirndorf," put in Hallam.

"I think it's a bit late in the day for that," said Riordan. "Kaltenbrunner left no room for doubt about his intentions. He's going to tell the Americans what he knows in an effort to save his neck."

"You should have killed him," grunted Sternberg, ever the realist.

Riordan debated whether to say he had tried to do just that. Eventually he decided to keep his mouth shut.

"Perhaps I should. Anyway, it's of no consequence now. What is, is what we do next. In my opinion we should get out of Nuremberg and move the stuff. We'll have to make the best deal we can, as fast as we can."

"I'd settle for getting away from this frigging hospital," muttered Hallam. "The snow's thinning. Before long someone's going to get curious about why we're sitting here while everyone else is running his ass off."

"Maybe this is your chance," said Riordan, pointing to where a couple of brighter than average MPs were trying to unsnarl the traffic jam in front of the hospital by creating a two-way stream, directing trucks off the forecourt as soon as they had off-loaded the troops. "Join the tail end." He signaled Granger in the adjacent Jeep to follow Hallam's lead.

Inside the hospital, Hadleigh received word that only two men had descended the fire escape; the third was still missing. Belatedly, the American major gave orders to stop and search all vehicles leaving the grounds. But by this time the remnants of Battle Group Sternberg were on the road out of Nuremberg.

TWENTY-ONE

~~~~~~

NUREMBERG
January 7, 1946

ALTHOUGH SEVERAL HOURS would elapse before they
learned from a despondent PFC that he had been duped
by the phony British captain, toward midday news filtered through about the two Jeeps leaving the forecourt
shortly after 11 A.M., vehicles that no one could account
for. While he lacked positive proof regarding the occupants' identities, Hadleigh had no doubt that the arriving SS and British Free Corps men had slipped through
the net.

With Colonel Masterson chairing the meeting in a
first-floor office made available to them by the hospital's chief administrator, Hadleigh, Quinlan and Petrov took stock of the latest developments. On the
plus side, Kaltenbrunner's three guards and his doctor
were in no danger and would recover after treatment.

Hannah Wolz was unharmed though considerably shaken after her ordeal. Since her captors had not intended her to survive the raid, they had not seen fit to blindfold her going to and from the Fürth backup house. She was therefore able to give Hadleigh its exact location. He had already dispatched a search team, but he did not expect to find anything. He was right. The birds had flown.

Of the two men shot at the foot of the fire escape, one (who would later be identified as Laidlaw) had died instantly; the other (Zander) had head and chest wounds and was not expected to live through the afternoon.

The man found shot in Kaltenbrunner's room had been lucky. The bullet had ricocheted off his fourth rib and passed cleanly through his body, missing the vital organs. He was in the process of being patched up and would be available for interrogation within the hour. Hopefully he would prove more cooperative than Kaltenbrunner.

Earlier, after breaking down the bathroom door, Masterson had found the Obergruppenführer curled up in a corner, shivering and whimpering. Not until he fully realized that his "rescuers" had vanished and that he was not to be executed out of hand or in any other manner mistreated did he recover his composure with an alacrity that was truly astonishing, assuming an arrogant, dictatorial posture and refusing to answer any questions. Within minutes, however, he had changed his mind, and in the presence of Quinlan, Hadleigh and Petrov announced, hinting that he had much to impart, that he would make a formal statement to the intelligence colonel providing he received certain guarantees.

He was being charged, he said, on three counts: crimes against peace, war crimes, and crimes against humanity. He had no scruples about saying he thought he could beat the first charge, that of planning, initiating, and waging a war of aggression, since he was too junior in rank at the beginning to have been privy to the higher counsel chambers of the Third Reich. While that charge could therefore remain on the indictment, he wanted the other two dropped. In exchange (which would be tantamount to a reprieve), he would tell the Americans anything they wished to know.

The conversation was conducted in German and Petrov spluttered with indignation throughout, interrupting frequently to declare that no deal could be made with war criminals without incurring the wrath of the Soviet people and government. So vehement did his objections become, ruining any chance that Kaltenbrunner could be persuaded to talk without concessions, that Masterson was compelled to pull him to one side and remind him sharply that he was in the US zone. The United States was not in the habit of exchanging clemency for information, unlike the Soviet Union who shot or hanged or turned over for trial ex-Nazis only if they proved uncooperative or useless. Current rumor in the French, British, and American zones suggested that Gestapo chief Heinrich Mueller, a known admirer of the Russian NKVD, was in Soviet hands and being treated leniently, his past sins forgiven in this new world of *realpolitik*.

Showing obvious signs of embarrassment, Petrov denied the allegation categorically while conceding that he might have been hasty in impugning the United States' integrity. He had not meant to imply that Colonel Masterson would accept Kaltenbrunner's terms.

Masterson did not inform the Russian that the decision was not his to make. While he had little doubt what the answer would be, he had a duty to pass on Kaltenbrunner's offer and let the commanding general decide what to do.

While Hadleigh summoned guards from the corridor, Quinlan brought up the subject of the fragments. In the excitement everyone had forgotten about them.

"We know about Tristan da Cunha," he said.

After seven months in captivity, Kaltenbrunner's

complexion was pasty enough. Even so, he grew paler.

"I don't know what you're talking about," he grunted, averting his eyes, obviously lying. The trouble was, *they* didn't know what they were talking about.

It was the implications of Tristan da Cunha that Masterson, Hadleigh, Quinlan, and Petrov were discussing in the first-floor office as lunchtime approached. Masterson would have preferred to exclude Petrov, but the Russian would have suspected underhanded dealings and cried conspiracy had he been asked to leave.

The snowstorm had blown itself out for the moment, and as a matter of priority Third Army engineers had traced the damaged telephone cables and repaired them. Unwilling to leave the scene until he heard from his superiors, Masterson had scribbled a summary of Kaltenbrunner's proposals on a page of diary and entrusted Max Judd with its delivery to General Lucian K. Truscott. Max had returned ten minutes earlier with the news that General Truscott had been in conference when he arrived; his adjutant, however, had promised to hand the envelope to the general at the first available opportunity. It should not be long before they heard the outcome of Kaltenbrunner's bid for immunity.

Quinlan was repeating his assertion, with which no one was arguing, that Sternberg's attempt to rescue Kaltenbrunner was because the SS general had the key to the Canaris fragments, when Max knocked and came in for the second time. Apologizing for the intrusion, he said that Fräulein Wolz wanted to see Major Quinlan —right away, if that were possible.

Quinlan excused himself.

"Is she all right?" he asked anxiously, when he and Max were outside.

"Sure. The doctor gave her a pill which will put her out for around twenty-four hours. She wanted to talk to you before it takes effect."

"Thanks. Where is she?"

"Third floor east, the door with a guard on it. I put a man there just to be on the safe side."

She was lying among a mountain of pillows, staring out the window. She looked beautiful and fragile and still a little scared as he came in. Taking the chair next to the bed, he resisted the temptation to reach out and touch her hands, which were lying on top of the covers. He felt awkward. He hadn't seen her in private since taking her to the Sündersbühl house on their return from Munich, which seemed a lifetime ago.

"In England we usually bring flowers or grapes when we visit hospitals," he said lamely. "I'm sorry I arrive empty-handed."

"It doesn't matter. Is it all over now?"

"Not quite. There's still a lot we don't know. How do you feel?" he added, giving himself a mental kick for asking such a damn-fool question. How the hell did he expect her to feel?

"Sleepy." She gave him a tiny smile. "The doctor made me take a pill. I told him I didn't want one until I'd seen you, but he insisted. It was very strange. He didn't recognize me, although I remembered him from the war years. He seemed quite surprised when I told him I used to work here."

"Thank God you did. It probably saved your life."

"I know. I have a lot to be thankful for."

She yawned and blinked. He had only a couple of minutes to say what he wanted to. God knows when he'd find another opportunity or the nerve.

"Look," he began, "about your father . . ."

She stopped him by placing one of her hands on his.

"You don't have to say anything," she whispered softly. "You weren't to blame for his death. He was a sick man. He could have died anytime. He knew it, I knew it. Even poor Ilse knew it."

"I was to blame," said Quinlan, forcing himself to look at her. "I'd like it to be different, but all the wishing in the world won't change the facts. I just don't . . ." He fumbled for the words, which came out in a rush. "I just hope it won't always be something that stands between us."

"It won't. I won't let it."

She was forgiving him, he realized, and perhaps there was more in her words than forgiveness. He tried to mumble his thanks. She shook her head as vigorously as she could in her sedated condition.

"You don't have to thank me. I've had a lot of time to think in the last twenty-four hours. I was convinced I was going to be killed, perhaps assaulted and tortured before they murdered me. I was frightened, very frightened. The only thing that kept me from going out of my mind was the belief that you would find a way to free me. Not Max or Major Hadleigh—you. Can you understand that?"

Quinlan said he thought he could.

"You'd better sleep now."

"I'll have to. I can hardly keep my eyes open. Will you be here when I wake up?"

"I won't be far away."

"Good," she murmured, "good."

When she was breathing evenly, he gently removed his hand. He wanted to remain with her, allow the peace and tranquility of the room to wash over him, retreat into a world that was as far removed as possible from the one that awaited him outside. But he knew he was being foolish. There would be a tomorrow. With luck there always was.

He found Max waiting for him in the corridor.

"I didn't want to barge in," said the American, "but word came through a minute ago from General Truscott. We make no deals with Kaltenbrunner. Not that it matters. The other one, the one who was shot in Kaltenbrunner's room, is sitting up. He tells us his name is Scharper and he's ready to sing like a bird."

*   *   *

Any loyalty Scharper might have had to Battle Group Sternberg evaporated when Riordan shot him. But more than that he remembered Kaltenbrunner saying he intended bargaining with the Americans, which would render what he, Heinrich Scharper, had to tell them superfluous.

So he talked. In the presence of Masterson, Quinlan, Hadleigh, Petrov, Max Judd, and a tape recorder, he told the entire incredible story. Some of the events he had witnessed personally; some were hearsay, some conjecture. Nevertheless, his audience listened in stunned silence from the moment he started to speak.

TWENTY-TWO

~~~~~~

FLOSSENBÜRG CAMP:
GERMAN-CZECH BORDER
April 6–9, 1945

IN THE BEGINNING (said Scharper) no one was quite
sure what part, if any, Canaris had played in the July
Plot against Hitler's life. The little admiral denied any
sort of participation and many people were inclined to
believe him. Had he not, after all, sent a telegram to the
Führer shortly after the explosion, congratulating him
on his providential escape? That he numbered several of
the known conspirators among his close friends was not
in dispute, and his arrest and detention were due less to
his relationship with Claus von Stauffenberg, who
planted the bomb in Hitler's conference hut, than to the
SS which, now that it had control of the Abwehr, was
paying off old scores.

Since arriving among the barbed wire, watchtowers,
and endless rows of huts of Flossenbürg on February 7,

1945, Canaris had received the same treatment as other "special category" prisoners. They were permanently shackled and allowed no correspondence. They were, however, adequately fed and exercised in order to remain fit for further interrogation. In Canaris's case, the SS was not convinced the admiral was the friend of the regime he protested to be.

The Flossenbürg guards knew that special category inmates regularly communicated with confinees in adjacent cells by tapping on the walls, using not Morse but a simple code that reduced the alphabet to twenty-five letters, omitting J. Canaris in cell 22 was no exception. He held long if limited "conversations" with the occupant of cell 21, Mathieson Lunding, a former Danish cavalry captain and a member of Danish military intelligence.

Although they had hidden listening devices in each cell and knew the code, the SS turned a blind eye to the exchanges in the hope of hearing something of value. But all they learned from Canaris's transmissions to Lunding were details of his interrogations to date, which they knew anyway, and that he expected to survive the war. Which he might well have done if his diaries, long hidden in a safe in the underground shelters of Camp Zeppelin, in Zossen, had not been found and passed on to RSHA chief Ernst Kaltenbrunner. At the customary midday conference in the Reich Chancellery the following day, Kaltenbrunner produced the diaries, which not only implicated Canaris with the July conspirators but also proved he had been in treasonable correspondence with the head of British MI 6, Stewart Menzies, as long ago as 1942.

Hitler gave immediate orders for Canaris to be killed. Kaltenbrunner objected; he was renowned for his dislike of nonjudicial murders. The lawyer in him wanted everything signed and sealed before delivery. Thus a drumhead court-martial was arranged for Flossenbürg on April 8.

Canaris received the news of the discovery of his

diaries and his impending trial (with only one possible verdict) from the camp commandant on April 6. Instead of protesting his innocence or accepting his fate, he asked to be allowed to send a message to Kaltenbrunner. When informed that that was out of the question, he warned the commandant that other heads would roll if Kaltenbrunner was not told immediately that the Zossen diaries were not the only ones in existence and that he, Canaris, knew all about Alt Aussee.

Concluding he had nothing to lose, the commandant relayed the message by phone to Berlin, expecting no reply. He was therefore astonished to receive a telegram within the hour stating that Kaltenbrunner himself and several aides would be coming to Flossenbürg on the seventh. However, Allied air raids and other urgent business in the capital combined to prevent his departure for twenty-four hours, and not until early evening on the eighth did he arrive by road from Berlin.

For the number-two man in the SS, the motorcade was unbelievably tiny. Later the camp commandant deduced that Kaltenbrunner had not wanted to publicize his visit more than necessary. Flanked by a dozen motorcycle outriders, his personal retinue consisted of just four men, one of whom drove the staff car. These were introduced as Standartenführer Sternberg, Sturmbannführer Scharper, Oberscharführer Flisk, and Unterscharführer Zander. The two NCOs, Flisk and Zander, were to be taken on the camp's strength, their presence recorded. Ever a stickler for doing things by the book, Kaltenbrunner wanted no documents turning up in the future saying that Canaris was interrogated by individuals who were not part of the Flossenbürg staff. His own visit was not to be logged. Neither were the names of Sternberg and Scharper to appear.

They saw Canaris in his cell. For the time being Lunding and the occupant of cell 23 were removed to another part of the compound, and the hidden listening device in cell 22 neutralized. Extra chairs and a table were brought in and Canaris's shackles removed. Kalten-brunner invited him to sit.

Round-shouldered and only five feet three inches tall, Canaris had never been an imposing figure to look at; nor had the months in captivity done anything to en-hance his physical appearance. When he spoke he was inclined to lisp.

Kaltenbrunner wasted no time getting down to busi-ness.

"What's all this nonsense about Alt Aussee and other diaries?" he wanted to know.

"Hardly nonsense, Herr Obergruppenführer, or you would not be here."

Canaris glanced nervously at the quartet who made up Kaltenbrunner's entourage. He knew the two of-ficers by sight and name from the days when he com-manded the Abwehr; the NCOs' faces were unfamiliar. They were typical SS, however. He had no doubt they were on hand to provide the muscle if the interrogation did not go according to plan.

"I also thought we would be talking in private," he added politely.

"This is as private as I care to make it, you treacher-ous bastard," snarled Kaltenbrunner.

Canaris seemed faintly amused at being described as a traitor.

"I'm not sure the Führer would regard your activities and those of your group as less than treasonable if he knew about them."

"Explain yourself."

Canaris chose his words carefully.

"The repository of looted art treasures in the Alt Aussee salt mine is what I'm talking about. These treasures were to form the basis of the finest collection in the world after the war, in the Führer's hometown Linz. Reichsminister Speer has already designed the building.

"Of course such a collection can no longer exist

because Germany has lost the war. If we had won, however, there would have been on display—and I will catalog only a few for the sake of brevity—the Ghent altarpiece by the Van Eycks, the "Portrait of the Artist in his Studio" by Vermeer, the Dierick Bouts altarpiece from Louvain, and Michelangelo's masterpiece, the marble "Madonna" from the Church of Notre Dame in Bruges. There would have been Titians, Raphaels, and Brueghels from the Naples Museum, canvases from the Rothschild, Gutmann, and Mannheimer collections, to say nothing of works by Rubens, Reynolds, Lippi, Palma Vecchio, Frans Hals, and others too numerous to mention. According to my information there are almost seven thousand paintings stored in the Alt Aussee mine, of which at least five thousand could be reliably described as Old Masters. The Führermuseum would have been the envy of the world."

Canaris paused for effect, his eyes never leaving Kaltenbrunner's pockmarked face.

"Naturally," he said slowly, "only a handful of people would have known that almost three hundred of the exhibits were fakes, painted by German, French, and Belgian art forgers in 1942 and 1943. The individuals concerned are no longer around to testify. I understand the SS had them executed when the work was done."

The long silence that followed was eventually broken by Kaltenbrunner.

"You have nothing to sell, Canaris, not to the Führer. He has known from the beginning what we were doing. We had his full approval. You're right about the forgeries, though I'd give a year of my life to learn how you found out. You're wrong that they would have been displayed at Linz. Had the war gone otherwise—and I do not accept for a moment that all is irrevocably lost—the real artworks would have hung in the Führermuseum. Now we have different ideas."

Canaris studied the giant Kaltenbrunner carefully.

"Which I must assume means ransoming the originals to their rightful owners at some future date. Secretly, of course. I doubt the present political climate in the world would tolerate individuals or governments doing business with what will remain of the Third Reich. I know where the real paintings are, naturally. As head of the Abwehr I made it my business to know. You can move them—though that won't be easy at this stage of the war. Neither will it do you any good. Once word gets out that part of the Alt Aussee repository is faked, you will find no buyers for the originals."

"And how," sneered Kaltenbrunner, "will word get out?"

But Canaris refused to be hurried.

"Let me see if I have this correct. You, Sternberg, Scharper, and a handful of others—the numbers necessarily small because of the secrecy needed—have stored fake paintings among the real ones in Alt Aussee. I freely admit I do not know exactly how many, or the identity of the works involved, but that's neither here nor there. When Alt Aussee is overrun by the Allies and the treasures recovered, what will they find? Why, with great relief they'll find, intact, priceless works of art from all over Europe. They will have no reason to suspect that booty so carefully concealed is anything but genuine. The forgers you employed were of the highest caliber, and any slight imperfections will be put down to hasty transportation or inadequate storage conditions. After examination and cataloging, the works will be returned to their proper owners. Afterward, you or one of your representatives will approach each individual or museum and tell them that what they have on their walls is worthless. You will offer to return the real painting for a price. If they refuse to do business, you will threaten to destroy the genuine article. If they dare talk to the authorities, it will become common knowledge that what they are displaying is counterfeit. And what collector would want that known? There are vast sums of money at stake and also the pride of ownership. Whether the ransom you receive is to be used for some absurd conception of a Fourth Reich or merely to line your own pockets I neither know nor care.''

Kaltenbrunner reached into his tunic pocket for his cigarette case. Scharper dutifully sprang forward with a light. Within the confines of the narrow cell the smoke was overpowering, however, and Kaltenbrunner soon ground out the cigarette with his heel.

''So,'' he said, trying to control his rage, ''you possess information I would rather not be made public. The fact remains that you are here, in Flossenbürg, incommunicado.''

''You underestimate me, Herr Obergruppenführer. My message to Berlin was that not only did I know about Alt Aussee but that other diaries exist apart from those found at Zossen. To be precise, they are not diaries but several pages of notes, setting out my findings and deposited in a Geneva bank. The number of the account is known only to me.''

''And with you dead,'' leered Kaltenbrunner, ''the account stays closed forever.''

''I'm happy to say you're wrong.'' Canaris gave the SS general a nervous smile. ''Long ago I devised a method that will enable several of my junior officers, without them presently knowing the number, to open the account should anything befall me. If I die, the plan goes into operation immediately. Even if they fail for one reason or another, the bank has instructions to release the documents to the world on January tenth of the year following the war's end—which will be next year, 1946, unless I am misjudging events; two years to the day since I made my trip to Switzerland.''

''You double-dealing bastard!'' bellowed Kaltenbrunner. He backhanded Canaris across the face, knocking him to the cell floor.

Alarmed, Sternberg and Scharper stepped forward, gesturing Zander and Flisk to help Canaris to his feet.

For Kaltenbrunner to succumb to one of his infamous rages would get them nowhere.

"Herr Obergruppenführer," said Sternberg gently, "perhaps we should hear what sort of bargain Admiral Canaris wishes to make."

"I'll see him hanging from a gallows before I strike a bargain with him!" screeched Kaltenbrunner. "The perfidious swine has probably told Menzies and half of MI Six what he's done."

Canaris wiped the blood from his mouth with his sleeve. Behind him, Zander and Flisk stood ready to do their master's bidding.

"Talk," said Kaltenbrunner, calming down only after a visible effort. "You haven't brought us all the way here to tell us how clever you've been. Let's hear your proposition."

"It's very simple," lisped Canaris. "In the first place, neither Menzies nor anyone else knows what is contained in the Swiss documents. I could hardly expect the British to keep such information to themselves, and that would defeat my purpose. Second, no specific signature is required to withdraw the documents from the bank. Anyone giving the correct number can do so. Third, you will be given that number in exchange for my freedom and that of my family, a sum of money to be agreed upon, and a passage via one of the SS escape lines to South America."

"Out of the question. The Führer has ordered your execution."

"Without a trial?"

"There will be a trial." Kaltenbrunner looked at his watch. "Prosecutor Huppenkothen and SS Judge Thorbeck will be arriving shortly. There can, of course, be only one verdict."

"Then I regret your little scheme becomes stillborn. On January tenth next year, or earlier if my men get to Geneva before, the world at large will learn what you have done and your intentions. You will find few takers for your proposition then, even if Allied troops do not locate the cache beforehand.''

Kaltenbrunner nodded his head as if coming to a decision. ''You have been your usual meticulous self, Canaris,'' he said, his voice almost friendly, ''except for one fact. Your plan contains a flaw. As we now know that you are the only living soul, for the moment, who possesses the number of the account, do you think we can't force it out of you?''

At a slight hand signal from Kaltenbrunner, Zander and Flisk advanced on Canaris and proceeded to beat him with their fists and the short rubber clubs they carried. Experts at their trade, they aimed their blows where they would cause the most pain—the groin and the kidneys—without rendering him unconscious. From the far side of the cell Kaltenbrunner, Sternberg, and Scharper watched impassively.

After five minutes Kaltenbrunner called a halt and asked whether Canaris was ready to talk. His face a mask of anguish but his spirit unbroken, the admiral shook his head.

Kaltenbrunner was about to sanction even harsher treatment when a faint rapping was heard on the cell door. From the corridor a tremulous voice begged that the interruption be excused and announced that Huppenkothen and Thorbeck had just arrived. The judge and prosecutor wanted to know when the *Kriegsgericht,* the court-martial, could commence. Judge Thorbeck had orders to report directly by telephone to the Führer when the trial was over and the verdict delivered.

''Tell them we'll be a few more minutes,'' said Kaltenbrunner.

Scharper opened the cell door a fraction and relayed the message.

Kaltenbrunner waved Zander and Flisk to one side. Canaris was crumpled against a wall, bleeding from the nose and mouth, the result of a wayward blow.

''Well?'' demanded the Obergruppenführer.

Canaris mumbled that he had nothing to say. His life depended upon remaining silent. They would certainly kill him once they had the number.

"We're in serious trouble if he holds out much longer," whispered Scharper to Sternberg, aware that Hitler would be waiting to hear from Thorbeck.

Sternberg agreed. "If I may make a suggestion, Herr Obergruppenführer?"

"You may not make a suggestion," snapped Kaltenbrunner. He thought for a moment. "Did you pass on my orders that our interrogation of Canaris was not to be recorded or even listened to?"

Sternberg said he had.

"In that case," continued Kaltenbrunner, "go to the control room and see that all communications from this cell remain cut off until I instruct otherwise. I want no eavesdropping by the duty watchkeeper. Do it now," he concluded in a tone that discouraged argument.

Sternberg went out.

Kaltenbrunner told Scharper to find Huppenkothen and Thorbeck and inform them that the trial would not be delayed much longer.

"Take Zander and Flisk with you. I want to have a quiet word with Canaris. Close the door behind you."

In the passage, Scharper waved Zander and Flisk on ahead and waited by the cell door just long enough to overhear Kaltenbrunner try a different sort of threat.

"You mentioned your family, Canaris. Think of them. We know where your wife, Erika, is. Also your daughters, Eva and Brigitte. Consider them and what could happen to them. Do you want them in the cell next to yours here? Or taken to Ravensbrück? Either can be arranged."

Scharper heard a muffled sob before following Flisk and Zander up the corridor.

Kaltenbrunner sought them out twenty minutes later. Sternberg looked at him expectantly.

"Herr Obergruppenführer?"

"Find an officer named Langenhain, Oberstleutnant Langenhain, one of the Canaris's cronies from the old days. He's the key."

Sternberg's expression was one of bewilderment.

"But did Canaris talk, Herr Obergruppenführer? Did he give you the number?"

"He did. For the moment, however, I shall keep it to myself. The fewer who know it, the better. Now, do as I say. Get on the telephone and trace this man Langenhain. He is the ringleader of the junior officers Canaris mentioned earlier. Call me in Berlin when you have his whereabouts."

"*Call* you? Aren't we all returning to Berlin?"

"You're not, not for the moment. I must attend a conference later tonight, but I want you four to stay here. I want to know from eyewitnesses I can trust that Canaris is dead. You may return after the execution."

He acknowledged their straight-arm salutes, and left.

"The bastard," muttered Sternberg when Kaltenbrunner was out of earshot. "I don't trust him."

Scharper shrugged his shoulders disinterestedly.

"He still needs us. The number means nothing once the account is opened and the documents destroyed. I think we can safely leave him to look after that."

"Maybe so," said Sternberg thoughtfully, "but we'll do as he ordered and find Langenhain. That way, we'll all have the number."

Canaris was tried, found guilty, and sentenced to death. At 10 P.M. on the evening of April 8, the duty watchkeeper heard the admiral tapping out a signal to Lunding, now back in his cell. For the benefit of Sternberg and the others, who did not know the code, he translated the substance of the text.

"Nose broken at last interrogation. My time is up. I was not a traitor. Did my duty as a German. If you survive, remember me to my wife."

"I think we'd better make sure he sends no more

messages,'' said Sternberg. "You never know what they might comprise.''

At a little before dawn the following morning, Sternberg was aroused by the camp adjutant. Accompanied by Scharper, Zander, and Flisk, he went out into the courtyard.

There were five men due for execution, among them Pastor Dietrich Bonhoeffer. All of them were naked, and one by one they were herded across to the gallows and made to mount a small pair of steps. A noose was then placed about their necks and the steps kicked away.

Canaris in particular took a long time to die, his frail body writhing for what seemed, to the witnesses, an eternity. But before the sun was up SS physician Sturmbannführer Dr. Hermann Fischer pronounced life extinct.

TWENTY-THREE

~~~~~~

NUREMBERG
January 7, 1946

"WE CAUGHT UP with Langenhain around the middle of April last year," Scharper said to a hushed room.

He didn't seem to care that he was implicating himself in at least several killings, for the way he framed the sentence revealed that Langenhain was as dead as Canaris. Probably he thought that the murder of fellow Germans in wartime was not an indictable offense, or that he was in so deep that holding back anything could only worsen his predicament.

"Canaris had told him the name of the bank but not the account number. All he knew was that he had to contact Hauptmann Arndt in Nuremberg. He had seen Arndt, we established that much, but had not obtained from him the first fragment or the name of the man who had the second."

"Wait a minute, wait a minute, interrupted Hadleigh. "You're going too fast. What does that reference to the fragments mean?"

"Don't you know?" Scharper seemed surprised. "We knew you had two and guessed you might have all four."

"We do. They don't mean anything."

"They give the account number," explained Scharper. "When placed together, Canaris told Langenhain, they would depict a group of islands in the Atlantic. By referring to a large-scale world map the islands could be identified. The longitude and latitude of the chief island is the number that opens the account. We knew that much but not which island group and therefore not the number. There are too many in the Atlantic for guess work. The South Orkneys, the South Shetlands, the Falklands, Cape Verdes, Tristan da Cunha, Ascension, the Azores, and dozens more."

"Christ," muttered Quinlan. The solution was so simple once you had the key.

Masterson was still bemused.

"I don't understand why Canaris chose such a complicated code."

Neither did Scharper, though he was willing to hazard an opinion.

"Complicated it may have been, but he was gambling with his life. He couldn't just give the number to Langenhain with instructions to remove the documents if anything happened to him. Langenhain might have taken them while Canaris was still alive, which would have left the admiral with an empty deposit box if Kaltenbrunner had agreed to his terms. The stipulation was that Langenhain should only approach Arndt when he heard that Canaris was dead. However, we know for a fact that Arndt was contacted long before April ninth. Langenhain's explanation to us was that he believed Canaris to be dead once he was told the admiral had been transferred to Flossenbürg. Sternberg did not consider that to be the truth. He reckoned Langenhain panicked when the war was nearing its end and wanted to get his hands on whatever was in the account before the Allies overran Germany. He did not know the contents of the documents, of course, or even what the despoit box contained. Perhaps he thought it held money; there's no way of telling. Anyway, Arndt refused to hand over the first fragment until he was certain the admiral was dead because those were the instructions Canaris had given him.''

The sequence of events was becoming clearer now. If things had gone according to plan, Canaris owuld have bartered the Swiss bank number for his freedom and that of his family. If the SS killed him and his murder became public knowledge, Langenhain would have obtained the first fragment and the second name from Arndt, which would in turn have led to the second fragment and the third name until the picture was complete. Langenhain and his friends could then avenge Canaris's death by turning the documents over to the Allies, earning the gratitude of the conquerors, and ruining any ideas the SS might have had about ransoming the paintings.

"How do members of the British Free Corps fit in?" asked Quinlan.

"Originally to act as intermediaries between ourselves and the real owners of the artworks," answered Scharper. "We realized that after the war it would be difficult for any German to travel freely, and for those of us who had served in the SS, impossible. The same restrictions would not apply to men who spoke English as their native tongue, especially if they had nothing to lose anyway. When we learned of the fragments and that they had to be found before January tenth, the British Free Corps contingent became even more important. Having caught up with Langenhain, we had to find Arndt. Riordan and the others were in a better position to walk the streets of Nuremberg than the rest of us."

Petrov had a couple of questions.

"Why was it necessary to forge paintings? Why not remove two or three hundred of the more valuable works from Alt Aussee and store them in a separate place until the time came to ransom them?"

Scharper had three answers to that.

"In the first place," he explained, "all the works were carefully cataloged at Alt Aussee. We couldn't have taken even two or three without someone commenting on their absence. Each genuine painting had to be replaced by a forgery, which is where Kaltenbrunner's authority came in. Second, it is psychologically superior to approach someone who believes he has his own property back with the news that what he really has is a fake. Third, the Allies knew almost to the last item what had been looted. An individual, gallery, or museum could not have a blank wall one minute and an Old Master the next without someone asking where the painting came from. We're talking about collector's pieces, don't forget, most of which even the man on the street would recognize."

Petrov accepted that. Nevertheless, he still did not understand why Battle Group Sternberg needed the fragments. "Kaltenbrunner had the account number and presumably the name of the bank in April last year. He might have found it difficult to get into Switzerland at that stage of the war; he would not have found it impossible. Why were the papers not simply removed by one of you?"

Scharper grimaced at what was obviously a painful memory.

"Because Kaltenbrunner didn't tell us the number. Whenever Sternberg asked him, he always made some excuse for keeping it to himself. For that matter he said nothing of what transpired between himself and Canaris in the cell. Even now I don't know whether he forced Canaris to divulge the names of the four men holding the fragments or whether he was quite happy just to have Langenhain's name and the account number.

Shortly afterward he dropped out of sight. Who knows the way his mind works? None of us ever did. He probably thought, as Canaris doubtless did, that being the sole possessor of the account number gave him an advantage over the remainder of us. Perhaps he would have told us eventually or slipped into Geneva to withdraw and destroy the documents. The war ended and he was captured before he could. We were waiting for him in Salzburg when we heard of his arrest."

"How can you possibly know he didn't get to Geneva if you didn't see him from around mid-April onward?" asked Hadleigh.

"I don't. We had to work on the assumption that the papers still existed."

"Which made it essential to free him before the tenth," put in Masterson.

"Either that or find the fragments," agreed Scharper. "Once we knew you had Arndt's, the second option became virtually untenable. We therefore had to rescue Kaltenbrunner or at the very least get the number from him. We had few doubts that if we had not done so several days before the tenth he would try to strike a bargain with you, because after the tenth the information would be public knowledge and therefore useless to him as a means of obtaining immunity.

"Liberating him from prison or the courtroom was a pipe dream. We all accepted that. When we heard of him being taken in and out of the hospital, however, we knew he was giving us a fair chance of getting to him without excessive risk."

"What about the Sherman tank?" asked Hadleigh.

Scharper smiled faintly.

"Sternberg expected you'd be worried about that," he said. "The tank was a red herring. You'll find it at the bottom of the river Pegnitz several miles west of Fürth, where ex-tank driver Granger drove it the night it was hijacked. Sternberg never considered using it against the Palace of Justice. Not that Kleemann and

Isken knew that. Not that Kleemann and Isken knew anything. They were not members of our original group. Sternberg picked them up in Salzburg to use as dupes. They firmly believed they were going to spearhead an attack on the Palace of Justice. We knew when you took them you'd find a way to break them.''

"You couldn't possibly have known we'd be waiting for them at the station last night," protested Quinlan.

"But we did." Scharper seemed pleased with their cleverness. "We learned where you were hiding Fräulein Wolz the day you all returned from Munich. We were originally going to kidnap her that night, to find out how much you knew, how close you were, if you had all the fragments. Then we had a better notion. If we left her abduction until yesterday, Sunday, the day before we were to try for Kaltenbrunner, that would work much more in our favor. We surmised you'd move heaven and earth to find out how we knew where she was living. We did not underestimate you. Either you would conclude one of you had been followed to Sündersbühl—and we took great care not to follow you —or that we had someone on the inside. We gambled— but we thought you'd suspect Gretl Meissner sooner rather than later. If you hadn't, we'd have tipped you off by telephone.

"Riordan *never* made contact with Frau Meissner on a Sunday. If on calling the Grand there was a message asking for a meeting at the Hauptbahnhof or the hotel, we'd know you'd set a trap. All we had to do was allow Kleemann and Isken to walk into it, following which they would reveal, under interrogation, that the Palace of Justice was to be attacked this morning. While you were there, we would be here. If there was no message at the Grand, if we were unable to inform you that Gretl Meissner was working for us, we'd have sent Isken and Kleemann out on some fool's errand and informed you anonymously where they could be picked up. Either way, you would have learned from them what they believed to be true, that we were to attack the Palace this morning at ten-thirty. If you suspected beforehand that Kaltenbrunner was the real target, you would surround him with troops. We would have seen them and known the ruse hadn't worked. However, it did work."

"To no avail," Masterson reminded him.

"The fortunes of war," said Scharper in a matter-of-fact voice. "You were too quick and Kaltenbrunner too cowardly. Otherwise none of us would be here now."

"Where would you have been?" asked Quinlan.

There remained much that needed answering. Who had raped and murdered Ilse Arndt and Angela Salvatini, for example? Who had killed Helga and almost killed Ingrid? Who had disposed of Willi Meissner, the tank crew, the original owners of the uniforms Battle Group Sternberg was wearing? But these questions could wait, as could the papers in the Geneva bank. What they all wanted to know now was where Sternberg had gone and the location of the real paintings.

Scharper licked his lips nervously.

"Does everything I tell you count in my favor?"

"I'm not empowered to make deals," Masterson said. "The most I can say is that a transcript of the tapes will be forwarded to the competent authorities, who will decide whether your cooperation is enough to warrant clemency should any charges be brought."

Scharper accepted the situation without argument. If he didn't tell them everything he knew, Kaltenbrunner might. In any event, the whereabouts of the hoard was in the Canaris papers and they now had the number of the account. A single phone call to the US legation in Geneva would give them the information they wanted in under an hour. Sternberg was going to need much longer than that to move the paintings.

"The cache is in an abandoned tin mine on the road between Bayreuth and Hof, a few miles beyond the Kulmbach junction. You get to the mine itself by taking a dirt road on the right of the Bayreuth-Hof highway.

The entrance is boarded up with corrugated iron and wooden planks, but that's a blind. I can explain it more clearly if I draw you a sketch. There are seven or eight tunnels inside, but only one leads to the cache. You'll find what appears to be a heavy rockfall at the end. Beyond the rocks is a cavern. The paintings are in there."

"How many of them?" asked Masteron.

"Almost three hundred."

"How do you know they're still there?" Quinlan wanted to know.

"There was a time when we thought they weren't. Kaltenbrunner made a private visit, we found out later, with half a dozen demolition experts from the SS Panzer Division Das Reich toward the end of 1944. That worried Sternberg and me so we paid a visit of our own. We thought Kaltenbrunner might have removed the rockfall with a series of controlled explosions and transferred the cache. We found no evidence to support that. Quite the reverse. If anything, the rockfall was higher and deeper than ever. Sternberg and I spent several hours digging out a gap wide enough to crawl through, and everything was as we had left it on the other side. We reasoned afterward that Kaltenbrunner had only wanted to strengthen the barrier. Perhaps he'd considered a double cross but found it impracticable."

"Why didn't you ask him, or ask the demolition engineers?"

"Because then he'd have known we were checking up on him. As for the Das Reich people, they just disappeared. Presumably Kaltenbrunner had them killed on the basis that the fewer who knew about the mine, the safer we'd all be."

"That was in 1944," Quinlan reminded him. "How do you know the paintings are there now?"

"Because we've been over the mine from time to time, most recently around Christmas. We even watched from a distance last year while a platoon of American troops removed the planking and explored the tunnels. They came out empty-handed. The paintings are still there, I assure you, as they have been since 1943. They are stored in metal-lined packing cases to prevent corrosion or mutilation by rats. The entire operation was planned to the last detail.''

"The ransom money doubtless to fund the Fourth Reich, as Canaris intimated,'' sneered Petrov.

"Not at all. Perhaps Kaltenbrunner had some such idea with himself as the new Führer, but that did not apply to the rest of us. Even as early as 1942 a few of us suspected we would lose the war. If that happened, the survivors would need money to escape from Europe and begin a new life elsewhere. I've read in the newspapers and heard on the radio that all SS officers have access to vast fortunes. I can assure you that isn't true. A handful of gold coins and a few Swiss francs perhaps; not enough to live on forever.

"The original conception was Sternberg's. He was a policeman in prewar Berlin and personally acquainted with many of Germany's top art forgers, who in turn put him in touch with Frenchmen and Belgians in the same business. He approached Heydrich with the scheme, but that bloodthirsty fool wanted nothing to do with it and even threatened Sternberg with a firing squad. When Heydrich was assassinated and Kaltenbrunner became head of the RHSA, he proved more amenable.''

"I don't believe you,'' said Petrov, as always looking for a conspiracy. "Hitler would never have agreed.''

"I regret to inform you Hitler didn't know about it, which was one of the reasons we couldn't spend too much time interrogating Canaris, not with Judge Thorbeck under orders to report directly back to the Führer. Kaltenbrunner lied to Canaris about that. Not even Himmler knew. There was only a small group of us, thirty at the most. The majority of those are now dead.''

"How many survived?'' asked Hadleigh. "What sort

of opposition are we likely to meet at this mine?''

Scharper countered that with a question of his own. How many had been killed or wounded this morning?

Hadleigh told him.

"In that case there are only five left. Sternberg, Flisk, Riordan, Hallam, and Granger. Hallam is an American,'' he added maliciously.

"A couple of platoons should be enough," said Hadleigh to Masterson. "If I remember the area correctly, the Kulmbach junction is around seventy miles from Nuremburg. I'll take Major Quinlan and Max to help me round up the troops while Scharper draws his sketch."

The trio left Masterson arguing with Petrov, who was already insisting that Soviet forces be present during the raid. Masterson was telling him there wasn't a chance, that the most he could have was himself and his two aides, take it or leave it.

"What about Kaltenbrunner?" asked Quinlan in the corridor.

"We don't need him anymore," said Hadleigh, "and I think we can safely leave Gene Masterson to pass on the good word."

TWENTY-FOUR

~~~~~~

BAYREUTH-HOF ROAD
January 7, 1946

THE REMNANTS OF Battle Group Sternberg had arrived at the mine just ninety minutes earlier, slowed down by a fresh snowstorm. For each of those minutes they had labored at the wall of rock using only their bare hands.

The knowledge that Kaltenbrunner was alive and ready to talk had caused Sternberg to abandon caution. He had neither hidden the Jeeps nor posted a guard at the mine entrance, which was several hundred yards from the rockfall. Every pair of hands was needed if they were to succeed in their task before Kaltenbrunner struck his bargain. Sternberg doubted that would happen quickly. A decision regarding immunity would have to be agreed to at the top and written guarantees prepared, which would take time. They had two or three hours' start, possibly a little more, and it said much about Sternberg's opinion of the human race that he did not consider for a moment the likelihood of the Americans refusing a deal.

Earlier, he had discussed with Riordan the problems they would face at the mine. Both men had agreed that trying to transport even one of the packing cases was out of the question. They had only Jeeps, and the cases were too large. Each, however, was labeled with its contents and rightful owners. They would therefore open those that held the smallest or most valuable paintings, or those belonging to men and institutions Sternberg judged most likely to pay a ransom. If necessary, some works could be slit from their frames, but the majority would have to be left behind, an unavoidable tragedy slightly mitigated by the fact that the ransom money need now be divided only five ways.

Sternberg had only an approximate idea of the value of the cache; some of the paintings were beyond price. Even so, in American dollars, the only currency he was inclined to accept, he estimated the entire hoard to be worth eighty or ninety million. Forty or fifty canvases, 15 or 20 percent of the total, would be enough to set up five people for life.

Breaking through the rockfall was a grueling task. Beyond the obstruction, in the cavern, were a score of full jerricans and a gasoline-driven generator hooked up to a lighting system. On this side, however, they had to work in semidarkness, the only illumination coming from strategically placed hand torches whose batteries were rapidly expiring. Between them, Kaltenbrunner and Sternberg had decided years before not to have electricity in the tunnels. The mine was meant to appear derelict; sophisticated lighting outside the cavern would have aroused suspicion.

Toiling alongside Sternberg, Riordan tore at the rocks at the top of the thirty-foot pile, cursing that the group was undermanned and wondering aloud just how thick the fall was. Sternberg was unable to tell him, though he recalled that he and Scharper had once taken two hours to create a gap big enough to crawl through. Theoretically, five pairs of hands should have been able to accomplish the same feat in less than half the time. In practice, however, while five men could expose a lateral opening 150 percent faster than two, what they needed was depth across a narrow range. They had kept getting in each other's way until they decided that they should work in couples for ten minutes at a time two at the rock face, three resting, and so on in rotation.

Nevertheless, progress was agonizingly slow, and at the end of two hours they had still not made a breakthrough. The major problems were the suffocating dust thrown up as the rocks hit the tunnel floor and the lack of oxygen, which impaired efficiency. Less important but annoying were bleeding hands and, when not working, the cold.

"I thought you Germans were supposed to be a logical race," grumbled Riordan, one time when Granger and Flisk were at the rockfall. "A child of ten could have figured out a better hiding place."

His tunic over his shoulders to prevent his muscles from cramping up, Sternberg refused to take offense. Including Hallam in his reply, he said that he and Kaltenbrunner had had many different ideas about a location for the cache at the beginning.

"Kaltenbrunner suggested shipping the paintings out of the country, to Switzerland or Argentina. I talked him out of that. We'd have needed special warehousing facilities and we had no guarantee that some inquisitive individual would not start poking around, wondering what was in so many packing cases requiring such meticulous storage. Neither could we guarantee that a ship or U-boat would reach its destination. Besides, I didn't entirely trust Kaltenbrunner. I wanted the paintings where I could see them if necessary."

"Then why not a bank vault?"

"In Germany?" Sternberg looked at Riordan scornfully. "If we lost the war, bank vaults would be opened by the Allies. Even if we won or managed a stalemate, our big cities were going to receive a pounding from the Allied air forces. The bank vault does not exist that can survive a direct hit from a thousand-pound bomb. As for a salt mine other than Alt Aussee, we considered that possibility before thankfully rejecting it. The Allies found them all—Merkers, Kochendorf, Heilbron, Lauffen, and many others as well as Alt Aussee. This was the best suggestion we came up with. We were not to know then, of course, that Canaris, working alone as he liked to do, had unearthed our little secret. When we found out, the Allied advance was too far forward to contemplate a change of location. Nor did we consider such a move necessary. Kaltenbrunner had the information to unlock the Geneva account. We didn't realize then that he had no intention of passing it on to us. Or that he would be captured before destroying the papers."

"We should have taken a few canvases the last time we were here," grunted Hallam, coughing as the dust caught in his throat. "As insurance. I said all along we were dumb to trust Kaltenbrunner. He could have tried to strike a bargain with the military government months ago and we'd have been none the wiser."

"Agreed," nodded Riordan.

Sternberg shook his head in disgust. *They were not only the scum of the earth, these British Free Corps men, they were also stupid.* Still, he needed them to help conduct the ransom negotiations. In spite of everything, they spoke English and he did not. From the Zirndorf backup house they could travel Europe with virtual immunity, fading into the crowd.

"*I* knew Kaltenbrunner would say nothing," he said haughtily, "not while there was a chance we could free him. Besides, you talk as though we're dealing with potatoes or apples. We're not. We're dealing with works of art, many of them hundreds of years old. If they're in less than perfect condition, we shall find no buyers."

"I don't see that bundling them into the back of a couple of Jeeps and driving across Germany at zero degrees Fahrenheit is going to do much for them," said Riordan.

"If you have a better suggestion in our present predicament, I should be delighted to hear it."

"We should have hijacked a couple of three-tonners back in September and moved the bloody lot." Riordan spat into the dust at his feet. "To Grossreuth or Fürth or Zirndorf. Then we needn't have risked our necks trying to rescue Kaltenbrunner or worrying about those bloody fragments."

Sternberg sighed inwardly. He was tired of telling Riordan that the paintings were worthless if the contents of Canaris's deposit box were publicized. No one would deal with them then, regardless, for to do so would be tantamount to a painting's owner saying that he didn't give a damn what the Nazis had done, that he wanted his Titian or his Rubens back at any cost.

The SS colonel was spared repeating this argument by a shout from above by Granger.

"I think we're almost through," he called down. "I can feel cold air."

Riordan and Hallam scrambled up the rockfall. Before following, Sternberg checked his pocket watch by the light of the torches. They had been working for almost two and a half hours and surely, by now, Kaltenbrunner would have talked.

Hadleigh and Colonel Masterson were also concerned about time as the small convoy of vehicles which their Jeep headed crossed the Kulmbach intersection without Max Judd taking his foot off the accelerator. Close behind came Yuri Petrov's staff car and half a dozen trucks carrying two platoons of dogfaces. Although the snow had eased in the last ten minutes, driving conditions remained treacherous, and Quinlan, in the passenger seat, juggled with Scharper's hand-drawn sketch while Max fought to control a back-wheel skid.

Scharper had indicated on the map that the turnoff for the mine was between two and two and a half miles beyond the Kulmbach junction, on the right-hand side of the highway. The reverse side of the sheet of paper depicted the interior of the mine and its branch tunnels. Quinlan hoped to God that they would have occasion to need the information, that the Sternberg group had not already left, taking what they could carry and destroying the rest as an act of malice. Max had led the convoy like a demon the whole way from Nuremberg, but the fact remained that Sternberg had more than a four-hour start.

"How much farther, Major?" asked Masterson from the backseat.

"Any minute now," answered Quinlan, peering through the windshield. "Take the next right," he said to Max, who slowed and signaled that he was turning.

No sign or any other indication told them that they were on the correct road, though Quinlan thought he could detect faint tire tracks that the snow had not quite erased.

"Pull over here, Max," said Hadleigh from behind. "If they've posted a guard, he'll have heard us by now, and we don't want to give him a big fat target to aim at. We'll footslog the rest of the way."

Grumbling, the dogfaces piled out of the comparative warmth and dryness of their trucks and deployed themselves on either side of the dirt road. They were under the command of a young infantry lieutenant, Joe Liddell, who came forward to find out what the next move was. Yuri Petrov and his aides remained in their staff car.

"Judging from the sketch," Hadleigh told Liddell, "there's only one way in and out of the mine. If there's a guard on the entrance, I want him eliminated, quietly if possible. Choose a couple of your best men.''

Liddell disappeared through the snow. Thirty seconds later a sergeant and a PFC went past the Jeep at a dogtrot, weaponless except for wicked-looking knives.

"Whether or not there's a guard," Hadleigh continued when Liddell returned, "we're going to face problems when we get inside. The tunnels are narrow and unlit. We'll carry torches, but if we take too many men, we're going to get in each other's way. There are only five of them, so half a dozen of your infantrymen should be enough. Plus you, Colonel Masterson, and ourselves, of course.''

"Don't forget Petrov," said Masterson.

"I wasn't." Hadleigh jerked his head in the direction of the Russian's car. "I'll see what his plans are in a minute. Pick guys who can move quietly," he added to Liddell, "and get the rest of your men behind cover where they can see the mine entrance. Leave someone you can trust in command. The guys we're after are wearing British and US uniforms and three of them speak English, one with an American accent. I don't want anyone holding his fire until it's too late because he sees drab-olive or khaki, and neither do I want anyone getting trigger-happy and sniping at us if we come out first. Maybe we should have a password.''

"How about Tintoretto?" suggested Masterson.

"Too much of a mouthful," said Liddell, shaking his head. "If you'll forgive me, Colonel, most of the guys I've got would think Tintoretto's something you drink with meatballs and parmesan. In the infantry we like to keep these things simple. How about cheeseburger since we're talking of food?''

"Okay, cheeseburger it is," agreed Hadleigh. "You can tell them to open fire if they don't hear it, though if the sketch is accurate there's no way anyone can get past us. Once we're inside we play everything by ear—except that grenades are out. On the other hand, the guys we're up against are facing a rope if they're taken alive. They won't quit without a fight.''

The two-man patrol came back wearing expressions of disappointment. No one was guarding the entrance, the sergeant informed Liddell, but two Jeeps were parked close by. These the sergeant had immobilized by removing the rotary arms.

''Petrov,'' Masterson reminded Hadleigh, who went over to the Soviet colonel and explained what he was about to attempt. To his relief the Russian did not want to accompany the incursion team. He and his aides would remain where they were.

''In your nice warm staff car, '' muttered Hadleigh.

He checked the sketch again at the mine entrance. About sixty-five feet beyond the opening, a major tunnel split into three branches; the one they wanted was on the right. One hundred sixty feet farther on came a fork. They again wanted the right-hand spur, at the end of which the rockfall divided the cavern into two. The distance involved was around six hundred fifty feet descending some sixty or seventy feet. Nowhere was the roof higher than ten feet, which came down to eight once they reached the second spur. The maximum width at this point was also eight feet, while the cavern was about a hundred feet across by forty feet high.

Rather than blunder forward in pitch blackness, Hadleigh gave orders to switch on the torches at the mine entrance. He was taking a big risk, he realized, even though the beams were partly masked with black tape. According to Scharper, Sternberg's group possessed automatic weapons. If the SS colonel had had the wit to set up a machine-gun position where the spur broke out into the cavern, the assault party was going to be a sitting duck.

They proceeded cautiously in two Indian files, hugging the tunnel walls, six feet between each man. Hadleigh headed one column. Level with him, Joe Liddell led the other. Behind Liddell came Quinlan, armed with an M 1 carbine he had borrowed from one of the infantrymen outside, and Max. Colonel Masterson shadowed Hadleigh. Equally divided, the six GIs brought up the rear.

After covering five hundred feet with no sign of opposition, Hadleigh shuffled to a halt. Somewhere in front he heard the sound of falling rocks and muffled voices calling to one another. The group also felt the dust creeping into its nostrils, eyes, and throats.

Keeping his voice down for fear it would carry. Hadleigh beckoned everyone forward. Sixty-five feet farther on, he explained, the tunnel took a shallow left bend which brought it into the cavern.

"With any luck they'll have their minds on other things. If they're still trying to get through the rockfall or if they're already through and ferrying stuff back to our side, it's possible we can rush 'em."

An experienced infantry officer, Joe Liddell was against dashing along a narrow passage in virtual darkness. The defenders would not have to see the attackers. All they'd have to do was shoot in the general direction of the tunnel mouth.

"They know the terrain; we don't. If there's only one exit, we'd be wiser waiting for them outside. They won't know we're there until we hit them."

Masterson rejected the suggestion, militarily logical though it was. By definition, once Sternberg and his group reached the exit, they would be carrying some of the looted artworks, which were certain to be damaged in a firefight. Masterson did not want an entry on his service sheet stating that he, as senior officer, was responsible for the destruction of irreplaceable paintings.

"No," he said, "we've got to go in after them."

Liddell shrugged. "Then one of us had better reconnoiter."

Quinlan volunteered, remembering the voice that had shouted "nail the bastard" the night he was driving from Humboldtstrasse, and the men who had abducted Hannah and who doubtless would have killed her. He had a bigger stake in this than the others.

Hadleigh understood.

"No heroics now. Look, listen, and come back."

"I'm not exactly a newcomer to this kind of thing," said Quinlan irritably.

He elected not to take a torch in case Sternberg had posted a lookout, and asked that the remainder be extinguished while his eyes became accustomed to the darkness. When he was ready he moved forward slowly, edging along the wall.

He felt his way around the left-hand bend in the tunnel, counting his paces. He stopped at forty. Surely he was close to the cavern now? He could feel cold air on his face and see what appeared to be a series of flickering lights twenty feet above his head and about twice that distance in front. Later he realized that these were torch beams coming from the far side of the rockfall and shining through the gap that Sternberg and the others had made. For the moment, however, he was puzzled.

He discerned no sign of movement in his immediate vicinity, nothing that might be a guard. Nevertheless, he remained motionless. With the aid of the darkness and the irregular configurations of the cavern, a platoon of troops could be concealed and they would not be seen until you were on top of them. Watching and listening, he forced himself to count slowly up to a hundred. Then, easing the safety off the M 1 and holding his breath, he continued forward.

From the tunnel mouth to the base of the rockfall was, he would later establish, fifty feet. He was halfway across when the stillness was shattered by the noise of a generator starting up. Simultaneously, a wedge of brilliant light spilled through the fissure above his head. After the dungeonlike gloom of a moment before, the cavern was suddenly as bright as day.

Although startled and temporarily blinded, Quinlan caught a glimpse of a man's head and shoulders silhouetted in the fissure. Then he was diving for cover as a Thompson submachine gun opened fire, kicking up dust and dirt as the marksman tried to pick him off with a long burst.

A minute earlier, leaving Hallam to watch the tunnel mouth from the top of the rockfall, Sternberg had led the way down the other side. Though the torches were very weak now, the German remembered precisely where the generator was. He filled the tank from one of the jerricans and pulled the cord to turn over the engine, using full choke.

Despite the cold and lack of regular use, the motor caught the first time, flooding the cavern with light and revealing dozens of packing cases, each the size of a large sea chest. But even as Sternberg turned to Riordan with a smile of triumph, Hallam was shooting.

"Kill the lights!" he screamed above the noise. "Kill the friggin' lights."

That Sternberg obeyed this exhortation almost before the words were uttered probably saved Quinlan's life. The machine gunner's panicky first burst had missed him; the second, as the marksman found the range, would have undoubtedly killed him—if the cavern had remained illuminated.

With Hallam firing blindly into the darkness, Quinlan sprinted back toward the tunnel mouth, weaving as he ran and not breaking his stride until the flashes from the Thompson's muzzle disappeared behind the left-hand bend. He collided with Hadleigh and Joe Liddell coming the other way.

"That's damned well torn it," cursed Masterson, when Quinlan, breathing heavily, explained what had happened. "Are you hurt?"

Quinlan said he wasn't. The back of one hand was

grazed and bleeding where he had scraped it against the tunnel wall, but otherwise he was uninjured. He'd also had the presence of mind to keep a firm grip on the M 1, for which he offered up a silent prayer of thanks.

"We're going to have a hell of a job getting them out of there," he told Masterson. "Even if they can't see us they can hear us. All the machine gunner has to do is aim at the noise. Under the circumstances, Sternberg has a first-rate defensive position."

"Damn the paintings," said Masterson. "If it were not for them, we could use grenades or a bazooka. I've half a mind to do so anyway and express my regrets to General Truscott later."

"What about teargas and smoke?" suggested Liddell. "There's some in the trucks and half a dozen respirators."

"Fetch it," said Masterson curtly.

"The trouble with teargas," said Quinlan, while Liddell was telling two of his infantrymen what was required, "is that someone's got to get close enough to lob a grenade through the gap in the rocks. Point a torch down here. Take the tape off. They know we're here now."

In the dirt Quinlan sketched a rough outline of the position in the cavern as well as he could remember it.

"That's where the gap is, roughly in the middle, at the top of the rockfall. I'd estimate the distance from the tunnel mouth at around twenty or twenty-five yards. It'd be tricky enough to throw a gas grenade accurately in broad daylight with no one shooting back. In the dark a man would need a lot of luck—if Sternberg decides to leave the lights out. I wouldn't. If I were Sternberg, I'd get the generator going again and take up better defensive positions on my side of the gap."

As though on cue they heard the engine restart. Fingers of light probed the tunnel mouth.

"Shit," said Hadleigh.

"What about the effects of carbon monoxide?" asked Max.

"Depends what sort of space they've got back there," answered Quinlan. "They might find it unpleasant, but I doubt if it'll be lethal for a few hours."

"So we're left with a Mexican standoff," said Hadleigh. "They're not going to come out with their hands in the air because they've all got a date with the hangman. We can't get close enough with teargas without taking unacceptable risks. Stalemate."

"Maybe not," said Liddell, cocking his head. "Listen."

They did so. In the distance they heard a voice calling, in English, for a parley.

A few moments after making the decision to restart the generator and illuminate the cavern in case they were rushed, Sternberg, Riordan, and Granger held a hasty conference. Dispatching Oskar Flisk with a second Thompson to join Hallam and giving them both orders to shoot at anything that moved, Sternberg, realistic as ever, spelled out their predicament.

"Time, gentlemen, is not on our side. There's only one exit and they're blocking it, probably in numbers and firepower much greater than ours. We can, of course, hold them off until our ammunition is exhausted, after which we shall be compelled to surrender or die here. The end product is the same either way."

"Keep talking," said Riordan.

"In my opinion they will not consider using fragmentation grenades or rocket launchers, which would certainly destroy what they are here to save. Nor can they rush us without suffering casualties. They can either try to starve us out or use gas, and my guess would be the latter. A few of them may die in the attempt. Sooner or later, however, a gas-grenade attack will be successful. When that happens, we're finished."

"If you're suggesting we give ourselves up, forget it," said Granger. "I'd rather take a bullet here than face the gallows in six months."

"I wasn't suggesting surrender," said Sternberg mildly. "I too do not relish the prospect of a rope. But we have something they want almost as much as our heads; they have something we want. We have the paintings; they have the exit."

He walked over to the nearest packing case and tore off the label.

"We'll talk to them," he said.

Hadleigh led the way to within ten feet of the tunnel mouth, where, by crouching to compensate for the angle of the roof, he could see the rockfall and the light beyond. Suspecting a trick, he advanced no farther.

"What do you want?" he called.

Out of sight, an English voice answered. Quinlan recognized the accent, though he had no way of knowing that this man's name was Riordan.

"There's someone here who wants to talk to you. He'll be happier speaking in German."

"He can speak in Hindustani for all we care," shouted Hadleigh. "We're listening."

Without showing himself, Sternberg revealed what he had in mind.

"I have in my hand," he called above the din of the generator, "a list taken from one of the packing cases, which contains two Titians, two Renoirs, a Monet, and a Reynolds, among others. Nine canvases in all. I am prepared to let you have these and the remaining cases in exchange for an unimpeded passage out of the mine. Should you refuse, these nine paintings will be destroyed in precisely two minutes. I will then repeat my offer with the contents of a second packing case. If you again refuse, they too will be destroyed. In under an hour there will be nothing left. I realize when that happens that my bargaining position will be nil, but you will have sanctioned the mutilation of priceless master-pieces. I wonder if you're prepared to answer for that? I regret I must hurry you. Your two minutes begin now."

"I think we can assume that was Sternberg and that the bastard means every word," said Masterson calmly. "Where the hell are your people with the teargas and smoke, Lieutenant?"

Liddell beckoned one of his GIs. "I'll send another man to chase them up."

"No, let Master Sergeant Judd go." Masterson gave Max a nod of dismissal. "You and your men are the in-fantry experts around here and we might have to come up with something fast."

"Ninety seconds," called Sternberg.

"Christ," muttered Hadleigh. "Titians, Renoirs, a Monet. I'd lay odds the frames are worth more than I earn a year."

"How about lobbing a few fragmentation grenades at them anyway?" suggested Liddell, whose knowledge of German was limited. It did not, however, take a linguist to deduce what was happening. "Just to shake them up a bit until the smoke arrives? I'll risk it as it's my idea."

Quinlan laid a restraining hand on his arm.

"Don't be a fool. Without smoke cover you'd be cut down before you could pull the pin."

"Major Quinlan's right," said Masterson, peering at the luminous dial of his wristwatch. "I want no dead bodies on my hands. We'll wait for the smoke, though if it hasn't arrived in fifty-five seconds the world will be minus a few Old Masters."

"Forty-five seconds," shouted Sternberg a few mo-ments later. "In thirty seconds we begin opening the first packing case. You're really being extraordinarily stubborn, Major Hadleigh. Or is it Major Quinlan? There are only five of us here, as you doubtless know. What can five lives possibly matter against a fortune in monetary terms and a heritage beyond price? Delaying matters will not help you. If you are sending for, as I suspect, teargas, at the first whiff I shall order every packing case destroyed by gunfire.''

"Here's Max," said Hadleigh.

Max had the respirators slung over his shoulder. Behind him, two perspiring GIs were struggling with open ammunition boxes. The stenciled markings on the side showed that one contained smoke, the other teargas.

Quinlan was first to grab a smoke canister and a respirator. Keeping close to the tunnel wall, he inched forward. When he reached the mouth he distinctly heard someone call up to Sternberg, who must, Quinlan reasoned, be tucked in behind the top of the rockfall, counting off the seconds. The voice was Riordan's, and he was speaking in German.

"There's something funny here," he yelled. "I've half got the lid off, but there's a bunch of wires . . ."

The sentence was never completed. The reason why the Das Reich sappers and Kaltenbrunner had paid a visit to the mine in 1944 hit Quinlan with the suddenness of a physical blow. The demolition experts' subsequent disappearance and probable execution also became clear. The SS general had not been reinforcing the rockfall. No one was going to move or in any other way interfere with the cache unless he was present. If he couldn't share in the spoils, no one else would. He had booby-trapped the packing cases.

"*Get down!*" screamed Quinlan, diving to the floor of the tunnel and burying his head in his arms.

A blinding flash of light was followed instantly by an ear-splitting explosion. Then another and another as the charges in the adjacent packing cases erupted, either linked in series or, more probably, set off by the first detonation.

A tongue of flame like dragon's breath leaped through

the gap in the rockfall as the jerricans of gasoline caught fire and went off like incendiary bombs. Blasts of scorching air whipped over Quinlan's prostrate figure, tearing at his clothes, burning his hair and flesh, causing him to cry out in pain. Somewhere up front he heard shrieks of agony, which were quickly silenced as the entire structure of the cavern began to collapse.

The rockfall was split asunder, hurling boulders large and small in all directions. Shrapnel-sized pieces of stone, white-hot like tracer shells, peppered the tunnel mouth, missing the prone Quinlan but killing Joe Liddell and one of the GIs, who were fractions of a second too late in hitting the ground. Their upright bodies took the first full force of the blast and, in the narrow tunnel, probably saved the lives of those behind them.

Quinlan knew he had to get out. Any moment now he could be killed by a flying boulder, lying as he was a few feet from the tunnel mouth. The shock waves might also bring down the ceiling, crushing him. He was astonished to find he couldn't move, that his body was refusing to obey his mind.

A massive sense-numbing noise like a dozen artillery barrages echoed and re-echoed in his ears, slamming into his brain, turning it to jelly. Now, however, the explosives were spent, the gasoline fires extinguished. What he was hearing was thousands of tons of rocks imploding, filling the cavern, annihilating everything in their path.

Then the noise passed, or rather became muted. He thought he had been deafened—except somewhere behind him Ben Hadleigh was calling his name.

He had no idea how long he lay there before forcing himself to open his eyes. He could see nothing, and the feeling of claustrophobia was overwhelming. Gingerly, fearful of making any sudden movement, he raised his head from his arms and reached forward. His fingers touched solid rock where, a little while before, the tunnel mouth had been. Gradually he realized that a huge boulder had blocked the entrance, sealing off the cavern and silencing the inferno beyond.

A torch beam pierced the gloom. Willing hands helped him to his feet. In answer to the anxious questioners asking him if he was all right, he could only nod. Making a nervous joke because he too was shaking from head to foot, Hadleigh said, ''I knew you had a class act. I didn't expect it to bring the house down.''

TWENTY-FIVE

~~~~~~

GENEVA/NUREMBERG
January 9–10, 1946

A LEGATION CAR flying the American flag from the
fender met Masterson, Hadleigh, and Quinlan at the
airport. All three men were in civilian clothes since
the Swiss disliked uniformed foreigners, whatever their
nationality, wandering their warless streets.

"I thought hostilities were over," remarked the be-
spectacled diplomat who greeted them.

They were indeed a sorry sight. Hadleigh and Masterson had suffered least in the explosion, but both had
been cut about the face and hands by flying debris. Still,
their injuries were minor compared to Quinlan's, whose
scalp and forehead were blistered and whose shoulders,
arms, and upper back, burned by blasts of scorching
air, were heavily bandaged beneath his shirt. The Allers-

bergerstrasse medical officer had wanted to hospitalize him for a few days. Quinlan had refused. "Just patch me up." Geneva was the last act. He was not going to miss out on it.

At the bank, they were shown up to a luxurious first-floor office and there given a simple form to complete. Hadleigh carefully checked the number in his diary, the latitude and longitude of Tristan da Cunha. They wanted no mistakes. Tomorrow, unless properly claimed, the information in the Canaris account would be made public, which was thought to be undesirable.

Hadleigh wrote: 12°30′ W 37°00′ S. He handed the form to a young male secretary, who took it gingerly between forefinger and thumb as though handling something contagious.

"Please be good enough to wait here, gentlemen," he said in impeccable English.

"Gentlemen." Quinlan managed a grin after the door closed. "I wonder how he addresses anyone who looks like a gentleman."

"Probably on his knees," grunted Masterson.

When the male secretary reappeared bearing a small steel box, apparently locked, he was preceded into the office by a tall gray-haired man wearing a magnificently tailored morning suit and a pearl stickpin in his silk tie. Quinlan felt an urge to spring to his feet. The man had presence. His hands, the nails beautifully manicured, looked as though they had never done anything so vulgar as count money. He would have minions for that.

The secretary placed the box on the desk, gave a short, stiff bow, and went out. The banker studied each of them in turn.

"My name is Dr. Beck," he said in English. "I do not wish to know yours. I mean no disrespect. It will simply not be necessary."

He referred to a black leather-bound notebook he was carrying.

"You have fulfilled the conditions of the account and that is sufficient. I take it you do not have a key to the box?"

"No." Masterson shook his head.

"I thought not. Never mind, it's of no consequence." He took a small bunch of keys from his pocket and selected one. "The box, you will understand, has not been opened *ever* by any member of this bank's staff. I do so now only with your permission." He waited a moment. "I have that permission, I take it?"

Masterson nodded.

Dr. Beck unlocked the box and returned the keys to his pocket.

"I will leave you now. My secretary is outside. Call him if you need me. If you choose to take the contents of the box and thus close the account, there are one or two formalities to be completed."

The box contained half a dozen sheets of paper covered with spidery handwriting and held together by a paper clip. All three men experienced the same sense of anticlimax. For so many people to have died for possession of something so commonplace seemed unbelievable.

That the words were those of Admiral Canaris appeared indisputable. Although they had never seen his handwriting, the address at the top of the first sheet was Tirpitzufer 72/76 and the notes began: *From Admiral Wilhelm Canaris to whom it may concern*. If any doubt arose about the authenticity of the calligraphy, it could always be checked against official documents.

To begin with, they had difficulty making out some of the sentences, so cramped was the writing. After a while, however, they found the reading easier.

"It is my fervent hope," the text began, "that no one will ever read this. If they do, I shall either be dead or have had to bargain for my life. If the former and it is you, my dear Manfred, use the contents wisely. If the latter and you are the reader, Kaltenbrunner, may you rot, for I am beyond your reach, one way or another."

There then followed a summary of the Kaltenbrunner-Sternberg plot, exactly as they had heard it from Scharper. How French, German, and Belgian art forgers had faked almost three hundred Old Masters and were subsequently executed. How the forgeries were mixed with authentic masterpieces in Alt Aussee. How the Allied recovery teams would believe the fakes to be real and return them to their rightful owners. How the genuine paintings were hidden in the tin mine between Bayreuth and Hof.

"If you have got this far, dear friend, you will surely wonder why I chose such a bizarre means of getting you here, why I handed fragments of photograph to Arndt, Bachmann, Butterweck, and Straub. Why also I told you only Arndt's name, the name of the bank, and the fact that all four fragments would reveal an island whose latitude and longitude become the key which opens the account. I'm sorry to say it was fear.

"Forgive me if I seemed to mistrust you. These days it's hard to know whom one can trust. You will recall I asked you not to approach Arndt until you had confirmation I was dead. I also instructed Arndt not to hand you (or anyone else) the first fragment and Bachmann's name until he was sure of my demise. I know not whether you stuck to the letter of our bargain. I hope so, but I would find it hard to blame you if you anticipated events and contacted Arndt before you heard of my death. With me in prison (where I must surely have been or you would not be reading this) you might have found it difficult to ascertain whether I was still in this world or entering the next. But there lies the rub. I intend bargaining with Kaltenbrunner: my life in exchange for the contents of these notes. If he agrees (and you must realize I am talking in the future tense here, because at the moment I remain free), you can imagine his reaction if he is informed by Dr. Beck that the account has been closed. For the same reason I cannot tell the British or allow any single individual to possess the number of the account. If Kaltenbrunner does not agree (and you know only too well his methods of persuasion), I hope I shall be able to hold out, revealing neither your name nor the account number. If I fail in either respect, I shall have encumbered you with an intolerable burden. Regrettably, there was no other way.

"If you are reading this and the war is over—if you, Arndt, and the others are alive—take these notes to the Allied military government. You will undoubtedly earn the Allies' gratitude and that, the state Germany is likely to be in, will be no small thing to have.

"If someone besides Kaltenbrunner is reading these pages because they have become public knowledge, then I am content. His scheme will have failed and I shall take the utmost pleasure in meeting him in hell."

"The word from on high," Masterson said the following morning, "is that none of it ever happened. Troops of the Third Army and a handful of hard-core Nazis were involved in a firefight at the tin mine, a normal mopping-up operation. The Nazis were killed in an explosion. The report will read that a stray bullet hit a secret ammo dump. There were no paintings in the mine, neither genuine nor faked. Paintings that are now or will soon be hanging on the walls of galleries, museums, and private houses are the real McCoys. Those are my orders from the brass, who've received theirs from government level. If it ever got out that a particular Rubens or Reynolds or Monet *could* be a phony, there'd be a major panic in the art world. There are billions of dollars at stake. Art, I am told, is big business, and big business can make or break administrations—American, British, or European."

They were sitting in Masterson's office—Hadleigh, Quinlan, and Max Judd.

"Let sleeping Titians lie," said Hadleigh.

"Precisely," agreed Masterson. "Even Canaris's

notes have been destroyed. I was present when they were
burned this morning. One or two of us wanted to keep
them for posterity, maybe under lock and key forever.
We were overruled. As we all know, locks and keys
don't guarantee anything.''

"What about Petrov?" asked Quinlan.

"No problem. The Soviets are being remarkably
cooperative. They had stuff looted during the war from
Leningrad, Kiev, Kharkov, the palaces of Peterhof,
Tzarskoye Selo, Pavlosk. Dozens of other places.
They've now got it back. They think. The trouble is,
none of us has an inventory of exactly what was in the
mine. Sternberg mentioned two Titians, two Renoirs, a
Monet, and a Reynolds, but which Titians and Renoirs?
And what else was in there? The lists were tacked to the
sides of the packing cases, which are now, together with
the contents, so much matchwood.

"As I said earlier, paintings are big business. They
can be sold for hard currency. Better to display a fake
that everyone thinks is genuine than to rock the boat.
According to General Truscott, the Russians are more
concerned about leaks from our side, though the small
number of people who know the truth makes that unlikely.''

"How many people?" asked Hadleigh.

"Apart from governments and brass and a couple of
bigwigs from CIC, just the four of us here. Lieutenant
Liddell is dead, and I doubt if his infantrymen thought
they were doing anything more than digging out a nest
of Nazis.''

"There's Fräulein Wolz," said Quinlan quietly.

He and Masterson had had a blazing row about Hannah earlier, with Quinlan arguing that she had a right to
be told everything after all she'd been through.

"And Fräulein Wolz," nodded Masterson. "I agreed
with Major Quinlan about that this morning.''

"For a price," muttered Quinlan.

He had agreed never to tell the story or leave behind

any diary to be published after his death. The journalist in him was enraged, and he was determined that one day he would find a way around his pact, Official Secrets Act or no.

"What about Kaltenbrunner, Colonel?" asked Max.

"Out of the clinic and back in jail, denying all knowledge of booby traps. He wasn't too pleased, I can tell you, that we didn't need his help. He threatened to spill the beans from the dock when he comes to give evidence. He won't, however. I made him a couple of half promises."

"Genuine?"

Masterson chuckled wickedly. "No, he'll hang with the rest of them, except he doesn't know it yet. We're not leaving any loose ends."

"Scharper's a loose end," Quinlan pointed out. He had raised the question of the former SS major when arguing with Masterson about Hannah. Masterson had avoided giving a direct answer. "Not only is he the only one left to face charges for the killings of Angela Salvatini, Ilse Arndt, Willi Meissner, and God knows who else, he knows exactly what was in the mine. Compelling me to silence doesn't make sense while he's roaming around, in prison or out of it."

"He won't be," said Masterson.

"How come?"

"He's dead. He fell from the fourth-floor fire escape of the Hallerwiese-Klinik while trying to escape."

"Christ. When?"

Masterson examined his wristwatch.

"In about an hour."

Quinlan was surprised to find that he was shocked.

"Don't be," said Masterson, reading his mind. "You said it yourself: Angela Salvatini, the little Arndt girl, Willi Meissner. We're just evening the score. With the verdict a foregone conclusion, a trial would have been a waste of time."

"Not to mention awkward if Scharper decided to conduct his own defense."

"Not to mention that. Money, son," said Masterson, "is what makes the world go around. The stories I could tell you . . ."

He shuffled a few papers into a neat pile to indicate the meeting was over. Telling Hadleigh and Judd to go on ahead and close the door behind them, he gestured Quinlan to remain where he was.

"There's one other thing," he said. "I've been getting some flak from my old buddies at British Second Army HQ, inquiring whether we still need you. I told them we did. For another couple of weeks. I don't want to see you anywhere near the office, however. Ben and Max will tidy up the paperwork, such as it is. Grab yourself a decent car and take that girl of yours to Austria or someplace for a couple weeks. Anything you need in the way of gas or ration coupons is yours."

"Thanks," said Quinlan. "I appreciate that."

"Otis," he heard Masterson mutter as he closed the door. "Some name for an Englishman."

"What did he want?" asked Hadleigh, who was waiting outside.

Quinlan told him.

"Hell of a two weeks the pair of you are going to have," said Hadleigh, nudging Max. "Patched up the way you are."

"You're right," grinned Quinlan. "I guess we won't get any skiing, tobogganing, or mountaineering in at all."

EPILOGUE

~~~~~~

NUREMBERG
December 4, 1949

SOMEHOW THE CITY would not have been the same
without snow, which was falling thickly, blanketing the
landscape and the new buildings that were going up.

They decided to leave the car at the station and walk.
It was their first time back in more than three years, an
unscheduled diversion. They had flown to Munich that
morning to see Quinlan's German publisher, and they'd
thought, why not? The round trip was only two hundred
miles on the Autobahn.

He was going to call his new book *Major Otis Regrets*, telling the whole story of the Canaris fragments as
fiction (for which he was gaining a considerable reputation), not fact, and changing a few names here and
there. Then let someone try reading him the Official
Secrets Act!

He already had the first lines. He would begin with

Sternberg and Scharper, as yet unnamed, gloating over
the fake masterpieces. Something like:

Beautiful, beautiful.

The two SS officers walked the length of the ware-
house, stopping occasionally to discuss the objects of
their admiration.

They crossed the river Pegnitz where Gretl Meissner,
a few days after learning of her son's murder, had
drowned herself in January 1946. The IMT verdicts had
been announced later that year, and on October 16
those to be hanged had mounted the scaffold. Ribbentrop, Keitel, Frank, Rosenberg, the near-idiot Streicher,
Seyss-Inquart, Sauckel, and Jodl. And Kaltenbrunner,
who finally seemed genuinely amazed that this could be
happening to *him*, who had run out of things with which
to trade.

Goering cheated his executioners by swallowing a cyanide capsule smuggled into his cell. Schacht, Von Pap-
en, and Fritzsche were acquitted, while the remaining
defendants drew long prison sentences.

But this was no day to be remembering such events.
Christmas was around the corner and they had to be
back in Munich by evening. Tomorrow they would
travel home to England where Ben Hadleigh, now a bird
colonel and on the way to his first star, was joining them
for the holidays. Max Judd had also promised to fly in
if he could get away.

On impulse they decided to visit one of the city's
newly restored art galleries, where they looked long and
hard at a magnificent Titian. After a moment they were
joined by a middle-aged German couple, who also stood
in awe before the painting and misunderstood their silence for reverence.

"A most inspiring work, is it not?" smiled the man
eventually, recognizing their nationality by the cut of
their clothes and speaking in perfect English.

"Actually," said Hannah, nudging Quinlan in the
ribs but keeping a perfectly straight face, "my husband
preferred the original."

ACKNOWLEDGMENTS

～～～～～～～～～～～～～～～～～～～～～

MANY INDIVIDUALS AND organizations helped with the research for this book. Regrettably but understandably the most important individuals wish to remain anonymous. These include three former German officers, one a former member of the Waffen SS, the other two Wehrmacht. A very elderly man who once served with the British Free Corps and fought with Waffen SS detachments during the last days of Berlin gave me invaluable assistance in describing the infrastructure and training schedules of the BFC. While I made it quite clear to this latter individual that I in no way sympathized with the stance he took, I respect his wish to remain unnamed.

The major organizations whose assistance was invaluable are: the National Archives and Records Service, Washington, D.C., and in England, the Public Records Office, the Imperial War Museum, the Royal Geographical Society, and the staff of the Tiverton Library, Devon.

306